To Katye
We've had lots of

Deirdre

A Woman from Clare

Fun & we'll have more
Peace, Health, & Joy
Chick O'Brien

By Chick O'Brien

PublishAmerica
Baltimore

ISBN: 1-60836-100-4
PUBLISHED BY PUBLISHAMERICA, LLLP
www.publishamerica.com
Baltimore

Printed in the United States of America

Dedication

I dedicate this book to my wife Grace, my lifelong partner, my main source of encouragement and my best critic. I also dedicate this work to my son Brian and my three daughters, Eileen, Maureen and Peggy.

Acknowledgment

To all of the many Irish writers, poets, song makers, Shanachies, mythmakers and story tellers who came before; who inspired, instructed, delighted and enthralled me. I thank you. I praise you. I am in your debt.

My story, *Deirdre: A Woman from Clare*, is my way of saying "Thank You."

To Joe Hsu who made me a gift of the Shian Bao and enabled me to add a drop of Asian spice to my story. I thank you.

Deirdre

A Woman from Clare

CHARACTERS

Deirdre DalCas	A Woman from Clare
Jay O'Neill	Lover and husband of Deirdre
Gregor MacGregor, Mac, Greg	Best friend of Sean O'Neill, Jay's father
Dermot O'Rourke	Cousin, & best friend to Deirdre
Maura Ni Coveney	Runs Coveney's Inn
Mary Rose Ni Coveney	Runs the Inn, with her sister
Declan O'Mahon (Dek linn)	Daring, fun loving, quick witted, IRB member
Donal Crowley (Doe null)	Older man, Irish Republican Brotherhood
William Burke, Wee Willie, Devil	Anglo-Irish aristocracy, Oxford Don, foe
Fritz Kunkel Von Meuser	Prussian Warrior/Scholar, highly intelligent
Father Rene Jean Batiste de la Salle,	French Jesuit A modern day Richelieu
Father Rory Beechinor, parish priest	Concerned, talkative, Irish patriot
The Good Doctor/Cracker Jack Surgeon	Cashiered British Army surgeon
Nurse, best surgical nurse in seven continents.	His Nurse, lover, companion
Flor Sweeney,	Mortician, businessman, smuggler
Florrie Sweeney, wife of Flor	Mother, housewife, empathetic

CHAPTER ONE

In a small elegant meeting room in an exclusive men's club in London, four wood and upholstered chairs were set around a low carved wooden table. Three of the chairs were occupied. The men were quiet, read their papers and sipped brandy; they apparently waited for the fourth chair to be filled. Reginald, a manservant, moved to the door and opened it. As if on cue a large middle-aged man strode into the room, swirled off his outer garment, and held it out behind him to the gentleman's gentleman who followed close behind.

"A brandy, Reggie me boy, and make it a large brandy. No. Make that two large brandies." Gregor MacGregor's speech had a pronounced Scottish burr to it, and it seemed at times to the other three gentlemen that English might be his second language.

William Burke gave a discreet harrumph while Rene Jean Batiste de la Salle exhaled loudly through his rather distinctive Gallic nose and Fritz, though seated, clicked his heels together in a display of Teutonic pique, but they all patiently folded their papers and set down their drinks awaiting MacGregor's explanation. Rarely was one of these four men late to a meeting. It was too important to them.

Gregor, hands clasped together, regarded each in turn and spoke to all three, "Now gentlemen, in one short moment we will begin our weekly indulgence, and I promise you an evening that will curl your toes, whet your appetites and quite possibly wet your knickers with excitement. And envy," he added with a large laugh. "Yes, envy. Ah. We begin."

Reginald knocked and entered carrying a tray with five brandies. Three of the drinks were normal and the other two were indeed extra large. A young man followed Reginald into the room. He was wearing the uniform of an officer of the United States Navy. Rene murmured a protest at this intrusion upon their exclusive group, while Fritz, after polishing his monocle, raised it to his weak eye, and Gregor sat back smiling. William raised a cautionary hand and they quieted, waiting. Reginald returned, placed a fifth chair in the place indicated by Gregor, set an extra large brandy within reach, and silently closed the door before taking his place in the room, on guard, and ready to serve.

After an approving nod from William, Jay took his place in the new chair, between Gregor and Rene and opposite William. He sipped his brandy; appraised the men seated with him, the pleasant room he was in, and he settled back with a sigh of relief.

It was early evening on the seventh of May 1915 with the long lingering twilight common to this part of the world at this time of year. Floor-to-ceiling drapes framed the windows on two walls and indicated a corner room. They allowed in enough light to illuminate many of the battle flags, banners and shields hanging upon the dark paneled walls.

Next to each of the wood and upholstered chairs, a small matching table held writing paper, pencils and brandy snifters. The room had a definite feel of age, of permanence, of single mindedness, as though it was conceived, furnished and used by the same people and no one else, for one purpose and none other, on a regular basis.

"I think it is time for introductions, all around," Gregor said to William. William was British, very proper and absolutely in charge at this club. As long as William approved, Jay could take his seat tonight and perhaps even return a time or two. William was an Oxford Don and a frequent consultant to the Foreign Office. He carried a diplomatic passport, which allowed him to travel anywhere, despite the hostilities raging throughout most of Europe since that unfortunate incident in Sarajevo. He was also a mystery writer of some repute, under a pen name of course, and the other three members usually acknowledged him as the leader of this group. He was the glue that bound them together and held them to their purpose. He was very British, a tad stuffy and at times he tended to be pompous.

William nodded to Gregor MacGregor. "Go on Gregor."

The big Scotsman smiled. "Thanks, Wee Willie." Then over his shoulder he said, "and Reg, I'd say bring us this fifth chair next week and the weeks beyond, 'till we tell you nay."

MacGregor was the only person in the world who could call William DeBurgo by his childhood name, Wee Willie, and get away with it. Except perhaps for Williams' own mother Wilhelmina, who preferred the modern version of their name and called herself Billie Burke and her son, Wee Willie Burke.

"Gentlemen," Gregor continued, "May I present the son of my best friend and comrade in arms. This is young Jay Jay O'Neill, the son of Sean O'Neill."

Jay blushed and held up his hands in protest. "Please Mac, one Jay will do, and drop the young part." Jay turned to Rene and William, "my father always called him Mac M'Gregor, King of the Scots. And if the Scots won't crown him King, why it's their loss."

The older men smiled and Gregor went on. "And I always told your father had he not gone to America, he would've been "THEE O'Neill, Clan Chieftain and *Ard Ri na hEireann*, High King of Ireland." Even William smiled this time. "Now Jay, there's a wee bit more explaining we must do before we proceed. Briefly then," Gregor eased into the situation the way a soldier picks his way through a minefield,

"On your left is Rene, a former Jesuit priest and the unsung pride of the French Diplomatic Corps. Rene could have become a modern day Cardinal Richelieu had he not retired and joined our small group.

To my right, the man with the monocle and dueling scars on his handsome Prussian face is our own, Fritz. Apposite us sits the Honorable William Burke, our chairman, our leader and sometimes our conscience. We four all carry diplomatic passports. We travel nearly anywhere at any time, have access to almost unlimited funds, and we may…."

William interrupted, "Enough said for now. We must move along, Gregor."

Gregor turned to his three companions and one by one he read their faces. "I promised Jay here my help, and perhaps your help as well. You've heard me speak of his father, Sean O'Neill," Gregor offered by way of explanation. "You may remember, Sean and I met in the Klondike region of Canada back in '97. We got snowed in and spent a perilous frozen winter in a wee cabin smaller than this room. And not elegant a'tall," Gregor grinned. He waved his hand to include their surroundings. "Unless you fancy eating icicles, we nearly starved, but we survived. We fought each other, we laughed and we cried. We told each other our life stories and probed each other to our deepest depths."

Gregor paused for a breath and shook his large shaggy head. "We fought. God did we fight: over the last scrap of bread, over the first fish we caught through a hole we chopped in the ice. Finally, we held it between us and ate it raw. Face to face with that fish between us. He took a bite from one side and I chewed on the other. We survived. And when the ice broke and spring came we were like two brothers. As though we two men were raised in the same house by the same mother, though perhaps fathered by different gents. Thoughts would arise in the mind of one and be finished in the mind of the other. A look or glance was all it took and we knew just what action the other would take."

Gregor paused and let out a long sigh. "But when the ice broke all hell came loose. 1898 in the Klondike was like 1848 and California all over again, but worse. The lure of gold is so pervasive. Digs right in under the skin and grows and festers in the marrow of men's bones. We made our reports. O'Neill to his government and me to mine, and we included the Canadians, too, by God. But none would believe us. No one acted. Thousands perished in that frozen north. They were frozen dead and stayed there or came out broken men, they did. Oh, a few became foolishly wealthy, but not many survived the gold and greed, the cold and dark deeds. Later on the poets told it best:

'There are strange things done in the midnight sun By the men who moil for gold.

The arctic trails have their secret tales That would make your blood run cold.'"

"Robert Service", Fritz exclaimed with delight, "THE CREMATION

OF SAM MCGEE," is one of my favorites. His poems, so full of manly men who battle cruel nature." He paused, "and you are correct. Most of them lose. Only the very strong prevail, Gregor. It is nature at its best, but of course it is harsh, yes."

Gregor went on, "We served together again in the Boer war, O'Neill and I, each for our own government. Supposed to be bloody non-combatants we were, but took plenty of fire. No one's too particular in the heat of battle. It's just Bang, Bang, and fire away.

Today, I ran into young Jay" Mac paused. "I met Jay on the train from Paris. He told me his story, and of course, I said I'd help him. I also promised him your ears and quite possibly your help. If you feel you cannot help, then I must have your promise of absolute silence on whatever is said here tonight. No one, no country, no government comes before our oath in this room. That has always been our way."

Gregor leaned forward; he was anxious and almost menacing. He faced each one and got a nod of agreement. Satisfied, he turned to Jay. "You see Jay, your president Mr. Wilson, who is your commander in chief, stays neutral and says this is merely a local dispute between the Serbs and the Austrians. But then the Russian Czar jumps in on the side of his little brothers, the Serbs. And the German Kaiser comes to the aid of his cousins the Austrians." Gregor paused and swallowed some of his brandy.

"It is all the same you see." William, always the Don, felt he had to clarify things. "Absolutely all the same. Caesar,… Kaiser,… Czar,…they all mean the same thing. All act the same too."

Fritz frowned but nodded agreement. His native Germany was at war with France and England as well as with Russia; it sometimes got a bit heated in this elegant meeting room.

Gregor put a hand on Fritz's arm, nodded thanks to Wee Willie and continued, "The French and we British came to the aid of little Belgium, which got in the way of the Kaiser's ambitions." He sipped more brandy and shrugged. "As a good Scot I've no great love for the English. But I am a loyal British subject, and Wee Willie's King is my King. His fight is my fight. Except in this room, here we set aside nationalities and act as a unified group.

To round out the bottom of the map, as it were, the Turks are in it too. The entire Ottoman Empire is faced off at us in Egypt and Palestine, so this small local battle has now become a World Wide War."

Gregor paused, sipped some more brandy and plotted his next step. He was the man in the minefield again. The others waited, letting him choose his words, trusting him to bring them all to the right place.

"But you know all that, Jay. Your Mr. Wilson will soon have to make a choice, and perhaps you'll play a part in that decision". Gregor turned back to his three comrades. "Jay is with the American Naval Intelligence and he will act for his country. And we four are like brothers in all but blood. Some of us are even related, though at a distance. In addition to being diplomats we are, in a manner of speaking, amateur sleuths. We are often called upon by our various police departments and many of the ministers within different departments of our governments."

"And military," chimed in Fritz, who sat up straighter and polished his monocle.

"The French Secret Service. And Belgian too," Rene volunteered.

"Professional government busy-bodies, we are," William contributed.

Gregor laughed and raised his brandy glass. "And not least, we are professional storytellers, weavers of tales, tellers of tall stories. We are all successful writers, Jay. Mostly travel books and mystery novels and the like. All of this story telling is accomplished under a variety of names, of course."

Jay leaned forward and swept his glass in a circle to include them all. "Ambassadors. Detectives. Spies. Warriors. And an association of professional writers?"

"*Oui*", Rene smiled and chanted, "*Le plume de ma tante.*" He gave a little flourish and a half bow, "in that sense we are a writers group."

Gregor flashed a big grin and turned to Jay. "Now laddie, let us have your story. Just the way you told it to me on the train from Paris. If you've remembered any more details, be sure to include them. We do love a good story, especially if there's some mystery in it. We are quite old fashioned, as you can tell from the lighting in our meeting room. We use only the old-fashioned gas lamps in here, no electricity for us, at least not in here. Now, just don't leave anything out, like a good lad. And Reggie, will you fill the glasses again, like the good man that you are. Doubles for everyone."

The four men settled back in their chairs, and an expectant hush filled the elegant room. The only sound was the gurgle of aged brandy as Reginald filled the glasses and then he moved silently to close the floor-to-ceiling drapes by each window and turn up the gas jets in the lamps mounted on the richly paneled walls.

The room darkened at first, then flared very bright. William Burke, in the center chair opposite Jay, raised his hand and turned toward Reginald as though to admonish him, but nodded and let his hand drop down to seek his brandy as the room settled into a pleasing medium glow after Reginald had adjusted each lamp.

The many banners, battle flags and shields seemed to leap right off the wall at Jay and come to life, as he regarded the well appointed room and the quite varied but very successful men in it.

Jay wondered how to begin his story. He desperately wanted their help and advice, and knew that he'd have to disclose everything to obtain it. Jay sipped his brandy to cover his hesitation. Maybe he would not tell everything. Not the waterfall and the pool and...

Jay quickly swallowed his brandy, cleared his throat, and leaned forward as he began to speak. "I was on a mission for my government, nothing very clandestine or dangerous. I was told to go out to the Far East and then come back through Europe. My people wanted me to collect impressions, be nosy; look into their food, their storage, the shipping and agriculture.

The ability to feed their armies is vital to all of the battling Empires, but especially the Russians and the Germans. How would they grow and collect the food, where would they store it, ship it, and what would that do to the price of food for the people left at home. Rice is critical in the Orient. Potatoes are vital in Russia, with wheat, rye and barley in all of Europe." Jay looked around to gauge their reaction.

"One very smart man, a commissioner in our War Department put it to me this way."

'Hey sailor. What's this war going to do to the price of beer? Or wine? Or vodka for that matter? Find out. That's your job. Fighting men need food, but they also get thirsty.'"

Jay settled into his tale. "I traveled in civilian clothes, mostly for convenience. With my State Department passport I wasn't technically a spy, and I was treated quite generously most of the time. Since I was an American, and a neutral, people responded to my questions." Jay shrugged. "Though I was careful not to appear too nosy and it all went well, most of the time."

Gregor laid a cautionary hand on Jay's arm and looked across the table to William Burke. "You look troubled, Wee Willie, so let us hear it. I vouched for the lad, but if you have a problem please share it with us."

William Burke exploded, in his own very upper crust British manner. "On your say Gregor MacGregor, and for the first time ever, we've allowed an unknown person, a new element, and an agent of another government into our...our sacred chambers. We are revealing our inner selves. We who are dedicated to fostering peace in this world." William sputtered and gestured with both arms. "Our world is at war. Why is he here? Why with us?" His lower jaw jutted out, and he was bright red in the face and neck.

"If you are finished dancing around the subject, Wee Willie, please do lay it out for us," Gregor retorted.

Sir William Burke, almost trembling now, exploded. "Why an American? Why a junior officer? Why would they send a Naval man, a young untested Naval man half way around the world to glean information on agriculture, food stocks, depots, loading grain cars. This son of your dear friend, your 'almost' brother," he sputtered. "I do understand your emotions Gregor, but I do not understand your motives. He is a junior Naval officer. He is too young, too unproven. And he is here, in our midst. This is utter nonsense."

Jay came to his feet as the other men were exclaiming over Burke's outburst. "For several hundred years, William Burke, the population of your own Northern Europe was held back; your nations were handicapped; your commerce was crippled." He had their attention now and rushed on. "Yes, your Northern Europe is now locked in mortal combat.... Again. The potato famine in Ireland wasn't the only food stock to cause a national calamity.

Ergot is the culprit. E-R-G-O-T." Jay spelled it out and paused to gauge his audience, "and I'll wager you have never even heard of it. Ergot. It's a type of food poisoning caused by a mold on bread, rye bread. It infects the growing kernels, replacing the grain with small shoots of mold, about a centimeter long. It goes right through the harvest and into the finished bread. It is unknown, unseen and absolutely debilitating in its effects.

People eat the Ergot and it can be devastating. It causes women to lose children before birth. It makes living children sick and adults have hallucinations and seizures. Witchcraft, and mental illness, and even prophecy can be blamed on this deadly, debilitating mold and it is still happening, still causing severe problems".

Jay had their complete attention, now. "In the Czar's court today, there is a monk advising the royal family using his so called prophetic powers. It is quite possible, nay, quite probable this monk is a madman infected by the Ergot mold on his peasant black bread."

He sat back down on the edge of his chair and continued his story. "As you know Mac, I was a city boy, born and raised in New York, and schooled there too. Before my appointment to the Academy at Annapolis, I worked down in Maryland for two summers, on a farm owned by distant relatives of my mother.

They were East Europeans, hard working, very old fashioned and I had first hand experience with the mold and Ergotism caused by mold on home made rye bread. I almost went into a mental hospital instead of the Naval Academy. But once I got home and back on my regular diet, I recovered. I was able to came back to normal and resume my career."

The room was quiet as Jay continued. "I never forgot the hallucinations and wild mood swings that consumed me. So, I studied Ergot. I researched everything I could find about it. I even went back to the farm and identified the growths on the rye plants. With the local government health agency, we helped them get rid of that mold on their farm and in the entire Polish immigrant community around them. That was very satisfying for me.

Thus, I became sort of a Naval expert on mold, grains, and food stocks in general. As for being young, well Mr. Burke, I'm working on that day by day." Jay sat straight in his chair and tried to relax.

Fritz smiled at each of the men. "I think now we can move onward, yes?"

William Burke, still red in the face, harrumphed twice and spoke in a cool but civil manner. "I accept your credentials, young man, but reserve my judgment on your presence in this room. You may continue." Wee Willie harrumphed again and cleared his throat. "However, should we ever meet again outside of this room, you will address me as Sir William Burke."

Rene on one side and MacGregor on the other each put a restraining hand on Jay. MacGregor leaned over and whispered, "Keep your temper, laddie. Your goal, remember your goal."

"Merde." Rene whispered. He gestured at Wee Willie Burke with a Frenchman's fine disdain. "The man has great pomposity." He smiled at Jay and closed one eye.

Jay eased all the way back into his chair, forced a smile on his face and continued as though he was never interrupted. "I took the train 'cross country from Washington to California—rolling plains, beautiful mountains, forests and rivers—in my romantic musings I pictured myself as Lewis and Clarke, Kit Carson, and every other pioneer who crossed the Missouri river and followed the setting sun."

"*Oui*," Rene interrupted again, "An' the *Voyageurs Francais* and Jesuit priests who precede them. St. Isaac Jogues, martyred by the Red Men."

William would not be outdone. "And our British chaps who followed the beaver and skinned a fortune for my family."

Fritz, having no family connections to the new world, smiled fondly at Jay. He alternated between rubbing his bad leg and polishing his monocle.

Jay continued, "In San Francisco I went to a small a shop on the waterfront. It was crowded with young sailors getting fitted for custom uniforms, but when I showed the clerk the sealed letter I carried, I was ushered right into a back room to a small Chinese man.

He spoke wonderful English, welcomed me to his humble shop and then proceeded to measure me and described what I would be getting from him: a traveling cap with a special band, full of small easily exchanged diamonds, and a travel coat with gold coins and more diamonds sewn into each sleeve and a money belt to be used mostly as a decoy in case I was set upon.

He instructed me to carry most of my money in the inner secret pocket of my new trousers. 'Take two or three days,' he said in his high singsong voice, and he put his entire staff to work, fitting my special outfit. There would be plenty of time to explore the waterfront and to absorb the special culture that was San Francisco. At least that's what I thought, but it never happened. I stayed in a room above the shop. It was room number three. Next door to me in room number five was my instructor, Wan Lee.

'You number three,' she said. 'Wan Lee next room, number five.' When she saw my puzzled look she exclaimed, 'Four bad luck. No number four room. When say Four in Chinese, sound same as say dead. No good. You three. Me five.' She clapped her hands together. 'First class very good rooms.'

Wan Lee was either the youngest daughter, or eldest granddaughter of the old tailor. She kept me busy by sending people to my room, both male and female. It became a regular parade of Chinese, Japanese, Mongolian and Russian people. They instructed me in certain words and phrases; they gave me addresses, and we talked about currencies and geography.

I memorized cities that I would pass through, houses where I could get or leave messages, money and help. Wan Lee was my taskmaster, tougher than any instructor at the Naval Academy. She would drill me over and over again, 'till I could repeat it in my sleep. At the end of each day she would repeat the lessons and grill me for hours.

'What city you stay? Which street? House number? Name of you?' She would clap her hands and whenever I tired or faltered she'd yell at me: 'you sleep on boat. Sleep many days. Learn now, with Wan Lee. Save your life, live long time. Die later, maybe so.' She clapped her hands to punctuate each point she made.

Too soon I had my new clothes. Wan Lee nodded her approval at my progress and she shrugged at the old man. The next thing I knew I was on the stern of a P. and O. merchant ship waving good by to Wan Lee and the lights of a city that I never got to see." Jay stopped for a breath and collected his thoughts.

William the Don purred, "Pacific and Orient Line. Very good line, a well run enterprise and quite a handsome return on my families' investment." He waved for Jay to continue.

"I posed as a young man recovering from an illness in need of a long sea voyage," Jay went on. "The first day at sea I collected my mail, which had been forwarded to me; I got to the officer's mess early, and as expected, found it empty. I sat down, read my mail, and found a small package wrapped in plain brown paper, no return address, and no stamps, just my name.

I ripped it open and inside was another package wrapped in bright red paper. Wan Lee, I thought fondly. I could hear her clap her hands and say 'open now, O'Neill Jay'. I tore off the red paper and found a small red cloth diamond in my hand. A bright red silk diamond, hand sewn, it just covered the palm of my hand and at one end was a small tassel.

'Shian bao,' said the man who sat down across the mess table from me.

'Jay O'Neill', I answered, surprised by the intrusion, but I held out my hand to shake with him.

'No, no, *Shian Bao* is Incense Fire Pack.' He pointed to the small red silk diamond in my hand. 'Incense Fire Pack, is *Shian Bao*. My name *Zhou*, first mate. Call me Joe'. He held out a large work worn hand and we shook.

The First Mate smiled at me. 'Someone wish you well. Good friend, but not lover. Red silk heart is lover. Red silk diamond is wealth. Red silk is good luck; inside is ashes of incense. Hold in hand, so. Tassel on end points to heart; other end of diamond shows way to go.' The mate smiled and extended his two hands, fingers together, and pointing like a spear. 'Diamond is for wealth and friendship, not love. Love is heart shape.'

He stopped and thought a minute. 'Sometimes diamond has little heart hidden inside diamond, but if you cut silk to find heart inside you lose incense ashes. Lose good luck, too.' The mate laughed. 'Best take diamond as is. Friendship with prosperity, and always go in right direction. Like compass.'

His round face beamed at me. Joe was wide in the shoulders and had very black hair. It was combed straight back and it stood straight up.

I held the silk Fire Pack and smelled it. It was Sandalwood. Wan Lee

20

often smelled like that. And maybe something else blended with it. I put the small silk *Shian Bao* into my shirt pocket".

Rene kept patting his left jacket pocket. '*Oui*. The left pocket. Near the heart, no?' His dark eyes twinkled as though he and Jay were conspirators.

"Near the heart yes," Jay agreed and went on with his story. "The first mate and I became friends and very often I'd stand Joe's watch with him. I was always a good sailor and a quick study, but I learned even more seamanship during the hours on watch. We navigated by the stars, and it was fine to be on a good ship on the deep ocean. I'd sailed a great deal off of Long Island and all over the Chesapeake Bay between Maryland and Virginia, but the rolling swells of the Pacific have a rhythm all of their own.

I also reinforced all my lessons from Wan Lee. Every night before sleep I'd hold the *Shian Bao* and smell her scent and hear her voice in my head repeating the drill, over and over, challenging me, and clapping her hands for emphasis. It was a good voyage for me. We had a brief stop in Pearl Harbor, and then came the long rolling sea journey all the way to Japan."

Jay paused and regarded his audience. The four men were all seasoned travelers and would be judging him. "I was looking forward to Tokyo and savoring a bit of home at the American Embassy. I'd get my mail; have some good Yankee food and plenty of easy, unrestricted conversations in my native American English language; but it just never happened. Our last night out, Joe pulled me aside and gave me an envelope and instructions.

'I have brother is captain of small freighter. Sail all Japan islands, Sea of Japan, all entire area. You meet him. Give him this.'

"Is it permitted for me to read this, Joe?" I asked, and he grinned at me.

"No can read. Is in my Chinese." He grinned at me. "Maybe I tell brother, "HELP YOU". Or maybe I tell him, "CUT OFF YOUR HEAD." His grin got bigger. "Follow diamond Shian Bao. Find brother of Joe. You will like him."

"And we left it at that. The next day was hectic. I went ashore and never saw him again. I reported in, picked up my mail, sent out some letters I had written while at sea, and then I was shunted off up the coast to a small fishing village. They had me billeted with a local family and I spent a few weeks learning to love fish and rice."

Fritz smiled, took off his monocle and chided. "Do not rush my young comrade, *Ja?* I know, there is much to tell, but we are traveling beside you, eh?" He was rubbing and massaging his leg as he spoke.

"I must admit I was having a hard time living in a house with paper walls. There was no privacy at all and going to the bathroom was the worst. It was a communal out house; a long narrow hut where you sit down in a line of strangers, and...

I was growing quite tired of it when a small freighter appeared just off shore and signaled my host. The fisherman took me out to the ship; we bowed; we shook hands and honestly, I think he was as glad as I was to say *Sayonara*."

MacGregor signaled to Reginald to refill the brandy glasses. "Give us all a small taste, Reg. Talking and listening is thirsty work. Go on Jay, we are all engrossed in your story."

Jay continued. "We meandered up the coast stopping at every small place that had a stone pier. And Joe was right. His brother was the Captain. I guess he liked me because he never cut my head off. Every time we met he beamed at me but he had no English, and his crew were a motley bunch from a dozen different island nations all across South Asia. I could never figure out what language they were using. Eventually, we rounded the Japanese island of Honshu and crossed between it and Hokkaido, the next largest island, and entered the Sea of Japan. Their charts called it the East Sea and we crossed over to *Chosen* and steamed into *Ch'ongjinn*, a regional capital."

Fritz gestured with his monocle. "Korea. Now called *Chosen*. The Japanese first made it a protectorate and then annexed the entire peninsular country in nineteen hundred and ten. They are a bit touchy about it, I hear."

"Yes," Jay confirmed. "As soon as we could see land, the Captain had me up to the wheel house and pointed it out on the map. He spoke to me then for the first and only time in halting but passable English.

'Ja..pan..ese man in Ja..pan....good man.' He spoke slowly as though to a child, exaggerating each syllable, then he assumed a fighting stance and drew an imaginary saber from his belt 'Ja..pan..ese man in con..que..red land,' ...'not good man.' He mimed cutting off the head of the young coxswain, who grinned and kept steering the ship. 'You no go *Chosen*. Stay on ship. Stay in cabin. My order.'

From a drawer he showed me a pair of manacles connected by a short chain. 'No trouble. My ship.' I nodded. He nodded. And I missed my chance to see *Chosen*, and the Japanese as an occupying army. But at least I kept my head," Jay shrugged and the other men smiled.

MacGregor clapped him on his arm, "good lad, always keep your head."

"For a day and a night I stewed in my small cabin. Even my meals were brought in and everyone acted as though I had a deadly disease. A short sail up the coast brought us to *Sosura*, the Northern most port on Korea's East coast. After a short stay we left and very quickly entered Russian waters. Almost at once, I was summoned on deck. The captain beamed at me again; the crew treated me as one of their own and I had the run of the ship.

We entered a small bay and docked at *Kraskino*. I stepped ashore and had my first glimpse of Mother Russia. It could have been China, Manchuria, or, I suppose, Korea. It was almost totally oriental. The sights and smells of the waterfront were so familiar and then I realized that it was very like New York's Chinatown or Wan Lee's place in San Francisco.

I patted the Incense Fire Pack in my pocket and enjoyed a good walk up the hilly streets of the town. Next morning early, we crossed the bay, made a fast stop in *Pos'yet*, and finally we steamed away to the Russian port of Vladivostok. Soon now my journey would begin.

CHAPTER TWO

"One by one I shook hands with each of the crew and the last was the Captain, Joe's brother. We shook. I said thank you. He beamed at me and I went down the gangplank and on to the next leg of my adventure. I never did learn his name nor the name of his ship. The Chinese characters on the stern were indecipherable to me."

Rene held up a hand to stop Jay. "Can you perhaps draw the ship's Chinese characters from the memory? Our Fritz is a master of language. He may give us a translation."

Jay shook his head no, and went on with his story. "Like *Kraskino*, indeed like San Francisco, and many other ports worldwide, *Vladivostok* was a city by a bay. It seemed well worth exploring but first I was determined to cash in a diamond or two from the band on my cap. Not only to have some local currency, but I was anxious to put my hard earned knowledge, drilled into me by Wan Lee, to the test.

The Russians and the Japanese had recently reopened trade after their war. So, I wanted a test of my skills and knowledge and soon I'd have my money belt, my secret pocket and my pants pocket full of local currency. Then I'd be on the train headed into the heartland of Asia and, I hoped, eventually into Europe itself.

Every night before sleep, I rehearsed what I knew about this next stretch of the road. I would put the *Shian Bao* under my pillow, like it was some sort of talisman. In my head I heard Wan Lee repeat each story, every lesson in her singsong voice and I could hear her clapping her hands and smell the Sandalwood scent that emanated from her.

The Japanese woman, the Mongolian man, the Eurasian woman and the old tailor, all had lived in many of the places I would visit. Everything anyone of them said, I heard Wan Lee repeat it and drill it into my mind. She was inside my head every night as I went to sleep. With her help I was ready for my next adventure and my God, it was exciting."

Jay looked again at the four older men in the room to gage their reaction to his story. To his left Rene was nodding and swinging his glass in time to a private tune. He seemed receptive to Jay.

Across the table from Jay, William Burke regarded him through half closed eyes, and gave a small nod. Was that approval from Burke? Probably not, thought Jay.

Next to William, Fritz held something in his hands. It appeared to be a passport and he was rhythmically caressing his leg with it while he stared at Jay. Of all the men, Fritz appeared to be enjoying his story the most.

Excepting, of course, Mac MacGregor, his father's best friend. To Jays' right MacGregor was regarding him affectionately and had a lopsided grin on his large face.

As Jay resumed his story, Reginald entered with more brandy, but William waved him away. Reginald nodded, and stopped to adjust a flickering lamp on his way to the door. Gently he crossed the threshold and closed the door silently behind him.

Jay collected his thoughts as he prepared to launch into the heart of his story and the first real test of his skill as a spy. His first encounter had almost been a disaster and his mission nearly scuttled before it really began.

"It began much like one of Wan Lee's drills. I walked up the hill and away from the waterfront for two blocks. There on my left was the *Barinov Hotel;* beyond it was the café, and next to that a small shop with the distinctive three balls hanging out front, the pawnshop.

I dropped my duffle bag at the front desk of the *Barinov*, obtained a train schedule and then went next door into the café to find the bathroom and slipped into a stall. The band on my cap came loose easily. I had practiced loosening it and I pried out two of the small stones, put them in my pocket and walked slowly back into the café to sit at the counter.

I ordered tea; *Chai,* they called it. I could have used something stronger to calm my nerves, but *Chai* would do. The counter man poured a bit of dark liquid into my cup, then he filled it with boiling water from the *samovar* and I inhaled the wonderful aroma of some unknown tea. I took a few sips, then added a bit of honey. I drank again and added a piece of lemon. It was perfect. I could've had another, but I was calm now and it was time to go to work.

The pawnshop next door was intriguing and I lingered upfront awhile admiring some of the things that were for sale. There were a variety of personal items, which someone had pawned, but never redeemed. They were little bits and pieces of personal dreams gone awry. Enough stalling, I thought and walked to the middle of the shop. It smelled like an old fashioned hardware store.

The man behind the counter appraised me as I approached and I gave my password in the form of a question. Maybe I should return when the moon is full? Instead of answering me he pointed with his left thumb to a small counter at the far rear of the store. I went back and sat down at the counter and he followed and sat opposite me and we stared at each other for a long time.

In very passable English he said to me. 'You look like someone who has taken a sea voyage to recover from an illness. Are you quite recovered?'

I nodded yes. My heart was in my mouth and my mouth was so very dry, I couldn't speak. Instead, I reached into my inside pocket and pulled out the two precious stones. They made a small tinkly sound when I dropped them on the glass counter between us.

He looked at me and he looked at the stones, and one by one he held them up to appraise them through the jewelers glass he held to his eye. He nodded at me and after examining each stone he would mention an amount in Rubles and then swing 'round and examine me through the jewelers glass, first with one eye, then with the other eye."

Jay paused, drew a big breath and continued. "I almost laughed out loud, but I was too nervous and it was so damned important, so I asked him to write it down in American dollars. Instead he reached under the counter and brought up a small metal moneybox. He opened it and began counting out a wad of bills.

As if on cue, the front door crashed open and several men in uniform came flying in. They were yelling, and swinging long clubs and one even had a gun drawn. The proprietor, or agent, or whoever he was scooped up the stones off the counter while I grabbed the big wad of cash out of the box and together we went through a door into a back room. I don't know where he went, but I was through the room and out a back window before I knew it. I heard shouts behind as me as I ran for my life.

The rear storage area was littered with barrels and crates, old shipping stuff and a high stone wall surrounded all of this. I ran for the back wall; leaped up and got one foot on top of a trash can, then another leap onto the roof of a small shed built against the wall, and on up and over the wall. I fell a dozen feet or so, and landed on some trash, breaking my fall. I picked myself up and saw that I was still clutching the wad of bills, so I stuffed them into my jacket pocket. Nothing broken but my pride sure was bent."

'Ah, *mon ami*, you were perhaps Set-Up as they say.' Rene offered. He turned to the German for confirmation. 'Fritz yes? A Set-Up?'

'*Nein*,' Fritz replied. The good Prussian was the best chess player, most nimble thinker and the most able problem solver of the group. 'Who gains? Who loses. More likely the Police or the Czar's Government agents have had him, the shopkeeper and diamond buyer, under watch. The Czar has many enemies and even more he has spies. Continue please, *Herr Jay*. Your story grows and my enjoyment increases.' Fritz had stopped rubbing his leg and the monocle hung against his chest at the end of its ribbon.

Jay carried on with enthusiasm, pleased at the reception his story was getting. "I bolted down an alleyway to the next street where I forced myself back against a building and caught my breath. I was scared. I was shaking and shivering and wet from sweat at the same time. So I forced myself to breathe deep, ten times, to regain my calm. Breathe in quickly, hold it, and release the breath slow; again, in and out. IN AND OUT ten times, just like I did before I tackled anything important. Then I made myself go slow. Walk natural. First left, two blocks, left again down hill to the seafront. Only it wasn't the docks and waterfront I came to. I had lost my way and walked into a small park."

Gregor regarded Jay with affection and growing admiration. 'Was this your first encounter with real danger, Jay?'

"Aye," Jay admitted. "Oh, I've had school fights, tough football games and the like, but this was my first brush with absolute danger; where death or capture was a possibility. I found a bench in a darkened area; sat down and breathed deep again. But after two breaths, I laughed out loud. I felt ten feet tall. I could run a mile in my bare feet. I could wrestle a bear. I laughed again. It was a good thing I was alone.

Then, for the first time I became aware of my surroundings. This park was a pure marvel. It was a tropical paradise with a huge old Banyan tree, Ferns of all types and sizes, Palms, Ginkgoes and others I couldn't name. They must have been special because there were plates with nametags, but I couldn't read them.

Sir William Burke smiled and again offered a bit of his knowledge. 'The identification tags were in Cyrillic, of course, and the reason for all the large tropical specimens in that part of Russia is that the glaciers never reached the Vladivostok area during the last ice age.'

The other men smiled at Wee Willie's need for titles as well as a display of his vast knowledge. Gregor nodded at Jay to continue.

"The Incense Fire Pack was still in my pocket. I could feel it warming me as I cautiously surveyed my area of this unique park. I was alone, but to make sure I stood up on the bench and made another careful look all around. When I was sure I was alone, I pulled the paper money out of my pockets, I counted it and put it away in various pockets. Then I began to relax. Maybe my recent encounter had been a success. Maybe I was ready for this kind of work, after all.

There was enough local currency for train tickets, food, good tips and maybe some exploring along the way. I wouldn't have to sell anymore little stones from my cap 'til I was through Asia and well into Europe. My cap. I almost swore out loud, and in English, another mistake. I didn't have my cap. It was gone. One hand went to my head, the other to my pocket, what the hell. Gone. Probably when I went over the wall.

I made myself sit down and breathe all over again. When I had control, I headed back and retraced my twisting path to the wall on the street in back of the shop and I never got lost this time. After examining the empty boxes and other trash that had cushioned my fall, I looked up and there it was; twelve feet above my head, caught on some broken glass at the top of the wall. I had to retrieve the cap. Either that or go buy a new one and lose the diamonds. An old woman, a babushki that I passed on my way back, had just yelled me at for not wearing a hat. She yelled, shook her finger, the whole bit. I had to get my cap.

Evidently it was common practice for an old woman to scold a young man not properly dressed. For the first time I noticed several tears to the front of my coat. Without a hat and in a torn coat, I was looking a bit ragged, but I was whole, healthy and free, and had enough money to get me most of the way. Or so I thought at the time. Little did I really know about money, and foreign travel, and traveling with a woman in a foreign land. But I was about to learn."

Rene seemed to brighten as Jay mentioned travel and a woman. "*Cherchez la Femme*, my young American sailor."

Jay raised his glass to cover his blush and then went on with his tale. "On my way down to the seafront, I had passed some young lads with strings of fish and long bamboo poles. Quickly, I bought the longest pole and a few pieces of bait and left the youngsters laughing. As soon as they were out of sight, I hopped it back to the wall and tried to use the long pole to fish my cap off the top of that damned wall. I got the tip in under my cap, raised it up, almost had it, and then it disappeared over the wrong side and it was now all the way inside the wall.

I could hear Wan Lee as though she were standing beside me. 'Never lose cap. Never lose coat. Keep you warm, keep you wealthy and save life, maybe.' She gave a big handclap and then, 'go careful, JayNeill.' By way of an apology, I reached into my shirt pocket and held my Incense Fire Pack. When I smelled my palm, I had a whiff of her scent, her Sandalwood. I grabbed the bamboo pole where it leaned on the wall, thinking to toss it atop the junk heap.

It felt heavier than before. Something was snagged onto the hook tied to the end of my pole. Could I be that lucky? Was Wan Lee still with me?

I climbed the trash heap and raised the pole high but whatever was caught remained on the other side. Nothing for it but to use an old boyhood fishing trick, so I flicked the butt end of the bamboo pole and my cap came sailing over the wall just like the snapper fish I used to catch when fishing from the sea wall every September, back home. My cap landed in the street. Thank you Wan Lee. I made a solemn promise to Wan Lee, to the U.S. Navy and to myself, never to lose my diamond loaded cap again.

I moved fast, but careful, and went the long way around to the *Barinov*, where I retrieved my sea bag, bought a ticket westbound on the Trans Siberian Railway, and purchased a meal to take with me. With Wan Lee's voice again ringing in my ear, I purchased a second-class ticket whereby I'd be one of four people in a cramped compartment. With three others in the same tiny space I'd have less room, but soak in more local color.

Finally, I indulged in a horse drawn cab ride to take me to the station. Along the way I regretted my decision to go second-class. Memories flooded in of my time in Japan in the fisherman's house. It was so crowded and no one had any privacy. I began to shiver again.

"Non, non, my youthful friend," Rene interrupted. "William Burke he is correct, *oui?* You are indeed young and it is to your great advantage." Rene flung his two arms wide and then hugged himself. "You possess my great admiration, Jay. I, *Rene Jean Batiste de la Salle,* could never travel in this manner. Not even under orders from Holy Father, the Pope himself. We all salute you, *eh."* He stared a challenge at Burke.

When Sir William declined to reply and stared into his brandy, Jay went on with his tale. "I resolved that if it became too cramped, I would pay more and move up to one of the better compartments. First class had just two beds rather than four and I would only have to share my space with one stranger. So, I leaned back and enjoyed my expensive cab ride. Finally. I was on my way." Jay felt better about his story, and his reception here in spite of Burke.

"I had been collecting information right along. Most of it was stored in my head, but I did have a small journal that I tried to keep sort of noncommittal and touristy in case I was ever stopped and questioned or searched and so forth, which never did happen. Way out East they didn't seem too concerned by a foreigner."

MacGregor made a steeple of his hands and queried his companions, "perhaps the war in Europe and the Turkish lands is too far away."

No one answered Mac and Jay forged on with his story. "And except for that one incident with the diamond merchant, I saw no sign of Czarist spies or secret police."

"They are cunning with experience of years, and your first trip is this," Fritz observed. "Perhaps you fail to see them." He then added gently; "spies and secret police. They are brutal, but well trained and good at this job. Very good." Having pointed out the obvious in his direct and sincere way, Fritz motioned Jay onward with their story.

"They'd had a mild winter and a good spring in that district, with plenty of rainfall. So far, the crops seemed plentiful. Everyone was well fed, although there wasn't a great deal of meat to be had. Whenever possible, I would eat with local families." Jay grinned. "It gave me a swell chance to escape my compartment mates.

Whenever the train stopped, or repairs were made, that sort of thing, I would flee. A young steward on the train acted as my guide and interpreter. Yurivich. I wondered whether that was his first name or his last name. He had a few words of English. I had a bit of Polish from my mother, and we both had two hands to gesture and point with. We got along fine.

I always paid the families for our meals, overpaid in fact, and they would fix a package of food for me to take back to the train. I knew they gave me their best. The hospitality they showed me was incredible, and it was right from the heart. They are wonderful people, out there. They live a life of oppression, hard work and minimal food. They have almost no variety, and none of the small luxuries that we take for granted. And yet they shared what little they had with a stranger. Back in my compartment I would give the food to my three compartment mates, my fellow travelers.

Burke asked in a careful, neutral voice, "Tell us about them, Mr. O'Neill. What did you learn from your compartment mates, as you called them?"

"Not a thing," Jay replied keeping his voice just as neutral. "An old man who kept himself drunk most of the time; an oriental woman and her young daughter who I never really saw. The old woman kept herself between me and the girl and she kept the girl bundled up from head to toe.

The old crone yelled at me if I failed to take off my coat as soon as I entered 'their' compartment. I felt like Jack the Ripper or somebody really vile. Even when I shared the good food I brought back, she never relented a bit, and they really needed what I gave them. They had very little money and couldn't afford most of the train food.

Yurivich explained, in a mixture of English, and Polish with hands waving and our chins pointing that it was rude to leave on your coat, once you were in a room; also never refuse a drink from the old man, and most important, never ever shake hands over a threshold. These are all rude and bad luck things. I was beginning to think the Russians were as bad as the Irish."

Jay turned to Mac and in a brogue reminiscent of his father he intoned, "Two men washing in the same water." He brushed his hands, then turned his head and spit into an imaginary sink. "One of the men must spit in the water to break the spell and ward off the bad luck."

Mac laughed and patted Jay's arm. The others smiled, even Sir William, and the tension in the room leveled off to a low hum.

"Oh yes," Jay went on. "Yurivich cautioned me to remove my shoes upon entering the oriental woman's 'home'. He pointed out the prayer rug on our compartment floor and said since I was an infidel, the woman and girl waited for me to leave before kneeling in prayer. After that, I made sure I was gone during prayer times each day and tried to bring back something nice for the woman and her girl from my foraging and spying trips into the countryside.

I took off my coat and shoes upon entering and we got along much better. The old one stopped yelling at me and once the girl even lifted her veil, pulled back her hood and smiled at me. I had a fleeting glimpse of strong, even, gold teeth and then she covered her mouth with her hand and veiled herself again, before the old crone turned around."

Shifting in his seat, Jay faced Burke. "Well...SIR William Burke, I..."

Fritz cut into Jay's monologue. "Here in this chamber, we use no honorifics, my esteemed young friend, *nein*. Else you must call Rene, monsignor, and of course Gregor MacGregor he is King of Scotland, and

I too carry a noble family title, *Wilhelm Frederick Von Meuser,* it is very heavy and burdensome for me. I seldom use it. I am just Fritz." Fritz put his well-polished monocle in place and smiled at Jay across the table. The tension seeped away into the four corners of the elegant old gas lit meeting room.

"Thank you, Fritz. I did learn one very valuable lesson from my roommates. One morning early, I left my compartment and went up forward looking for Yurivich. I wanted more tea or maybe on this day I'd get the coffee he had promised me. I was two cars away, when I realized my cap and coat were back in my room. I went charging back, afraid of losing everything. My room mates were so poor, they had nothing."

Jay spread his hands and shrugged. "The prayer rug was down, unrolled, and the old drunk and the young girl were kneeling on it, praying. The cranky old woman had my coat in her lap and she was busy sewing the places I had torn going over the wall in *Vladivostok.* She smiled, showing a mouth full of bad and missing teeth, and then she reached over, picked up my cap and tossed it to me. When I caught it I could tell my treasure was still intact.

I put my cap on and went hunting for Yurivich again, feeling, if not ten feet tall, at least eight or nine feet in height. If you do something nice for someone; they'll find a way to repay you." Jay paused and looked a challenge at William, while Fritz and Rene nodded.

He appraised the other men and decided he could share this bit with them. It had no real military value and would not violate his American neutrality.

"I did learn something from my roommates. Yurivich told me the story when he and I shared tea in the dining car while my three companions were praying in our compartment.

The old man was pressed into the Imperial Army to fight in the Russo-Japanese war. He was badly wounded, left for dead, then captured and never received proper care for his wounds; certainly not from the Japanese, and not even when he was safely back in Russian hands. He is quite bitter. He feels let down, his country, his government, his Czar, abandoned him.

His wife is even more bitter. Yes, the old woman is his wife and the girl is his daughter. He drinks for the pain. His wife feels bad about the pain and even worse, the drinking. It violates their religion. But she tolerates the drink because she loves him and the alcohol helps his pain. He hasn't worked, can't work, since his military service. They revile the Czar. Curse him. Blame him for all of their bad luck and misfortune. They curse the last war and they curse this new one, even though it may change their bad fortune.

Now, they travel to meet an important General who will give him a medal for his past bravery, and his wounds. The old woman hopes for a pension too and perhaps a little medicine for the pain, which would allow him to work at a new large food depot and railhead being built near their home village.

Yurivich said they would not share this with me because I am a stranger. They hate the Czar; consider him arrogant and vain and dangerous to all the people. They'd like to see him replaced, but they would never say this to an outsider. Bad as he is, the Czar is one of their own. One more thing, the old man exhibited many of the symptoms I had when I was sick from the bad bread, the Ergot. His problems were not all from old war wounds and drinking as the old woman thought."

Fritz set his monocle in place and smiled at them all. "William is correct in that one regard. Czar, Kaiser or King are all the same. A new war needs new young men to fight it. What better way to attract them than to give medals and small pensions to their fathers and uncles who fought for you in the last war. Dress them up. Show them off. Bang the drums and blow horns. Young men will come and help you make a new war."

Fritz turned first to MacGregor and then to William Burke. "Your bagpipes are excellent for this, yes? A small gold coin in the hand; bang the drums, skirl the pipes and young men march away. Excitement and blood, pain and death." He rubbed his bad leg, then turned to Jay and motioned him to continue.

Jay paused and sank back into his seat. His voice changed and he had a dreamy look on his young face. "We were four days out, with lots of stops and breakdowns and delays. I really don't know when she got on the train or if she got on as I did in Vladivostok. But there she was on the other side of the aisle and up forward of me. I tried to keep my attention fixed on the landscape as we chugged our smoky way westward. I tried to estimate the fields of crops and cattle and chickens, but I found myself daydreaming and looking at her.

She was beautiful, breathtaking really. She had a classic face; her eyes were wide-set and slightly tilted up at the outside corners. With prominent cheekbones, she almost could have been a local woman. Did she have mixed blood in her? I wondered whether she was Eurasian? In any case, she was stunning, with long dark hair, wavy, bouncy, rolling around her shoulders as she moved. It kind of cascaded around her face when she turned her head. I knew I'd have to meet her. Not knowing when she'd get off, it seemed important that I meet her right away. And in the right way."

Jay grinned and took a small drink. "And so, of course, being young and a man and aggressive, I stacked the deck in my favor with a little bit of money and told Yurivich what I wanted. That evening I went to the dining car early and selected my seat facing away from the direction I knew she would come. As instructed, Yurivich filled up all the other tables and left mine empty. When she appeared he smoothly escorted her to my table and held the chair out for her to sit facing me as though it was the most natural thing in the world.

And there we were face to face and she was even more beautiful up close. I tried to act nonchalant, but it didn't work. I began to stammer a bit and then she smiled at me and the world rocked in its orbit. Really rocked. Or maybe there was an earthquake. Or the train ran over a bad stretch of track. Her mouth was wide with very white teeth and a smile. Oh my God. Her smile would make the angels in heaven weep with envy.

The train settled down and resumed its steady thrumming again, and I was back on my game. We sat there and stared at each other for what seemed an eternity. Finally, Yurivich came with the wine bottle, filled our glasses and handed us menus. He gave a little half bow to my lovely companion and I could swear she winked at him and something passed from her to him."

Gregor gave a bellow. "Laddie. That steward Yurivich got a tip from both of you. She stacked the deck as well as yourself. Good lad. And good lassie, as well."

Jay blushed and went on. "Maybe. In any case, it was fine. It's so easy to begin when you're discussing food and wine and likes and dislikes and then small personal things slip out. By her questions and her answers I knew she was not Eurasian. She was not from that country. She was just a traveler, much as I was. She seemed just a tourist, and yet she was traveling alone. This was unusual for a young woman. She was poised and very comfortable as though sitting at home in her own drawing room. I couldn't pin down her accent. It was mostly British, with the odd French word here and there, but some of her phrasing, her choice of words sounded the same way my father put his words together.

She drank very little; part of one small glass of wine; said no to the vodka when it came; and no again to the brandy; but yes to the tea. She liked good tea she said. She mentioned several teas that she really liked. I made a mental note of her favorites and wondered where I could get some. She was so easy to talk to. She had me at my ease, and I guess I made her feel the same way.

We kept it informal and started out with first names only. I told her I was Jay, and she told me to call her Dee. This set off a whole new train of thought for me. Was it D for Dorothy or Dee Delores? Deborah? Diane? D-e-e, or D. Hah. I couldn't think of any other girl's names that started with the letter D. All that popped into my head was delightful, divine, delicious, delectable, delirious, desirable. Dee? I felt like a poet or songwriter, not a naval intelligence officer. I was lost in her name, in her smile, her eyes, her form. I couldn't see much of her form, but what I saw and what I imagined was truly wonderful.

She had on a white blouse and a dark skirt down to her ankles and a sort of traveling cloak over that. The cloak had a sort of a half cape affair at the shoulders and down her back. Her hands were well made and strong and her neck and skin seemed fair and quite lovely. I wondered briefly about the rest of her and then pushed those thoughts out of my head.

We stayed at the table and talked well into the night. Poor Yurivich. He earned his money that night. She drank cup after cup of tea from small ceramic pots finely made and hand painted. I finally had some vodka. It was strong but I didn't care. I was drunk already.

At end of the evening I walked her to her compartment. We said a long goodnight with meaningful looks and a handshake and I knew we'd be friends. I wondered if it would lead to more and I knew I wanted more than a just a friendship. I wondered if she was wondering, too."

William motioned to Reginald and said. "Speaking of tea, Reginald. I think we all could use some. Jay, would you prefer coffee?" William asked with careful civility. Jay, engrossed in his story, shook his head no. Reginald immediately collected the glasses, and set off to get their tea. And then each of the men nodded at Gregor as if to thank him for bringing this young man and his story into their group. They had each been in love, some of them several times, and as men and as writers they were extremely interested in how Jay's story unfolded.

"Next morning, I shaved very close and dressed with care. I chose a shirt and trousers that I knew flattered my trim figure and put on a loose jacket over it: my-special-hand-made-by-an-old-Chinese-man-jacket. In the dining car there was just one table open. It was the same one we had last night. I approached it from one end and she came in from the other end of the car and we sat down together. It was right out of a stage play and oh she had a fine walk. Good posture, a firm step and so confidant and yet so womanly. Our conversation picked up just where we left off the night before, and it all seemed so natural.

And it went like that for several days. Dee and I ate at the same table, three meals a day. We became an item. People, total strangers, would applaud when we entered the dining car. I sure didn't earn my Navy pay on those days. Between meals we'd sit together, or stand out on the platform holding hands. We were invited aft to the crew's car. The crew even invited us to come up forward to visit with the engineers in the cab. It was all very fine, but the problem was, we had no privacy at all.

"A*lors.*" Rene smiled, "They were making wagers on which compartment, yours or hers, where you would end each night. *Oh non mon ami.* You 'ad the drinking man and a praying woman with a bashful daughter in your bedroom." Rene laughed and slapped his knee. Then he held his head between his two hands and rocked from side to side, laughing again. "Old drunk man. Praying woman. Shy young *femme* with golden teeth." He laughed and wiped his eyes.

Jay blushed and rushed ahead. "One morning I awoke to see the young daughter kneeling at my bedside. She had my *Shian Bao* cupped in her two hands and had been holding it under my nose. That's what woke me, the smell of Sandalwood. She took and shoved it under my pillow where it usually was each night, and indicated it had fallen to the floor. The way she handled it, she must have thought it was some sort of religious icon for me. I thanked her and she tiptoed back to her bed."

MacGregor smiled, "She had been a keen observer of your actions, Jay. She knew that you often smelled the scent of it, and that you slept with it under your pillow."

Fritz added, "and you valued that diamond shaped silk quite high, yes?"

"Yes fritz. We reached a level of civility in our four person compartment but all that was about to change. That morning, right after breakfast, the train ground to a halt with a lot of whistle blowing and shouting in many different languages. The steward came and cleared our dishes, the teapot and cups, and then a man in uniform came through and announced there had been a mishap, a big storm, a flood and great damage. The bridge was out. A train was coming for us on the other side of the river. We should get off now. All the cargo and our luggage would follow. They provided us with a sort of jitney thing, like a bus, but horse-drawn. People were spilling out of the train into this contraption. The day was mild so we didn't really need any extra clothing. We were told everything would be brought from our compartments to the new train, and we trusted our Yurivich to take good care of us."

"As we were approaching the steps to go down, our magnificent steward came up and pulled us aside. The official was there with him and they explained to both of us that our Yuri Yurivich had a cousin who lived in this district. The cousin owned a horse and wagon and would take us, just us, to see some of the countryside, have a picnic lunch and then cross the river and meet the train. Yes there would be several hours' delay before the new train arrived at the other side of the river. It sure beat sitting for hours in one of those jitneys. And we'd be alone. I thanked Yuri and the official. Some more money changed hands and Dee had a big smile on her face. She was holding a picnic basket that Yuri had provided for us. She looked like a country girl off on an outing. And we were, of course."

Reginald set the tea things on the table and Fritz spoke out, "A perfect opportunity for you, *Herr Jay*, for you both."

Rene almost crooned. "A young man on an adventure with a beautiful maid. *Bien*. I hope there was wine in the basket."

"I went to take it from her, and go down the three steps to the ground. She motioned me ahead, so I stepped down, turned 'round to help her, and she stepped down flipping her skirt out of the way to give me a glimpse of a fine left leg. She swirled her skirt again, and showed her right leg. They were wonderful legs, both of them. She swirled it again but didn't step down, and when I looked up Dee had a big grin on her face. She was enjoying watching me watch her."

"I made a gallant bow, reached up for the basket and helped her down. She was still grinning at me. And as we walked away, swinging the basket between us, the entire train cheered us.

CHAPTER THREE

"It was a mild sunny day, a perfect spring day. We walked away from the crowd, swinging the basket between us and sure enough there was the wagon with his cousin the driver waving us on. There were three horses. It was a real Russian Troika and the driver, the cousin, was a small wide man with mustaches flowing down beyond his chin.

His clothes were right out of an opera. He wore a large black wooly hat, a bright red coat with golden epaulets on each shoulder, a wide black leather belt and long, baggy, green trousers stuffed into over-the-knee brown felt boots. I asked him his name and he said Troika. Maybe he misunderstood, or maybe that was how he was called.

I put the picnic basket up in the back of the wagon and went to help Dee, but she had already clambered in. I just barely had time to swing up next to her when he cracked his whip and we were on our way.

We were laughing and screaming and he was laughing looking back at us with one eye on the road, slapping, snapping his whip over the three horses. We drove down stream away from the train and then splashed across a low spot in the river and went on and up a small hill on the other side. And then Troika turned and we went back upstream again and kept going about a mile or two.

Finally he pulled the horses up and motioned us to get down and take the basket. We were all alone on a dusty rutted trail that fell away steeply on one side. It seemed cooler and we could hear the roar of a rushing stream. We looked over the side and sure enough there was a beautiful waterfall below us. He motioned with his hands moving as though he were climbing down the rocks. And then he held up three fingers and made a motion as though a hand was spinning on a clock. And I assumed he meant he would be back for us in a couple of hours."

Jay Paused. "Mac, I need directions to the men's room and maybe some more tea when I come back. My kidneys are bursting and at the same time, I'm quite dry from all this talking."

"Reginald, please direct our young story teller to the men's toilet and bring us more tea," William said, and nodded in approval at Gregor and the other two men.

Jay sagged against the wall in the rest room and faced his dilemma. He wanted their help. He must have their help; use their collective ideas, wisdom, and contacts. Gregor had told him to include everything. All details. Don't leave anything out. But some parts of his story were private, meant for himself and Deirdre alone, they were too private to tell others.

It was so fresh in his mind it might've happened this morning and yet parts of it seemed like a dream. And so he sank down onto a plush chair and relived in his mind their wonderful encounter, which now seemed hazy and almost unreal. It was his dream, his and Deirdre's. He closed his eyes and relived this part of his story in private, and only to himself.

'I would go first, to help her climb down but she said no. I was to take the basket. She would go first. Dee got three steps down and I heard a little shriek, and she came back up. She looked up and down the road. We were alone in the middle of nowhere. Troika and the horses were gone.'

She said, "turn around please." I did so, and a minute later, she laid her skirt over my shoulder. "Please fold my skirt and put it on the picnic basket with our coats." Quickly then, one-two-three slips followed. I folded them and put them on the basket between the handles. Next came two shoes for my pockets. And then she draped two stockings around my neck. They were wonderful stockings, still warm from her legs and they smelled so good. They were warming my neck and filling me with the scent of Dee, and while I was enjoying her stockings around my neck she bowled me over with her directness.

"Close your eyes, Jay O'Neill from New York and the American

Navy.—don't you look. Please—I peeked at your passport—don't look at me—on the train." From behind me her two hands held my head from turning and she spoke almost into my ear. "I am Deirdre DalCas from County Clare, Ireland. I'll show you mine later. My passport, I mean." She giggled and then she was gone.

I opened my eyes and looked around and she had almost disappeared down the rocky path. I grabbed the picnic basket and followed after her and without too much of a tussle we got down to the bottom and there she stood in her blouse and bloomers. They covered down to her knees and were tied at the bottom. She held her arms out and pirouetted and she was a fine figure of a woman. A sweet girl indeed, except for her devilish eyes and wide full mouth in a big grin after putting one over on me. She wrapped her coat around herself, placed her hand in mine, and we started down the trail.

Soon, the waterfall was so loud we had to shout to hear each other. We rounded a bend still holding hands and stopped. We stood, totally silent, and admired the scene before and above us. We were awestruck at the might and majesty of the moving water and the overwhelming sound it produced.

There was the waterfall towering high over us. It fell for a hundred feet or more, but not straight down. It fell and twisted, splashing, fell and turned back, split and rejoined. It was just fantastic to see the water dropping down, dashing against the rocks and sending sheets of spray in all directions. Overall, a bright rainbow arched over and down, shimmering colors on all that water. At the bottom was a pool rimmed all around by large boulders.

We found a big flat rock back from the spray, laid out her coat and my jacket and the other clothing and then opened the picnic basket and sure enough there was a blanket, so we added it to the pile. Deirdre asked if I was hungry. I said no, not yet. I can wait a bit. She took her stockings and tied them around my eyes and said, 'Close your eyes', and the next thing I knew she was squealing and splashing in the cold water of the pool and the rest of her clothes were on our flat rock next to me. I shouted, but she couldn't hear me so I mimed her closing her eyes. She nodded yes she would, but there was that big grin again.

I undressed anyway and dove in. I held my breath underwater and swam completely around her and had a good look at her under the water and my God, she was beautiful. When I came up sputtering, she was laughing and then it was her turn. She took a deep breath, dove underwater, and I felt her swimming around me, completely around me, and I knew she was having a good look for herself. I guess we each liked what we saw.

She came up spitting water at me, 'well Jay O'Neill of the United States Navy.' She looked into my eyes for the longest time, and in a husky voice she said 'I approve. Do You?'

Yes and yes and again yes and then we were chest to chest, warm breast to warm breast, our legs twisting, winding, seeking the perfect fit around each other in the icy cold water. Too soon we both realized it was time to get out and get warm. And we did, and we made love on the blanket and the pile of clothes, and our lovemaking was new and exciting, raw and smooth, gentle and demanding. We were the first man and the first woman, as ancient as the rocks we were on, as strong as the flow of this river, and as new as each rainbow soaked drop of moisture.

Our shouts and cries of delight got lost and mingled in the roaring waterfall that filled us and surrounded us. We rubbed each other dry and helped each other dress, and then we ate, and finished the wine. Just in time for we saw small stones bouncing down near us. It was Troika. He was above us, shouting, jumping, and throwing rocks to call us.

On our way up the steep, rocky path I repeated her name, Deirdre DalCas several times. I had my woman, a real woman, and I had her real name, Deirdre DalCas from County Clare, Ireland.

I knew my father would be pleased too, and I could picture him smiling, saying her name and his eyebrows rising as his smile got bigger; 'a girl from Clare is it, Jay? Deirdre DalCas from County Clare,' and he would smile wide and shake his head the way he did when he was pleased. 'Your mam would've liked her Jay. 'Twas well known that she liked the Irish.' And he'd chuckle and give another shake of his head. I need to bring them together now, my father and my woman. I knew she would like him, too.

Troika got us to the new train in plenty of time. I gave him a ridiculous amount of money as a tip and he kissed us both three times, twice on one cheek and once on the other. Troika leaped up onto his wagon, made a great whoop and from a standing position gave a wild swing of his whip at the three horses; and with a wave of his hat he was gone. We three watched him go, Deirdre and I from the dusty rail tracks and cousin Yuri awaiting us up on the train.

Yuri kept looking at us and nodding his head. He announced he had been forced to give me a first class accommodation on this new train and therefore I owed him money. Trying to hide my relief, I agreed. He beamed at me and led us to my new bedroom. The compartment was a bit larger and had only two beds.

My duffle was sitting on one bed and Deirdre's bags filled the other. Yuri looked long and puzzled at Deirdre to gauge her reaction and then turned his face to me with a questioning look. Deirdre and I began to laugh and that answered his question. She grabbed Yuri Yurivich and gave him three big kisses. I of course followed her lead and shoved a wad of cash into his hand while kissing his bearded cheeks. We three joined hands, made small bows to each other and then Yuri left us alone. The door had barely closed behind him when we were pressed together, kissing, caressing, celebrating our first moment in our own private rolling bedroom.

But this part of my story would remain private, just ours alone, just mine and Deirdre's.'

On his way back to the meeting room Jay saw William down at the end of the corridor speaking to someone. It was a man, and not one of the men from the meeting. It did not seem to be Reginald, either. Perhaps, he thought, it was just another servant in this stuffy men's club. Jay walked back, knocked and entered the elegant meeting room.

The tea had been refreshed and scones were set out on a large silver platter. Jay poured himself some tea but ignored the food. He had spent too much time inactive while on the train and on the ship before that, and eating all that heavy Russian food had not helped. His trousers felt a bit tight at the waist, and he pledged himself to resume his normal training routine just as soon as he found his Deirdre.

"Well come on lad. William has stepped out somewhere, but the rest of us are antsy to have more of your story," Gregor said.

"In the picnic basket was the wine, yes? As Rene has proposed?" Fritz asked.

Jay sipped his tea and gauged his three listeners. "Yes, there was wine, there was good food. We were alone at last and we had a wonderful picnic."

Sighs of understanding, disappointment and regret came from his audience and Jay quickly moved on. "In the new train, I was assigned a first class compartment with just two beds. There was much more room and you'll never guess who my roommate was."

This time the three men exclaimed in delight and took pleasure in his good fortune, or good planning, or whatever it was that brought an exciting young woman into his compartment to share his journey.

"There were two major incidents along this stage of the journey," Jay resumed his tale as soon as they would allow him to leave the story of his sleeping arrangements.

Rene and Fritz and Gregor were all exclaiming and the level of excitement climbed higher. "Press on my good *raconteur*."

"Proceed my dear Jay, with haste, *ja?*"

"Tell on, laddie, tell on."

"The old man, yes, the drinking man, or wounded veteran as I now thought of him, with his wife and daughter, were leaving the train. He to collect his medal and perhaps a pension, and they to watch him in this, his delayed, but deserved, moment of glory. He was no longer a man who broke all his religious laws by drinking, no longer a shame and burden upon his family. He was now their hero, the head of the family and their hope for the future.

The change in the old man was startling. Except for a small beard, he was clean shaven, wore a clean and pressed suit and was as bright and shiny as a big new English copper penny. His eyes were clear and he had a great smile as he helped his wife and daughter down from the train to their waiting automobile. The woman and young girl also wore fine, clean new outfits. Their ensembles were quite old fashioned, but the woman looked presentable and the girl with the golden smile was fetching.

Yurivich came up and explained to Deirdre and I. 'Everyone in their village made a contribution and loaned them some clothing so they could attend this most auspicious ceremony. Is very good, yes?' When we had agreed it was good, he pointed to the large open touring car 'A cousin loaned us the automobile but he cannot drive us, today. I myself am willing, but cousin says NO.' Yuri wagged his finger back and forth. 'Yuri not so good a driver. We wait now. Maybe cousin's driver will not come too late for this affair. Train will not go forward anyway until after big ceremony, after big General Kamzarov leaves, all military will leave, then this train also goes ahead.'

"Yuri shrugged his shoulders and held his hands out, palms up. It was a very Russian gesture, eloquent, pleading and I could almost see tears in his eyes. Of course, I offered to drive. Deirdre, as usual in these matters, was way ahead of me. She had a picnic basket by her side, and a smile on her lovely face. So, the three of us joined the family in the grand touring car and we were off to a happy event for my former travel mates, and to witness a strategic military affair. It was also a political good will mission and very important for the Czar's government. And of course it will look good in my report so I drove with Deirdre on my arm, so to speak, and the day turned into a huge success for everyone. It was better than we could've imagined.

It was wonderful. The air was warm; the low clouds stayed on the horizon, so the sky remained sunny and Deirdre settled into her seat beside me and kept smiling. I truly loved watching her enjoy herself. We followed the crowd with me driving the big open car. I went ahead slow and careful. At the sight of the shiny, expensive auto, people waved and saluted us, some of them even bowed to us.

The old man took it right in stride, bowing and waving back. This was indeed his party. The old woman, though, remained stiff and stared straight ahead as though scared of the event. The young girl, her veil gone now, showed her gold teeth in a huge smile, first to the left and then to the right, but always to the side opposite the old man's bows and waves. Deirdre and I enjoyed their varying reactions while Yuri was his usual competent self. The crowd parted for us and we drove slowly past, smiling, waving, saluting and on out to the large parade grounds."

"There is Mayors Palace," Yuri pointed to an imposing building at one end of the grounds. "Palace is place of all Czar's government for this district. We will drop old man by lines of chairs facing Palace. Please, go by other side of, how you say, square field. Do not drive into military band on this side. They will play music for us, ver' soon."

"I drove past ranks of soldiers to the first row of chairs facing the Palace. A young officer in fancy parade dress uniform jumped to attention and saluted us all. He sprang to the passenger side and opened both the front and rear doors, then resumed his salute. Yuri stood and saluted the old man, called him our honored veteran and held his salute as the old veteran stood ramrod straight and returned the military honorific as he stepped down and limped over to an empty chair."

"We can park over there," Yuri said and pointed to the left side of the large drill field. "This is important automobile. Park us in prominent place, and in plain sight of all onlookers and also with good view, please."

"I pulled ahead towards the Palace, then backed and turned into a spot next to another large car with a flag on the fender. The General's official car? Yuri nodded. He was pleased with our vantage place. We had a terrific view for the ceremony. To our left was the Palace, to our right were seated the honored veterans awaiting medals and behind the old veterans stood rank after rank of Russian soldiers. Straight ahead of us was a platform for the speakers. Beyond the platform at the far end of the rows of seats and facing us, was the military band.

They began tuning up the instruments and we sat there admiring all the ceremonial bunting, banners and guidons and the flags snapping in the breeze. As a military man, I admired the brave show they displayed as they prepared to honor their living heroes.

Deirdre turned to Yuri and asked about a ladies rest room. He assured her the Mayor's Palace had such a room and if she hurried, before the General came to the podium, it will be all right. When Yuri asked, the old woman shook her head no and again no for the daughter. I wanted to escort Deirdre but she said she'd find it herself and I should enjoy the Russian Army in all its glory. Yuri, the petrified old woman and the now buoyant young girl enjoyed the Russian Army while I enjoyed watching my woman as she walked over to the Palace. Deirdre had great posture and the walk of a country girl. She kept to a long stepping, arm-swinging brisk pace with just the hint of a sway. She was a pleasure to watch.

The band warmed up with a stirring march and we were all applauding when Deirdre appeared and began her solitary march back to the car. One of the drummers picked up her pace with a short TAT...TAT...TAT, on the edge of his drum with each step she took. Soon another drummer joined in and it was RrrraT...TaT...TaT. RrrraT...TaT...TaT. RrrraT...TaT...TaT, with every step and finally all the drummers were in the game, giving a rolling drumbeat to every step she took. Deirdre, chin high, her arms swinging, smiled wider and began to sway her hips as she marched back to us. It was incredible and she was a delight to watch.

First, all the old veterans rose to their feet and cheered her on. Then the ranks of soldiers stood and began cheering, flinging their caps high in the air, calling out and clapping for her. I almost threw my own cap into the air, but I thought of Wan Lee and left it on my head. In back of me the young daughter was standing on the seat, yelling and cheering with both hands raised high. The old woman was mortified and tried to pull her down, while Yuri on her other side, steadied her by holding her waist. Deirdre was glowing as she reached the car, climbed in next to me, and gave me a big kiss. It was a fine moment.

Just then the General appeared. He thought the drumming and cheering was for him, so he smiled broadly and swaggered and waved his way to the podium and saluted the veterans who were still standing and cheering. It was a wonderful moment. The men were cheering and General Kamzarov was glowing, basking in the cheers he thought were for him.

Yuri shouted above the crowd noise, 'this is good for all old veterans. General Kamzarov is pleased. Is very good also for our wounded old drunk man. The General, he is very Russian. He will now be generous, thinking that all his men love him. Maybe Kamzarov will regret it later, but now he will be good to these old men. He will give them medals and pensions and maybe gold coins, too. That was a golden cheer we just heard.' Yuri turned to Deirdre and bowed. 'Thank you, beautiful Irish woman, Deirdre.'

I had never heard Yuri Yurivich give such a long speech, but my attention was focused on the commotion in the rear seat. All of this walking and drumming and cheering and even Yuri's words were lost on the old woman. She was busy trying to get her daughter back down into the car. When the drumming began, the girl had climbed onto the rear seat of the open car and cheered first for Deirdre. When Deirdre got in beside me, this girl with the golden smile turned, and with her arms raised high, she yelled and cheered at all the young soldiers.

They of course kept cheering and waving and the general loved all of it. When she turned at last and sat down, our girl with the golden smile was breathless and flushed from the excitement. She enjoyed the scene immensely; it was written all over her animated face. It was clear that she wished with her entire young body that she too had gone to the Mayors Palace alongside of Deirdre."

Rene was clapping, keeping a beat to Jay's story. "*Ah oui.* That young one will relive the story, *eh?* She will picture it is herself walking, arms swinging and men cheering wildly for her, until that memory in her head will become hers, and she will be the marching girl, not Deirdre."

Fritz seemed pensive as he polished his monocle and regarded Jay. "Did your woman meet that Russian general, *Herr Kamzarov,* do you think?"

"I asked Deirdre that same question, Fritz. She said they met briefly in the hallway. There was a tense moment of appraisal between them. Deirdre said she curtsied as an old fashioned girl might and the general made a deep bow, bending his knee and sweeping his hat across his chest in an equally old fashioned way. He immediately turned into an office doorway, while she came outside and back to the touring car. The bow and the curtsy was the extent of their meeting. Why do you ask, Fritz?"

Fritz just shook his head and rubbed his bad leg with long vigorous strokes, the way a groom would rub a thorobred horse.

Jay poured himself some tea and gathered his thoughts. He had promised them two stories from this stage of his journey. He wondered how to tell this next episode without upsetting or offending anyone.

Before Jay could begin, William came in, took his seat and put a slim leather folder on the table in front of him. William spoke first to Jay, and then included all of them. In a clipped and very serious tone he commanded Jay to hold the balance of his story for another meeting. "Next week may be more appropriate," he intoned. When the others all objected, he revised his demand and insisted that Jay cut short his story, and proceed directly to the part where he met Gregor in Paris. "We must authenticate some of the details within your story before we commit as a group, to aiding you, you see. Of course we are willing to help and you may simply tell the rest of your story at another time. Harrumph." William cleared his throat amid more cries of outrage and anger by the other men. "Time is slipping by, and we must make best use of what time we have, my fine young fellow."

"*Mon Dieu*," Rene exclaimed. "I am most interested in this story, William Burke. Go on, Jay O'Neill." Gesturing with Gallic gusto to both Jay and William.

Fritz polished his monocle with great energy and blurted out, "*Mien Gott, Wilhelm.* You are too...too..."

"Bloody bossy." MacGregor exploded, finishing Fritz's thought for him. "We are co-equals in this fine group, Wee Willie, and don't forget it. Jay, we accept that your tale is 'true as told' and will help you as much as we are able." MacGregor glared at Burke. "With or without you, Honorable Wee Willy bloody Burke."

William Burke held up his two hands, palms out, in a silent plea for peace and gestured them all to be reseated as he sat down himself.

Jay continued in an almost trancelike tone. "I'll go directly to the puzzling part. The train was approaching Paris. I went ahead to the dining car after packing all my stuff, figuring I would catch an early breakfast. Deirdre mentioned that she would like some time alone, packing and planning and..." Here, Jay shrugged and shook his head. "Being a woman, I guess."

Rene agreed. "*Cherchez la femme,*" he exclaimed. Then remembered he had spent the better part of his life as a celibate, and so he subsided and urged Jay to continue.

"When I got back to the car the compartment was empty. All of our bags were gone, hers and mine. Quickly, I found a porter and asked him and he said our bags were on the platform awaiting our arrival at the station, ...in Paris. We were due in at any moment, and sure enough there on the platform was my duffle, but none of Dierdre's bags. I went back to our room and it was still empty. Next I went back to the dining car where I had just finished my breakfast. She wasn't there. I walked the train from front to back, but no Deirdre.

I was beginning to panic. Back again to our compartment. Still empty and the corridors were filling up with people milling around, ready to end their journey in Paris, making plans, meeting people. A hubbub in four or five different languages was going on. I didn't know where she could be and didn't know why she wasn't in the dining car, why her bags were not next to mine on the platform.

Finally, I saw one of the cleaning crew pushing a sort of laundry cart. She was just coming out of our compartment. I asked if she had cleaned the room? Was it bare? Did she find anything at all? As I turned to go she grabbed my arm, shoved a newspaper in my hands and motioned that she had found it in the cushions. By then the train had stopped and people were all around me, getting their bags, stepping off, calling out, greeting each other.

I got out and ran up and down the platform looking to see if they had put her bags on another platform, or another car. Did she get off the train? I couldn't see her anywhere.

My heart jumped when I remembered; during breakfast there had been a whistle and a brief stop at some little village just outside of Paris. The train stopped for just barely a moment, and I couldn't figure out if that had anything to do with Deirdre. Had she left the train at that stop? That tiny place? Why there? Did she leave me without a word? But Why? What was going on? Did I do or say something?" Jay shook his head, still in disbelief.

"And that is when I saw him", MacGregor took over the story. "Son of my best friend all grown and looking the image of his father, but in a great deal of turmoil. We got his bag and scoured the station. We then scoured it again, and asked the local *Gendarmes* to help us. Finally, after we'd exhausted every possibility, we took the boat train to London and under my prodding, and a few early morning whiskies, I had the story from him, or most of it in any case."

Jay was alive, alert and back to his old self. He took over his story with a nod and a thank you to MacGregor. "I gave the paper from our compartment to Mac. It's my only real clue. Mac said he'd hand it to the one man who could find any hidden message and decipher any clue therein. Is there is a clue? Did Deirdre leave a message? If there is a message, is it for me? What did she say? Is there anything you can tell me?"

"*Ja*," Fritz exclaimed proudly and clicked his heels together for emphasis. "I find buried treasure hidden in plain sight." He adjusted his monocle, looked around and removed it from his eye. When he was sure of their undivided attention, he began. "Scholars of my Germany would study old parchments to understand our Teutonic Culture, *ja*? They find many notes in some ancient tongue, made by missionaries of long ago."

"*Mon dieu*. Of course. Monks from Ireland spread Christianity to all of Europe," Rene exclaimed.

Jay leaped to his feet demanding hard information from Fritz or Rene or someone, and William held up his open leather case and pointed to the papers inside, but Fritz would not be cut short in his moment of disclosure.

"*Ja Herr O'Neill*," and Fritz struggled to his feet, "I am comfortable in this old tongue. I have studied ancient Gaelic, the language of your father and his fathers before him."

"An ancient form of Irish Gaelic," William the Don interjected. "German scholars had to go to Ireland and learn the Irish of today, a dying language, in order to decipher and fully understand the voluminous notes in their own old Germanic manuscripts."

"*Ja*, and from the Gaelic notes, and many other sources, the German scholars founded a culture which leads to unity of purpose and made a strong nation." Fritz offered.

Mac sighed, "and today we are at war with that strong nation. Good for the monks."

Jay almost shouted. "What was the message? What is the clue? Did you find anything, Fritz? How do I find her?"

"Deirdre DalCas is her name, that is a beginning," William spewed out the information with pure venom. "It is not a proper surname at all, but an ancient Celtic clan name. The eleventh century High King Brian Boru, was one, and the Kennedy clan, and the O'Briens, the O'Mahoneys, they all came from this DalCas Clan. As far as we are concerned, my own English people and our British Empire, they are all trouble makers. They live in our back yard and are a constant danger to us. Always have been, and they always will be."

Fritz, unperturbed, gestured with his monocle, "We approach the finale of your so interesting story, *Herr Jay O'Neill.* I find there are clues from that paper. Her name," Fritz made a stiff small bow to William Burke, "is Deirdre of the DalCas Clan. And a named place, perhaps a church or abbey is included, with a series of numbers." Fritz shrugged, "perhaps it is a telephone exchange. It is there, perhaps, in that church or Abbey, where she will be found."

"The Holy Ground it is called." William spat out the name. He was very red in the face.

"The Holy Ground", Jay repeated, almost reverently.

"And a number," Fritz continued. "Probably attached to a telephone, which will give us a town or city."

"Where? What place? Which city. For God's sake, help me. Give me the information, Fritz," Jay pleaded. "I must know everything there is to know." He was desperate.

"Queenstown," William declared. "The main harbour for Cork City, and the principle point of embarkation for our soldiers from all over the Empire heading to the warfront in France and Belgium. We are at war, you know." He glared at Jay and then at Fritz. "Your fine new culture and nation have become a war mongering empire, my good Fritz. Right now, men are dying, even as we speak."

"On both sides," Rene murmured. He made a small sign of the cross on his breast. "In war men die on both sides, my learned comrade."

Fritz wasn't finished yet and he ignored William's tirade. "C-o-b-h," he spelled it out, "or *Cove*, is the way the local Irish call that town. And another consequence of those dear monks from by-gone days is that the German scholars studying the *old Irish language* awakened in today's Irish scholars a thirst for their own language and customs." Here Fritz shook his monocle at William and spoke with passion. "Two peoples, two stirrings toward nationhood." Here he was gesturing with both arms, while leaning, favoring his injured leg. "All from some scribbling in the edges of old parchments. An awakening for these two peoples." Fritz smiled, made a small stiff bow and sat down, satisfied with his performance.

"And possibly TWO wars with those stirred up nationalistic peoples," William shuffled the papers in his file. "We soon will have an armed insurrection with those so called Irish Patriots right here in our own back yard, whilst we fight the stirred up Germanic peoples on the continent."

Gregor, the large Scotsman, shook his head in dismay as his group seemed to slip further into discord. "Perhaps, Jay, it was a mistake to bring you here into this gathering of men who are supposed to be dedicated to peace, while our own nations are at each others throats." He looked to Rene for support, but Rene shook his head and shrugged with both hands. He could never fathom man's passion for military things and wars and killing.

Jay leaned towards Gregor and ignored William's tirade. "My father always called it *Cove*. Never Queenstown. It's the place he sailed away from when he left Ireland as a boy, and if that's where Deirdre is, then that's where I'll go."

"Just one moment there, Jay O'Neill, you young Junior American Naval Officer." William fairly sputtered at Jay. "You have prior commitments and besides The Holy Ground...."

"Wee Willie, hush your gob," Gregor turned and grabbed Jay by the shoulders. "I'll tell the lad," and he held Jay until everyone settled down and the room became very quiet. "Queenstown or *Cove* is indeed a great harbour; and on a hill overlooking that harbour is the Cathedral; and up behind the cathedral is The Holy Ground, well known to every sailor and soldier since the days of Wellington. Jay, The Holy Ground is a brothel. Look at me. Yes laddie, a brothel. It's one of the best in Europe and well known to military people, soldiers and sailors alike, since Christ was a corporal."

Jay closed his eyes as though by shutting out his sight he could amend his hearing. "Look at me Jay. Hold my eyes now, with your own, my lad. And know that sometimes things are not what they seem." He paused and said over his shoulder, "Reggie, take away this tea. Bring us a bottle of your best whisky. And be damned quick with it."

Sir William rattled the papers in his file and pronounced his judgment. "Your young woman is very probably a prostitute and quite possibly an agent for those Irish Rebels who wish to start a rebellion against our King and Empire. The Holy Ground, in addition to being a brothel, is a known hangout, a meeting place, for the Irish Republican Brotherhood. That is a secret organization whose goal is the violent overthrow of British law and rule in Ireland. As an American officer, you shall not meddle in the internal affairs of our Empire."

"Wee Willie, sometimes you have a vindictive streak in you a furlong wide and just as deep." Gregor drew a deep breath and continued with annoyance, "and you are too chummy by half with that crowd in the War Office. Hold your tongue 'til we all get our thoughts going in the proper direction."

Over his shoulder Mac bellowed, "Reginald, where in hell is that whisky. Now Jay, Wee Willie is correct in that one regard. You must report in at once to your headquarters."

"Of course," Jay retorted. His head was rocking and his world was falling apart but his training took charge and he answered automatically, "My admiral is at the American Embassy. I expect to see him first thing tomorrow morning. He'll want a full report. And I will give it to him, Mac. He will know everything that I know."

Gregor waved his hands and continued. "Excellent. Then we'll take a few days and see about a trip to Queenstown, I mean *Cove*, of course. Thanks Reg." Reginald entered with a bottle and whisky glasses on a silver tray. MacGregor poured a drink for each and handed one to Jay. "Now lad, get yourself outside of that fine whisky while I give you some good news for a change." Gregor pulled a telegram from his jacket and opened it up.

"Thanks Mac." Jay took the whisky in one gulp and held his glass out for another. "I'll go to the embassy and see the admiral first thing in the morning. He'll be delighted to see me. Now Mac, I hope that good news is something special."

Gregor began to read his telegram, "To Mac M'Gregor, king of the Scots. Stop." He looked over at Jay and grinned. "Arriving Liverpool by ship on the 8th. Stop. The 'Greyhound of the Seas,' a fine ship. Stop.

Check shipping news for arrival time. Stop. Jay expected in England any day now. Stop. Check our embassy and bring him with you, if possible. Stop. My best regards always. Stop. Your brother Sean, The O'Neill."

Jay rose up, grabbed the whisky bottle from Reginald, and with a flourish he re-filled all of the glasses and smiled at everyone including his nemeses, Wee Willie Burke. "Gentlemen, will you join me in a toast, please." The men rose and their glasses met and clinked over the center of the table as Jay gave his toast. "I give you good health and long life to my father Sean O'Neill and his best friend and brother, Mac M'Gregor, King of the Scots."

They drank and Jay grinned at Mac, but MacGregor's eyes were fixed upon Burke across the table. He had not joined them in the toast. William Burke was huddled back into his seat looking pale and very upset. He had his leather file case open in front of him.

"My dear God in Heaven." William held wide his arms in a plea to the others and in a stricken voice muttered a sincere apology. "Gregor. Jay. I had no idea. None at all. I'm sorry. So sorry." From his leather case he selected an official dispatch. "This is from the Admiralty," and he began to read.

"7 May, 1915 at 1430 hours the Lusitania sank off The Old Head of Kinsale, in the South West of Ireland. It is believed a German U boat, U-20, fired one or more torpedoes. The 'Greyhound of the Seas' went down in 18 minutes. Astounding. Many, perhaps most, feared dead. Rescue operations, as such, are being undertaken from Queenstown and other points on the southern coast of Ireland."

The men sat down and no one spoke. No one made eye contact. Except for the hissing of the gas lamps, there was immediate and total silence in this elegant old meeting room.

CHAPTER FOUR

At the embassy later that evening, the Admiral had been stern about the debriefing. "Be thorough, Jay. I want it all, every encounter and every thought. Now grab your duffle and get over to Waterloo Station. I'll have an embassy staff member there to travel with you. He'll take it all down; transcribe your report nice and neat. You will sign it and he'll bring it back to me, and honestly Jay, I am most anxious to read it."

The Admiral relaxed and regarded the younger man with some affection. "It's all been laid on, Jay. A special train to Swansea in Wales and a Royal Navy frigate to Queenstown, Ireland." The Admiral rummaged through the files and papers on his desk, until he found the small box he'd been looking for.

"The Lusitania has become an International incident and we may be dragged into this war because of it. So many of us Americans aboard; so many died." He winced as he thought of Jay's father. "A Maritime Board of Enquiry is being set up, but that will take months, maybe years to sort out, so we have a sort of Ad Hoc International Committee to look into the sinking right now. There are the British of course, and our Embassy, a French agent and even a Swiss chap. You are part of our delegation, but feel free to pursue your own search.

It seems there were two explosions on the ship. German agents both in New York and Washington claim the Lusitania was carrying munitions for the British war effort and therefore the ship was fair game and open to attack. Civilian passengers should have been warned of this, but they were not. The munitions caused the second explosion. According to the Germans there was no second torpedo.

The British say there were no munitions aboard, no contraband. There was a second torpedo, and that is what caused the second and larger explosion. Thus the attack was totally unprovoked and against the rules of war." And under his breathe, the Admiral added, "as if any war has rules."

The Brits want us in, Jay, on their side, of course. We share the same customs, same language, Mother England, and so forth, as though we hadn't already fought two wars against them. The Kaiser would like us to remain neutral, but REALLY neutral. So, keep your eyes and ears open while you are about your personal business, Jay. We need to report on up the chain of command so President Wilson and the Congress can make the right decision. Do we go in, and if so, on whose side? Then it's when, where, and how do we go to war? Is it to be a full out war effort or just money, material and a few token forces?"

The Admiral was totally understanding about Jay's father. "Officially you are part of our Embassy team Jay, but you will be independent and have a free hand for your search. I hope to God you find him alive, Lieutenant." The Admiral handed Jay a small box containing a set of First Lieutenant gold shoulder bars and Jay snapped his hand to his brow in time to return the salute the Admiral was giving him. It wasn't often that an admiral saluted a junior officer. "Congratulations Mr. O'Neill. You are now one of the youngest First Lieutenants in our United States Navy. Those bars were mine when I served on the old USS MAINE." He held out his hand and Jay took it. "Good luck son. And if you have to take his body back to New York, I'll see to that too. Whatever you need."

On board the British warship, Jay watched as the secretary from the embassy packed up his notes and slipped them into his briefcase. The man, a career State Department official, was younger than Jay and both of them were glad to take a break from the debriefing and get away from the very small stateroom that Jay shared with a crusty leftenant of the British Navy, the First Officer on this frigate.

When the First Officer went on watch, the secretary had swooped into the tiny cabin, eager to begin the debriefing. He was anxious to hear the story from Jay's own lips, having heard many rumors about this young officer who traveled around the world collecting things. Collecting what? No one knew. Now he would hear it first hand.

At least it would be some compensation for this terrible trip. He wasn't quite seasick, but it was close. The constant pitching and rolling was bad, but the rise up and over one wave and down the other side into a trough, was worse. And every few minutes, it seemed as though they changed course. He couldn't get into the rhythm of the ship and that added to his discomfort. After four hours of hearing and transcribing everything from the trip, that cabin seemed even smaller. Jay was talked out. The secretary's hands and fingers were all cramped from writing and he was still uncomfortable. They both needed a break.

The secretary headed to his own bunk to finish transcribing his notes, while Jay shucked his uniform jacket for a gray wool turtleneck, pulled on some oilskins and sea boots and headed for some badly needed time out in the open. Body mind and soul, he craved fresh air. So, down two ladders he went, through a passageway and out a hatch onto the open deck. He stepped out into the blackness of a raging Atlantic storm.

The night was dark and starless as the ship made its way across the Irish Sea. Jay, full of turmoil, wondered if anyone had ever made this crossing with peace and joy in their heart. There had been so much war and hatred between these two island peoples. The ship brought him back to reality as a sharp wind caught him and drove water into his face. Jay tasted his lips and it was clean, sweet rainwater. He made a dive and caught the rail as the ship rose up and then heaved down into the trough of the next wave. Spray washed over him and this time it tasted salty.

He was on the port side a bit forward of amidships. There were no lights and they were zig-zagging their way through the pitch dark of a stormy night on the Irish Sea. It was standard wartime operations made even more serious since the Lusitania went down and German submarines were known to be in these waters. A tack to starboard and his back would feel the lash of sea spray, while a port tack would fill his face and soak the front of him. Jay's heart was pumping in his chest.

The Incense Fire Pack from Wan Lee was hung around his neck on a chain and it seemed hot against his skin as he moved to the rhythm of the ship. He should be feeling down, he thought. His father was lost at sea. His woman was gone, disappeared, maybe deserted him in Paris, but out here with the elements he felt clean and strong and positive. He was on the move and it was good to be outside, on the heaving deck of an ocean going vessel, battling wind and rain. At last, he was doing something.

The thought of food almost drove him inside and down below to the galley, but he stayed on deck. Jay felt at home on a ship at sea and he reveled in the cold, wet wind and stinging salt spray.

I will find my father, he promised himself. He felt it and he knew it. And his woman, ah Deirdre, I will find you too and I will love you and cherish you and protect you. The thought of Deirdre connected in any way to a brothel dismayed Jay. The thought of Deirdre as a rebel, connected to the Irish Republican Brotherhood secretly excited Jay and filled him with wonder and admiration.

What a couple they made. He was a spy and his woman was…what? Jay shook his head and faced into the slurry of wind and rain lashing across the deck. Whatever the answer is, I will find it. Wherever the truth is, I will seek it out. There must be some strange and wonderful reason for her connection to that brothel, "The Holy Ground". He could feel it. He leaned forward into the wet wind, thankful for the boots and oilskins. Exhilarated and excited, peering through the dark, he could just make out the forward gun turret and he knew that the men on watch up there were taking a great deal more wind and spray than he was.

"Sometimes," his father used to say, "'tis best to take a wee short holiday from your problems. Let the inner mind sort through the clutter and when you go back to it 'twill often have a surprise for you, Jay."

And so, he left his future problems for the future, and alone at the rail he went over everything he had told the American Embassy secretary.

—His mission statement as outlined by Naval Intelligence: Food stuff, and the growing, shipping, storing and distribution of it, with a sub plot concerning the Ergot problem. Was there a problem? How extensive was it? What, if any, are the repercussions?

—All the teachings of Wan Lee, her old grandfather, and the Incense Fire Pack or Shian Bao as she called it.

—*Zhou* or Joe and the fine watches they stood together crossing the great rolling Pacific Ocean.

—His brief, unsettling stay in Japan, which took off some of his 'American Shine,' and showed him the value in even the strangest, most difficult of cultures.

—Joe's brother the sea captain, who took him to Russia; but forced him to miss Korea. Because of the Japanese occupation there, he was kept safe aboard, locked in his cabin.

—The diamond caper and the chase, up and over the rear wall. He lost his cap and the scary bamboo pole incident to recover his cap and the rest of his diamonds.

—The drunken man, the old woman and the young girl with the golden smile, who shared the compartment with him. They taught him so much about Russian ways and the old woman, thankful for his small favors. She had sewed up his torn coat.

—His attempt to explain Ergot to them and then spending Navy money so Yuri could buy all of their home made black bread from them and toss it away, in the hope that a better diet might help the old man. Jay remembered his own sickness with Ergot driven nightmares.

—This was his first occasion to see the disease up close since his own bout with it and he wondered if the old man would improve and how long would it take him, once off the bread.

—The wild ride with Troika, the rail and bridge problems and of course his romance with a young woman, which, while not strictly 'by the book' of Navy regulations did give him good and plausible cover when he went on information gathering jaunts.

—Would the Navy understand? Would his boss, the Admiral, understand?

—It was so natural, so plausible. When he and Deirdre traveled as a young couple on a romantic jaunt, people accepted them, accepted him. It put the locals off their guard. People opened up, answered questions, and showed him things. It was a great advantage, having Deirdre with him. He certainly hoped his explanation would suffice.

—The old man's loathing of his overlords, and his story of abused Army veterans. The hated Czar now giving medals and pensions to veterans of his Russo-Japanese War in hopes of attracting fresh recruits for this new war. That information about the new depot and train installation that was being built at the old man's village was very important.

—Deirdre's drum roll walk at the Medal Giving Ceremony. The "Golden Walk" Yuri called it with pensions and coins to the old veterans, from a beguiled General Kamzarov.

—The dinner and meeting they attended after the generous General Kamzarov had gone. Yuri explained that they were dining with Comrades from a fledgling new "RED ARMY." It was mostly a Citizen Army, but it contained many experienced soldiers and officers.

—The speeches in Russian were long and boring. Yuri explained that he liked some and disliked others, but the singing was electrifying. Almost two hundred voices raised in The Internationale and other rousing worker songs. Poor Deirdre winced; he held her hand so hard. Would these Comrades fight the Czar's war against Germany? That was a question.

—The great shock when the old man's daughter, she of the golden smile, turned up at the dinner on the arm of that young Russian officer. The one who had saluted them upon their arrival. She stood atop a table, sang out and waved at them and flashed her golden smile.

A rogue wave caught Jay and sent him back across the deck and smashed him into the bulkhead. Dazed, he grabbed a lifeline, and shook his head to clear it. Instead he heard a clapping sound and then a singsong voice. "You forget O Jay Neill. Rule Number One. Hold on. One hand is for ship, one hand for Jay. Forget teaching of Wan Lee? No live long life." He could see her wagging her head and clapping her hands. "You think of two Gold bars on sleeve. Make you forget rule number Two, KEEP hold on. Live long time. Soon have many gold stripes on sleeve. You live, Jay Neill. Be Captain, even. Like Wan Lee cousin Zhou and his Captain brother in Japan Sea."

Jay struggled to a sitting position. Was Wan Lee related to first mate Joe and his brother, the Captain? He spoke aloud to her as the wind ripped the words out of his mouth and sent them into the wet darkness around him. "What else are you keeping from me, Wan Lee?" He heard her laugh echo off the steel bulkhead. 'You have *shian bao?*' He pressed his hand to his heart and felt the Incense Fire Pack against his bare skin. He nodded, yes. 'Is shape of diamond, yes? Not heart. Wan Lee good friend you, not lover. Never confuse number one friend and number one love.' He heard her laughing.

'Wan Lee send you to lover. You cherish her, Jay Neill. Rule number three, you remember Wan Lee.' He heard her hands clap and she laughed. 'Good bye O Neill Jay.' More laughter. He asked why she was laughing? 'Jay man grow old. Lover woman grow old.' More laughing. 'Forever young is Wan Lee.' Above the fierce wind Jay heard her laughter again and then a loud clang.

"Is that you, Wan Lee?"

The hatch had slammed open and Mac stepped out carrying two large steaming mugs. He too was dressed in foul weather gear. "Get up, laddie. Close the hatch and grab a mug. You must be destroyed with the wind and the waves battering you about." The wind force dropped some as the ship turned onto a starboard tack and the men moved to the rail and together peered out into the black sea, all flecked with white foam.

They clinked mugs and Jay gasped at his first sip. "Good English tea laced with strong Jamaican Rum, lad. This is the British Royal Navy, Jay. Not that pale imitation you belong to." Mac put back his head and gave a great guffaw. It was heard above the wind and possibly all the way to Ireland. "We must keep our wits sharp and our humor wrapped around us like a strong wool cloak. Us Celts, every last one of us, have a deep streak of blackness in us, Jay. We must never descend into it. The climb back up is perilous."

Jay interrupted, grabbed Mac's arm and pointed forward and to port. "A green light Mac, about eleven o'clock." The men up in the forward gun turret were also pointing and shouting to the bow watch.

"Aye. A channel marker, more than likely, a lighted green buoy. We're in the channel now, just a few more hours to go. Jay"...He hesitated and leaned down to put both arms on the rail. The wind had dropped and the sea was much calmer. "No matter which way it goes about your father, and your girl too, for that matter. Don't let it take you...don't let it destroy you. Death and grief are certainties. 'Tis only the when and the how we have to wait for and wonder about."

Jay joined Mac leaning over the side and clinked his mug again to Mac's mug. "You're thinking of my Da and your wife too, then?"

"Aye, and your mother as well and her passing. Your Da and I, best of friends, we were separated by an ocean, and each of us grieving alone. Did you know that, Jay? We were made widowers within a few months of each other. Each of us so deep into our own personal darkness we couldn't even write or telephone to find out about the other or console the other. Mutual friends told each of us of the other's loss.

I imagine your Da suffered terribly. I know I did. My Regina was my life. She was beautiful and strong and gifted, my wonderful black haired Welch woman. She had the second sight and often would laugh at the mention of loosing her youth and beauty. 'I don't fear it, the old age.' She'd say. 'I'll never have it.' And she was right, so damned right."

Mac pounded one hand on the port rail. "And I almost lost my Maria, my only child as well. I ignored her, gave her over to Regina's sister to raise, so lost in my grief, was I. Do you know lad, I always harbored a secret wish that Sean's son, Jay, yourself that is, would meet and favor my daughter Maria. You two would love and marry and Sean and I, though without our wives, we could share some grandchildren. Oh, aye. If wishes were fishes...we'd never know hunger, would we now."

"Sorry Mac. I am in love with Deirdre; and I'm committed to finding her. My father first, of course, then I'll find my woman. We always considered you part of our family, Mac, our overseas family, and I always looked forward to meeting you and getting to know you and your family."

"Ah young Jay Jay." Mac grinned and grabbed him by the shoulder, "We'll find your Da. Then he and I will both help you find your missing love, your mystery woman and we'll become as close as any blood tie family. And don't worry a bit about my Maria. She's off on her own pathway and doubtless has no time for romance at the present."

"I want to meet her one day. I'm sure we'll be friends. Her and Deirdre and I."

Mac drank some of his tea with rum. "We were mending fences and making a damn good job of it, when Maria tells me she's been acting in a theatre group up North. Wants to make a career out of it. My daughter an actress, in the theatre. I guess I didn't react very well, lad. In truth, I was against her doing it and told her so. She stormed out and since then our father, daughter rapprochement, as Rene would say, was put on ice."

"People are changing, Mac. My mother was a young, single woman when she traveled alone, from Poland all the way to New York, where they met and married. My father loved that about her, her independence. It's one of the charms that draws me to Deirdre."

"Aye, lad. I went up North and saw Maria perform; never told her I was coming. My God, she was mesmerizing. Held me fast to my seat. After the performance I could not go back stage. I was too ashamed of my objections and the way I criticized her chosen path. So, I went out, got the biggest and best bouquet of flowers to be had and sent it to her with a letter of apology and my sincerest congratulations. Told her I expected to see her leading a cast very soon on the London stage and I even used her stage name, Maria Scotland.

She wired me right back and I carry it with me now, always. 'My Dearest Da. I love you so much. Thank you for coming. I cannot wait to see you in London and you will have the best seat in the house. Did I say I love you? Your daughter, Maria Scotland.'"

They stood silent leaning against the rail and watched the black sea become calm as they raced closer to the coast of Ireland. Ahead lay the answers for all of their questions. A few points off the starboard bow a red light appeared. Jay pointed to it and Mac broke the silence. "Another channel marker. Getting closer, now. Are you hungry, Lad? They'll have a meal going now; a good bowl of stirabout or perhaps some rashers and eggs? They may even have coffee, knowing we have foreigners aboard."

"Now that you mention it, my stomach is empty. I'll have some of each, and coffee will do me fine, though I could get used to that tea with rum." Jay grinned and headed for the hatch.

MacGregor called after him, "when you dress to go ashore, put on your best, lad. We'll want to impress them all to get their full attention and help. We want their unqualified assistance."

"Do you mean the Irish?" Jay turned half way back to Mac.

"I mean the bloody English. They tend to be protective of investigations, the more so, if they're the ones who have mucked things up." Mac resumed his silent vigil into the dark night. After a short while he heard a step, and turned just in time to grab an arm. He steadied Rene, and helped him to the rail.

"*Alors. Gregor,* you are like *Jesu Christi* calming the seas for us fishermen, *no?* I 'av been inside waiting for wind and rain to cease so I can 'av my walk on this fine night. The sea is calm now with a gentle roll, eh?" Rene stretched and made circles with his arms. "We must pump our blood, yes. 'Av you seen Fritz, my good King of Scots?"

"Good Jesus God in Heaven, is Fritz aboard?" Rene nodded yes and gave one of his famous Gallic shrugs. "Rene! Does Wee Willie know?" Gregor asked in disbelief.

"*Oui.* Our Wee Willie Burke protest with vigor against his inclusion, but Fritz is no longer a legal German. Fritz carries now, Swiss papers, uses his mother's name of Kunkel and disavows his father's titles, and so forth and so on." The way birds fluttered about a fig tree, Rene's hands reinforced his words with agile motions. "Though he is still very much a war veteran with his wounds and he is still a German. But Willie Burke was ridden over by higher up people and must make room with us for Fritz Kunkel, the Swiss neutral observer for this Lusitania sinking. So, now Burke is angry and will make mischief for you and most especially for our young American friend, Jay O'Neill." Rene pointed behind Mac towards the bow where Sir William Burke was bearing down upon them. "Now the sea is calm, I will walk the plank deck, no?" Rene turned and walked towards the stern, wriggling his fingers in an over the shoulder wave. As he walked he rolled with the ship.

"Was that Rene I saw," Burke asked, "walking away from us? I'm surprised to see him on deck in rough seas like this." Gregor nodded and Burke went on. "I waited for the rain to abate, but I'm out on deck now. I rather like a rough sea, don't you, Gregor?" Gregor nodded again, concealing his smile and Burke rushed on. "Fritz is aboard too, you know. I rather encouraged his coming with us, now that he is accredited as a Swiss observer." Burke faced aft to resume his walk and missed Gregor's wide smile at this remark.

He turned back; came up close to Gregor and in his most infuriating pompous manner declared. "Gregor, it was I who managed that train to Wales and now this Naval vessel which will carry us all to Ireland. You know that, do you not?" When Gregor didn't answer, he rushed on. "I will help you locate your friend, O'Neill, in spite of his son, that Junior Officer. He makes me uneasy, Gregor. I have real doubts about your judgment, my friend. He should never have been brought to our meeting. As for that woman he is seeking. Yeack. After O'Neill is found, I intend to have the son followed and apprehend that DalCas woman.

If she is only a prostitute I'll have her freed and he can do as he pleases with her, but if she is, as I suspect, an agent of that secret society, that rebel Brotherhood dedicated to the overthrow of King and Country, of all that we hold dear, I will clap her in irons. Being merciful, we shall spare her life. However, she will serve years in prison and be an old and broken woman before she is free again." Burke turned and moved away, pompous, pleased with himself, holding the rail and carefully lifting high one foot and placing it squarely upon the deck before lifting the other foot. He was the worst parody of an English Gentleman.

Mac shook his shaggy head and spit out over the rail. "Ye bloody pompous twit, Wee Willie Burke." Now he had an entire new set of problems. As was his wont when puzzled he mused aloud. It helped him when he thought, and spoke and heard himself all at the same time. It gave him three of his senses at work on the problem and speeded up the process.

"Choose a side. Must I? Yes, of course I must. But which side? Sean, I hope to God you're alive to help me be straight with your son Jay. Ah. Yes. Accept Willie's help to locate Sean. Alive or dead, that's first. But we must be nimble. As soon as the father is found, the son must disappear to seek out his woman. I must get him away. But Burke will be watching me and the son and The Holy Ground, where the lad will go first to look for her.

But Willie can't lean too hard on the lad. I'm sure the Admiralty ordered him to be nice, since we must convince our American comrades to stand alongside us in this war. Willie must be nice; the Admiralty are after all his masters. Here, all these years, I thought he was independent of any sitting government the way Rene is, and Fritz and myself. Perhaps I can use that. Find the father; then get the son the hell out of Ireland. That's the answer, and the end of my involvement. I owe nothing to that girl. Never met her. And yet, she's about the same age as my Maria. And the lad loves her and she him. And I love Sean the way I'd love a real honest-to-God brother. And his son, Jay, is…is…well admit it. I wish he were my son. Ah, Christ in the guardhouse." Gregor bellowed and threw a punch out into the black night.

"Nothing else for it, I must help them all, the father, the son and the Holy Ground woman." Mac laughed at his play on words; he raised up his two arms and gave a tendon snapping great stretch, reaching his fingers to the stars in the sky while inhaling to the bottom of his lungs. "In for a penny, in for a pound. William Burke and all his kind be damned and to hell with them. Excepting, of course, his mother Billie Burke. She's a decent sort. And the whole damned British Empire is big enough and grand enough to take care of itself. It surely doesn't need my help to persecute a young man or prosecute his young woman.

Find Sean first. Elude Willie. Find Deirdre. Convince all three to flee Ireland. If Sean is dead, procure an extra large coffin and hide the girl in with the father's body. Good Christ, we're not even in Ireland yet and I'm thinking the way Sean does in the wee hours of the morning, and him with a drop taken. It's time for me to have a short lay-down. After, I'll dress in my best Scottish duds; have a meal on the Royal Navy and we'll all go ashore."

Jay felt almost rested after an hours nap, a hearty sailors breakfast with coffee, a fast shave and a bath and now he was back on deck, ready for whatever the new day might bring. He was dressed in his best Navy Blues, with gold stripes on his sleeves; new gold bars on his shoulders and pants that were pressed, sailor style, under the mattress while he napped.

He knew he should be concentrating on his father, but there was nothing he could do until they went ashore. Deirdre and her message occupied his entire universe and filled him with hope.

In his temporary quarters, while dressing, there had been a knock on his cabin door. He called, "come in", and when he turned around, there stood Fritz.

He rubbed his bad leg and asked Jay, "May I sit down, *Herr Jay O'Neill?* Sea voyages should be *verboten* for old soldiers." Jay smiled, indicated his bunk and went back to knotting his tie. "I would rather sit on a bad horse during a cannonade than be on a ship in the calmest sea. It is never stable, *nein?*"

Jay grinned at the landlubbers discomfit. "I heard you were aboard, with Burke' s help?

Fritz smiled now, acknowledging the inside joke. '*Vee Villie* did his damnedest to keep me away, but the British Admiralty likes the idea of a Swiss as an onlooker. So I am here.'

Jay finished dressing and asked, how does it go for you with the ship's company, The British officers?

'They like me not, but they are seamen and British, so they are civil and correct. They see me as another warrior, even though I am the enemy. When I come near, all conversation ends or goes to the weather. No talk of submarines or the Lusitania when I come into the wardroom. My meals are quick and finished. But I have no enmity. I would feel as they do.'

Jay understood. He'd had some of the same very civil and very correct treatment, and he was a neutral not an enemy. He stuck out his hand. "We'll not be enemies, Fritz."

Fritz took his hand and shook it with warmth. 'I will not keep you, Jay, but I am on this mission, most of all, for you. This is why I come now, to you, in private. I have for you a message.' He handed Jay a folded sealed sheet. 'This is for only you. I would not disclose in front of the others.'

Jay tore it open and read, ...J. SON OF SEAN. COME TO ME. FIND ME PLEASE. I LOVE YOU. DEIRDRE... THE HOLY GROUND. 8 010. Fritz was just stepping into the passageway when Jay caught him and spun him around. Their eyes locked for a long moment, then Jay grabbed and hugged Fritz and whispered, "thank you, thank you so much."

The blackness became gray and soon Jay could see banks of fog rolling off in the distance. Suddenly, he could see a dark shape in the water, moving along just in front and keeping pace with them. Jay hollered to the men in the gun turret above and to his right, but they pointed starboard where a strong light shone. No. It was not a submarine. It was their ship casting a shadow on the water. And then the sun was up in the East behind them, and the fog was lifting.

Off the port side, through the lifting mist, Jay could see the green hills of Ireland and as the sun rose behind them and the last of the fog cleared before him, the green hills were bathed in golden sunlight.

My father would love this, he thought. He always talked about coming home to Ireland and always in the same way. He would be on the bow of a ship with the first light of dawn shining on the land. My father would close his eyes and he'd recite his favorite poem, "THE EXILES RETURN", by John Locke. Jay began reciting, saying the first line in Irish and in English the way his Da always said it.

"Th' Anam Tho' Diah,
My soul to God. But there it is:
The dawn on the hills of Ireland"
MacGregor's voice behind him took up the poem.
'God's angels lifting night's black veil
From the fair sweet face of my sire-land!
Oh Ireland, isn't it grand you look,
Like a bride in her rich adorning'!
And together they finished Sean O'Neill's favorite poem.
"With all the pent-up love of my heart
I bid you the top of the morning".

"I can't tell you how many times I heard Sean recite that poem. Nor how many times I said it right along with him." Mac cleared his throat and Jay did the same. "Jesus, God Almighty, aren't we a couple of right old weepin' widows. Keening away here, holding a wake and him not even dead yet, not for certain, not 'til we see his cold body. Sorry Jay.

By God, let me look at you in all of your finery. Navy dress blues, new stripes, new gold bars, congratulations lieutenant." Gregor saluted and Jay returned the honor with tears in his eyes.

They stood on the gently rolling deck and admired each other's outfits. MacGregor was dressed in full clan tartans from his bonnet and badge to his jacket, his red with green plaid kilt and a worn leather sporran at his waist. He wore brogues and high wool socks with the handle of a dirk sticking out of the right sock at his knee.

"Our Family motto is *'S rioghal mo dhream*. My race is royal. The MacGregor clan was outlawed, you know. 'Twas a capital offence to bear the name MacGregor from 1604 'til 1774, when we were made legal again. Sassenach bastards. During those times, we bore the name in secret and the MacGregors were known as 'Children of the Mist'. I am well qualified, Jay O'Neill, to help you find your woman and smuggle her out of Ireland before Wee Willie Burke has his way with you and with her. We will thwart him, you and I."

"I was afraid of that, of Burke. Sir William", he said with disdain. "A right two faced bastard, Mac. Sit in a room with you, smiling, while plotting against you."

"Well said lad. We must, now, act in the same manner. We will use him. Burke has been ordered to be nice to Americans. The Lusitania's sinking, if handled well, could bring your chaps into the war on our side. He'll help us find Sean. He has all the connections and we'll use his help. Then, as soon as your Da's fate is known and dealt with, we'll slip away, the three of us." Gregor narrowed his eyes, "Or just us together, lad. We'll find your Deirdre and get her to safety. Look, Jay."

Coming towards them at a fast pace was a great troop ship heading out to sea. Mac took a small shiny brass tube out of the Sporran at his waist, slid it open and held it to his eye. "She's flying all her battle flags. They are signaling to us. If I remember my wig-wag stuff, she's headed to France and the trenches and is wishing us 'Good Hunting.' 'Get The Hun,' and some other things too. It may be in code."

He offered the glass to Jay who studied the ship from stem to stern and then it was alongside and passing them outward bound while they headed on into port. Salutes and silent cheers were exchanged between the ships; but no signal lights, no sounds, no wireless, passed between them. It was wartime and enemy submarines could be anywhere.

The rail of the troop ship was crowded with young soldiers, some catching a sunrise at sea, others wanting a last glimpse of home or of the land itself. Suddenly an officer appeared. He shouted something, which Jay and Mac could not hear, but all the men on deck came to attention and gave a right hand salute to Jay and Mac as they passed them by. "That officer must be a Scot and he recognized my MacGregor Tartan." Mac smiled.

"A brave ship Mac, full of courageous young men off on a jaunt."

"Off on a journey to hell, more like. They say the trenches in France and Belgium, especially those near Ypres, are full of pain and misery, sickness and death. The damned Germans dug in on the high ground so our generals, in their infinite wisdom, had the Allied trenches laid out in low ground. Aye lad, they laid our trenches in a bloody bog.

The men stand in water for days till their toes rot off. They call it Trenchfoot. A lost limb and a trip home would be a blessing for some. And a lifetime of aches and lost youth; just ask our Fritz. And he's right, you know, Fritz is. Bang the drums, skirl the pipes, and they'll come. All the handsome young men; dress them up in fancy duds and all the beautiful young maids will be there to admire them and see them off."

Together Jay and Mac walked forward, around the bow and headed aft down the starboard side. Jay waved to the men on the gun turret as they passed by and he stopped amidships near the gangway where his duffle and Mac's gear was guarded by a young seaman.

"Mac, we need to find out if any survivors are still being found, it's sixteen or more hours in that cold water. And who is picking them up? And where are they being taken? There are so many unknowns. Do you think it's only the dead they are finding now? Sixteen hours is a long time in that cold water."

Jay didn't really expect an answer and none came.

CHAPTER FIVE

The harbour and the Town of Cobh were lovely in the early morning light. The docks and waterfront had clean lines and appeared to welcome the visitor. Back and above the dock area, the cathedral dominated the scene and ranks of buildings rose up behind and Jay knew that The Holy Ground was in there somewhere. "It looks inviting, doesn't it, Mac? Clean and welcoming, I'd say."

"Aye, lad. From a few hundred yards out, it is. Further in, well, we'll see very soon."

"It reminds me of the last few lines of John Locke's poem my Da always recited, the part about Cobh.

And doesn't old Cobh look charming there,

Watching the wild waves motion,

Leaning her back against the hills,

And the tips of her toes in the ocean."

To an untrained eye the dock area was utter chaos. Men in a motley assortment of uniforms and work clothes moved in every direction with motor cars carrying people, lorries loaded with goods, horse and mule drawn carts, wagons and vans threaded in and out of everywhere. Horns blared and voices shouted, cursed and ranted. The draft animals seemed calmer and better behaved, by far, than the men who drove them. The smells were good or bad depending upon where you were and which way the wind blew.

To the trained eye of a seaman it was all a smooth and oft repeated dance. Each person, horse and vehicle knew exactly where to go, when to move and how to get there. Jay and Mac watched as the mooring lines were heaved ashore. There the workmen leaned and pulled and plied the lines and made their practiced knots almost silently, using arm and hand signals, some on the bow and more at the stern, and the ship was eased into her berth, the way a child is gathered into the arms of its mother.

Both men were anxious to get ashore and pursue their goals. The older one to find his best friend and the younger man to find his father and regain his lost love. The next hours or perhaps days would bring them the answers they had been seeking and the end might not be pleasant. So, they stayed at the rail of this warship and enjoyed the sight of men toiling in the early morning sunshine of a May day. Some were coiling rope and adjusting knots on the big mooring lines, others collected tools and a few moved away to the next job.

Wee Willie Burke came blustering up to them. He was full of his own importance and made a sharp contrast to the workers Jay and Mac had just been watching and admiring. And so they smiled at him. "You two will be first ashore," Burke approached, puzzled by the smiles, but he began his prepared speech. He stopped almost speechless and absorbed the sight of them smiling at him. They were both dressed in full regalia. Jay, representing the American Ambassador was now a full Lieutenant. He was the equal of a Captain in the British Army, and not to be taken lightly. MacGregor in his clan tartan was just a bit frightening, but Burke rushed on. "I'll have a seaman take your bags,…"

MacGregor cut him off. "Bloody hell you will, we'll carry our own gear, Wee Willie. Damn it man, we are not bloody tourists, here on a lark"

"Yes, of course, Gregor. I see. Well then, you both are first down the gangway. I've arranged for you to have…"Here Willie pointed to a large automobile parked close to the ship. A soldier stood at attention by the front wheel. "That's it just there. A motor car and driver. Jay, he will take you to the hospital and all the temporary medical shelters where the survivors are being treated. I wish you the best of luck finding your father. MacGregor, after he drops Jay, the driver will take you to the City and

Military Morgue as well as any other facilities for the dead. I understand there is a warehouse set up...He's yours,..."

Burke stopped talking and turned from Jay to Mac and back to Jay again. "He's yours for as long as you require him and I'm sorry, but this is the best that I could manage. I could not arrange for two separate conveyances." He waved to the waiting soldier, pointed to Jay and Mac and waved again.

Just then the gangplank went out and down to the pier and the two men were free to depart. They grabbed their gear, saluted the flag at the masthead, saluted the Officer of the Deck, and moved down and off the ship. Wee Willie Burke called out to them. "This way at least you can divide your labors and save time. Good luck, MacGregor, ...and O'Neill." He added the last almost grudgingly.

Jay set first one foot and then the other foot gently down upon the quay and whispered softly to himself, 'Hello Ireland, land of my father's people.' He looked beyond the crowded pier and town of Cobh with the Cathedral above and the green hills embracing it all and thought of his father, Sean O'Neill. 'I'm home, Da. I'm back in the land of the Macs and the Os. With a bit of luck and the help of your brother, your friend, this Gregor MacGregor who says he is one of the Children Of The Mist, I will bring you out of this and I will bring home a bride as well.'

For the first time, Jay realized that he intended to marry Deirdre. It was the first time he had said the words, Jay and Deirdre and marry, even to himself. He felt a jolt and a surge of energy race up his spine and instinctively he reached inside his shirt and held the *Shian Bao*. 'Thank you Wan Lee.'

And now he had a plan. Find his father, first; then find Deirdre; marry her and get her a passport and whatever American papers she would need. This will put her beyond Wee Willie Burke's schemes. It will put an end to any danger to his love, his woman, his bride. But first he must find her.

"Go on and do it, Jay. Kneel down and kiss the old sod of the homeland." Mac smiled but he was serious about it. "Forget the onlookers, lad. This entire mission is one of the heart not the head." Mac imitated Sean. "'Tis not about regulations a'tall Jay. As the poets say, we'll soon be striding around on the stones and bones of Holy Ireland itself."

Jay smiled and enjoyed a quiet laugh. Mac must've been reading his mind.

"Shall I stow your gear in the boot, sirs?" The driver saluted them and stood at attention, waiting for orders. He wore the stripe of a private on his sleeve, but the close-set eyes in his wizened face gave him a cunning look and the many battle ribbons on his uniform belied his rank. They told a story of a man with many years in service and several campaigns in different parts of the British Empire. Without waiting, he saluted again, grabbed the bags and walked to the rear of the car and stowed their gear in the boot.

Jay headed around the car to the far door, opened it and then knelt down in the dust, as though to tie his shoelace. He kissed his finger tips, touched them to the soil of his father's land and said, "welcome me home da. I'm so glad to be here with you." Brushing his trouser leg, he jumped in beside Mac and gave him a grin. "Let's go," he yelled to the driver, and then to Mac, "Sir William Burke is a first class pompous ass," Jay declared with fervor.

The driver threaded his way around the many lorries, military vehicles, parading troops, and autos, which nearly choked the waterfront area. There was a great deal of honking horns, shouting and cursing, threats and arm waving and then they were in the clear and moving with ease. "Take us to the mortuary first," Jay instructed. The driver nodded and Jay slid shut the glass partition, giving himself and Mac some privacy.

"Aye lad. Wee Willie is that, a total ass. But, at least he had the good sense to have you search among the living and it's me sorting through the dead. Wee Willie has a Saxon head on him but somewhere in there beats a Celtic heart. He must get it from his mother, Billie Burke." Jay looked surprised. "Oh yes laddie boy. Billie is Irish. She is one of those women who grow lovelier with age, as though it takes time for them to become themselves. She was a Fitzgerald, she was, one of The Geraldines of Irish history. Do you know any of the stories?"

"I do", Jay rushed in, eager to talk about his father. "Da loved history. When I was in school he would quiz me about American events, and so learn it with me and then he'd tell me Irish history in the old way. 'The best stories are those that are told, one person to another, Jay, he'd say to me.'

Then Da would get out a map, pick a spot and give me all the main events from that area. 'The Fitzgeralds were mostly rebels through the years. Lord Edward, shot in the Rising of 1798. And Silken Thomas Fitzgerald, he led the rebels in 1534.'"

Jay was eager to tell Mac what his father had told him, though he was certain Mac had heard it all before, directly from his father. "Three great families contended for leadership in the Province of Munster in the South of Ireland.

The House of Thomond, the O'Briens, were the native Irish, descended from Brian Boru, high king in the eleventh century.

The House of Ormond, the Butlers, were Normans and mostly loyal to the English Kings. They take the family name from their position as Butler to the king.

And third, The House of Desmond, the Fitzgeralds or Geraldines as they were called, were also Norman, but they became fiercely Irish and mostly fought the foreign Parliament and English crown.

Most of the time, the three families, being Irish, would rather fight each other than their common enemy, the English; and allegiances often shifted, depending on who wanted what and from whom."

Mac shook his head, "Aye and include the Scots in there, too. Had our Clans ever really united, why the English would never have prevailed." He sighed and regarded Jay. "Sean and I have been through all this a hundred times, lad. And it's a pleasure hearing these words again and now from your own lips. Sean taught you well, lad, well indeed."

Jay went quiet as the driver stopped at the mortuary. "Thanks Mac, for listening. I know Da has told you these stories. Told them many times. Thanks for everything, Mac. Thanks..." Jay began to choke on his words.

"*Ah tosca sin innis a warra,*" Gregor MacGregor comforted Jay in Gaelic and in English. "Hush now Jay, me boyo. One of us will find him, either myself here in the morgue or yourself in hospital, and we both must accept what is. We cannot change what has happened. But, by God, we can and we will put our stamp on the future." He grabbed Jay by the shoulders and held him with a stern gaze. "If you find Sean, let me know, but not through,..." Mac inclined his head towards the military driver. "Willie will use any method, including spying on you to find your Deirdre.

He will follow you to get to her. Be careful, Jay. I have no doubt that young man up front is earning more than just his military pay. The Burke family has great wealth and Wee Willie knows how to employ it."

Mac stepped out of the vehicle and leaned back in for a final word. "Find another way, Jay, but do let me know and I will, of course do the same. Once we've located Sean, I will handle all the details and you can slip away on your other quest. Use Rene or Fritz if you can. They are with us in this matter. Are we agreed, then?"

Jay and Mac locked eyes and gripped each others hand in a solemn promise. "Indeed yes. We are in total agreement, Mac."

"You sound just like Sean, Jay." Mac smiled, turned and quickly walked into the mortuary.

Jay counted seven steps up and three long paces before he was through the heavy oak and glass doors and inside the hospital. He paused and allowed his eyes to adjust. It was quite dim after the bright sunshine and glare from the water in the harbour. A long corridor ran off to the left and another corridor to the right while a third hallway went ahead and many doors opened from each of them. Where to begin, he wondered. It was just a bit daunting.

He strode to the paneled booth in the center and faced a forbidding older woman. "O'Neill. Jay O'Neill. I'm looking for my father. He's a survivor, at least I think he is. I hope he is," Jay finished and saw that he had not impressed the woman, at all. Without uttering a sound, without even looking up at him she handed Jay a clipboard with a pencil and turned away to talk to another black clad hospital person.

"Lieutenant John J. O'Neill of the American Navy?" Jay spun around to face a sergeant of the Royal Marines. He was about Jay's size and age and wore a clipped moustache in the British manner. The man gave a smart salute, said he'd been expecting Jay, and would he kindly follow him. "I have news of your family, Sir. This way, if you please." He turned and strode down the center corridor and Jay had almost to run to keep up with him.

His heart pumped fast, both from the sudden brisk pace and from anticipation. Thank God, and thank you Wan Lee. "News. What news?"

They burst through the rear doors and out into a sun filled courtyard and Jay could contain himself no more. "What news? Where is he? Is he alive?" Before Jay could get an answer they were at another car. This one had an open front seat for the driver and an enclosed rear cabin. The Marine motioned Jay into the rear, but he refused. "I want information, damn it. I can't leave. There's another car waiting out front for me, and a friend is checking all the Morgues. Tell me about my father. Tell me where he is. Damn it. Say something."

The Marine smiled. "We have a location for your father. He is not in this city, sir. I will take you to that location directly after we pick up our next passenger. Please sir. Time is short." The marine again indicated the enclosed rear, and without waiting for Jay's reply he entered the open front seat and started the engine. Jay entered the rear cabin and sat down.

As the car pulled away, Jay spoke to the Marine sergeant. "Our next passenger is a big Scot, my father's best friend. He's been at the morgue looking over the bodies, the one near the harbour and you can't miss him. He's wearing his full Scottish attire, Clan MacGregor plaids, his kilt and he even has a long dirk at his right knee. At last we're getting somewhere," and he smiled as he said it.

Jay began to feel a bit better and settled back into the luxurious cushions of his private car. It made him think of the horse drawn cab ride he had treated himself to from the *Barinov* hotel to the train station in *Vladivostock*. He reached inside his shirt and pulled out his lucky charm, the Incense Fire Pack, his *Shian Bao*. It still smelled of Sandalwood and reminded him of Wan Lee. "Maybe everything will go alright, or am I just whistling in the dark," he wondered.

He must have day dreamed because when he began to take note of their travel he realized they were above the city on one of the hills. He looked all around and to his right and below he could see the harbour and the frigate he had come in on. He opened the sliding partition and asked the Marine sergeant if they were being followed. "There's a motorcycle and sidecar with two men about a block behind. I think they are following us. Have you noticed them?"

"Yes sir," he replied. "They are my men, Royal Marines. You are precious cargo for us, Lieutenant O'Neill. I will, however, caution them to be less obvious, sir. In any case we are here."

The car came to a smooth stop. Looking back Jay saw the motorcycle pull to the curb a block behind them and when he looked forward again, he could not see the water. On his right side and rising up from below was the huge gray bulk and spires of the Cobh Cathedral.

"On the left side now, me boyo, that grand old house is the Holy Ground, Jay O'Neill." The Marine had lost all trace of an English accent. It was pure Irish now.

The door flew open and a figure clad in a long, black, hooded cloak came tumbling in on top of Jay. He knew immediately from the scent of the cloak that it was Deirdre. His emotions went spinning out of control and he breathed deep, inhaling her very essence and he was made whole again. He held her tight and couldn't believe this was happening.

"It is you," he whispered. He pulled back the hood and began kissing her dark hair while she opened his uniform jacket and wound her arms around him, getting as close to him as she possibly could.

The door slammed shut from outside. They were alone and private now. Jay held her against him with one arm and caressed her face with his other hand. He kissed her neck and her lips and tasted the sweet wetness of Deirdre 's mouth. Then he kissed her eyes one after the other, and with his tongue, Jay tasted the salty tears welling up from each of her blue eyes. "Don't cry my Deirdre," he whispered into her dark hair.

"You came for me. Ah Jay. My own love. You came and found me." Deirdre turned her head and sought his mouth and tongue with her own mouth. They kissed again and kept on kissing, even while talking, asking questions and giving answers, between their kisses.

"I found you. We're together." He could feel her entire wonderful, soft, strong, young body pressed against the length of him. Thoughts of the waterfall and the pool and he and Deirdre pressing hard against one another flashed into his head, but there was no pool of cold water this time. Now they were wrapped in the warm cocoon of a black wool cloak.

"You're not angry at my leaving? I had to leave. Ah, my love, you found me." She wiggled around until she had his one arm under the cloak where he could caress her body.

"Hush now, I love you and we will stay together. Nothing will..."He held her tight as they were jostled on the seat as the big car pulled away from the curb and raced ahead. "Where are we going?" he asked her.

Jay knew one way they could be separated. If Wee Willie ever got his hands on Deirdre, he would do his damnedest to keep them apart. But this will never happen, Jay swore an oath to himself on his mother's grave and his father's...? Life? Grave? He must ask Deirdre about his father. Then he became tangled in his emotions and his lust for her as she moved against his whole body. My God. My father. I was supposed to find my father first.

"Jay, I love you, so. I did miss you." She smothered him with her kisses. "I'm so sorry. I must've brought pain and doubt into you. We'll not be separated, not ever again. I promise you." Deirdre turned and lay with her back to Jay, her head on his shoulder, where she could snuggle her face into his neck. He reached under the cloak and held her and cupped his hands around her warm full breasts.

She leaned a bit forward to the sliding window and spoke to the sergeant, the driver. "*Go raibh maith agat, Diarmuid.* Thank you Dermot, for bringing him to me." She leaned forward and grabbed Dermot's hand that he thrust through the sliding window. "Jay O'Neill, meet Dermot O'Rourke, he is my cousin and fellow Patriot."

Jay reached out and added his hand to the other two. "How many are there, then?"

"Cousins? Or Patriots? Dermot asked.

"A dozen cousins and I haven't a clue the number of Patriots," Deirdre replied. "But enough, I think for the job at hand." The three of them laughed and squeezed each other's hands. "Where will you take us now, Dermot?"

"A short drive, only, Deirdre. We go to The Hill of Fire. First, up the road to Ballywilliam and thence take the hill road to the top. Some 300 feet high is that hill, the highest point in the area. A great lookout it was, and in the long ago, a holy place for the Druids on every feast day. They kept grand big fires going all through the night. Ah sure, they have them still. The people burn a big fire on that hill at the turning of each season, and on *Samhain* especially. All Hallows Eve, or Halloween you call it, Jay.

It can be seen from most everywhere and a good long way out to sea, as well."

"Ireland is such a Christian nation, and yet I think if you scratch an Irishman you'll find Pagan blood seeping out." Jay spoke with wonder and awe in his voice and the other two laughed at his observation.

Dermot turned onto a small road and downshifted as they began climbing and twisting their way up to the top. "A slight deviation, Deirdre, I'm to go straight away to the morgue and capture Sean O'Neill's best friend, a big Scot, one Gregor MacGregor. He's to travel with us to West Cork."

The big touring automobile climbed up the last of the hill. They leveled off and turned away from the road and went across a meadow and parked under some large trees. "All that you need, cousin, is in the boot."

Just as soon as they stopped, Deirdre went to the boot and called out to the two men, "Jay O'Neill meet Dermot O'Rourke, my cousin and best friend. Shake hands again, will you."

The two men shook hands again, appraised each other and then smiled as Deirdre glared and admonished them in a fierce tone. "Be nice now will you, so. You're both important to me and I love you dearly. Both of you," and she smiled with the radiance of a woman fulfilled.

Jay and Dermot walked into the clearing at the brow of the hill and had a perfect view below them of the church spires, the British frigate at the dock and the harbour and bay and the wild ocean beyond. "Dermot, are all the DalCas clan so bossy?"

"Only the women Jay O'Neill, and may God help you." He smiled and pointed away to the right. "See the water, there. That's Passage West, it leads on into Lough Mahon and thence up the River Lee to Cork City, itself. But we'll not be on the water, Jay O'Neill. There's too much activity entirely, for our liking. We'll be moving by road." Before Jay could question him, Dermot smiled and stuck out his hand. "Deirdre has your answers. I'm away now. I must pick up another part of our puzzle, and then I'm back to you, both."

They shook hands again and turned to go back to the car. Dermot went ahead but Jay was held awestruck by the sight of the fire pit. Off to his left was a half circle of large boulders standing upright and with the open side facing out to the water. The stones themselves were blackened and crusted from centuries of bonfires. Logs and kindling were piled on one side as though in preparation for the next ceremony.

Jay could almost see the Druids, with their wands held high, lighting the fire while the faithful huddled and trembled nearby, hoping for a blessed season with no sickness, no starvation and free from savage invaders.

The automobile drove away but Jay never saw it, never heard it. His eyes were riveted on Deirdre as she stood before him on the small grassy meadow between the Stone Circle of Fires and the edge of the hill. Her deep blue eyes had a fire burning in them and they spoke to Jay of a lifetime of passion and the eternal promise that he would not travel his way alone.

Deirdre remained silent, as he took one end of the blanket from her, backed away, and together they pulled it open and let the white wool float down towards the green grass of the meadow. Before it had fully settled on this grassy place they strode upon it, and met in the middle, where Deirdre and Jay knelt down and began to undress each other.

They knelt there, eyes locked together, while their hands unclothed and explored each other, caressed and made promises to each other; promises that would be kept by their lips and loins and by their entire bodies. One of the couple faced out onto the open air vista with the town below and the changing gray sea beyond. The other lover faced a half circle of blackened boulders in this unchanging ancient place of pagan rituals.

Their love making was as old as fire and as new as the next breath. It was youth and beauty with lust and love and each knew they were changing their partner and being changed themselves. The man, thrusting into the woman, felt he had come home, while the woman, opening herself to him, was filled by her man and fulfilled in her destiny.

Sean, the father, had left this country, driven out and forced to make a new life across the sea. He was home now, drowned in that wild ocean, and his body washed upon the shore of his native land.

The son, Jay, found and claimed this woman and now with her help, he would find and claim his father and gather the remains to himself.

Then Jay must secure a way for his woman to leave her land and begin a new life with him in that far off place called America. That place chosen for him by his missing father.

The man, descended from the *Ui Neill* kings of Northern Ireland, and the woman was a *DalCais* of Southern Ireland. The *DalCais* were usurpers who wrested away that High Kingship of Ireland, in a battle some nine hundred years ago.

These children of ancient foes were now made one by their love and by their passion. They would create a bond and begin their own clan in that new land across the sea and all future battles between them would be waged within the confines of their love and their marriage.

Jay and Deirdre sat on the white wool blanket, on the very edge of the Hill of Fire. With their arms wrapped around each other and further warmed by her black cloak over them, they looked out beyond Cobh at the white-capped water of the Atlantic Ocean.

That white water was fast disappearing as a violent storm swept in towards them. And the sweeping clouds, constantly changing, had shoots of lightening in them. The darkness was lit from within, and in the way of so many menacing events, from a distance; the darkness had great beauty. The man and woman, leaning against each other, were quiet, and content and almost purring.

"We'll have to move…soon," he kissed her dark hair.

"I know…not yet," she snuggled closer, looked up and kissed his chin. "Dermot will return soon and we'll be dry inside the big motor car."

They watched as the Harbour below them disappeared under the storm clouds. The wind picked up to a brisk blow, and then the Frigate was gone and her arm tightened around him as St. Colman's Cathedral below was lost to the blustery black clouds.

Whirls of earth rose out of the ground like tiny tornadoes and marched up the hill towards them. Fat raindrops followed and made puffs of dust as they hit the ground below and came ever closer up the hill.

Deirdre shrieked in delight as the first cold wet blobs of water pelted them. "Come on now, my Jay." She snatched her cloak and got up running. Jay scooped up the blanket, grabbed her hand in his, and together they ran to the large Fire Stones.

"Around back…we'll be in the lee, out of the wind," he shouted against the rising wet noise of the storm. On the lee side, two of the stones leaned back, creating an overhang, almost like a small cave. It was dry. It was out of the wind and they could sit up in it.

Jay and Deirdre crawled in and as before, cloaked and warm and dry, they sat and hugged each other and watched the storm soak the meadow and the trees on the lee side of the Hill of Fires. It moved across and on down the landward side of this ancient and sacred hill. The violent storm passed and washed clean everything it touched as it went on by.

"He went away from us, Jay." Deirdre was close and spoke to him in a whisper. Jay turned to face her and make sure he heard it right. She reached up and cradled his face in her two hands and pulled him to herself.

"Your father went down with the ship. He and two others were seen as they tied infants into baskets of wicker and life jackets, trying to save them. 'Moses Baskets' they called them. He got away from us, Jay, and he died that others might live."

She held Jay against her breast as she softly told him the story as it had been told to her by one of the rescuers. "One of the richest men in the world, Jay, one Alfred Vanderbilt, and another, a playwright Carl Frohman, and your Da, Sean O'Neill. The three of them stayed and died trying to save those children, those wee infants." He moaned and nodded, moving against her. "We'll go to him, my dearest Jay. Soon now, soon." She crooned and turned his face, bent and kissed him, tasting his sweet mouth and the saltiness of his tears.

"He's clean and nearly undamaged, Jay. He has a lump on the back of his head only. He got away from us very fast, my love. Something must've fallen on him, hit him from behind, they said. Sure he never felt it, not a bit. And he died helping others. It fits in with all you've told me of him. I'm so sorry Jay my darling. I love you and I will keep on loving you, to make up your loss. I am your family now, and you are mine"

The storm was moving inland and the sky became lighter when the sound of an engine straining and gears grinding alerted them. This was followed at once by another higher pitched engine winding up the hill towards them.

"Company coming, the car and motorcycle, too" Jay smiled and caressed Deirdre's soft face with the backs of his fingers. "Marry me, Deirdre. I love you and..." Jay bumped his head on the stone roof above as he struggled to get onto one knee from a sitting position. "Damn. Ow. It's not funny."

Deirdre stifled her giggles and quickly held his head and kissed the bruise on the top of his head. "I will of course, marry you. I love you as well, Jay O'Neill. I want you close to me always, the way I want to be with you."

They came out of the cave and stood and held each other in one long last kiss before walking out into the soft lingering rain and joining the newcomers.

The motorcar slithered across the wet meadow, and pulled in under the trees almost out of sight. The motorcycle too, roared into view and stopped by the big automobile. The sidecar was empty now and the driver appeared younger than the others, almost flamboyant from his white silk neck scarf and soft helmet with goggles and earflaps to his well-cut military jacket. "A grand lovers hideaway here, I'd say," Declan pronounced with a grin.

"Close your gob and drive your machine, Declan O'Mahon." She yanked off his helmet and ruffled his reddish hair. They all laughed and Deirdre made the introductions. "Jay O'Neill of New York, this *amadan* is one of us, and my cousin on the far side of Dermot's family. Meet Declan O'Mahon, Jay. And Declan, this is Jay O'Neill of New York, my betrothed, my lover, my husband to be and my best friend in the wide world." She curtsied before all of them and then went even deeper into it as she noticed Gregor MacGregor in all of his Scottish finery as he stepped out of the car.

Gregor pulled the long knife from the sheath strapped to his leg, flipped it end for end, and held it out handle first to Deirdre, as though it were his sword. She touched the hilt briefly and released it back to him. He made a formal bow, while appraising her loveliness. "Gregor MacGregor, your servant, Deirdre Ni DalCas."

He came up from his bow and raised an imaginary glass in a toast. "To Deirdre, the unmarried daughter of the DalCas clan. May your life be long; may your children be many, and may your husbands be few." He kissed her on both cheeks and she kissed him a third time in the Russian fashion. He then grabbed Jay in a bear hug and whispered, "She's everything you said she was, and then some, me boyo. She's lovely and she is yours and I'll keep her safe, Jay as I would my own daughter."

Jay grinned and sighed in relief. "We must marry as soon as we can. I need to get her, her papers. As the wife of an American citizen she'll have some rights in this country, and then we can all relax. She'll be safe from Wee Willie Burke's grasp." Jay looked over to the motorcycle where Deirdre was engaged in a heart to heart with Declan.

"Aye Jay, but remember 'tis war time and Burke is not easily thwarted. You should marry all right and obtain the correct papers, but more important you two must get beyond the borders of these Isles. And along the way we'll collect your Da, and carry him away with us. Yes, Dermot told me and I'm heartily sorry, I am. Sean…your Da was the best."

MacGregor became very quiet and appraised his friend's son in his usual direct way. "Life…like death itself, is only for the living, Jay. The dead have no need for either." The two men were quiet, thinking about Sean, but then taken out of their reverie by a shout from behind.

Dermot was all business now. "Children, Rebels, Conspirators and Lovers, gather round me and listen for we have plans to make and distant places to go." All smiles, they clustered around him. "I know. I feel quite festive myself, but we must hurry. There's a wedding to plan and a funeral to attend and more important, we've an enemy to elude."

"Aye Dermot. But as we say at home in Scotland, we need to come in out of the rain for a meal, while we plan our success."

"Well said MacGregor, does it rain in Scotland, as well?" Declan mounted his cycle.

"In Scotland it rains so hard, me boyo, there are times they say the tide comes straight down." Mac exaggerated his Scottish accent.

Not to be outdone, Declan threw out a challenge. "Well then, we need a name for this motley group. Look here, an American Naval uniform, a Royal Marine, and a lovely colleen." He pointed to each. "Donal is British army from the waist up and a farmer below the belt and I'm almost a Royal aviator." He laughed and indicated himself. "I say we call ourselves The Motleys."

"How about the O'Motleys," Jay chimed in wanting to be close to these people who would help him protect his Deirdre.

"Thank the Gods no one has suggested we call ourselves the MacMotleys. My MacGregor ancestors would awaken angry from their eternal sleep."

"O'Motley, MacMotley, whatever. The Motleys we shall be." They were still laughing as Declan roared away on his machine and Dermot looked after him in surprise. "Where in the name of God is he off to?"

"I sent him home after some things I'll be needing." Deirdre looked unhappy at having upset Dermot.

"Deirdre, do not, ever….", his voice kept rising and his face became red.

"Dermot, if I'm to marry, I must have my things. The necklace, and pin, the brooch and my rings as well as the white gown."

"Jesus, Mary and Joseph," Dermot shouted at her. "You CAN NOT EVER send away one of my men. You must ask me…."

"It's a short run only, and he'll meet us in Courtmacsherry. He has the plan in his head, Dermot."

"LOOK AT ME!" Dermot roared and smashed his fist into his chest indicating his British uniform. And then he pointed after the motorcycle, "Declan as well. We're dressed in the stranger's uniforms, so. They'd shoot us in the blink of an eye, and laugh at us while they shot us. Is that what you want, cousin? Two men dead so you can have some baubles and a white dress for a wedding. Is that it?"

Deirdre stood speechless. She was white with anger, regret and even shame at having been so wrong and now being tongue lashed in front of strangers. MacGregor was bad enough but Jay too had heard it, and though he was her beloved he was still a stranger when it came to family matters or indeed, Irish Republican Brotherhood business.

The men probably agreed with Dermot, and some part of her too, knew she had been wrong; but she would not, absolutely not, cry in front of them. Not one tear would fall, she resolved, and feeling her eyes fill, she pulled her hood up over her head, turned and walked across the meadow and under the trees to the far side of the hill.

Jay watched her walk away and was amazed. The hood covered her head and the cloak fell to the ground, covering all of her, even her feet, and Deirdre appeared to float across the meadow. He was charmed beyond reason. Who was this woman he was so committed to and for a lifetime. She was stunning and he was bewitched.

A line from a 1902 play by Yeats popped into his head. He must have said it aloud. "Did you see an old woman going down the path."

"I did not. But I saw a young girl and she had the walk of a queen." Dermot answered with the next line of the play. He looked at Deirdre, shook his head and turned away.

Jay agreed with Dermot. She should never have sent Declan on a private mission, not without the leader's knowledge and consent, but she was so excited and in love and planning a wedding while on the run. It was understandable. I should've taken her side even if she then flared up at me. I should've spoken up for my woman.

Jay was about to run after her when Donal appeared near the road from his lookout post lower down the hill. He waved an all clear and Dermot urged the Yank and the Scot into the rear of the car. He drove on, picked up Donal and made introductions as he backed across the meadow to pick up Deirdre.

Donal Crowley was older than the others. Closer in age to MacGregor, he had graying hair and far seeing eyes of the same color. His tanned, lined face spoke of more time spent outdoors than in an office or shop. He seldom spoke and seemed ill at ease in the English uniform as well as the English language. Donal Crowley climbed into the open front seat next to Dermot and cradled his rifle between his knees.

"Time to go, cousin. We're off to West Cork." Dermot thought to soften it a bit, "The Motleys are off now with a stop for a meal along the way." Dermot was very matter of fact when he spoke and so was Deirdre's response.

"Yes, of course." She walked around the front of the car and using her thumb, motioned Donal out of his seat and into the enclosed rear with Jay and Mac. He complied at once and she took his seat, pulled her hood up close around her face and without a word the motorcar lumbered away, down a steep track, around the other side of the hill and by back trails they headed to the main Cork road.

They were on their way to find Sean O'Neill.

CHAPTER SIX

The silence was almost deafening and was so unusual in this group. Finally, and very business like, Gregor leaned forward, slid open the glass panel and extended his small brass telescope out front. He began a visual sweeping of the road ahead. "If that's our way and that's the main Cork road up ahead there, we'll pass some military traffic, in short order."

"Aye. 'Tis our way indeed." Dermot pulled over to the side of the road and gave his orders. "Deirdre cousin, you must become a nurse. Donal, you are our invalid. Sit in the middle of the rear, pull the rug over you and keep that trusty rifle of yours hidden but at the ready.

Gregor, you take the seat behind me. Open the window and show off that fine outfit of yours. Any English troops will appreciate those MacGregor Plaids. Jay you have the other outside position, behind Deirdre, and next to the soft shoulders and stonewalls. When we approach any troopers, just slouch down some and be natural. They'll see a uniform, but not see that you're a Yank. That's grand. The Motleys will get through this fine."

Jay watched as Deirdre piled her hair on top of her head and pinned it in place. She was fast and graceful and it seemed to him that putting up a woman's hair was a very intimate process. He made a mental note for the next time they were alone, to lift her hair and kiss that sweet vulnerable place where her dark hair met her lovely white neck. She then pinned on a nurse's cap, donned a pert jacket with Red Cross insignia and passed her full black cloak into the back seat. Jay grabbed her cloak, folded it and held it on his lap.

Their eyes met as she turned and he was entranced by the change in her appearance. Jay wouldn't mind being sick or wounded for a nurse like Deirdre. Within two minutes they were under way again, and Jay chalked up another amazing facet to this woman, this very separate and amazing being he felt so attuned with, and he loved the smell of her cloak.

The Motley group turned onto the Cork Road and almost at once, they began passing military vehicles headed to the port behind them. Dermot kept to a steady high speed and overtook many civilian cars. He used his English uniform, the big expensive auto and the nurse beside him to bully other drivers into giving way for them.

Suddenly MacGregor warned of a roadblock ahead and soon everyone could see it. The motorcars were bunching up and forming a line on both sides of a barricade on the Cork road. Military lorries pulled sideways formed the block in the road. Dermot announced a cache of guns and ammunition in a hidey-hole beneath Jay's seat. He insisted Jay and Mac arm themselves and cautioned Donal to be ready. The tension in the enclosed rear of the big vehicle was electric as Jay pulled out three revolvers and loaded them. He handed one each to Donal and MacGregor and kept one for himself.

Mac took the deadly weapon but put it on the seat behind him. He was still peering through his spyglass and announced that no one should shoot. "Do you see the battle flag attached to the lorry, ahead there on the left. I've served under that symbol, and just today, I'd not like to kill someone who is protecting it. Besides, there's a heavy machine gun mounted upon that armored car and those chaps manning the gun are not recruits. They'd have us in pieces before we got off a second pistol shot."

He collapsed his glass and put it away. "It's guile we'll use, fellow Motleys. 'Tis your own plan after all, Dermot. We've a wounded man headed to hospital in Cork. Deirdre, I promised Jay that I'd protect you as my own daughter and by Christ, I will. Keep your guns down and well hidden, gents. Dermot, slow speed ahead, is what is needed here. Pull out into the oncoming lane and don't stop for anyone or anything."

MacGregor opened wide his car door, swung it all the way back, and stepped out onto the running board. He leaned back against the open car door and it was a wild sight the English soldiers beheld coming at them and their roadblock.

A large expensive touring car with a Marine sergeant driving, flanked by a nurse and on the running board stood a big Scot in full parade dress. He yelled in a loud voice that rang out down the road, carried over the stone walls and into the green meadows. "Give way. You, open up there. Wounded man. Give way. Errand-of-mercy. Give way."

Then Mac began singing out a recent dance hall ditty that was very popular and had become the marching song of the Connaught Rangers and everyone of The Motley group in the car joined him in a rousing sing-along.

"It's a long way to Tipperary, It's a long way to go. It's a long way to Tipperary. To the sweetest girl I know." People along the way joined in and then the soldiers took their fingers off the triggers and they too began singing. "Goodbye Picadilly, Farewell Leicester square. It's a long long way to Tipperary but my heart's right there."

They bluffed and sang their way through the roadblock, past the saluting singing soldiers and the deadly machine gun. When they were beyond danger, Deirdre turned to Jay, reached a hand back and grinned at him. She locked her fingers with his and both felt a surge of energy as the danger passed. "Thank God for Jack Judge and Harry Williams." When Jay looked puzzled she added, "Words and music by them a few years back."

They held hands and remembered her bold march from the Mayors Palace to another motorcar amid the rousing cheers of Russian soldiers. "Yuri Yurivich would have enjoyed this trip," Jay said and Deirdre nodded. It was exhilarating for both of them.

They went along then in a pleasant way. Donal was humming "Tipperary" a bit off key but no one minded. They all were enclosed in the bubble of well being that comes after a scary happening. The green grass glistened and the gray stone walls shone under the bright sun after the recent storm and the sky was blue over it all. The storm itself had gone well inland away from them and they felt safe now.

A brown military motorcar zipped past and MacGregor shouted,

"Jesus Jay, the same car. That's the one picked us up at dockside and that same pinch faced spy is driving it."

Donal was all business now. "Have ye the looking glass, so?" Mac nodded and dug it out of his Sporran. "May I have the lend of it, then." Donal swung around and peered through the back window. "He's braking and slowing, so. Now he's swinging around in a farm yard. Dermot, give a hard push on yer throttle, if ye please. He's coming right after us."

But Dermot had been on the gas pedal from the moment Mac recognized the car and shouted his warning. The Motleys were fairly flying down the road to Cork City.

Donal faced front now, "Beyond this small hill is a hard road off to the right hand. Tis the road to Watergrasshill. Take it, but ye must veer off to the left at yer first chance. That's it. Now, go left there on the soft road and left again just ahead. That's it. We're grand, now."

Dermot broke the silence with his shout, "Pistols everyone. Safety off and be ready. I don't think there was anyone else in it with him, was there, Mac?"

"Aye, he was alone," MacGregor answered.

"Himself alone," Donal said. "Now drop me there round that bend and go on ahead, so." Donal grabbed his rifle, changed places with Jay while they were still rolling and vaulted out the door when they were nearly stopped. He clambered over the gray stone wall and as the car pulled ahead, he ran crouched down behind the wall to find a good firing position.

They accelerated fast up the long hill ahead of them and just before they crested they could see the other car. It was a long way back but it still came after them.

Dermot took the motor car out of gear, cut the engine, and they coasted down the other side of the long hill in complete silence. No one spoke; they rolled and rolled in silence until it seemed an eternity. But nothing at all happened.

They coasted on down the long hill and the local blackbirds made a loud sound cawing in the trees around them. Jay's hand was on the sill of the sliding window and he felt Deirdre's fingers seeking his. It was so quiet. They could hear the cows moving around in the fields while the wind rustled the long grasses and caused rolling wave after wave of green in the meadow. It looked like some ghostly green army passing silently by. Deirdre dug her nails into the palm of Jay's hand as the tension grew and they rolled on, but nothing happened.

CRACK. The rifle shot rang out and inside the car they all jumped at the sound, even MacGregor's feet leaped off the floor. The birds screamed in fright and anger as they flew off. Cows in the field close by mooed a protest but they never moved. Dermot started the engine, turned the car around, and drove them slowly back up the long hill and none knew what to expect. "He's a marksman, Donal is. I've seen him take the eye out of a deer at a hundred yards."

Donal could be seen in the distance pushing the other car through a gap in the stone wall, into a field. When they got abreast of him, he shoved his rifle through the window to Jay and from the boot of the other car he took a brand new rifle, a web belt with a hand gun and pouches of bullets on it and a full metal ammo box. These items he stuffed into the boot of their car.

"Never throw nothin' away that costs money, for ye'll need it some day." He passed a leather satchel to Dermot, another long barreled revolver on a lanyard, some papers and a wad of cash. "Judas money, no doubt." Donal pronounced and came back to the car.

"Donal, change seats with me, will you? I need to be enclosed, the while," Deirdre asked. She got in the rear between Mac and Jay, leaned back and with her fist to her mouth made a sound like a stifled sob and her shoulders shook.

Jay put his arm around her and held her tight to him. He kissed her brow and he whispered to her. She leaned her head forward and he kissed the back of her neck and whispered again into her ear. Her quiet sobbing slowed and became a long sigh and she leaned into him for protection and comfort and healing. And Jay gave her all that was in him.

They were moving again, towards Cork, and on the same back road. "Is he dead?" Dermot asked.

"I took him in the shoulder, only. In and out, clean like."

"You should've killed him, Donal." Dermot was quite emphatic as he stared at Donal.

"Aye", MacGregor seconded that notion. "You should've done for that one. The bastard knows both Jay and I by sight and sound and now he's seen Deirdre and Dermot and this distinctive automobile. He's a spy you know. He hides behind that soldier suit, while he's in the pay of a civilian who has no authority to spy on us or anyone else. He's Wee Willie Burke's man and it would've been better for us if he were removed from this equation."

"He's Devil Burke's man, is he?" Dermot repeated himself. "You should've killed him Donal. That Burke is half Irish, half Devil and all English Sassenach bastard."

"How bad is the man?" Jay was anxious for Deirdre, not for himself or the others.

"He'll be out for awhile only, but the pain may put him out again, so. I stopped the most of the bleeding, fore and aft, like. And there's cows in that field so they'd likely find him by milking time."

They drove on a bit and Donal exclaimed with great sadness. "Sorry Dermot. I could've taken a head shot." He pointed, "Go on now and make a left turn anywhere. We'll cross the River Lee at the far edge of Cork and go on down below Bishopstown. There's a grand Country Inn there, owned by one of our own. We can stop and have our meal in peace."

Dermot began to smile again. "We must ditch this vehicle now and beg or borrow another. Jay, have you any American dollars, still?"

"Yes I do and the Admiral gave me leave to get whatever I need to take care of my father. We can rent or buy a car or a truck. Whichever is best. Is there a nearby place, a dealer?"

"Good Christ Jay, if the Irish countryside is like the Scottish, then everyone out here that owns a motor car is a dealer, and ready to trade at the sight of a coin."

The others all laughed and once again the worry quotient of The Motleys, dropped to a more comfortable level. "Dermot, stop at the corner a bit." Donal, the protector and guide had something for them.

"Jay and Deirdre d'ye see that big church with the red and white steeple, the one with the clock in it. St. Ann's at Shandon, 'tis a famous Cork landmark."

Deirdre brightened and sat up "Ah Donal, I remember Shandon and the old rhyme, 'With thy Bells of Shandon, that sound so grand on, the pleasant waters of the River Lee'."

"Aye lass. The very one. Well t'would be a grand church for you and Jay to be married in."

"We need a Catholic Chapel Donal and St. Ann's, though very nice, is a Protestant Church. It will not do, Donal Crowley, but thank you indeed for thinking of us."

"Drive on anyway, Dermot. When you cross the Lee you'll see the road to Bishopstown. Ye see now, Jay. The steeple on that grand church has a clock on each of the four sides of it, North, South, East and West. Four clocks and they all tell a different time." He chuckled, "here in Cork we call it the four faced liar."

"You know a good bit about Cork, Donal", Jay smiled to encourage him.

"Indeed, I do know Cork. From Bantry to Baltimore, from Bandon to Ballincollig, and from Skull to Skibbereen." Donal waved his arms in wide swings and almost knocked Dermot's military cap off of his head and out of the moving car. "Sorry Dermot. I nearly took the head off yer shoulders, so." He smiled and his gray eyes danced with pleasure.

"Donal, I've never in my life heard you talk this much. You are brilliant, man, absolutely brilliant, and quite loquacious," Dermot declared, half serious, half in jest. He put his cap back on and adjusted it to his liking. "Is it the shooting gives you the gift of gab?"

Donal's arms came down and his face fell. Then he looked at each of them in turn. "I don't like to kill things, Deirdre, not a'tall. Not one bit, Dermot. Not an animal and never a man, Jay. I'm good at it, I know, but I don't like it and I'm glad right now, MacGregor I never killed that English soldier, be he spy or not. I'm relieved like, is the way of it, so."

They drove on through Cork City, crossed the River Lee, found the Bishopstown road and followed it out of town. The Motleys, all five of them, in the large touring car were relaxed now, almost in perfect harmony, heading out into the country. They had begun to know each other better; begun to like each other and there was a trust building between all of them. Donal had revealed his carefully guarded truth; though a crack shot, he was reluctant to kill.

The Yank and the Scot were no longer suspect strangers; Dermot's leadership was firmly established and Deirdre was restored to her rightful place as a woman of the rebellion and best friend of the leader. And most important she was a woman who loved and was loved in return. The Motleys were beginning to fit like the thumb and fingers of one hand.

Out in the country beyond Bishopstown, Donal had them slow and turn in at a sign for Coveney's Inn. He guided them past a parked auto in the front of the Inn, and around back to a secluded parking area and private entrance. Dermot turned and backed in so the car was pointed out in case a quick exit became necessary.

In response to their knocking a young woman came out, recognized Donal and put her finger to her lips. In silence she guided them along the side of the building until they reached a heavy wooden door.

She unlocked it and led them into a large walled garden. Inside the walls the garden was furnished with several plank tables and wood benches, a few white lawn chairs near a small rock fountain and a pond with gold fish. Several espaliered trees with young fruit on them were flourishing against the north wall of the garden.

The other walls were busy, in a relaxed Irish way, with red and yellow roses, green ivy vines and colorful flower beds, with some herbs and vegetables mixed in with the flowers.

The woman wore a cloak like Deirdre's and when her hood was pulled back she appeared young and quite attractive. "I am Maura Ni Coveney," she said and repeated each new name and her own name as Donal introduced her one by one to each of the Motleys.

Deirdre and Jay were the last to be introduced... "And Jay O'Neill, I am Maura Ni Coveney. A pleasure indeed to meet each of you." She paused for a breath and with her gaze on Dermot, she said to all of them, "at the moment, we have strangers inside having a meal. A man and a woman headed to Bandon, I think. Once they have gone away, I will bring you in. It will be a short while only." She made her promise directly to Dermot.

"The garden will do fine, for this Motley group, Maura Ni Coveney," Dermot assured her and as he pronounced her name, Maura glowed with pleasure. "We'd be pleased to have our dinner out here in your lovely garden with all the sunshine and fresh air, Maura. Is that at all possible now, Maura Ni Coveney?

"I will make it happen for you, Dermot O'Rourke. You all are welcome and please be at home." Maura turned to enter the small side door of the Inn but was stopped by a question from Jay.

"Maura Ni Coveney? It's a lovely name, and a fine cloak, too. It's the same as Deirdre's, isn't it?" Maura shook her head as Jay gestured to Deirdre, who joined them. "My betrothed, Deirdre Ni DalCas." The two women smiled warily and studied each other, especially each other's cloak.

"No two cloaks are ever the same, Jay." Deirdre linked her arm through his.

"Indeed not," Maura smiled proudly. "Do you see the fine stitching here on the inside of the hood?" Jay was invited to examine the embroidery inside each of the hoods. "When the front of the hood is folded back the distinctive markings are shown. No two of them are ever alike, Jay O'Neill."

"I see the difference. And your cloak Maura, it smells like candle wax and incense."

"And well it should. I am only a short while wearing it," she said sadly. "The cloak, Jay O'Neill, is a link from one generation to the next."

Deirdre put her hand gently on the other girl's arm. "Your mam?"

Maura nodded. "Nearly a fortnight, now."

"Blessings and tradition are the very warp and woof of the garment," Deirdre explained to Jay while Maura took Deirdre's hand and held it between her own two hands in a gesture of thanks for her understanding and sympathy.

"The possessor of a cloak, and she going to die, will pass it down to another in the family, usually a young one in the first blush of womanhood. And always with the admonition, 'wear it to Mass. Remember me in your prayers'."

Dermot joined Jay and the two women who were now holding hands like old school chums. "Did you know Maura, in days past, the cloak was worn in many colors. Anything but black would be a rare sight today, since the famine and the hungry times."

"Dermot O'Rourke, surely you must know more of our history than all the rest of us together." Maura smiled at Dermot and winked at Deirdre. "Will you ever come inside and freshen yourself, Deirdre. I can get you upstairs unseen by those others." To the men she said, "there is another, outside toilet, 'round back of the garden. Come Deirdre."

"Before you go, do you have the time, Maura? The hour? My own watch was soaked on the trip over here. We had quite a rough crossing."

"It is just past midday, Jay O'Neill. *Ard na Greinne,* we call it, the height of the sun."

"Almost a full day since the ship went down," Jay whispered softly with wonder in his voice. He looked at Mac and they nodded together in mutual sympathy.

The Motley group then, made themselves comfortable. MacGregor took a chair by the fountain with Donal, and Dermot leaned against the end of the long wood table near them. Jay made the rounds of the fruit trees, raised bushes and herb beds, smelling and tasting as he went. There was dill and basil, rosemary and thyme and several types of mint flourished.

Maura came back and spoke to all, but she looked directly at Dermot. "And a young priest is riding with the strangers. He himself is known to us and just now returning from a retreat up at Maynouth Seminary. His bishop sent him away for prayer and mind changes."

Maura gave a shy smile. "He is said to have Irish National sympathies, and maybe even knows some in the Brotherhood." Here Maura's smile came on stronger. "Will I have him stay on, after the strangers leave?" Receiving no answer she went on, "I'll send out food and drink to you then, at once." Her smile was full and radiant as she gave a curtsy directly to Dermot. He grinned and made her a gracious bow.

"Maura, do not send anyone out to us. I'd prefer you yourself would take care of us."

"As you will, Dermot." Maura had a glow around her as she whirled to go into the building and her cloak and the garment under it flared out from her slim body.

The door was barely closed behind Maura, when MacGregor and Donal began speaking at once, but Dermot held up his hand and said, "I know. I know. Sit down here, now."

Deirdre came back outside and over to the table. Now she and the group of men were all together. "We must get that stranger to swap cars with us." Dermot exclaimed.

"We must convince him to buy ours, and use his as part payment." Jay grinned as he said it.

"We need a bit of guile here." MacGregor smiled and rubbed his hands together.

Deirdre looked wistful and said, "We need Declan with us now. He's the cute one. Declan has more guile in him than a Tinker at the fair, trading horses."

"Indeed. I would dearly love to see that man and his woman driving our large expensive motor car to Bandon and all points beyond. 'Twould be a grand dodge for ourselves now wouldn't it," Donal closed his eyes to picture it and then smiled as a British patrol raced after the strangers in hot pursuit, with sirens blaring and lights flashing. He shared his dream with the others and they all smiled, appreciating the irony of it.

MacGregor smacked his palm onto the wooden planks of the table and declared, "we must make it happen. Indeed, we will make it happen."

Maura entered the garden carrying four pints of porter, a bottle of sherry and a glass for Deirdre. She had shed the cloak and now wore a large green apron with a gold harp embroidered upon it. Her sun yellow frock went well with the green apron. "I will have dinner for you soon. Is there anything you need or want, Dermot?"

She served the black porter to the men and poured a glass of amber sherry for Deirdre, and the bright sun overhead made her hair sparkle and appear the same color as the wine. She included all of the Motleys but her attention and questions were for Dermot alone.

"We're here on business, Maura, so after this, there'll be no more drinks to any of us." To soften his words and make them easier on her ears, he took one of the roses Jay had cut; the yellow one, and fastened it to her green apron just above the gold harp.

"I'll bring out some tea to you then, will I Dermot?"

He nodded. "Maura, listen to me now," Dermot began and kept his eyes locked on Maura's as he raised his glass and took small sips between his words. "What else...sip...can you tell me... sip...about the man...sip...and his woman,...sip...inside, there."

He had soaked his moustache in the foam of his drink and now some of it dribbled down his chin. Maura grabbed a linen napkin and rushed to dab the drips before his uniform became stained. Dermot caught her hand and under the pretext of drying his moustache with the white linen, he managed to press her fingers to his lips.

Her eyes widened and she made a small sound deep in her throat. "I'm so sorry, Dermot. The other girl is waiting on them, my young sister, I mean, and I have no knowledge of the strangers. Not a thing do I know about them except of course, he is a surgeon and the doctor is going down to help the survivors in Bandon. But I will find out something. I will find out everything, Dermot." Once again Dermot pressed her fingers to his lips. "Surely, I must get the tea now, Dermot. Excuse me." Flushed and smiling, Maura almost ran from the garden.

"Dermot O'Rourke, you should be ashamed of yourself." Deirdre smiled, dabbed at his chin and pressed her fingers to his mouth to be kissed. "Declan isn't the only one full of guile on your side of the family, is he, cousin?"

Dermot grinned and pushed her hand aside. "Behave, woman. Your man is watching you."

Jay, seated next to her at the table jibed at him, too. "Careful with Maura Ni Coveney, Dermot or The O'Motleys will be going to a double wedding."

Dermot allowed that strange but pleasant thought to ricochet off of the corners of his mind. He shook his head and declared, "It's down to business, boys and girl." He pointed to Donal. "Outside, please and clean out our motor car. Top to bottom, bonnet to boot, every corner, shelf and cabinet. There'll be nothing to link us to it. Mac will you help him and pile it all here in the garden on that other table."

MacGregor rose to follow after Donal. "Mac is it!" His smile told Jay that he was pleased to be accepted as one of the bunch. "Gregor MacGregor is now just plain Mac. Or should I say, MacMotley. It seems

I am to be the Scottish Auxiliary for the Irish Republican Brotherhood."
He saluted on his way out of the heavy wooden door.

Outside the walls of the garden, they heard a high pitched whine and
a pop-pop-pop. The motorcycle backfired as it was shut off. "Declan."
Deirdre and Dermot exclaimed almost together.

"Dermot, don't be hard on the lad. Sure it was my fault. I sent him
away, after all."

"Deirdre, what's done is done. No one is angry with anyone anymore,
besides the anger takes too much energy and we have sooo much to do.
Now cousin, leave your cloak here, and see will Maura lend you an apron.
I want you to work that dining room where the strangers are eating. Get
close to the man and his woman. See and hear whatever you can find out
for us, that we may use it to our advantage. We must have him swap cars
with us."

Declan burst through the door, his face beaming. "God Bless all here."
He was loaded down with a suitcase and a grip, a leather dispatch case
hung around his neck, and a pack was strapped onto his back. "God Bless
all in this garden, and we must hurry. There's gobs of military doings along
all the roads."

He unloaded his burdens onto the table, slid the carpetbag grip over to
Deirdre and gave the suitcase and leather dispatch case to Dermot. "I'm
sorry, Dermot. I should not have run off like that without telling you."

Dermot stared at Declan. "Asking me, do you mean?" He smiled to
soften his reply.

"Asking you, then." Declan indicated the suitcase. "Here are some
things your mam sent along for you. And also she sent to you a God Bless,
a caution, and a kiss. But I'll not kiss you Dermot. I will kiss Deirdre and
she can pass it on, so." Declan looked uncomfortable and the other two
cousins smiled. For all of his bravado Declan was quite shy about hugs,
kisses and any sort of personal closeness. He approached Deirdre with
caution. Instead of offering her cheek, she held up her hand and Declan
kissed her fingers with relief. "To you from your aunt Fiona." He kissed
her fingers again. "To Dermot from his Mam, Fiona."

"Now cousin, go inside please and hurry. Secure an apron from Maura
and get Declan the information he'll need." Deirdre held her fingers out

for Dermot to kiss and so get the kiss from his Mam. He pecked at her hand and with a grin said, "Thank you Mam. Hurry now Deirdre, and if you fall down so, don't stop to rise."

Dermot swung around to Declan. "Now you, cousin. We need you out of those clothes. Open your pack and let's pick out a costume for you and put together a plan. I'll explain what we want. Nay, what we need, what we must have. Then you tell me how we get it."

Together Jay and Dermot gave young Declan the highlights of their trip thus far. The way they sang 'Tipperary' and made their safe passage through the machine gun roadblock. Then the chase by Devil Burke's spy, and finally Donal's shot and now the need to get rid of this car and get another before something bad happens. "Deirdre's freedom, perhaps her life, depends upon it, Declan," Jay finished. He was eloquent and urgent.

Maura came into the garden with a tray. "Here are the tea things, Dermot." She saw Declan half undressed and stopped. "I am Maura Ni Coveney, welcome sir. And aren't you the young man made eyes at my sister Mary Rose Ni Coveney on the Friday last?" Without pausing for breath she hurried on. "Dermot, there will be no bargaining with that stranger inside. The man is an amadan," she turned to Jay, "a fool, Jay O'Neill."

"Thank you, Maura for the tea. It looks grand." Dermot took her hand in his own and gently asked her to go on.

"Well, he fought my sister, Mary Rose Ni Coveney, on the strength of his bill, his reckoning. Too much he says, and then after ordering a bottle of our best wine, he's denying me payment. He'll not even leave a customary wee little something for the staff. After he ordered them about as though they were indeed, his own indentured slaves."

Deirdre entered the garden in time to hear the last bit. "Ach Dermot, we're in luck. The man is a skinflint, a greedy ha'penny miser. Insists the woman with him drink his wine, makes inquiries about the price of a room, but when she leaves the wine untouched he refuses to pay. And then he cancels the room."

She smiled in anticipation. "Declan darling dear, he's all yours. His greed will be his undoing, surely. Park our shiny expensive motorcar just outside that big window. He'll see it from where he is seated. Come back inside, Maura. You'll finally have some joy out of this stranger and we must keep him busy the while." The two women left the garden bubbling with enthusiasm.

"Jay have you a white dress shirt. I need one with a collar. Oh, and a black tie? And can you take away that Navy gold braid and insignia from your cap? Dermot, ask Maura if she has a jacket in the house would fit me. Someone in her family used to be a chauffer, her Da or an uncle or somebody. And I need a sheaf of papers. Legal looking papers to look like a Last Will and Testament, seven or eight pages anyway." Declan went through his own pack, Jay's duffle and Dermot's suitcase to assemble a possible costume for himself.

Donal and Mac brought in the last of their goods from the big car. They piled it all on the far table and began to sort it. "Two rifles with twenty or so rounds," Donal counted.

"Three revolvers, a case of ammo and another handgun with holster and lanyard," Mac sorted them by barrel size. "Two long, one short and one snub-nosed for close in work."

"Two blankets, one white, one brown, a dented helmet, a gun cleaning kit and repair tools and a travel bag of some sort," Donal finished lamely. He pushed it over to Mac.

"An actors theatrical kit. Wigs, hairpieces, eyeglasses, a nose, moustaches and the like, there is enough here for us all to go on tour." Mac was shaking with laughter as he moved over to help Donal clean and oil the guns.

Maura came out with a dark jacket for Declan and as she was headed back inside, Dermot asked her to send out the priest who had been riding with the strangers. "I'd like him out here beside us and out of the way, entirely. Declan will need a free hand, so."

Declan assembled himself in the white dress shirt and tie, the too big jacket, dark trousers and his own motorcycle boots. Jay's Navy cap stripped of any insignia gave him an almost chauffer look, a disheveled one indeed, but it fit his story as he outlined it to the group.

"I'm sure it will work. And so, we become more 'Motley' every day and in every way." Declan placed the toe of one boot behind he heel of his other boot and did a smart about face with his arms outstretched to show off his new outfit. "Wish me luck, lads. You'll soon be safe as a nun in church and driving away in another motorcar, Dermot."

Declan drove the big auto out of the yard and off the property. He turned and came roaring right back. Those in the garden heard brakes squealing and gravel spraying as Declan came to an abrupt halt just outside the large front window. He jumped out and went slamming through the main door into the Inn.

"Landlord, will you ever bring me a pint, something dark and wet. I don't care if it's Murphy's or Beamish or Guinness. I want it wet and in a glass and I want it now." He slammed down the sheaf of papers as Maura handed him his pint of porter. He drank a bit then slammed down his cap and pointed to the window. "D'ye see that grand big expensive automobile? 'Tis mine. All mine. Willed to me this glorious day." Declan held up and rattled his sheaf of papers, then slammed them down onto the counter again.

"'Tis the most beautiful, most expensive thing in the world ever owned by the likes of myself. And then he has the gall to fire me. That damned butler. Would you ever believe it." He looked at Maura, then turned and looked at the doctor and his woman who were staring out at the fancy car. "The likes of you wouldn't believe it. Not in seven lifetimes. Naagh. Not in seven times seven lifetimes". He made a long derisive sound in the back of his throat and turned back to Maura as she was cautioning him and clucking and soothing him.

"What exactly did happen, young man?" The doctor inquired. His attention was off of the car and full on Declan and his eyes narrowed as he waited for a reply.

Declan ignored him and spoke to Maura. "Never mind clucking at me like an old mother hen. I'll be needing a good writing pen and a pot of black ink and some clean white paper, like these here in this Last Will and Testament. Left me her motorcar she did, but that butler stripped away my neat chauffeur's uniform and nearly had the shirt off me back. Nothing now but these ill fitting duds. Still I'll make a sign and put it in the window. 'FOR HIRE'. Or maybe, CAR AND DRIVER. Man and Machine? What do you think, missus?" Declan throws down some coins and counts them, three pennies, two ha'pennies, and two six pence. "Do I have enough here for another pint?"

Maura looked at the money and stated flatly, "You have just enough there to pay for the one drink, and you have nearly finished it. I suppose you haven't eaten all day, either."

"Young man," the doctor made a visible effort to swallow his anger. "I may be able to help you." The woman leaned in and whispered to the doctor who pushed her away. He said to Maura, "will you kindly show my companion to the necessary."

Deirdre, dressed in an apron, walked over and cut in front of Maura. "I'll take care of her, Maura my dear. You've got your hands full here." She linked arms with the woman and led her out of the large dinning room to the women's toilet.

"You're offering to help me, is it? Have you the need of a car and driver, then? Will you hire me and my wonderful expensive motor car?" Declan turned to the window and stared at his car in rapt fascination.

"No certainly not. But I will buy you a pint and listen while you tell me your story and if I deem you worthy, I may have a solution to your problem." To Maura he called, "Miss, a pint for the chauffeur here and I'll have a brandy, if you please."

"Doctor, you already have a large account which is in dispute…"

The doctor cut her off. "A misunderstanding my dear." He produced a fat wallet full of large bills and handed a guinea note to Maura. "That should cover it and leave a generous something for yourself and the serving girl too."

"Yes sir and thank you very much sir. I will bring the drinks straightaway."

Declan approached and pulled out a chair next to the doctor and facing the window. "I must sit where I can watch my automobile, and you sir, should be careful flashing around a wallet full of money the size of that." He made a big circle with his two thumbs and fingers.

"I am well able to defend myself." Here the doctor twisted the handle of his walking stick and drew out a foot of steel, enough to show a long, wicked, blade concealed inside his walking stick. "Twenty years a surgeon in the Army. Been all over the Empire, I have." Maura served them and left. "Now we have our drinks, let's have your story."

Declan took a long pull at the pint, wiped his mouth with the back of his hand and began to tell his story. "I started when I was a wee lad of ten years. A stable boy at first, then a gardeners apprentice." He tapped his forehead. "Seeing as how the engines and motor cars were becoming all the rage, I became a helper in the garage, and then I drove for that good old woman for four years. One year ago she bowls me over and buys this elegant, fancy, big motorcar. I nearly wore out my two arms polishing and dusting and caring for it. Drove her everywhere, I did, and just the way she liked it. Slow and easy like." Here Declan joined his hands and made them plane through the air, slow and easy.

"Would you ever enjoy seeing the inside of it? I must figure a good window to place my 'FOR HIRE' sign. And thanks for the pint. I'm a bit short just now. Here I own a grand big wealthy man's car and I haven't a farthing to my name."

The doctor and Declan went outside and shortly thereafter Deirdre escorted the doctor's lady to the door and pointed her to the big car. Back inside she said, "My God Maura, she's as greedy and shallow as he is. They deserve each other, those two."

Maura smiled and told Deirdre that the bill had been paid and a generous tip given as well.

"He probably flashed some money to impress Declan and thus get to buy his car. I wonder Maura, what did the priest think of the pair of them? Did he offer any opinion at all?"

"Mostly, he thought the two were rather shallow people. Empty headed, he said except in one narrow regard, and that is their chosen profession. They told a bunch of stories, driving down from Dublin, all glorifying themselves of course. It seems that he is in the way of being a cracker jack of a surgeon, a wizard with the knife, as he tells it and she the best surgical nurse in seven continents. Wounded early on in France, he's back home now and goes where he is needed for delicate operations, and it seems, she goes where he goes."

"Married are they," Deirdre asked, matrimony being uppermost on her mind.

"I think not, Deirdre. At the lofty level they see themselves on, one can ignore the local social niceties. Marriage does not seem important to them, Deirdre, not one wee bit."

"Well Maura, marriage is important enough to us. I'll be out in the garden if you need me."

Outside, on the far wood table there was a map of Cork County laid out and the men were gathered around it. Deirdre walked up, took Jay's hand and kissed his cheek.

The young priest, part of the group now, was surprised. "Here I thought you one of the serving girls, inside."

"I am when I need to be, father." She stuck out her hand to the priest and with a sly glance at Dermot and imitating Maura she said, "I am Deirdre Ni DalCas, a member of the rebellion and betrothed to this big Yank, seated alongside and as close to me as he can get."

"Deirdre cousin, how goes it inside? Time is getting short and The Motleys need to move out, without delay. Have we our new transportation yet?"

"Soon Dermot. Declan has the greedy doctor drooling in anticipation. He'll close the sale any minute now."

The priest smiled and shook her hand. "I am Rory Beechinor, a priest who has just been chastised by Bishop Connor Westbrook. I am too sympathetic, by far, to the rebel cause."

"Excuse me father Rory," Jay interrupted. "I need to speak alone with Deirdre. We'll talk some more on our way. You are coming with us, aren't you?" Rory nodded yes and Jay and Deirdre, holding hands moved to the other table where all of their luggage lay.

Beaming at Jay, Deirdre took a small, very old, oak and leather chest out of her grip. She set it on the table between them and opened it with joy and obvious pride.

At his table, Dermot moved to the other end and said, "Donal, Mac, will you two see to all the guns. After you clean and oil everything, I want them all loaded." When Donal raised his eyebrows, Dermot backed off. "I know, I know, you are the expert. Just see to it, please. As soon as Declan's finished bargaining with the strangers, we'll have Maura serve us a meal and then we're off. Our way is selected and our line of march is clear. The Motleys are headed to West Cork, into rebel territory. And, we can be sure, the British Army is on the move as well; they'll be looking for payback."

Mac, with experience in that very army offered, "With one of their own shot, they'll not rest until they've caught and punished someone. They require blood for blood."

"He's right, Dermot," Donal chimed in. "We need to move." Donal started with the rifles, and Mac selected the pistols, one by one, taking them apart, cleaning, oiling, reassembling and loading them.

"Aye Aye skipper," Deirdre at the other table chimed in with some bravado, but her hands shook as she began lifting pieces out of her jewelry case. Jay covered her hands with his and held on until she was steady. After this morning's episode, guns and war talk upset her.

Rory moved over to the fountain and took out his prayer book. "My presence may be of some help to you later on Deirdre, but for now, I'll do what I do best."

"And what is that, Rory?"

"I'll pray. My prayers are for all of us here, of course, and that man, that British soldier who was shot, and the other man, the one who sent him out after you, as well. I feel that we all will need help and guidance before this is over and done." Rory raised his hand in a blessing, which included them all. *"In nomini Patris et Filii et Spiritu Sancti, Amen."*

Deirdre took out a square of dark linen and laid it on the table, then one by one she selected pieces and set them out on the cloth. "This brooch now, it belonged to my mother's grandmother. The large emerald set in gold filigree has a pin underneath. It was used as a clasp to hold a cloak together. There are earrings to match which will go to Dermot's bride, when..."

"If." Dermot looked up from the map. He was always aware of Deirdre, her words, her needs, and her actions, as though the two of them were connected by an unseen force.

"IF Dermot ever marries. And there's a ring to the set. I suppose we'll have to flip a coin for it." Deirdre saw the ring in the case and brought it out. "Dermot. The ring is in here. Your mother must've put it in?"

"Yes. I'm sure she wants you to have it. You're like her own daughter."

Jay was puzzled by all of this cousin closeness. "I grew up in New York as an only child and both of my parents were immigrants. My father, of course, was from Ireland and my mother from Poland. Neither of them had any family nearby, so I have no experience with all of this cousin stuff. Were your mother's close, when you two grew up?"

"Hah. I'll say close." Dermot turned to face them. "My Mam is Fiona. Deirdre's Mam was Fionnoula. They were twins. Close indeed, the way the left arm and right arm are together."

Deirdre laughed out loud remembering. "The wild Gilmartin girls they were called. Beware, people said; the Terrible Twins are coming; people would cry out. Then people laughing would say of them; 'more energy than a prize bull; more determination than the salmon swimming upstream, more beautiful than the Goddess Dana', and they were loved and known from one end of the Barony to the other. They would be at a Ceili dance all night and still the two of them would be up at dawn making breakfast for the men in the family."

Dermot smiled. "They loved life, surely. And they loved each other as well. And loved each other's children as their own. Deirdre and I grew up in that circle of magic the two sisters created. Sure there was no 'her house' or 'my house'. We were at home in either house."

Jay was enchanted by the stories his woman told about her large extended family. He watched her lay out a necklace and rings, a bracelet, more rings and some gypsy looking bangles. Each piece had a story and even the old oak and leather box had a history.

Deirdre held the open jewelry box. "One of our ancestor's found it on the sand centuries ago, after a ship from the Spanish Armada was destroyed nearby. The English chased the Spanish ships and then a storm caught them near the coast and drove several of the Spaniards onto the rocks where they sank. The local people rescued and hid the Spanish sailors from the English Army and many of them stayed on, married local girls and today we have the Dark Irish, many with olive skin and dark eyes. This small case once contained a fortune in Spanish jewels and gold coins, but one coin only and these few lovely pieces of jewelry are all that's left of the original treasure." She set the box down on the table.

Deirdre took a plain gold band and slipped it onto a finger on Jay's right hand. "The Spanish lady gives this band to her man at their wedding." When Jay protested, she put her finger against his lips to silence him. "Yes we are married Jay O'Neill. That day in Russia at the waterfall when I undressed in front of you and dove into that cold water and then we swam together, and dried each other, and made love under the sun and the sky. I married you there on that day, and you married me as well, didn't you?"

"Yes love, of course. I knew you were the one for me the first time I saw you sitting on that train before we ever met. But Deirdre, I feel so bad. My marriage to you is the most important day of my life and I have no ring for you. I'm not prepared and I'm sorry. But I do have a small treasure to give you." Jay reached under his shirt and lifted the red silk Incense Fire Pack off of his neck and laid it down upon the dark green linen among her jewelry. The bright red diamond shaped silk with the gold tassel and silver chain actually looked elegant and at home amid her jewels. "A sailor on the British frigate fixed it on a silver chain for me, on the way over here."

"Ah Jay. Your good luck charm from the Chinese woman." Deirdre picked it up and held it to her cheek. "It's warm from your body."

He took it from her hand and put it around her neck, lifting her dark wavy hair, and then settling the Incense Fire Pack inside her blouse. He let the red silk diamond fall gently against her breast. "Now my Deirdre, you will warm the *Shian Bao* and it will protect and guide you as it has me."

Inside himself he prayed, 'Wan Lee, this is my woman. You led me to her, now please transfer all of your protection and guidance to my love, my Deirdre.'

CHAPTER SEVEN

Declan and the doctor walked briskly back into the dining room. The woman would have followed but the doctor shooed her back outside. He told her to wait in the car. She went directly to Declan's big expensive motor car and sat down in it.

"And that was the way of it, so." Declan continued. "My employer, my 'Old One' as I thought of her, had a telegram delivered by my own hand, that I'd had from the hand of the bicycle messenger himself at nine o'clock in the morning. Her sister. That is the 'Old One's older sister had died in the wee hours of the morning, and she, the sister that is, up in Dublin itself and us down here on the estate in Cork County."

"Get on with it man. Finish your story. By my sacred oath, if words were coins, you'd be a wealthy young man, indeed."

"Aye, yes. We're right at the finish line, so to speak. Well, she, my 'Old One', that is takes to her bed at once and sure she got away from us before dinner time. I remember the tide was at its lowest at noon of that day." Declan shook his head at the wonder of it all. "She went out with the tide, like. Her and her sister both died on the same day but in two different houses in two separate counties. Now isn't that…"

"So here we are then." The doctor bullied his way into the conversation. "You are broke. You are unemployed. You haven't even a place to live, a place to lay your head, tonight."

"A fleeting situation only, mister."

"You should get rid of that monstrous big automobile."

"I'd never in a million years part with it."

"Your only worth lies in that automobile sitting on the ground, outside."

"The one your lady friend is sitting in? I wouldn't take a thousand guineas for it."

"Hah." The good doctor narrowed his eyes. A price had been mentioned and now he was fishing in familiar waters. He put his arm around Declan and led him to the table. They sat down in the same chairs as before. Both had a fine view of the car with the lady sitting in the open front passenger seat. "There's a war on, my penniless young friend, and you are sure to become a part of it, sooner or later."

"I'd rather later."

"I could see you driving one of the generals through the back lines, going from one command post to another. A chauffer never has to go into the trenches you know. He'll never go into battle." Declan cocked his head as though listening and the good doctor set the hook. "You would drive him to parties, too, you know. Generals are very big on parties. The best food, the finest wine and the girls, why the girls love men in uniform."

"You make it sound so grand."

"I'd give you a hundred pounds for it. In cash. Right now."

"Never in my lifetime." Declan jumped up out of his chair. "That is insulting, mister miser."

"Plus my car, of course. I thought that was understood, that we would make a trade plus a bit of cash thrown in for good luck".

"Too little cash and you haven't thrown it far enough IN to cause any kind of good luck for either of us." Declan, acting a bit mollified sat back down and stared at him eyeball to eyeball. "Your car for my car..."They both nodded. "And eight hundred pounds, thrown in like." Declan glanced up and noticed the woman was gone from his car. Had he overplayed it?

"Car for car and two hundred pounds." The good doctor blinked his eyes and licked his lips. He just couldn't help himself. Trying to rectify his momentary weakness, he blurted, "Think of the parades when this war is over. You will drive the victorious general at the head of the Grand Parade. Think of the medals on your chest. I can see stripes on your arm. You will have a pension for life. And the women will crowd you."

"Six hundred, is my final offer to you, sir."

"Three hundred." Shouted the doctor, smelling blood.

"Never in five hundred years," shouted Declan.

They both stood up face to face and the doctor brandished his sword filled cane while Declan jangled the keys to the big car in the doctor's face.

"Three hundred guineas, I meant to say." The good doctor smirked at Declan, feeling sure of himself.

"Five hundred and not a ha'penny less."

"Four hundred." The doctor smiled. He was winning.

"Guineas. Four hundred guineas." Declan dropped the keys onto the table and folded his arms across his young chest.

"Pounds. Four hundred...and ten pounds." The doctor added. He split the difference. "Or I'm out the door and I will drive away in that trusty car I arrived in."

"Done." Declan pushed the keys on the table in front of his adversary. He spit in his palm and held out his hand for the good doctor to shake.

The doctor dropped his keys on the table in front of Declan. He put a handkerchief in his palm and they shook hands. Next, he pulled out a wad of bills, counted out ninety pounds for himself and dropped the rest onto the table. "Four hundred and ten pounds, young man. You did quite well for yourself."

"You'll want to shift all your stuff into the big car and then I'm away." Declan announced. He gazed longingly out of the window at his former prized possession, but inside himself he was jumping for joy. He was elated with his success and eager to brag to all the Motleys.

"It has already been shifted young man. Our trunks and personal possessions are out of your new car and into our new one as we speak. My nurse has been busy while you and I discussed numbers. Good luck to you and it has been my pleasure." He rattled the shiny keys to his new expensive motorcar and gloated his way to the front door. The good doctor opened it, turned and held up the ninety pounds and shook them at Declan. "Another five minutes, sonny and you would have had these as well." He folded the bills and put them into his pocket, and then he swaggered out to his new car where his nurse gave him a warm, wet kiss before they drove off together.

"What did this cost us?" Asked the best surgical nurse in seven continents.

The cracker jack surgeon smiled at his nurse and replied. "Five hundred pounds, my dear, and worth every penny."

Declan went back to the kitchen and called, "Maura, Mary Rose. Can you bring us our dinner out to the garden." Mary Rose met him at the door and he pressed a ten pound note into her hand. "There's a dance over in Ballincollig next week, Mary Rose. Would you ever get yourself a new frock, so."

"You're a bold one, Declan O'Mahon. Are you asking me to the dance or telling me."

He gave her a big, warm, wet kiss, patted her bottom and said, "I'm telling you Mary Rose Ni Coveney." He closed the Inn door behind him and grinning wide, he made a little dance step into the garden to the applause of his comrades in arms. His fellow Motleys were busy working at the tables but they all stopped to hear the good news and cheer Declan, the hero,

"We have a new motorcar," he announced, and the keys sparkled in the sunlight as they tumbled through the air from his hand to Dermot's.

Without seeming to look up, Dermot caught the keys and allowed them to drop onto the map in front of him. "Details? My young genius, tell us all about your devious machinations."

"The greedy doctor paid us four hundred and ten quid, and I should've had five hundred, but near the end I got lazy and played it safe."

"Better be safe than sorry, as the bishop said to the virgin." Donal shook his head in admiration. "I could nary do that in donkeys years. Tis a real talent you have within you, Declan Roe O'Mahon."

"A grand job Declan, 'tis exactly what we needed," Deirdre congratulated him.

"He's well rehearsed in the music of bargaining, that good doctor is. It seems we both studied under the same maestro, the way we went at each other".

"How so?" Jay asked. He was in a mellow state and felt quite relaxed. They had a safe car to travel in, Deirdre and he would marry, and he'd get his father's remains back home.

"Well Jay O'Neill, and you may want to remember this for your own good fortune. When there's something you really must have, when you approach the seller to buy it, he'll ask you ten. What he really wants is eight, but he'd likely take six. Now you can really get it for four, but you must first offer him two. Do you see what I'm saying. Do you see how the numbers all fit together, like? 'Tis simple mathematics is all that it is."

Jay grinned at Declan, and then at Dermot and at Deirdre and keeping his eyes on her he said to MacGregor, "Mac, I keep learning things about Ireland and the Irish, even my father never told me."

Dermot held up his hands and slowed the merriment. "First, Declan, listen to me now; you will change back into your military costume. Jay and Mac pack away your military duds and travel in something comfortable. I want people to see three country gents and a priest accompanying this lovely lady. I'm her brother. Mac, you are her father, and Jay, handsome Jay, well you're the lucky lad will marry her." He stopped and looked around at his group and nodded in approval. "Hurry now. The Coveney sisters have laid on a sumptuous pre-nuptial feast for our delight. Let the festivities begin." They had come a long way in a short time and Dermot was pleased.

The table was laden with an abundance of food. Maura, Mary Rose and the cook, an older woman relative of the recently deceased Mrs. Coveney, had carried everything out in an endless procession of trips from the kitchen to the garden. At the center of the table was a large platter of potatoes boiled in their jackets. A great silver salmon on the one side and a big steak and kidney pie on the other flanked the potatoes. Smaller bowls of carrots, beet roots, turnips and greens added color and variety. Plates of home baked bread, tubs of butter, dishes of salt and other spices for the fish plus two fine pots of tea with sugar and cream were all placed within easy reach. Fresh cut flowers from the garden graced the table along with dishes of parsley, mint, chives and marjoram. It was a festive table for a joyous occasion.

"You Coveneys have done yourselves proud," Father Rory Beechinor said from his place at the head of the table. On either side of him were Jay and Deirdre. Next were to them were Donal and Dermot and finally Declan sat across from Mac. Rory offered the blessing and as the Motleys dug into the food Mac called for a toast.

Dermot stood and said, "Fellow Motleys, a tea toast is all we'll allow ourselves, lads and Deirdre. This is a working dinner and we've much to accomplish before we bid goodbye to this eventful day." With tea in hand, he offered a toast, "to my wonderful cousin Deirdre, my best friend and childhood companion, and to my newest friend, her betrothed, Jay O'Neill. I wish you many children to be raised in freedom and with peace,...in your lifetime."

Donal speared a large potato from the top of the pile, held it on his fork and with his knife, he peeled back some of the skin, made a small slit for the pat of butter he applied and next he sprinkled a good amount of salt on it. With a shearing motion of the knife and a quick bite he had nearly a third of the potato gone.

He quickly prepared another bite, rose and excused himself. "Dermot, with the thought of freedom and peace uppermost, I'll take a stroll along the outside perimeter. And Declan, don't eat all the *praties*, while I'm away from this table."

As Donal left the table, Mac cut the head from the salmon, wrapped it in a napkin and handed it to him. "I usually savor this part myself, Donal, but you also look like a man who would enjoy the head of this fine fish."

The meal progressed and Maura and Mary Rose kept busy refilling teapots, plates and bowls until everyone had their fill. There were jokes, and banter and some good natured ribbing at Jay for his eating with the fork in the wrong hand. "Damned Yank," someone said and they all picked it up. "The Yank told me...The Yank does it this way...The Yank..."

"Wait now," Jay protested. "At home in New York a Yank is anybody from Boston or Maine or somewhere in New England, and that's not me. New York and Maryland were my playgrounds, Long Island Sound and the Chesapeake Bay. I'm an American yes, but I'm not a Yank"

Declan burst out with, "hah. A Yank over here is any Irishman who left early on and went to America, made his fortune over there and now he's back, ready to buy himself a Province or maybe he just wants a County if there's a bit of modesty in him." His voice rose and he nearly shouted the rest. "In any case he can't wait to tell us locals how to do this, how to run that or how to fix the other thing." He laughed till his eyes squeezed shut and tears ran down his boyish cheeks. His emotions were so very high after his coup with the good doctors car.

Jay felt like he had to even up the score a bit. "Declan, tell me why," Jay asked, "all of you have names begin with a 'D'. My own love Deirdre, her cousin Dermot, yourself Declan and Donal too. Is it a family thing or has the D to do with the Irish Republican Brotherhood"?

Declan started in again, laughing as he shouted. "That's it Jay. 'Tis the answer, of course. We're the 'D' squad of the Cork Brigade of The Irish Republican Brotherhood, The IRB. Had you landed here a day or two sooner you'd have fallen in with the letter 'C' bunch. You know, Con and Connor, Conan and Cormac, Ceiran, and the like. Dermot darlin' who else is in that 'C' crowd. The ones we call the Celtic Crusaders." He was having a high old time, drunk on the glory that was his, after redeeming himself by bringing in the car they so desperately needed, and some extra cash, which might well be needed at some point.

Mary Rose was concerned and wanted to caution him, but after all it wasn't the drink moving him and then she thought of the dance next week and she decided to let him be.

Even with no drink except strong tea, the noise and excitement level rose way above dinner conversation. Mac, noticing her concern for Declan, spoke to Mary Rose about it. "He's excited about his car exploit and to be honest we're all relieved that the danger seems to have passed." Mary Rose nodded and excused herself and Mac went to the head of the table where he pulled up a chair between Jay and the priest Rory and sat down facing Deirdre.

Rory seemed puzzled and he said to Mac, "a bit ago, I stood up, arms outstretched, with my palms open and offered a blessing to this group. Everyone was engrossed entirely in their conversations. No one paid any attention. They neither heard nor saw my blessing. No one even knew I had given one. I sat back down stunned. Are you following me at all?"

Mac felt his humor rising but he stifled a funny retort, knowing that this priest was very serious. "You mean did the blessing work. Did it register with God. Do the people receiving it have to know they've been blessed for it to work?" The priest was on the edge of tears and Mac hurried on. "Is your role here any the less because no one saw you give us a blessing"?

Mac leaned in close. "Look Father Rory, the monks living behind the abbey walls, or the nuns locked away in a convent, they pray and sing and fast in God's name. Surely he hears their song and counts their prayers." He indicated Jay and Deirdre and then the others. "Love and friendship, breaking bread together, talking and laughing, telling jokes, surely these are all some sort of a blessing from God, Rory."

"As you see, Mac, I am somewhat conflicted. My heart as well as my teaching tells me this love is grand," Rory spread his hands to indicate Jay and Deirdre, "but it must be blessed by the church in holy matrimony. Are they to be married, then? And when? And more important where will they marry? And who will perform this marriage?"

"Let's ask them, Rory. They're not a bit shy." Mac leaned in, took Jay's hand and placed it over Deirdre's. "Rory here is concerned about your wedding. Specifically he wants to know when and where, and I guess, by whom will you two happy young lovers be married? Can you enlighten us at all? Will you share your joy with us now?"

Jay smiled and deferred to his love, "I think my lady should decide the where and by whom, but the when is mine and I vote for right now. Mac you will be my best man?"

Deirdre squeezed his hand, "I'd prefer a bit more time and preparation my love, but we can talk about it on the ride down. We should see to your father first Jay. Rory, you are coming with us, aren't you? Perhaps you will perform the ceremony for us. We'd like that, wouldn't we Jay?"

"We'd be honored Rory, to have you marry us." Jay held Deirdre's hand as he spoke.

Rory rose up to his full height and cleared his throat. He was clearly agitated now and unsure how to begin, so he just plunged in. "I have just spent a week on retreat at the seminary in Maynooth. There, I was singled out, berated and tutored by bishops from several counties around the country. It was a most unpleasant week. For me at least."

He kept his eyes cast down at the table, unable to meet the gaze of any of the group and especially Deirdre and Jay. "I am instructed to deliver this message everywhere I go. Spread the latest word, as it were, of my bishop Connor Westbrook, and all of your bishops". Rory paused to clear his throat and catch a deep breath.

He was on the edge of tears. "All members of The Irish Republican Brotherhood, active or inactive, are hereby denied the Sacraments, …denied all Blessings, …and denied even membership itself in the Holy Roman Catholic Church. By direct order of the Bishops of Ireland." He almost gagged on the words. "You are excommunicated."

There was a brief moment of stunned silence as each member of the group searched within to see how this edict would affect him or herself. Would this hold, this bombshell from the Bishops. Perhaps it was just temporary, because of the war against Germany and Austria. Was it political or religious? Did the Bishops have the right to do this to them? Was Rome consulted? Was there an appeal? And lastly, so what, was it really damning? And do I have a soul? Is freedom worth it? Do I carry on, or knuckle under to the church.

"The Bishops of Ireland have spoken. There is no appeal. There are no exceptions. This will be read out next Sunday from every pulpit in this country, from each and every Catholic Chapel and every Church of Ireland Anglican Church and may God help us all."

Maura emerged from the side door into the garden carrying a miniature wedding cake and Mary Rose came right behind her with a fiddle and she began a wonderful slow rendition of 'The Wedding March'. Maura sang and Mary Rose played and the girls came right up to the table where Maura set down the small three-tiered cake before she noticed anything was wrong. The fine familiar notes played out into the sun-filled afternoon air of the garden. They seemed very loud in the total silence around the table. 'Here comes the bride, All…' Maura's 's voice rang with sweet earnestness until she looked around at the stricken faces of the others. She stopped singing and hushed her sister and the music faded and died away.

Deirdre stood and poured her heart out in great cries of "NO. NO. It's not fair. It's my country. It's my church. They can't deny me. NO. And no again. I will not be done this way. Not by you or not by any black robes, nor purple garments, no not even a cardinal and he wearing the red hat. I WILL NOT".

The two Coveney sisters helped Deirdre, one on each side guiding her towards the door of the Inn, when suddenly she turned and pleaded, "Jay, I cannot marry you."

"JESUS…" Jay saw Rory and changed his outburst. "Jesus Mary and Joseph, Deirdre. Listen, damn it. I'll marry you Catholic. I'll marry you Protestant. I'll marry you as a Jew or a Turk. I don't care anymore. Let's just get married. NOW.

Rory, appalled at what he had done with his pronouncement, tried to be helpful, "France would be dicey with all the fighting going on, but you could go to Portugal or Spain."

"I will not." Deirdre pleaded and then shouted at Rory. "When I marry it will be in my country, in my church, and by a priest. And you, Father Rory Beechinor," she derided him, "You, you thought you'd have me begging, thought you could make me give up my beliefs, thought you could make me cry. But I never cry, Rory, never. Ask my cousin Dermot." And Deirdre began sobbing, great racking sobs that absorbed her entire body and her soul.

Deirdre gulped air in and let out long anguished cries of loss and frustration and fear. Feelings that had been bottled up inside her came out in anguished, choking sobs. The one love that she felt so secure in was now being denied her and by her own church in her own country. Between sobs she lashed out again at Rory. "*Ruairi, mo leir,* you Judas. I am betrayed, and by one of my own."

The Coveney sisters held her and steadied her as Rory backed away from them. Rory had no mechanism for dealing with this outburst of anger that came at him in waves. He, a celibate priest grew up in a house with only one female and when she, his mother, was angry with him, he usually ran. "The bishops encourage, nay they insist we give all of our loyalty to Britain in her hour of need," Rory offered by way of apology. "This terrible World Wide War has killed and maimed thousands and still today young Irishmen are enlisting to fight in the trenches. The bishops say we must be loyal to the English."

Mary Rose, the younger sister, hissed at Jay. "Jay O'Neill. Mr. Yank. You're wanted over here. This is the time for hugging and patting and shah shah shahing your own beloved woman. Come to her now, sir."

"It's time to be on our way," Dermot said. "The Motleys must move on out." He pointed to the far table and asked Mac to find Donal and load up all the bags, duffels, rifles and handguns. "Declan, you and Donal are riding in the machine again. I'll handle the car. Rory, you're up front with me. Just keep showing that Roman collar. Mac, you will have to keep the peace in the rear of the car as we go. Come on everyone, we must move out now, 'pronto' as the Yanks say it.

Jay and Deirdre stood close together and he caressed her hair, patted her back and made soothing sounds as Mary Rose had suggested. Deirdre stopped crying. She was breathing normally now and took the handkerchief from Jay's hand. She dabbed her eyes and blew her nose and gave his cheek a kiss as he hugged her and whispered to her.

Suddenly she stepped away from him as though bitten. "What did you say? John Joseph O'Neill what did you say to me?" Deirdre looked ready to take a swing at Jay.

"I said that I love you and want to marry you and we must marry NOW for my plan to work. I can keep you safe from Wee Willie Burke."

"And how does that plan work?" Her eyes were narrowed and her tone was flat.

"As soon as we marry, you will have rights as an almost American citizen. As the wife of an American Naval officer, you are beyond Burkes power..."

"No. I will not." She exploded in Jay's face. "I will never marry you just to thwart some Anglo-Irish twit, some half Irish bastard. That *Gombeen* man, that Devil Burke, he has the Cardinal and the Bishops doing his bidding while he follows orders out of London or Dublin Castle, or wherever. That's not who I am, Jay O'Neill. Nor will I ever be."

Jay stood silent. He was stunned and confused. He had merely offered her a path out of their dilemma. It was so simple, so logical. "Why in the name of God are you so upset with me and about my plan?"

Donal, loaded down with bags and guns knew, as an old huntsman, to always seek another approach when blocked from your quarry. He thought another direction might help so he offered some insight to Jay. "The Gombeen man Jay, is the one who collects the rents for the absentee landlords. 'Tis he who takes his orders from the Lords in England. Hence their name LAND LORD. He carries out the dirty work and mostly he even goes beyond simple rent collecting. Thinking to curry favor with the Lords of the Land themselves, he'll very often exceed his warrant with threats, evictions, even prison on trumped up charges, thus keeping the tenants in their place."

"The Gombeen men, the sheriff and the soldiers, all work together", Dermot added.

Deirdre turned and pushing Maura ahead with Mary Rose following, the three women went into the Inn. Immediately, Mary Rose came stumbling backwards out of the door, with Deirdre pushing her out of the way. Mary Rose almost fell flat but managed to land sitting in one of the garden chairs. Deirdre was no longer sobbing. She was beside herself with anger and frustration.

"You may as well know now, Jay O'Neill, who I am. I am not a woman to marry for safety sake. I will not take a man just to be secure. I will not hide behind a uniform nor a piece of paper. Not American. Not British. Not even some trumped up Irish concoction that owes allegiance to some ninny sitting on the English throne. That's not me. Not at all."

She paused for breath and the silence was large. Maura was transfixed where she stood behind Deirdre. Mary Rose, sprawled in the chair, sat with her mouth open in astonishment and stared up at Deirdre.

"I am a woman. I am not a chattel, nor a chair nor stick of furniture," here she kicked out at a leg of the chair under Mary Rose. "I am no slave. No indentured person. I am no Raparee, no transported convict and this is not Van Deimans land." She was stentorian now with her arm raised and finger pointing, "here in my own homeland I may own nothing at all, not one single thing. I cannot vote. I have no voice in my own destiny. I cannot even control my own body. The only freedom allowed me, is that which I take with a gun. So much for justice. So much for those old men in wigs and robes. A curse on they who allow this, this travesty to go on." She pointed at Mary Rose. "Fill me some wine and bring it to me."

The younger girl jumped as though shot out of her chair. She curtsied and ran for the wine bottle. Never had she heard a woman speak this way to a man, let alone to a group of men. 'Deirdre was amazing. She was almost blasphemous. She was wonderful', thought Mary Rose Ni Coveney. She went and filled a wine glass and brought it and the bottle to Deirdre.

The men themselves were silent and respectful of Deirdre's thoughts and feelings. They were also marveling at how a person, any person, especially a woman, could move from abject despair and uncontrolled sobbing to angry leaps of logic with rapier like cutting effect. So, they stood and listened as Deirdre made her points.

"Jay would have me in America. Will I be free, once there, my love. May I own property in my own name in America." Here she pointed to her small wood and leather jewel case. "Or may I keep only baubles and trinkets like some Tinker woman. Will I have a voice in our government in New York, Jay? Will I have a vote? I read in the news that American women are marching now for a voice, a vote, a say in how their lives will play out. And the police and the soldiers in America round them up and put them into prison. Jay, you are my life. I love you more than life. But tell me why would I go from here to there."

Deirdre raised her glass in a salute and drank. "Why would I go anywhere if the outcome is to be the same? I am. . .A Woman from Clare." She paused. "I am. . . A Woman Of Ireland."

"And you Rory. When you or any priest or bishop or indeed a cardinal say mass, you need young boys on the altar to serve with you. *Et introibo adaltari dei.* "She chanted at Rory the opening line of the Latin Mass. "I go to the altar of God. And the response from these boys is. *Ad deum qui laetificat juventutem meum.* To God, the joy of my youth. Where will you get these boys, Rory? You plant no seed. You raise no young. Where in the name of your Holy Roman Catholic God will you get them? When Irish mothers see their sons dead from fighting for a strange king, when Irish women hold their legless sons, maimed in battle, fighting for unjust laws, they will not have another child. There will be no more boys marching to the altar of God. There will no longer be any joy of their youth."

"And you Dermot, when our freedom is finally won, you will want

124

young men for your army, won't you. But from where will they come? NO MORE, will you take the limbs from a child of mine". She drank the rest of her wine and turned to Declan. "Will you be my chief bargainer, now, Declan? I want no money. Not even pay for all the cooking and sweeping and, …and everything else a woman does for a man. When I and my sisters have our rights. When all women in Ireland, and America too, can cast a vote and hold an office; when we may own our own land and pay no ground rent to a man across the sea. Then I will spit in my palm and offer to shake hands with some politician, some man."

She spoke directly to Jay, "then will I open my legs and accept your seed. Then will I produce a child for you, Jay O'Neill." Deirdre paused and then low and fierce she said, "But not until then."

Deirdre's legs became wobbly and she dropped down into the chair Mary Rose had occupied. She closed her eyes and when she opened them again everyone was silent and in the same places as before. No one had moved.

Except Mary Rose, who knelt in front Deirdre. She refilled her wine glass and whispered very low. "How did you do that, Deirdre? You are brilliant, my sister. Where did all those thoughts come from? I nearly peed myself listening to you speak; I was that excited. I must go now and write it all down. I won't forget it, Deirdre, not a single word that you uttered. You were grand, and I love you for that." She jumped up and ran inside.

Donal busied himself lugging everything out to the car and the motorcycle. Mac would have helped him load up but he stood transfixed as though rooted in place in this walled garden. He thought of Regina his dead wife, and Maria his daughter and how they would have relished Deirdre's words. He wished with all his heart that these three women could have known each other.

Dermot and Declan gathered at the map and assured each other they knew exactly the route they would follow, what evasive action they'd take if necessary and they marked off two safe places to meet should they be discovered or separated.

Jay stood next to Deirdre who still sat in the chair, and for the first time since they met, he was unsure of his course. He saw her shiver so he took off his jacket, and gently he leaned her forward enough to get his jacket around her. She settled into it gratefully and held it close around her. In a minute her shivering stopped and her hand came up seeking his. He squatted down, took her hand between his two hands and she leaned against him. "I am always open to you, my Jay. My heart, my entire body and my immortal soul are yours. Treat me well." Deirdre kissed his hands and he felt her tears spill onto him. He pulled her up and they stood together, their arms around each other. All of his doubts washed away.

"Deirdre, we will marry if I have to tie you up and force you to be my wife." He felt her relax in his arms "I will get you out of here safe and married to me. My solemn promise to you." She leaned into him, her body against his. "When we get to New York I will encourage you to march for Women's Suffrage. I will even buy you a pair of special marching shoes, with shiny silver buckles on them."

Deirdre seemed to shake and he heard her chuckle. "I'll march alongside you and we'll bring our children too. If the cops come, we'll all go to jail together." She broke out into a full-throated laugh and stopped just long enough to give Jay a long passionate kiss. She pushed her body hard against his.

Dermot folded his map and stowed it in his leather case. Declan went out to his motorcycle and Mac gathered the last of the gear to bring out to Donal to be stowed in the boot of the new car, the good doctor's car. He set down the gear and watched Jay and Deirdre pressed together in a passionate embrace. Mac shook his head and announced to himself, "like his Da. He'd talk the trunk off of an Indian Elephant. They're well matched, that pair." He went out to the yard and helped Donal and Declan prepare their machine and the sidecar.

Jay and Deirdre walked to the wooden door and stepped out into the yard, leaving Dermot alone in the garden.

Maura seized her chance and came straight from the Inn to Dermot in the garden and into his arms. He was delighted and asked her softly. "May I kiss you, Maura Ni Coveney?"

"If you do not, Dermot O'Rourke, there will be another fight in this garden this very day." They kissed and he caressed her and she almost caressed him in return. Maura leaned back within the circle of his arms, "Will you come back to me, Dermot O'Rourke?"

"Will you be here to welcome me, Maura Ni Coveney?"

"I will, Dermot O'Rourke. Indeed I will." She watched him go through the garden door and heard him shout to the group.

"We're away, lads and lassie. The O'Motleys or The MacMotleys or whoever we are, we've miles to go before this day is done. It is time for us to be away."

Dermot drove and Rory sat next to him and made sure that his white roman collar could be seen. In the rear seat Jay and Deirdre and Mac made do with a bit less room than they had in the other bigger auto. Mac had stowed a rifle and two pistols under their feet in the back and Dermot had the new pistol and lanyard within easy reach.

Declan on the machine had a revolver concealed under his jacket and Donal had the other rifle shoved out of sight in the sidecar. Dermot gave a beep on the hooter and they began to roll. Suddenly Mary Rose came running out of the wood garden door and cried, "Stop you. Wait. Will you wait, so." She ran to Declan who stepped off his machine and waited for her.

She rushed into his arms and gave him a long, wet, warm kiss and in his surprise and excitement Declan almost forgot to kiss her back. "Declan, there's a dance next week in Ballincollig and you will take me to it."

"I will?" He was still surprised and embarrassed to be kissing Mary Rose in front of his cousin and his friends.

"You will, Declan O'Mahon, you will indeed." Mary Rose Ni Coveney kissed him again and reached behind to pat him on the bottom. "And don't be late, Declan. Do you hear me now?"

Declan jumped on his machine and roared out of the driveway with his white silk scarf flying bravely behind him. Dermot drove away fast trying to catch up. Rory rode up in the front seat and Jay and Mac together with Deirdre rode in the rear seat. They waved out the windows at the two Coveney sisters who stood in the yard with arms linked.

Maura waved them away and called out after them, "Good Luck to you Motleys, God Bless."

"And come back to us," Mary Rose shouted and waved after them.

CHAPTER EIGHT

They drove on in silence for a few miles, but silence was not easily maintained in an enclosed tight space populated by a group of Celtic people. Especially when the group of five included three Irish, an American, one Scot, a woman and a very talkative priest.

"I don't think we have…" "Would you want to…" "In the Name of the Father…" "It's a long way to Tipperary,…" "I truly am sorry, Jay and…" It almost became a contest to fill the silence and they all spoke at the same time. Finally, Dermot as leader, imposed some order on the group. "You first, Deirdre, since you are the…"

"Don't say it, Dermot. For God's sake cousin, we all know I'm the only woman here. All right. I am here. I am a woman. Done and done. Now, I am sorry Jay and Dermot and Mac and Father Rory if I offended you back there." Deirdre leaned forward and spoke in a low voice. With each word she tapped on the seat back in front of her for emphasis. "I have no idea where it all came from, but that was me." She turned and spoke directly to Jay. "All of that was me. And you must take me as I am."

"Cousin, my cousin." Dermot grinned and drove as he talked. "I've known you and loved you all of my life and I will not stop now nor will I ever stop. I 've wiped your nose. I have bandaged your bloody skinned knees and I've held your hand and consoled you at dances when a boy you liked took someone else out onto the dance floor. I have enjoyed watching you grow into your own skin. We're kin my lovely cousin and nothing will change that."

Mac smiled at her, "and quite a beautiful skin indeed. If Jay does not marry you, I stand ready to assume that burden myself."

Jay jumped in at once. "Ah Mac, your generosity is exceeded only by your great Scottish good looks. But have no fear, I'll marry this woman if I have to take on the whole damned British Army and it's no burden to me. None at all."

Deirdre faced Jay. "I haven't scared you away from me?"

"Never. I love you and am delighted by the fierceness of your thinking and your ability to speak it. Many of the things you said, I agree with." Jay held up his hands in defense. "Some few things, I will need time to think about."

She took his hand and squeezed hard. "What things, Jay?"

Jay raised her hand and kissed her fingers. He spoke with quiet gentleness. "Don't push me, woman. Give me time. I need to think and form my own thoughts, but I promise you this, Deirdre mine. Our marriage will be a union of equals." He grinned. "I just hope to God I can keep up with you."

Father Rory Beechinor turned to Jay and Deirdre, "that was a lovely walled garden at the Inn wasn't it? What? What are you all laughing about".

Mac reached forward and gave Rory a clap on his shoulder so that he joined in the laughter though he still didn't get the joke. When the merriment slowed down to a ripple, Rory became serious and said to all, "I hope to God this Motley bunch survives and me with you. Survive as a priest, I mean to say. The Bishop was veiled in his threat to me but he made it abundantly clear that my job as a parish priest was on the line. I am…on…on…"

"Probation", Jay offered.

"That's it," Rory answered. "If it becomes common knowledge that I left the company of that good doctor and his nurse to ride in with you…"

"With the likes of us O'Motleys, you mean," Dermot said over his shoulder, more to the group than to Rory. "Has the good Bishop in his infinite wisdom, given you a specific threat, Rory?"

"There is an Abbey in the far cold North of Scotland. It's all stone, the walls are bare and cold and it sits on a point of rocky land jutting out into the wild North Atlantic. It's close to but even more remote than the Orkney Islands. Provisions are meager and communication is almost non-existent. There is a round tower, a sort of watchtower, where the monks used to pray and keep a lookout for the sails of the Viking Raiders. It is high, and cold, and lonely." Rory paused and looked down at his black shoes. "I'd rather not go there." He turned and faced Deirdre. "If I have anything more to do with any I.R.B. members, well the Bishop says my place in that round tower is waiting for me. There will be no appeal and no coming back. It is a lifetime assignment. It's either a cold lonely cell in that stone tower, or I must leave the priesthood." Rory groaned and whispered, "and that is the one thing that I can not do."

"I know the place," Mac said. "Or at least, I know of it. That Abbey is so far removed from everything, it is still a Catholic Abbey. King Henry the eighth left it stand and the Anglicans never wanted it. Henry is supposed to have said, 'let Rome keep it. It's punishment enough just being there.'"

"Rory, I'd better drop you off soon. You can't risk being with us, man." Dermot was very moved by the priest's predicament.

"I'll stay with you. I can be helpful and I know quite a bit about West Cork. I have been a student of local history and lore for the two years I have been here. That is my wish, so let us drop the matter now." Rory opened his prayer book and began to say his office.

They rode in silence for a bit, then Dermot handed the map to those in the back of the car. "Take a look at our map. You'll see just where we are headed. Turn it upside down so Cork City is at the bottom and the ocean up top."

Gregor MacGregor smiled as he turned the map. "Damn it Dermot, I have read maps, from the white Arctic to the darkest Africa. Be easy now and just tell us our final destination and how we will get there."

"Ah yes, Mac. I keep forgetting. You have more experience than I do, bags of it. Now look you at the top of the page, the ocean side of the map. There's a place looks like the back of your open hand." Dermot held up his right hand, thumb extended and showed them the back of it. On your left, the thumb if you will, is The Old Head of Kinsale"

"Where my Da went down with the Lusitania." Jay said it quietly but it had an impact on them all. Deirdre reached for Jay's hand and squeezed it. "God, it's just one day ago," he whispered. She held his hand between hers and kept squeezing and caressing it.

"Aye, Jay. Sorry. Now, where the ends of my fingers are is called the Seven Heads. I know, I have only four fingers and there's seven heads. It's a wee bit like the way Declan uses numbers, all right. So, the Old Head on one side and Seven Heads on the other. In between is Courtmacsherry Bay and the town itself is where we'll find your Da."

"The Royal Irish Life Saving Service rowed out into the wild Atlantic and were the first rescuers to the Lusitania survivors," Rory offered. He closed his prayer book and went on. "They, The Courtmacsherry rowers are one of the oldest Life Saving Services in these Isles. They are truly gallant men. Their leader is a man named Keohane; he is their coxwain."

"I'm told they brought in your Da along with the living, thinking he could be saved." She snuggled her arm inside Jay's arm and held his hand again in both of hers. Softly she consoled him. "I'm so sorry he didn't make it, my love."

"Jay, if you would like, I can handle the details, the paper work and such," Mac offered.

Jay in a low voice said, "let's get Deirdre and all of us safely to him, and then we can work on the details. All right, Dermot, we know where we are and where we're going. Now what about the stretch in between, are there any dicey places, any precautions we should take."

"Aye, there is. We will avoid the main route and travel alongside it, so. We'll avoid all the towns as well, especially Bandon. It's a walled town and an Orange Order stronghold. I have no desire to be inside a walled city when we are wanted the way we are.

So, if we keep Ballinhassig off to our left hand, and avoid the Owenboy River, then come on through Upton and we get to Inishannon the back way. There we should safely cross the Bandon River and then we're in West Cork, safe and sound, with the help of the good doctor's car."

Rory closed his prayer book again. "Almost safe, Dermot, almost. We still must cross the Argideen River and go through my home parish at Timoleague. I have seen a constable on that bridge over the Argideen. Grand fishing there as well, MacGregor."

Rory turned to face Mac. "You get down on the mud flat and watch for a small bubble or a hole in the sand, then quickly dig in and catch a tiny, spiny little crab and tie him on your hook, then as the tide comes back in, you cast upstream. I caught a grand big...."

"RORY," Deirdre shouted. "For God's sake, Rory, keep the fishing tales for tonight around the fire, when our business is done." She seemed calm but Deirdre was still tightly wound.

"Sorry, Deirdre and Jay, both of you. I am so very agitated and I tend to talk on and on about small things. It is another failing of mine, and Bishop Connor Westbrook said he would part me from it, the next time we meet."

Dermot jumped in, "It's all right Rory. We all have our small failures, don't we cousin." He looked at Deirdre in the rear view mirror. "Now, to get on with my travelogue. We keep Ballinadee to our left, skirt Kilbrittain and come out to the coast road at Harbour View.

Once along the coast road we are in the way of being at risk. So. Daring Declan and dangerous Donal are our scouts, as they have been the whole way, or almost the whole way." Here he looked in his rear mirror again. "With one small absence or interlude, you might say." Dermot smiled into the mirror.

"Those two on the motorcycle are in the way of being our own 'canary in the coal mine', so to speak. As long as Declan is wearing that white piece of silk around his neck, we're on our way to Tipperary. Any questions? Mac will you keep that glass of yours handy, so."

Just before the coast, Dermot eased the motorcar to the side of the road and stopped. Mac went over the gray stonewall and scrambled up the long green grasses to the hilltop. He shouted down. "The white scarf is streaming out behind him. It's a long way to Tipperary."

They followed the coast road, keeping the motorcycle in easy sight until Declan rounded the Burren Rock where it jutted out into Courtmacsherry Bay. Dermot adjusted his speed downward and eased around the bend. Even with the naked eye, they all could see that bit of white silk, streaming out behind Declan.

Rory murmured, "We're still headed to Tipperary." They had told him the story of the roadblock with the machine gun and each explained it to him in their own way.

Mac called it, "rolling past the fixed gun positions".

Deirdre's eyes had been closed so she never had a clear view of the gun, but her imagination built it into something fiercer than just shiny oiled metal.

Donal claimed he was so ill, he never knew the gun was there.

Dermot declared it was simply British bravado. "They never in this world would've fired upon us."

Jay likened it to sailing past the enemy's guns under a cloak of darkness, "in broad daylight, no less."

However they told it, whatever he believed, Rory loved the story and sang out, 'Tipperary', each time he saw the bit of white cloth up ahead. In later years, his version would include a miracle and he'd declare, "Someday, I will erect a roadside shrine upon that spot on the main road from Cork to Cobh. Perhaps we'd call it the Place of the Motley Miracle."

Dermot backed uphill into a driveway at a derelict house, shut the engine off and they all got out to stretch their limbs. They could see the entire length and breadth of the Bay; the coast road curving away on the right, and on into the town of Timoleague; thence they could follow the road across the bridge and around Courtmacsherry Bay to their destination.

Almost directly across the Bay from them was the small shipbuilding, seafaring and smuggling town of Courtmacsherry, Cork County, Ireland. A commercial yawl was tied up at the quay and they could make out the tiny figures of men offloading crates and boxes.

Jay was first to exclaim over the vista before them. "My God Deirdre, it's beautiful. Look at the sweep of this view."

"This is Harbour View, Jay. It is well named, isn't it."

"Yes. Come with me." Jay borrowed the brass spyglass from Mac, and taking Deirdre's hand, they crossed the road and climbed out on a jumble of large rocks. The rocks were placed there to hold the land fast against the constant surging of the wind driven waves.

The Bay was at full tide and the afternoon sun made the waves sparkle and dance as though showing off, knowing their time was short for the tide would soon turn, and all of the salt sea water would drain away leaving only a narrow channel winding through a large mud flat. Here and there would be a few puddles, maybe one with a fish flapping and gasping and a crowd of hard beaked birds digging for cockles in the muddy tidal flats.

Jay aimed the glass down the road till he picked up a flash of white. He adjusted the focus and saw Declan and Donal seeming very relaxed as they rode along. They looked like a young man taking an older man, perhaps his father, for a Sunday drive along the scenic coast road. "Here Deirdre, have a look."

"Ah, Jay. It's grand. I can see Donal has his pipe in his mouth," and she laughed. "I can almost smell that terrible old tobacco he burns in it. This is grand Jay. I can just make out the bridge over the Argideen River and beyond it the remains of the old Abbey."

Rory and Mac joined them on the rocks. They each had a hand fishing line with a sinker on the end and several hooks were attached to the line, spaced about a foot apart. A feather covered each hook.

"Scotch feathers, they are called. They dull the fish's natural caution and allow him to take the hook," Rory declared. He loved to tell stories.

"Great deceivers they are, those feathers. At home in Scotland, Rory, we call them Irish feathers." Mac grinned as he teased the gentle priest.

Rory shook his head and laughed as he tied the free end of the line to his left wrist and began twirling the weighted end with his other hand. Round and round it went and then he let it go. The sinker and hooks sailed out a good ways and dropped into the blue water. "Perfect." He laughed again. "Irish feathers, indeed. Now Mac, wet your line and mayhap we'll have fresh fish for our tea."

Rory watched Mac and when his line was out in the water, the priest said, "ah, good man Mac, you have done this before." Mac nodded and Rory went on. "Some will whistle for a fish to come on their line; others sing or hum a tune to attract the fish. I myself like to talk to them. I don't usually pray for a fish. Me having been ordained and all, it seems a bit unfair. What? What are you all laughing at?"

Jay had the glass again and followed the coast road around the bay to the small town of Courtmacsherry and beyond it to the point. Past the point was the large open expanse of Courtmacsherry Bay and beyond that he could just make out The Old Head of Kinsale. "That's where the Lusitania went down, off the Old Head, just out there in the open ocean."

Deirdre stood close in back of Jay and wrapped her arms around him, as though she could lessen the pain of his loss by absorbing some of it into herself. "Soon my Jay. We'll have him with us in a short time, only." He lowered the glass and allowed her warmth and love to flow into him. His Deirdre was very giving, in spite of what she said back in the garden.

"Out there, beyond the Old Head, it's a straight shot to New York. I can almost see the Statue of Liberty and she's smiling, waiting for us." Jay turned his head and kissed her.

Deirdre tightened her arms around Jay and whispered to his back. "Find a way. Find us a way we can marry, Jay, because I want to be with you always."

"JESUS, Mary and Joseph," Rory crossed himself. He was nearly dancing on the rocks. "I've got a fish, maybe two, or one big one." He began hauling in his line, hand over hand, while Mac gave his line to Deirdre and went down to the edge of the water to help land Rory's catch.

"Easy now, Rory. I can see 'em, or two, no by God you've got three fish on there, Rory boyo. Three mackerel. Here, I've got 'em." Mac hauled in the fish and when they were safely on the land he called to Jay. "How's Declan? Keep a sharp eye on him, now. If we cannot cross that bridge, we've got a detour of several hours through the back country, nearly to Clonakilty and around to get us just there." Mac pointed directly across to Courtmacsherry village. "Hell, Jay me boyo, if we had a boat, I could row us there in ten minutes."

Deirdre said, "Jay, help me. There's something on here. It's trying to pull me off the rocks into the sea."

Jay slipped his arm around Deirdre's waist to steady her and tried to keep the spyglass on the motorcycle with his other hand. "Mac, Declan is over the bridge, but he has no white scarf now. He's moving along on the other side. Now he's stopped and I see flashes. Must be a pocket mirror. He's signaling us. I have it; H..O..L..D. He repeats it, and a third time, HOLD. HOLD. HOLD."

Dermot walked down and crossed the road to them. "Did you see it?" When they nodded, he laughed. "Jay, will you ever give me the glass and help my cousin before the mackerel have her for their tea." Deirdre was leaning back and holding fast to the line, and Jay had half a hold on her waist, but her feet were slipping on the rocks almost into the water.

Now Jay wrapped both of his arms around her and together they pulled in four large fish. "Dermot we'll have to invite the Coveney sisters to come have tea with us," Jay announced from a sitting position on the rocks. The two lovers were laughing and gasping together while sitting on a large flat rock. The four caught fish were flapping, gasping, and fighting on the same flat rock to get free of their hooks and bounce back into the sea.

Rory was already casting out again in the same spot and he was busy chatting away to the fish, to himself, to no one in particular. Dermot held up his hand and everyone but Rory fell silent. There, up on the road was an old man watching them, standing next to his bicycle.

"Grand day," Dermot greeted him while he walked back up to the road towards the man.

The old man nodded his head, looked at the sky and offered the opinion that they would have some rain later in the evening or perhaps towards the morning. After looking around, the man motioned to his own back, then to Dermot's back and asked, "Will you hook more of them mackerel, or are you planning to shoot them, so?"

Dermot's hand went to his back and felt the revolver there, tucked into his belt. "Damn," he muttered, and started walking up to the man. "I suppose I should be wearing a jacket or a gansey," he said in an easy manner.

"Aye, the heat is gone from the sun, this time of the day."

When Dermot reached the old man, they exchanged more pleasantries and then Dermot declared that he, his wife, the priest and two friends were on a country outing, fishing and enjoying the sea air. He pointed to his car parked in the lane and the old derelict house behind it. "Have you any knowledge of that place? Would it be for let or for sale?"

"Neither," The old man warmed up to telling a story. "Four or five acres only and all of it poor land. If you could sell stones, there's a fortune to be made there. A family struggled on it for years and paid the ground rent to a man across the water in Leeds. The wife left him in despair and then when the father died the two sons left, as well."

"America, is it?"

"Nay, not a'tall. The two sons never got along. A strong dislike flourished between the two of them. Canada, the one. Australia, the other. As much space between them as God and the Ocean will permit. The Leeds man, now, says he wants no more tenants on that land. Plans to build a grand big guest house type of a thing, soon as this war is over."

Dermot cocked his head in an unspoken question. "Oh, aye the war. There's good and there's bad in it, don't you know. I sell milk and I make some cheese and begod if the prices I get aren't higher now and looking to go up from here." He smiled at Dermot and nodded his head. "And my cows eating the same grass as they always ate. I and my wife and children milk them gratefully two times every day."

"No sons in the war?" Dermot probed his man.

"Thank the good Lord no. Two daughters only. I'd not like a son of mine to take the King's shilling and go and fight on foreign soil." He spat into the roadside. "Mister, I was looking forward to Home Rule for Ireland. We were promised free elections and our own parliament, like the one we had before Napoleon scared the English so hard. Then came this war and now they say, wait till it's finished and we'll give you Home Rule. Well maybe. And maybe my cows would milk themselves if I let them. Mister revolver man, some day I would enjoy an outing up to Dublin. I'd love to sit and listen to our own learned men in our own parliament debate our issues of that day. Well, grand day to you, sir. I'm away, so".

He mounted his bicycle and Dermot held the handlebars and mentioned the names of a few people he knew in the Barony. The old man turned a bit pale and said he knew one of them and had heard of the others. "Hold on now." Dermot said in a mild tone. "I think my wife wants you to take home one of our fish and have your wife fix it for your tea."

Deirdre came up to the two men with the largest of her catch. She carried it with two fingers slipped into the gills and offered it up to the old man. He muttered a thank you, and a God Bless, put the fish into his basket and he pedaled away with never a glance backwards.

"Your wife indeed, Dermot O'Rourke. If wishes were fishes we'd all live in the sea."

"Hah, Deirdre Ni DalCas. Who needs you in any case. I can have one of the Coveney girls any day. Nay, maybe I'll have both of them, so."

"Dermot, you will not. God will get you for that thought." She gave him a dig in the ribs. "Besides, Declan will have something to say about Mary Rose Ni Coveney." They bantered their way up to the car where Dermot grabbed a burlap sack for the fish and a satchel with food and drink in it. They had been teasing each other this way ever since Deirdre learned how to talk. They kept at it, back again to the group, who were still fishing on the rocks.

"Jay, Mac, Rory, there are flasks of tea, some biscuits and pieces of my forgotten wedding cake in here. The Coveney sisters were very good to us. Come everyone, tea and cake."

Rory was busy talking, showing off a bit of his local fishing expertise. "Do you see, Mac where the sea birds are swooping after wee small bait fish jumping up out of the water. Cast right into that spot. Just there, the big fish underneath are causing the little ones to jump."

Mac twirled and cast his line and Rory gave his approval. Jay offered a bit of his expertise, "It's the law of nature. The big fish eat the little fish and man survives by using his knowledge and eating both of them."

Dermot offered a mocking assessment. "The small fry have one grand big hellish choice Rory, don't they. Stay in the water and be eaten by the big fish, or jump up and be taken by the birds. Much like the choice the English give to the Irish, or the Africans, or the Indians and the Egyptians and Moslems. God almighty, I am sick to death of The British Empire and all the money grubbers who run it."

"Easy Dermot. What happened with that old man to set you off," Mac kept his voice casual.

"I had to threaten him to assure his silence. Nothing real bad, I just mentioned a few of the lads by name. He said he knew one and had heard tales of the others." He nodded to Deirdre, "the fish helped a bit, maybe, and thank you cousin. But I hate myself when I have to lean on someone, especially that old man. He and his kind are the very reason I carry a gun. It's why I resist the police, the army, and our so-called government. I should protect, not threaten him. Mac, will you take the glass and keep watch by the car? Maybe if I fish the while I can get out of myself." Dermot took Mac's line and walked to the rocks.

Jay cried out all excited. "Wait, it's Declan. He's gone back over the bridge into the town. He's stopped; he's turned around and now he's crossing back over the Argideen and this time I see the white silk around his beautiful, young neck." He whooped and grinned and whirled Deirdre in a tight circle and gave the glass to Mac.

"Pack up everyone." Dermot was the leader and felt like himself again. "Rory, here's a sack for the fish. Reel in your hand lines and we're away. The Motleys are on the move again."

Rory held up the burlap and read the printing. "Murphy's Spuds. Dear God, no one in Ireland eats Murphy's potatoes. They ship all the Murphy harvest over to England."

When he had his laugh from the group he took the sack to the water and washed it out, then carefully packed the catch. They had eleven fish now. "Counting the one you gave away to that poor man, we had a dozen fish, Deirdre. Enough for The Last Supper, eh?"

When they were packed and loaded, they resumed their seats and Dermot drove at a moderate speed towards the town of Timoleague and the bridge over the Argideen River, and the last leg of this part of their journey. Soon, they would be on the other side of the bay and headed into the small town of Courtmacsherry, and finally they'd recover the body of Sean O'Neill. One half of Jay's quest would soon be fulfilled. Then it was on to a wedding.

"They tell a grand story here in Timoleague," Rory implored Dermot for a detour around to the old Abbey. When Dermot shook his head no, Rory carried on with his tale. "As we cross over this bridge, look now to the right. That roofless ruin once was a flourishing Abbey, a local spiritual center. Well Cromwell came with his savage army, spreading death and destruction from one end of Ireland to the other. He destroyed us from the Giants Causeway up North, down to Mizen Head here in the South.

He sailed right up to the bridge here, and destroyed the town and the Abbey. All the monks were killed or scattered. The local parish priest was so angry, so incensed, he prayed night and day for a miracle from God. 'Never again will an army sail into this town.' Well now, within a few years the Argideen and this end of the bay silted up so bad that no ships could ever again sail in here with an army. The parish priest had his miracle, but sad to tell, the Abbey remains roofless to this day."

"Jay. Jay my love, my heart, wake up. We're here at the mortuary. You slept the last few miles. We're here now. Can you go inside? Are you ready, or do you want to rest the while? Mac, can you help me?" Deirdre was beside herself with worry and grief for her love.

"Jay. My son." They were here to identify and accept the body of Sean O'Neill, and Gregor MacGregor made a formal acknowledgement that he would now stand as Jay's father. "Shall I go in and make the identification, or do you prefer to go?.... Alone?"

"Together. The three of us. I want my family with me," Jay said and embraced them both.

The entrance to the basement morgue looked like a dark tunnel. Upstairs, the mortuary itself could be seen in the twilight. Inside it was dimly lit, against the coming of evening, but down here, in the basement mortuary, all was dark.

Inside the cold dark room, Dermot put a match to a candle and created a circle of light to guide them in to him. "Come, and listen to me, now. Declan took father Rory back to Timoleague. He must report in to his pastor this night or by early tomorrow, for sure. He'll be back with his kit to give your father his last blessings so, and offer prayers for the dead."

Deirdre's mind was churning at a hundred miles an hour. "Sean O'Neill is not nor ever was he a member of the Brotherhood. Rory can say a Requiem Mass for him, so."

"Indeed, cousin, yes he can, and if you were to be completely safe, I'd recommend it. Hellfire woman, I'll serve as his Altar Boy. But only if I know you are safe and alright."

Jay took Deirdre's hand in his. "You're right Dermot. Deirdre, we can have a mass said for my father later, when you are well and truly out of danger. I know his soul is fine. Now, I want a last look at my father, at his body. Will you come with me?"

Donal stepped out of the darkness of the room and with a nod he walked past them carrying his rifle. "I'm beyond now, outside there in the coming darkness. Listen for the owl. One Whoo is safety. Three fast Whoos, get out of it, so."

Dermot held his candle high and cast a flickering circle of poor light as he marched into the morgue. Jay stayed close behind him while Deirdre, holding Mac's arm, put her other hand on Jay's shoulder. The cold hit them and crept into their skin like sharp knives. It was a large room and at a quick glance Jay estimated there were forty or so coffins. The hair on his neck was standing straight up; goose bumps made his skin crawl and he seemed even colder.

Deirdre's hand slid up and warmed the back of his neck and Jay almost cried with relief. The thought of his warm loving woman and his cold dead father made him shiver and he feared losing his Deirdre as well. It must not happen, he vowed.

There was an aisle between the coffins and at the far end Jay could see a raised platform. On the platform was an open coffin with candelabras on each side holding seven candles each. The level of brightness was better but the total effect was eerie.

As Jay mounted the platform in silence, Deirdre came to his side, took his arm, and leaned into him for support. She was feeling this as deeply as he was. Mac came up on his other side and together they took the three steps across the platform to the open coffin.

He tried to be stoic but a groan escaped him and Jay sagged down onto the kneeler. He placed his hand over the cold icy fingers of his father and then he became somewhat calm as he studied the peaceful face of Sean O'Neill. This was the man who had caused his birth, had loved him beyond reason, protected him and taught him and made him who he was. He crossed himself and said prayers for this good man who had died at sea. It was ironic, thought Jay. Here am I, the sailor, holding a wake for my dead father, drowned at sea.

He stood up and Deirdre knelt and said her prayers. Someday, through Jay, she would carry this man's seed and create a new generation of

O'Neills. Waves of emotions washed through her. Deirdre was saddened and curious and elated by turns. Then the cold returned and she stood and embraced her man for his strength and warmth, and she gave the same back to him. Together they stood on the platform by the coffin and held and warmed each other.

Gregor MacGregor knelt at the side of Sean O'Neill who had been his friend since both were young men. He crossed himself in honor of Sean's religious beliefs, and then prayed in his own mostly Protestant fashion. Silently he wept until his entire body shook with grief and the two lovers behind him each put a hand on one of his shoulders.

Jay was filled with sadness for his father, apprehension for his woman and a clear sense of joy for the future. He wanted to have children with his Deirdre and give to her and the children what he had gotten from both his father and his mother. Life must go on.

MacGregor reacted very differently. He wanted answers. He wanted someone to take responsibility. He wanted revenge. He knew this could not, would not and maybe should not happen, but he wanted revenge with every drop of his Scottish blood. An old Celtic custom rooted in the Eye For An Eye tradition; he knew it led only to blindness for all.

He stood up to his full height and bellowed out in a rage. His voice echoed in this cold vault of a room. "Sean. Who did this to you? Was this some bloody stupid English foul up. Did that ship have munitions on board. Was she running war goods on a civilian passenger liner, against all Maritime law, against all Rules of Engagement, against common decency. No warnings prior to sailing, no contraband listed in the cargo manifest, no choices were given to innocent travelers, therefore I say someone in charge has broken faith with the human race. Someone must pay for this butchery.

Or was it some vicious German submarine captain and crew, seeking glory in the watery graves of hundreds of victims. Two explosions Sean. One torpedo? Or two? Concealed weapons and munitions? Tell us will you. For the love of The Christ who died for us, tell us. We are your family. We are the ones you love. We are the ones loving you, Sean O'Neill."

"Mac", Deirdre sat on the edge of the platform looking back at

MacGregor. She was cold and she was afraid. "Please Mac." Jay stood on the floor in front of Deirdre looking up at MacGregor. He was struck dumb by this outburst, and had no idea what to say or do.

"I am on a commission to find answers," Mac went on. "The truth is what is required here, Sean. I will ask questions. I will demand answers and by God, I'll get them, because I will keep on asking, until I do get them". Mac's big Scottish voice and its' many echoes were still audible and bouncing off the walls and the ceiling and swirling around the forty black coffins when suddenly the door to the tunnel crashed open.

Dermot came surging up the aisle between the coffins and stopped halfway to the three on the platform. "Declan is back. He has news. Urgent news."

"Bring him up here to the light," Jay said in a stage whisper. "Tell Donal to be extra sharp."

"I have, Jay O'Neill, I have." Dermot and then Declan came running up the aisle. Rory the priest was just behind them, slowed down by trying to bless every coffin as he passed it. His right hand was a blur of action as he kept making the sign of the cross at each coffin, on both sides of the aisle. Finally Dermot and Declan picked him up bodily, one on each side, and they carried him and stood the priest, who was still making blessings, up onto the platform.

"Now Rory, will you bless Sean first, like a good priest. Then give a general blessing to all in our silent congregation." Declan made a wide swing with his arm. He encompassed the entire cold, dark cavernous room, and he included both the living and the dead.

Mac came back from a foraging trip under the stairs that went up to the main floor. "Dermot, just back there is an old door and more chairs." He erected two coffin stands and set up several chairs. When Dermot came back they laid the door on the stands and now had a working table. Jay grabbed two chairs and he and Deirdre sat up on the platform next to Sean's coffin. They looked down at the men seated around the makeshift table.

Rory finished his blessings. He had given one to Sean with special prayers for family. He then used the aisle as a divider, and gave blessings to each side of the room. When he was satisfied that at least the minimum had been done, he sat down at the table. "I have never seen anything quite so cold, quite so gory and yet so…"

"Father Rory Beechinor. Time is short. Stay only on our subject, please." Dermot gestured toward the coffins. "More lives could be at stake. Please begin, Rory. Declan took you to your parish house. And…."

Rory took a deep breath and it all came out in a rush. "There was a big automobile out front. It was official looking. I had Declan take us around back. I went in first and cook shushed me but I was already being quiet. She motioned me over and we listened at a crack of the door. Slightly ajar it was." Dermot made a hurry up motion. "Cook whispered to me, 'I'm to prepare a tea for all of them strangers. A big one. A fancy tea, mind you; and himself with nothing in the house for me to cook and no extra money given to me a' tall. Not a farthing'.

Declan comes in about then. He hears all this, of course, and cook is looking him up and down. He is much younger than her, but cook likes him, I think. She likes his white scarf especially, and doesn't he invite her to touch the silk. Over her head he grins at me, and to her he says, 'have you a sharp knife or a cloth cutter?' She produces a cutter from a cupboard and he flings the silk scarf onto the table, long ways do you see. Right as rain he cuts that white silk in half, long ways, then he takes one half and gently wraps it around her large neck. Well, glory be to God, the look on cook's face. If she wasn't working in a Catholic priests house, she would've had Declan on the floor, and me fast running away."

Dermot was making circles with his hand again, trying to speed up Rory's story. Declan sat there with a big smile on his face and his hands in his pockets. Jay asked in a gentle voice, "Rory, do you know who they are and what brings them here?"

Rory nodded. "Declan is a rare marvel, indeed. He holds up a ten pound note and asks her if she'd mind getting provisions. Go out you, and buy great gobs of food, he says. Enough to feed that crowd inside and another meal entirely for seven or eight, which he will take away with him. He stopped her protests with a smile and a squeeze. I will hire a serving girl for the evening, oh, and he says to cook, get plenty of wine. There is another ten quid for yourself when I take that meal out of here. Cook snatches the ten pound note and is out the door in a flash, then pokes her head back in and she winks at Declan, a great big pagan sort of a wink. Do you know what I mean?" Rory asked, looking around at them all.

"For God's sake, Rory, who are they. Get to the point, man." Jay spat it out, clearly agitated, but Mac sat serene and comfortable. He was thinking three jumps ahead of all of them.

"Declan and I, we crept like a pair of church mice." Jay and Dermot leaned in towards him. "All right, all right. We listened at the door. It's none other than some sort of commission to study the sinking of the Lusitania". Rory stood up then, clearly agitated, and made the sign of the cross once again, over Sean and the other coffins. He sat down and waited.

A collective sigh rose up from the rest of the Motley group. And then the questions came flying at Rory. "Did you get any names?" "How many in the group"? "Why are they in West Cork?" "Why at your pastor's house?" "When did they get here? And how long will they stay?" It was becoming loud and their voices and shouts were creating echoes.

Dermot stood and held his hands up to shush them, then made a two handed half-circle motion and pointed with both hands to Mac as though passing the ball to him.

"Let me start with the easy ones, first. Declan that extra food is for us here?"

Declan nodded and added, "here or wherever you will be when I bring it."

Mac went on. "The serving girl you will hire to serve these guests in the Pastor's house. This is Deirdre is it not?"

Declan nodded and looked at Deirdre. "Have you the apron still, from Coveney's Inn?"

Her eyes sparkled. "I do, but tell me Declan, just who is it will I be serving?"

Rory jumped in, "One was a foreigner with a bad leg. He kept changing seats, seeking his comfort, and I could hear his cane against the finely polished wood floors of…"

"Did he speak with a German accent"? Mac asked, cutting Rory off.

"Easy Rory. Let me pick up the pace," Declan was in his glory on this evening. "He claimed to be Swiss, but yes, the accent may have been

German. The other foreigner seemed French. I caught the name as Ronnie, or Rene. Then there was another Yank, Jay. But he sounded younger, maybe?" Declan grinned at Jay the Yank, and Jay returned a smile.

"I see some possibilities here," Mac looked at the two lovers sitting, leaning against Sean's black wood coffin. "There are problems, of course. And opportunities as well. Go on Declan, or Rory. Finish if you please, but make it quick."

"I could tell the Pastor's voice. It had that ring of authority; comes from years of preaching and telling people what's best for them. Oh and one other man who spoke as if he should be listened to. His voice was English, but there was a soft layer underneath all the bluster. He may be Anglo-Irish, but I couldn't tell from his voice if he's Church of Ireland, Church of England or a Catholic. Whichever it is, he and the pastor got on famously."

Mac leaned back tilting his chair onto the back legs and looked at the ceiling. "Wee Willie Burke. Here in West Cork. This is interesting."

The Motleys erupted, very loud and all at once. "Devil Burke is here?" "Burke?" "Wee Willie?" Deirdre hitched her chair closer to Jay and he put his arm tight around her.

There came a clattering noise from the back stairs. Dermot jumped up to greet the man coming down. He was the owner, an astute business man, a mortician and a smuggler. He was a large man and a sometime comrade in arms with Dermot. "God almighty, Dermot. They can hear you across the bay, so. And look you, this is supposed to be a cold room. All your warm bodies and candles will make it too hot for these poor devils." He waved at the coffins. "I happened to overhear some of your talking. Now Dermot, I will not have that pastor, or some of those men nor any other authority, come into my private room. Be they clergy, coppers or commission members, this is private, like. Mostly the way this room is used is to store goods and things. Untaxed things. Maybe I have one or two dead in here at any one time. But that's between you and me and the Cunard Line insurance chappies."

Jay stepped up and Dermot made the introductions. "Flor Sweeney, meet Jay O'Neill, the son of your client, there. And this is Gregor MacGregor. He's a half brother to the deceased, Sean O'Neill."

Mac assumed the lead. "We'll be out of your way in two shakes, Flor. Jay and I want to thank you for a grand job on our Sean." He kept edging Flor Sweeney over to the stairs. "I will join you up there immediately to sign the death papers and perhaps we may do a spot of business as well." Flor smiled at everyone. He shook Mac's proffered hand and allowed himself to be guided to the stairs and up he went. The Motleys breathed a sigh of relief.

Jay took one of his small diamonds out of an inside pocket and handed it to Mac. "We need a hearse or a truck or something. Rent it or buy it if you have to. Also Mac. Buy another, better casket, something nicer than this." Jay grinned, but he had tears in his eyes. "Buy something my Da would have complained about. You know how he is…or how he was."

Mac imitated Sean. "Jesus and Mary, young JayJay, you're mad, to spend good money on a fancy box and then bury it in the ground." He accepted the diamond from Jay and then he wiped his eyes. The group all smiled at this understandable quirk of the dead Sean O'Neill.

Declan called to Deirdre. "Come now. Get your green apron with the gold harp upon it and we're off. We've a meal to serve and all the enemies plans to learn and steal while we serve them. Mac, be sure now to use my style of arithmetic when you bargain." He pointed upstairs and grinned. Declan wished he could stay and bargain for them.

"The fish," Deirdre almost shouted. "Declan, we have a grand big bag full of fresh caught Mackerel. It's in the boot of the motorcar. We'll take it with us and serve it to them."

Dermot claimed the lead again. "Away you go Mac." He pointed upstairs. "Bargain hard but bring us a vehicle which will hold…. what? Two coffins. Declan, take the car now, instead of the motorcycle. Take Jay and Deirdre with you, so." Jay nodded a yes. "We'll have Flor Sweeney move Sean into the better casket, then Donal, Mac and myself will clean up here and load the new vehicle with the two coffins. Am I clear to you all?"

The Motleys nodded, one after the other and Dermot went on. "We'll meet you, Jay, behind the wall at the old Abbey. And Deirdre, as soon as you've served the meal and cleaned up after, come to us there. It will be dark. We will devour whatever food you bring to us. You can tell us their plan while we eat and whatever it may be, we will thwart them completely. Then this Motley bunch is away. We can drive the main roads in the dark of the night, and we'll be in Dublin before the sun greets us tomorrow."

Mac nodded yes, and Jay agreed. "Sounds like a good plan and Dublin it is."

There was a loud wail from Rory and Dermot stopped giving orders. "Great God Almighty, Rory my good man. I'd have left you here in this cold room giving away blessings. You're so quiet I forgot to include you. Are you all right, Rory man?"

Rory stood to his full height and extended his two arms the way Moses might have quieted the Israelites. "You can not leave here, I mean this West Cork area. You cannot leave here tonight. You must listen to me." Rory the priest gave a stern look to each of them.

'Good God, thought Deirdre, is this another thunderbolt from the bishops.' "Rory, what are you going on about? Why cannot we leave this West Cork area?"

"I found some papers in my room," Rory declared. "I knew there was an answer for you my dear Deirdre. And for you, my friendly Yank, Jay. It was nibbling away there in the rear of my mind. I knew there was a way to keep your faith intact, Deirdre, and at the same time make a leap around and get behind the good Bishops. We can circumvent them, entirely." Rory briskly rubbed his two hands together, from the cold and from his excitement.

"How. Tell us how, Rory." Jay was the loudest, but Declan and Dermot and Deirdre were all asking the same question. "Hard facts only, if you please, father Rory. Quickly now."

Rory, still standing, extended his arms out again and the Motleys all groaned in dismay. "There is a place where they used to have Mass all the time. It hasn't been used in donkeys years, but it is still usable. My research shows it still is a sanctified place, a church."

"The old Abbey?" asked Deirdre.

"That's too open, too exposed entirely," Dermot claimed. We'd attract attention the way flies are drawn to..., well anyway we'd soon draw a crowd, then the constables would come, and the soldiers soon after and then we'd be in for it."

"Hold. Hold on, now. Not the Abbey, though I would dearly love to say a Mass in that old Abbey. No. This is out in the country. Next to an active farm field, there is a large wooded area. In the woods is a sort of shallow glen and down at the head of this glen is a huge flat stone. Almost as high as a man, twice as long and flat on top, it is a big big rock."

"An old Mass Rock?" Dermot was skeptical. "A real one? I've heard of them, of course Rory Beechinor, though I've never seen one."

"What is it?" Asked Declan.

Rory sat down and assumed his favorite role, that of the storyteller. "During the last century when the English Parliament imposed upon us their Penal Laws, it was a terrible time to be an Irishman, or woman." He made sure to include Deirdre. "None of us could speak our own language; it was forbidden to learn it. There was no schooling. None could read, nor write. A few made it to Irish schools in France or Spain and a few brave souls came back and taught here. Living as outlaws they were known as Hedgemasters, always moving about, teaching and looking over the shoulder."

Dermot was making his Hurry Up motions again, but Rory continued in his groove. "Hearing Mass or harboring a priest were capital offenses. Anyone caught would lose their lands, their title and even their life. In spite of that, word would go out; there is a priest in the Barony. People would come to the hidden place of the Mass Rock and there would be a Mass, confessions heard, or sometimes just a group absolution. The priest would baptize any children born since the last visit; he'd marry those ready for it; he would bless the sick and the dying and visit the graves of those who went away from us. Lastly he would take any promising youngster and see they got to one of the schools overseas."

Deirdre, her eyes shining, sat on the edge of the platform at Rory's feet. "Rory. Are you certain beyond any doubt this Mass Rock is still an active site. Is it within the permission of the Church to have a Mass? To have a wedding?" Her two hands were holding each other under her chin. "Have you asked your Pastor?"

Jay reached down and wrapped his hand around her two hands clasped at her chin.

"Indeed not. Listen to me now, I would not involve him, Deirdre. He is a good man, a good priest, but he is a bishop-in-waiting, if you take my meaning. I came across this Mass Rock while studying antiquities. The owner of this field and the wooded patch with the small glen and the Mass Rock in it, well he and I; we have become quite friendly. He too is an amateur historian and archeologist, and a very fierce Irish patriot.

I keep trying to convert him, but unfortunately he is also fiercely Protestant. However we do seem to enjoy prodding each other over religion, history and the like. He has shown me all the deeds, the papers, everything having to do with the history of the rock. The Church sanctified it as a dedicated church site well over a hundred years ago and they have never removed their approval, never 'cranked it down' as my friend has it."

"Rory," Dermot went carefully so as not to hurt his cousin. "Aren't the most of these very old places, these Mass Rocks, aren't they pagan sites. Places of Druids and pagan worship?"

"Aye. Indeed they are and this one is too."

"I don't care, Rory." Deirdre was on her feet and ready to fight. "Jay, forgive me. I've come over to your thinking, now. Sorry, love, that I took so long. Rory, if that Mass Rock is fine for a Mass, it is certainly good for my wedding. Jay marry me. Tomorrow at the Mass Rock. I don't care if it is Pagan or Christian, or Jew or Turk. Marry me, Jay." Deirdre pleaded.

Deirdre stood next to Jay, holding his hand. She looked at Rory and bowed her head. "Marry us, Father Rory. Please. Tomorrow, out in the woods." She made her plea again.

CHAPTER NINE

"Marry us, Father Rory, please. Tomorrow, out in the woods."

"I am sorry, Deirdre. I can not."

"But, Rory, no one need know."

"I will know. And soon others will know. Country people will talk, especially Irish country people. And then I would be gone. I am sorry, my dear. I cannot marry you."

"I want a chance, Rory. I must have my chance." She turned, first to one, then to another, with an impassioned cry. "Jay, please. Dermot, help me. Declan, can you do something."

"I have found you a church, Deirdre. Do not ask me to be your priest, for I cannot. I will not leave my calling to the priesthood and I cannot go to the remote north of Scotland. I could not live at the top of a stone tower and hear the wind and see the snow and ice coming at me from far off Norway and Finland.

My God woman, in the short time you have known me, you must have observed one thing about me. I am a talker, a compulsive talker. Even before the priesthood, I was a storyteller, a Shanachie. I must have listeners. I need an audience. It is the one thing that I must have. It would kill me, Deirdre, to be alone."

"And, Father Rory Beechinor, this unmarried state I am in, could well be the death of me. Soon enough we will all be like these." She indicated the black coffins lined up in neat rows in front of them in the cold dark morgue room.

Mac had come downstairs and quietly rejoined them. "Neither of you two need die over our situation. I have the answer for you both. Rory, much as Scotland would welcome a great Irish talker like yourself, your place is here, helping your fellow patriots. And Deirdre, beautiful Deirdre Ni DalCas, betrothed to my son, Jay, I have a priest for you."

Deirdre sat back down on the edge of the platform. "First a church and now a priest. Is he willing and able to marry us, despite the harsh pronouncements of all the Bishops in this poor sorry Ireland of ours?"

"Declan said there is a Frenchman in that group of committee members at the pastors house. You know him, Jay, and you've met him. He is Rene Jean Batiste de la Salle. Our Rene. He is a friend of mine and more important to you my dear; he is a priest. As a Frenchman and a Jesuit he is not bound by the politics of the Bishops in Ireland.

What's more, Rory, like your Mass Rock itself, Rene too is a bit out of date. Though he is not currently an active priest, he has never been, ah, decommissioned, as it were. He has all the rights and privileges, all the faculties of the priesthood and yes my Deirdre, he can unite you and Jay in the sacrament of Holy Matrimony."

Deirdre sprang at Mac and gave him three kisses and a fierce hug, getting her tears all over his face. "Thank you Mac. You will always be a part of my family, our family."

Jay followed and hugged Mac and then hugged Deirdre and then hugged both of them together. "This is the best news I've had since Yuri Yurivich got us into the same compartment on that wonderful train. AND we'll marry right under the fat pompous nose of Wee Willie Burke, that half-Irish two faced bastard. He's well named, that Devil Burke."

Dermot jumped upon the platform and raised his two arms high. "Enough. Enough, now." He clapped his hands for action. "Declan drive the car. Take Jay and Deirdre and Rory back and serve that meal. Listen, learn, and get to know our enemy.

Jay, you must not be seen, not even by the cook. Deirdre you must get a message to the French Priest. Mac will you compose a few words now, and see that Deirdre has it. Clear out of there at the earliest and bring us back a meal. Come back here to this place. Outside."

He gestured to the door, down at the end of the long aisle of black coffins. "Donal will be out there waiting, and he will know where we have gone and taken the body of Sean O'Neill." He smiled and grabbed his cousin in a bear hug and gave her a big kiss. "I do wish our Fiona could be here. And now Mac, at what time tomorrow is the wedding to be?"

"Shortly after sunrise." Mac turned and looked from Jay to Deirdre who nodded, Yes, Yes, YES. "Perhaps Rory, you would say a Requiem Mass for Sean at the Mass Rock after the wedding? As sort of a cover, if we need one." Rory began to speak, then just nodded yes.

"All right Motleys, it's time to move out. NOW, GO. Please." Dermot first ordered and then implored them and they filed between the rows of silent black coffins and went on outside.

Flor Sweeney was almost giddy with the success of his many business ventures and now this one came to him right out of the deep blue. It was way over the top. He dropped the keys into Dermot's hand. "Here's your new transportation, me lad. Listen to me now, that black paint is new and the engine and such are grand, all tuned up and begod she'll go seven times around the world for you. You'll never find better transport anywhere, I swear to God.

At various times she's been an ambulance, a hearse and even a sort of a bus for the outings of some nuns from the convent over in Clonakilty. And Dermot, I did like the Scot, that MacGregor. Says he is a 'Child of the Mist', outlawed by the English, his MacGregor family was. He's nearly an Irishman, that Scot, I swear to God Almighty."

Dermot cocked his head. "He's a good man in a fight, too, Flor. Keeps his head about him."

"Indeed. And he bargains like an Irishman. Very good he is, and he has more heart than some I've known. I want you to know the deal we made, he and I. Listen now, Dermot, lad. Keep it more than a week and it's yours, free and clear, bought and paid for. Bring it back before the week is out and you have a bit of money coming back to you, a nice tidy sum, altogether." He and Dermot stood face to face, eye to eye, testing each other.

"Florence Sweeney, you must know that this is a two way street that you and I travel. The I.R.B. has a long memory, Flor." Sweeney turned to walk away. "Someday you must make a choice. You are in or you are out. What is soon coming at us is not a sometime thing."

Sweeney came back and tried to use his height to intimidate Dermot. "Listen to me now, Dermot O'Rourke. You haven't been in this Rebellion business more than a few years. And the I.R.B. isn't so very long in the tooth a'tall. I and my father and his father before him have been smuggling goods along this coast for…. for a good long while, now."

When he saw Dermot was not impressed he stepped back a pace. "Ach Dermot, there will be several hundred pounds you may put to good use for The Brotherhood. I have taken a small sum only for this service here tonight. And the night's stay up at the big place is included, barring anything broken or taken." Flor stopped and again he peered through the dark into Dermot's face. He tried to get a read on Dermot, but saw only a stern commitment.

"The coffin is loaded in, alongside the new expensive casket with the brass handles, and Mr. O'Neill's name plate which I placed on the lid myself." He went on talking faster and louder.

"The two coffins now, are held fast to the floor and will not shift on you. There's room for the driver and a helper up front and a bench seat behind, between you and the coffins, so. The bench will hold three people, easy. I sometimes have family who wish to ride with us. My son will ride with you now to show you the way, like. As for Donal, now he is welcome to come and wait inside." Dermot shook his head, no. "Ah well then, I'll send him out some tea in a short while, like. The papers are all in the pocket at your right hand and you driving. Thank you Dermot and good luck, so."

Flor spit in his palm. Dermot spit in his and they smacked hands together and shook. The business side of it was accomplished. Flor Sweeney, like many small businessmen in Ireland, tolerated the Irish Republican Brotherhood. They made deals; they even made contributions of goods and money. Whether or not Flor would ever take the oath and formally join the secret society was not known at this time. He went his own way.

At the Parish house, Rory led Jay up the back staircase to his room. They tiptoed quietly so Jay's presence would not be discovered. Once the door was closed Rory began to show Jay his collection of books on Irish history and antiquities. Each book, of course, had it's own history with a story attached. Rory explained, "now Jay, the way this rare book came into my possession was strange, indeed. It happened at a fair up in Macroom." When Jay never answered him, Rory looked and saw the exhausted Yank sailor was fast asleep on Rory's bed.

Below stairs in the kitchen of the pastor's house, Declan introduced the two women and backed out of the way. They regarded each other with caution and cook began a long list of projects in minute detail when Deirdre stopped her. "I have a good bit of experience at serving and I will earn my pay this evening, cook."

Deirdre stepped over to the older woman and put a hand on her shoulder. "Oh, I love your white silk scarf and the way you've tied it. Isn't that the way the French chef's tie them? Can you teach me that knot, when we have time?" Cook seemed pleased that her helper was experienced and even knew the look and the knot of a French chef.

Deirdre put on her green apron and cook admired the harp embroidered on it. "How many for dinner, then? And cook, shall I set the table now?"

Declan jumped for the wine, "I'll go freshen their glasses and collect any empties. We're feeding six, isn't it, cook."

While cook was in the pantry, Deirdre and Declan took a moment to look each other over. They gave each other silent approval and Deirdre whispered, "I'm going to give the performance of my lifetime, Declan."

"Begod Deirdre I'd marry you meself, if I wasn't so busy." Declan dodged her poke in the ribs and went in to announce dinner. As the men filed into the dining room from the lounge he seated them by rank. The pastor, Reverend William Conklin sat at the head of his own table. To his right was his old school chum the Honorable William Burke.

Next to Wee Willie was the young American officer and on the pastor's left sat an honored guest from Switzerland, *herr Frederick Fritz Kunkel.* Beyond Fritz a place had been left for father Rory Beechinor and at the other end of the table sat Rene Jean Batiste de la Salle, a retired diplomat and Jesuit priest.

Rene, once seated, continued his discourse from the other room, "*Ah oui*, father William; were I still active I would much prefer the life of a country priest." He indicated father William and now included Rory who had entered late. Rory seated himself quickly, made a small nod of apology to his boss and tucked his napkin under his chin.

Declan had already learned the name, rank and importance of everyone here. He made the introductions while the pastor merely nodded and ignored Rory for the rest of the dinner. William Burke and William Conklin had been away at school together where they became close friends and they were still reminiscing. The pastor was almost sentimental. "Those were fine days, weren't they, Wee Willie. I think it all started that first time our parents came to visit. The entire class heard Mr. Burke called by his nickname Wee Willie, and I was called Big Billy. Of course the names stuck and of course, boys being boys, together we would thrash anyone who called us that. We have never lost touch, have we Willie."

Big Billy, the host, tinkled his little glass bell and Deirdre entered with a large tureen of leek and potato soup. He waved her away, and in a righteous tone of voice, said, "no, no girl, serve my guests first, I am but a simple country priest." Big Billy smiled.

Deirdre stepped over to the side of Wee Willie and holding the Tureen, offered him the ladle. Willie scooped up some soup for himself, replaced the ladle and as Deirdre turned he stopped her. "Marvelous needlework, my dear." He reached up and caught the edge of her green apron between his thumb and two fingers.

Pretending to admire the golden harp stitched into the apron, he moved the backs of his two fingers against her breast and slid them back and forth, under the apron, caressing and pressing her breast. "Did you make this yourself?"

At first she was thunderstruck, thinking, 'this pig Burke is feeling my breast in front of these three priests.' Then Deirdre was embarrassed and felt herself going red in the face. She stood there holding the tureen of soup as he continued to brush and press her breast with two of his fingers. "The apron was a gift, sir," she answered meekly and then Deirdre became angry and understood why her Jay called this man a pompous bastard.

Wee Willie brushed his two fingers back and forth, up and down and babbled on about the fine art of hand stitching. Big Billy could not see this blatant act of aggression against his hired woman. Deirdre's body was turned and blocked his view.

"Wee Willie," he chided his friend. "You haven't changed one bit." Then to the other dinner guests he said, "don't you know he was always chasing after local art and hand made items. He would be touching one thing and handling another." Pastor Big Billy sounded annoyed as he looked down the table at his curate. "Father Rory, are you ill?"

Rene was spared this seedy little episode. He could only see part of Deirdre. Deirdre, her anger rising, smiled sweetly and was just about to dump the hot soup into Wee Willie's lap when Rory saved the day.

He saw the sneak, Wee Willie Burke, feeling her breast, but at first could not believe it. Then he acted, "Miss will you serve me my soup at once. I am famished." Rory withstood the withering stare from his boss, Big Billy, and was rewarded with a silent 'thank you' from Deirdre. She moved away from Wee Willie and continued to serve the dinner as though unaffected. She did, however stay out of Wee Willie's reach.

Declan was clearing glasses and wine bottles from the next room. He saw the episode and admired the way she handled it. Later in the kitchen he caught her eye, gave her a thumbs up and blew her a kiss. She came to him immediately and whispered, "Not a word of this to my Jay. He's liable to shoot that grubby grabby Anglo-Irish bastard."

Declan kissed his fingertips and touched her cheek. "My lips are sealed, love. I passed the note to that Father Rene and he did leave the room once, so we can assume he has read it. But let us hurry and get to hell away from this house. Big Billy and Wee Willie, indeed, they are a right couple of bastards."

Deirdre overheard Willie and Billy gabbing on and on when Rene and Fritz, after thanking their host, said they would stop in the kitchen and thank the serving staff. She motioned to Declan and he managed to entice cook out to the scullery and out of the way. Declan wanted to give Deirdre some time alone with Rene, and Cook wanted some time alone with Declan in hopes of a hug or a squeeze or maybe even a pagan kiss or two.

Rene and Fritz let the kitchen door close behind them. Fritz clicked his heels and bowed to her. Rene took one of Deirdre's hands and kissed it. "*Mam'selle*, Deirdre, such a lovely name. I, that is we, 'ave so much of you from your Jay and we are enchanted to meet you at last. You 'ave been in our thoughts and prayers since first Jay mentioned you to us."

"I have heard so much about both of you and from the same source." She kissed each of them on the cheek and impulsively she took Fritz's monocle from his hand, raised it to her mouth and blew her warm breath on it. With her apron, she polished it clean and returned it to him. "Thank you for finding my note and getting it to Jay. I was so afraid I had lost him." Fritz made another bow and the dueling scars on his forehead seemed to turn bright red.

"And father Rene, you will marry us tomorrow?"

Her eyes were wet and she would have kissed his hand except that now he held her by the shoulders and whispered to her. "Just Rene, *oui?* Tomorrow, when I perform your wedding, you may call me Father Rene." He wagged his finger at her. "At all other times, I remain just plain old Rene, yes?"

Fritz shook her hand and patted it as a goodbye. "Villie and Billy stay here. Rene and I go to the next house for sleeping. You and Jay will come for us at dawn, yes."

"At first light, yes. And again, thank you both from my heart."

Declan stuck his head in and pointed up the back stairs. "While we're slaving away here, your man is having a nap for himself up in Rory's room. Back bedroom." His curly reddish brown head disappeared back into the scullery.

Upstairs, she opened the door and tiptoed in. Jay was sprawled on a diagonal across the narrow bed. To Deirdre he looked like a young boy who had run wild all day and now slept a sleep of innocent exhaustion. He still had a boyish face, except around the line of his jaw. The darkening stubble added to his determined look.

She sat for awhile studying him and then asked herself one last time. 'Is he the one'? Softly she answered her own question. "Yes, yes, oh yes. John J. O'Neill, you have my heart forever. Tomorrow, you will have the rest of me. Forever."

Declan followed close behind Donal and the motorcycle. They turned away from the bay and traveled a short way on a winding soft road. Jay, sitting in the front seat next to Declan saw a high brick wall in front of them. It receded left and right into the dark night and seemed to go on forever. Two large trees flanked the arched entranceway. There was a big iron gate ahead and the young lad jumped out of the sidecar and swung it open it for them.

They drove in and the high brick walls hemmed them in on both sides. Jay turned to Deirdre. She sat in the back surrounded by large covered pots, baking pans, baskets of bread, and butter and flasks of hot tea and bottles of wine and porter.

"Looks like quite a place."

Declan answered him, "Built like a fortress, it is. This setback entrance and gate are for safety. They'll have a small gatekeepers flat built into the wall on one side of the gate, and blacksmith or machine shops and such on the other side. The main house is ahead there across the courtyard. There are many of these Anglo-Irish great houses scattered about the countryside. A great big square of brickwork contains it all inside of the walls, the gentry, the help, the stables and gardens too. Famine built I'd say, wasn't it Deirdre?"

"Aye. During the hungry times labor was so cheap. Workers were paid in food only and they'd take home a few bites to keep the wife and little ones alive."

Donal stuck his head in the car. "Indeed. My own father laid some of these bricks as a young lad. It kept him alive and growing." He nodded and grinned. "And years later these bricks allowed me to be born into this cruel old world. This was a grand place in its day. Me Da took me here once, and he with a few days work in it. Closed now, the owners are back in England. Some say it will be a hotel for tourists, come the end of this war. And providing, of course, we don't have our own little war right here in West Cork."

Alone in her room above the kitchen, Deirdre wished she had another woman with her. The men were grand and Donal treated her the way he'd treat his own daughter. He got her grip and bag up to her and served a private meal for two in her room. Then he helped her shoo a sleepy Jay into the room next door. Donal had to talk and sooth and cajole Jay into it.

"Women are always right about these things, Jay. 'Twould bring bad luck and you seeing her just before the wedding, so. There's only just the thickness of a wall between you and herself. Not enough to lose any sleep over. God Bless and goodnight now."

She hung her white wedding dress and unpacked the few fine things she owned in addition to the jewels in her oak and leather case. The bed looked adequate and there was a small tub, a toilet and a bidet along one wall. Deirdre sighed and wished she had Fiona with her. Dermot's mother was very good at these feminine things like hair and nails and make-up too. Someone knocked and she called come in.

"I am Florrie Sweeney. Flor is my husband." She smiled. "I know, two persons named Florence, in the one house." Her laugh was musical and pleasing. "I've come to help and I've brought along some things a woman might need and she being married tomorrow."

Florrie was a bit stout and rounded whereas her husband Flor was lean and flat. She opened her bag and laid out scissors, nail clippers, files, brushes and combs. "And I've some things for a real ladies bath. Flor and I have married off two daughters; I know the routine of the night before." She fussed around the room and fussed over Deirdre too, prodding and poking, cutting and filing, tweezing, trimming and talking to her the while.

"I see you've eaten already. Some fish and a meat pie, some wine, and that is a wedding cake is it not? Bless me. My old mother, Lord have mercy on her, she always held that food was God's reward to us for having to be here in this world."

Deirdre shut down her hearing and sort of coasted along on the rhythm of Florrie's verbal flow, hearing just a word here and there. She smiled and nodded whenever the older woman's voice rose in what might've been a question.

She smiled to herself and remembered the compartment she and Jay shared on the train through Russia and into the heart of Europe.

Sometimes Jay would sit behind her on the bunk and brush her hair and hug and kiss her shoulders and then brush some more. He would tell her the wildest tales about America. The grand big cities, rivers as wide as an ocean, the rolling plains that went on forever and still had a few buffalo and Indians. His stories and his hair brushing were magnificent. She believed completely in Jay but maybe not quite everything in all of his stories. He was an O'Neill and half Irish after all.

A knock on the door broke her reverie. Florrie answered and she heard Donal's voice, then the door closed. Florrie came back carrying a large steaming kettle and the little cap on the top was dancing and whistling.

"Into the tub now dear. Donal will bring another kettle and I'll add enough cold water to keep it comfortable. Here's some nice Essence de Fleur from the apothecary. It bubbles up. It smells grand and it will oil your skin, so. Flor brings me a bottle every year on our anniversary. He is a dear sweet man. He never forgets."

Deirdre settled into the small tub and swished the water with her two hands to mix the hot water with the cold and to raise more bubbles. It was so grand, so relaxing to have someone take care of you. She could sit up and stretch out her legs under water, or bend her knees and lay down with her shoulders under the water. Both positions suited her fine.

Below her in the kitchen she could hear muffled voices, sometimes a shout, or laughing and a great deal of singing. Declan had a fine clear tenor voice. It stood out from the others and rose up so sweet. Dermot would join in while Donal and Mac provided harmony.

They sang their favorite marching songs, 'Clare's Dragoons' and 'The soldiers' Song' Deirdre smiled as they began to sing "Tipperary" again. That seemed to be the theme song for the Motley's. "It's a long way to Tipperary, it's a long way to go. Deirdre sang along."

Out of the tub, Deirdre had her nails done; all ten fingers and all ten toes were cut and shaped, filed and painted. She never in her life had her toenails fussed over by someone else, not even in France when she went to school there. Florrie took her brushes, comb and scissors and cut, trimmed and shaved hair from Deirdre's head and body, under her arms and all over her. She fussed and encouraged her like a mother would and

161

suddenly Deirdre laid her head on Florrie's plump shoulder and began to cry. It was a soft slow sort of an emptying that Deirdre went through. Florrie held her and patted her; she brushed her hair again and again and she kept saying, "I know, I know, I do know my darling, I know."

"Your Mam is gone, is she?" Deirdre nodded. "You have no one, now," Florrie asked?

"Fiona, my aunt Fiona. She's my mother's sister. Her twin." Deirdre smiled thinking of her Fiona, Dermot's mother. "You would like her, Florrie."

"I know I would, love. Now, would you ever wrap yourself in this nightie and get into bed." Florrie took a glass vial and emptied the contents into Deirdre's wine glass. "Drink it down, so." She held up her hand to forestall any questions. "Bride's Drink on the Wedding Eve. It has a mixture of brandy and herbs, some prayers and even a bit of magic in it. Drink it down, dear. You'll sleep like a babe and awaken when you are ready to begin a new life with that man of your choosing. It is so important that you chose him." Florrie looked pleased with her work. She tilted her head side to side and admired her handiwork.

Deirdre drank most of the Bride's Drink and felt sleepy at once. Was it the bath, the fussing, the weeping or the drink. "I'm sorry I cried like that, Florrie. And you were so nice to me."

"Ah girl, it's just the Bride jitters and not knowing who you will be after tomorrow. Drink the last of it now. I'll clean up a bit here and tip toe out and on home. Just remember Deirdre when you marry off one of your own, write to me and I'll send you the recipe for the Bride's Drink. Good luck and joy to you, my dear."

"The committee members are all snug and dry in that pub that looks out onto the quay." Dermot sounded tired. "They were called to be witness for the loading of the Lusitania coffins onto lorries guarded by the Army early this morning, but the rain would not let up. Not even for the dead and so the members are all in there. The Swiss with his eye piece, the Yank from your crowd, Jay, and Rory's there to give a blessing; Devil Burke is there, the one you call Wee Willie, and of course that French Priest who will marry you and Deirdre."

Dermot had a long drink of tea. "Flor said they're packing away kippers and eggs, gobs of ham and rashers of salt bacon, tea with brandy and plenty of bread. The brandy is for the chill and this damned weather. Sorry Jay. The wedding is delayed."

Deirdre entered the kitchen in time to hear the last part about the wedding being delayed. She took Jays arm and the two of them stood at one end of the long kitchen table and faced Dermot, Declan, Mac and Donal at the other end. The two lovers were like a couple who had just arrived at their hotel to find that there was no room at the inn.

Declan jumped up, bid them be seated and poured out mugs of tea for them. "You look different, Deirdre, something about you, your hair?" He studied her close and went on.

"In any case, someone rang the Post Office in the wee hours. Soldiers are coming here with the lorries, they said. There'll be Government agents, Maritime Insurers and the soldiers. They will take all the coffins from Flor this very morning, they said. Most will go up to Cobh in the lorries and be closely guarded by the British Army. Though why in the world they need foreign soldiers to guard the Lusitania dead is beyond me. Some are identified and some are not. They'll make one last try at identity in the Cobh mortuary, and then bury them as 'Unknowns'." Declan grimaced and shook his head at the thought of being an 'Unknown'.

Mac spoke up, "I suppose because there are dead from so many nations here, and there will be more questions and inquiries for years to come. The presence of the British Army, foreign or not, Declan my lad, is their attempt to see that nobody mucks it up, at least not any worse than it already is."

Donal spilled some tea into a saucer and blew on it. "Flor will not let any copper nor soldier into his cold room. He likes to keep his secrets." His tea was still too hot and he blew some more. "He's had two men working since the call came, middle of the night, like. They're knocking together a few wood and canvas boxes that the coffins will go in, so as to keep them dry till they're loaded onto the covered lorries."

Declan sliced some bread and set it down in front of Jay and Deirdre and then a dish with a slab of butter. "Now, there's also a small steam coaster tied to the quay. It seems some of the coffins will go by sea to Liverpool to be buried in England. Some others will go out onto the ocean off of Kinsale to be buried at sea. The sea going coffins of course have all been identified and they are carrying out the last wishes, like." He shrugged and smiled at them.

"How does all this affect our wedding?"

"Sorry Jay. Sorry cousin." Dermot sounded tired but very determined. "The place is crawling with soldiers, constabulary, officials and the like. Courtmacsherry town itself is overrun with them, the quay, the bay, everything."

Declan kept busy making tea and filling mugs. "And the road and bridge into Timoleague are posted with guards. Donal says the back roads are awash with all this heavy rain, so it's the main road or nothing. We've no way to go a'tall."

Deirdre got up to help Declan and examined the leftovers from last nights feast.

Jay asked, "How do you read this, Mac?"

"Flor Sweeney was here for just a moment and he was very strong on it. 'Hold tight' he said and repeated it several times. The lorries will soon be loaded, the rain will let up and the soldiers will all go away. Also the tide will be at flood soon and the steamer will be away, as well. Problem solved, says Flor Sweeney, just hold tight."

"Forget Sweeney, Mac. How do you see it," Jay was impatient and eager to take action.

"Jay my son, your bride is at risk, but I'd be very tempted to try a bold move. We pack up now and move out. If we hold at the edge of town and then pull up behind the last lorry load of coffins or soldiers, whichever, we join the caravan and we're off like yesterdays knickers." Mac looked around at the other Motleys for some kind of reaction.

"What about Rene and Fritz?"

"Send someone into the pub." Mac pointed and imitated Declan playing a role. "There's a gent outside in that motor car would like a word with you. Would you ever step this way?"

Deirdre smiled for the first time this morning. She had been glum since she woke up and saw the rain coming down in buckets. She set down fresh tea and more bread, butter and jam, then she sat down next to Mac and Jay moved down the table to be near them.

Donal quit blowing on his saucer of tea and spoke up. "Flor says we should wait a bit."

"Damn it, I'm in charge of this operation." Dermot was red in the face. "Flor Sweeney has his own agenda and it always involves money flowing into Flor's pockets." He got up and paced the large brick kitchen.

"Deirdre cousin, you and Jay take the Motleys on a ten shilling tour of this grand house of bricks, would you. Maybe a good walk inside here keeping high and dry in this brickyard will clear our heads and let us think. Begin at the front entrance and I'll catch you up. I need a word here with Donal." Jay and Deirdre led the Motleys out of the kitchen.

"Donal, I haven't a clue as to what the hell is going on here. I can smell mischief in this wet rain, but what in God's holy name is Flor Sweeney up to?"

"Be easy, Dermot. Near as I can tell, many things are happening now and at once; things that should be happening weeks apart, so."

"For instance?"

"Rifles, Dermot. Rifles and the rounds to go into them."

"Sweet Jesus on the Cross. That shipment is not due for a fortnight at the earliest. Deirdre was to be well out of harms way before the rifles came, and they were never supposed to come to Courtmacsherry at all." Dermot began pacing again, back and forth, back and forth. "So Flor Sweeney has those wood and canvas coffin covers as a blind. Bring a coffin to the steamer, it goes below decks out of sight of the soldiers. Another coffin or just the box comes out covered by the canvas and the box is loaded with rifles." He glared at Donal.

"Not loaded, maybe a dozen or two rifles at any one time. It shouldn't look too heavy coming back off the ship. Will you slow down your running Dermot. I'm dizzy keeping an eye on you, and you going back and forth like a tennis ball at a match."

Dermot came over and sat facing Donal. "Let me guess. The rifle filled box goes back to Flor's cold room."

"Aye. Four boxes at a time on the donkey cart."

"And Flor repeats the process till the ship's manifest is filled with coffins and Flor's cold room is full of rifles and ammunition."

"Not quite, Dermot." Donal looked pleased but unhappy. "Once in the cold room, some of the rifles come out of the wood and canvas boxes and are put into coffins. Empty ones, like."

"Jesus. Flor is a cute one, isn't he. He's much smarter than I gave him credit for." Dermot stopped his pacing and was staring at the fire in the kitchen stove. "Coffins loaded with rifles go on the donkey cart, are brought over and loaded onto the lorries. That's bold."

"Aye, You've got it now, Dermot." Donal's unhappiness faded away, leaving him pleased.

"And the British Army stands guard over our new, smuggled, Irish Brotherhood rifles as they are hauled up to Cobh for us." Dermot and Donal shook their heads in admiration.

"About half of them. The rest will go out into West Cork as originally planned."

"And the lorry drivers, do they know? Are they concerned with the risks?"

"Most of them are Connelly's men. They will be grand, Dermot. Not to worry, not a'tall."

Jay strode into the kitchen. "Son of a bitch, is it Sweeney has us trapped in here?" He dropped down at the table next to Dermot. "Is he responsible for all the soldiers? Is Flor Sweeney putting Deirdre and all of us in danger?" Jay's voice rose and his face was flushed. He stared at the two men who should be protecting his Deirdre.

"Sorry, Jay. It isn't your problem and it shouldn't even be mine. But Flor is not the reason we're in this fix."

"No." Jay spoke in a low voice. "I'm the reason my Deirdre is at risk. I needed help to find her; I brought her to the attention of Burke. I told my story and he, that two faced bastard, set the wheels in motion so he could follow me to find her and harm her."

"Sure to God it's Manannan MacLir." Donal saw the blank look on Jay. "The Celtic God of the sea. Listen now, He's angry with us Irish, but He's enraged at the English. Mayhap he still likes the Welch and the Scots, time will tell on that. Look, he took the Lusitania down. Dragged her under in eighteen minutes." Donal crossed himself in quick short moves.

"Next thing, through storms and such, he caused that Dutch coaster to stop here for a load of coffins and discharge the rifles here, today, in the rain. That Dutchman wasn't due in here for a fortnight. Supposed to go beyond Clonakilty Bay, down near Galley Head she was. 'Tis Manannan MacLir's doing, I tell you." Donal crossed himself again with great fervor.

Declan and Mac came back and took seats at the table. Deirdre went to the stove and put on a kettle for another of the endless pots of tea. No one was to blame and everyone had their own piece of the entire story. The missing parts were easily filled in.

Mac began the unraveling. "We did not eavesdrop on you, Dermot. We would not do that to you. We respect your leadership too much. It was the openings." Mac pointed to the grates overhead. "They allow the heat to rise up and we overheard you. This kitchen warms several of the rooms above, and you and Donal's talk flowed up to us like the word of God Almighty." Mac cleared his throat and sipped the tea Deirdre put in front of him.

"With Sean lying there dead, Jay is my son and his Deirdre is my daughter. Married or not matters naught. We are one family. Several things are paramount now, and we must avoid them, defeat them or negate them. First, we are all guilty of high crimes and treason against the crown, and in a time of war. Like it or not we are all involved. If caught we may be hung or shot." Mac swallowed his tea and watched for reactions.

Declan's spoon made a loud sound as he stirred sugar into his mug of tea.

Mac went on. "I ran into Jay in Paris. He was frantic looking for you, Deirdre. I took him to London and sought help for him from my colleagues. It was I who introduced Jay and his story to Wee Willie, who is now seeking to destroy you, Deirdre. And it was Fritz, who helped us by unlocking your message to Jay. And Rene was there too. Rene, who will marry the two of you today, if we have any luck at all." Mac took a moment and appraised each of his companions. "So it was I Deirdre, who set you up and put a target on your back."

The Motleys all protested Mac's harsh indictment of himself, and Mac held up his hands for silence. "Though inactive, I still hold a commission in a Scottish Regiment, and it galls me to fight against my King and the Crown. However, I will lay down my life to protect everyone here and I'll take whatever comes as my portion. It is my just due."

"No." Declan jumped up and moved to Deirdre's side. He crouched down next to her. "It was me was supposed to carry the letter of credit to that Russian General. Me. A young innocent lad with a gift of gab, what could go wrong? Who would ever suspect me of anything but maybe running away from a terrible war. I was supposed to go, but when it came time, I told Dermot I was sick. And I was." He paused. "I was sick with fear."

He looked up at Deirdre from his crouch. "I was scared out of my mind. Forgive me, please. I'm sorry. It was me got you into this." Declan couldn't help himself. He sobbed and Deirdre held him until his shoulders stopped shaking.

"Declan, Declan darling. No one doubts your bravery. I see it with my own two eyes each day, and you grow stronger and more valuable to us every day that passes. Thank you for telling me, cousin of my cousin." She rumpled his curly head, looked over at Jay and winked. "Suppose now, you had gone to Russia to meet General Kamzarov and Jay met you on that train instead of me. Do you think he'd have fallen in love with you instead of me?"

Declan began shaking with laughter instead of tears and he sat down on the kitchen floor, then he lay flat out on the flagstones. "Jay, I think you're a grand man but I'm having a hard time seeing us holding hands and traipsing through the waving fields of grain in old Mother Russia." He rolled over laughing and Deirdre gave him a playful shove with her foot.

Donal put down his saucer of hot tea and exclaimed in a serious tone, "Listen to me now. It was I who put us in this unholy scene of grief and despair. Begod, had I taken a fatal shot on that spy, that Devil Burke's man, we'd not be stuck here in the wet rain and all."

Dermot stood and stretched. "Enough. Enough, you Motley bunch. This is a kitchen not a bloody confessional. If you do not stop I'll have Father Rory back here to give us all a general absolution and a long heavy penance for each and every one of you.

Mac, it was not you, and Declan it was not you either. I sent my cousin on that mission. I gave her the letter of credit. I put that target on your back my dearest cousin Deirdre. I will regret that decision to my dying day."

"*Diarmuid macushla.* I wanted to go. There's an end to it now, for all of you. I put myself and all of you dears into this terrible grand situation when I had Yuri Yurivich stop the train and let me off just outside of Paris." She put her hand up and caressed Jay's face.

"If I'd been caught and you were with me, we'd both be in a French prison. I had to protect you, my love. The papers I carried entitled the bearer to take possession of the rifles and ammunition and you were innocent, my Jay. I knew you were a spy of sorts, collecting information, always asking questions of everyone, and that little notebook you kept.

But you had nothing at all to do with the guns. I had to protect you, so I left you, and hoped you would come after me when the danger was past." Deirdre held his face in her two hands. "Forgive me Jay, please?"

Jay took her hands and kissed each in turn. "I came for you. I will always be where you are. You will not, ever, shake loose from me again."

Mac got up this time and walked around the table pouring tea for everyone. When he got to Deirdre she stopped him, "But Mac, how can I be guilty of gun running? I never touched a gun; I never even saw one. I simply brought a letter of credit to a certain General, and carried papers from him to a shipping agent in Holland."

"Picture this for a bit, Deirdre. Here we are in the highest court in the land. Deirdre, you are the accused in the witness box." Mac grabbed Declan's make up kit and put on a blond wig. "This is my powdered wig." The Motleys all smiled but the smiles dimmed as Mac pressed on.

"The Crown prosecutor will say, Madame, did you carry a letter of credit across several international borders? Ah. You did. Did you hand deliver it to a certain Russian General? I see. Was that letter redeemable in Swiss gold?" Mac leaned right into Deirdre's face.

"And madame. What was it you expected in return for your Swiss Gold? Was it, Potatoes? No. Rye bread? Of course not. Perhaps cases of good Vodka? Or Russian rifles which is itself a double crime. One. The rifles will be used against the Crown. Two. The rifles you bought will diminish the value of the Russian Army fighting as our Allies in this war."

Mac was nose to nose with Deirdre and spoke in a hushed whisper. "Madame. Perhaps we should hang you twice." Deirdre winced and drew back. "Or maybe we'll be lenient. We will shoot you and then hang you."

Jay went behind Deirdre, put his hands on her shoulders and supported her. "Easy Mac."

"On the other hand," Mac straightened up. "I spoke to a chap in the War Office just before we left London, Jay. There is no specific gun running caper on their agenda. There is no ongoing search for a young Irishwoman, who has recently traveled abroad. Nothing. What we do have is Wee Willie Burke putting two plus two together and coming up with his own conclusions of four, five and maybe six.

There is no warrant for Deirdre, or you Jay nor anyone here. He's using his own money on a hunch, hiring thugs, hoping it will lead to his knighthood, or Order of The Garter, or medals and the Honors List. He has become sickening. Sorry, both of you, but this could get very dicey and in a flash." Gregor MacGregor turned away from them all.

Mac went to the window and looked out as though he could stop the rain by staring hard at the clouds. "Jay we need one of your American Indians to do the opposite of a rain dance."

Jay thought a bit, "Donal, is there a prayer or a sacrifice we can make to this Manannan MacLir, God of the sea?"

"Aye, Jay O'Neill but we need one of the ancient Druids or the poet Amergin to get his attention. You'd nearly want to be out on the deep blue ocean for Manannan MacLir to notice you a'tall."

Mac spun around from the window. "Dermot, Donal, is there any way in God's green earth we could get aboard that Dutch coaster and be out of here at high tide. We have Sean, who is our own Motley corpse. We have his son Jay and Jay's wife Deirdre, his brother, myself and however many of you cousins want to go sailing on the salt sea. We could even Shanghai Rene out of that pub and he could marry them at sea. Would it work?"

Dermot jumped into action. "Mac that's brilliant. It's risky of course, but at least we'd be away from this dead end we're stuck in. Donal, put on your raggediest looking duds and get down to Flor Sweeney and see how far along they are. Deirdre cousin come, let us clean up and clear out of this damp old pile of bricks."

Dermot's face lit up. "Jay me boyo the Motleys are on the move again. Best we put your Da back into the old coffin. It'll match all the others. Mac you and Jay pull the new expensive casket out of the hearse and bring it here into the kitchen. We'll leave Flor's lovely hearse out on the quay when we go aboard the Dutch steamer. Declan, you and Donal will wait for the troops to leave. Bring both the car and the motorcycle. You will catch us up somewhere. Oh God. I don't know where you should meet us. I'll get word to you, somehow."

He looked around at the flurry of motion he had caused. "That's it, that's it. We are moving now." They were changing clothes, packing bags, cleaning the table, banking the fire in the Aga cooker, while Jay swept the floor. "Activity with a purpose. I love it. I swear to God I love it. Declan we'll have to change our name to the Efficient Motleys"

Donal, pulled on his Wellingtons and offered, "mayhap you can bribe the ship's Captain to drop you near to Clonakilty. We could all meet there and head up to Dublin by road."

Declan scoffed. "Hah. Wouldn't that look grand, altogether. Three men, a handsome woman and a black coffin, all sitting on the slippery rocks out in Clonakilty Bay."

"God bless all in this house." A young boy, their guide from last night, stood in the doorway.

"Flor's son," Donal identified him. "How's your Da, son? Is the loading nearly done, so?"

"The loading is done. The lorries are full up and the soldiers will soon be gone away altogether. The Dutchman is making steam now and will leave at any moment." The boy saw the puzzled looks they all gave him. "His load has been lightened and he's riding much higher, over the waves. No need to wait on the tide. Sure he'll clear the bar easy, so."

A long blast of a steam whistle rattled the windows of the big brick house. "The Dutchman is loose from the quay. I'm away, now. Good luck and God Bless." The lad turned to go.

Dermot jumped for the door. "Thank you son and thank your father and mother, as well." He gave the boy a half crown coin. "Have you any brothers and sisters at home?"

"One of each, sir. Both younger than meself." He grinned as Dermot doled out two shilling coins then he tossed them into the air and caught all three coins with one swoop of his quick left hand. "I've two other sisters as well, both married and moved away."

Dermot showed him his fist in mock anger. The boy laughed, turned, and he was gone.

"A chip off the old Sweeney, isn't he," Donal said. He followed the boy as far as the front door.

Declan sighed. "Here we are making and executing our plans. Ach No. We changed the plans. We'll do something else, instead. No wait now. We're back on our plan again. I should've called us the Nimble Motleys." The group laughed as he grinned and took a bow. Then Declan looked for approval from Deirdre and Dermot "What now, oh mighty King Dermot the first? Oh glorious Queen Deirdre, successor to *Grainne Ni Mhaille?*"

Dermot put a hand on Deirdre. "Sorry cousin, there'll be no Atlantical wedding at sea for you. This is Irish history in a nutshell. We have missed the boat. You are surely right, Declan. The Nimble Motleys are on again at the Mass Rock. At least we'll have a bit of breathing room with all the soldiers gone away.

Declan you must get the French priest out of that pub and into the hearse. Jay, you and Mac will drive the hearse. Declan you're pushing the motorcycle again and Father Rory goes in the sidecar. God be praised you will find him. I've become right fond of Father Talking Rory Beechinor, parish priest and story teller extraordinaire."

Jay chimed in, "and Declan, don't forget to grab Fritz as well. The Swiss, German fellow. Oh, of course you know Fritz. You served him dinner. And Deirdre will ride with us in the hearse."

Dermot had a pained expression on his face as he moved toward Jay. "I would feel much stronger about her safety Jay, were she to ride with Donal and myself in the good doctor's car."

"That's not going to happen, Dermot." Jay squared his shoulders around so he and Dermot faced each other with just a pace separating them. The rest of the Motley men stopped all of their activities and watched this confrontation play out. They had expected something like this would happen, sooner or later.

Jay kept his voice soft, but he was deadly serious. "I will never again be separated from Deirdre. Not by anyone. Not for any reason. Not while I am alive, Dermot."

Deirdre quickly put herself between the two men with a hand on each man's arm. She looked at each of them in turn, then reached up and kissed Dermot on the cheek. She stepped to Jay's side. Quickly, Deirdre lifted his arm and pulled it around her waist.

"Come you all." The Sweeney boy's voice rang out loud and clear. "Be quick. Come now to the great hall and up the stairs so. Come, follow me."

Donal was first and the others ran just behind him. They went through the large entry hall, and up the stairs and followed the young Sweeney lad along an open hallway that overlooked the large entry hall. The boy led them through a glass double door out onto a balcony. They could see below them the courtyard, the enclosing brick wall and beyond the wall the trees fell away to a cleared space and they saw the cliffs and the blue water of the ship channel.

Suddenly, the Dutch coaster was there. It was close in to the cliffs. They could see the higher parts, the wheel house and smoke stack and a slice of the deck on the port side from bow to stern. The rest of the small ship was hidden by the cliffs. A man wearing a seaman's cap stepped out of the wheelhouse. He looked up at them standing on the balcony and a puff of smoke came out of his mouth. With his pipe in his hand, he made a huge wave to them, going left and right and left again. He smiled and waved again.

The Nimble Motleys waved back, each with a private thought about the ship. Some had regrets, wanting to be onboard. Some were filled with joy; their feet on solid ground and they not having to face the long Atlantic swells in a small ship. The seaman went back into the wheelhouse and the ship gave off a long low whistle, then two short blasts and it passed out of sight around the point and into choppy Courtmacsherry Bay and on out to the wild Atlantic Ocean.

Deirdre leaned in to Jay and he put his arm around her and held her close to him. "It seemed so nice and safe, that ship. I wish we were on it." She shivered; and he held her tighter and kissed her dark hair.

CHAPTER TEN

It was so simple, so fast and so easy that they laughed about it later. Jay drove the hearse with Mac in the seat next to him. Deirdre sat behind Jay on the bench and behind her was Sean O'Neill in his new casket with the empty black wood coffin along for the ride.

"What is it now, me boyo," Mac looked over at Jay. "You've got a grin a yard wide on that O'Neill mug of yours."

Jay's grin got even wider. "There's a good looking wench behind me, breathing down my neck." Deirdre laughed out loud and the two men smiled, glad that she was enjoying herself.

They were part of a slow, stately procession as they moved along the main road back into the small town of Courtmacsherry. The neat houses and commercial buildings on the left were all painted bright pastel colors, which never seemed to change. The water on the right was always changing. At low tide it was the Argideen River flowing out into the Bay. When the tide was filling, as it was now, the Bay came rushing back in and forced the River to double back on itself, betraying it's seaward journey. The life in the water seemed to thrive on the constant change in salinity and sea levels. There was always an abundance of cockles and mussels in the tidal mud and big fish eating smaller fish in the water while sea birds with their hard beaks and shiny flat eyes preyed on all of them.

Declan wore a white shirt with a black tie and in his chauffeur's outfit, he looked almost elegant. The hat to his uniform had gotten lost and the

Navy cap had gone back to Jay, so Declan wore a gray cloth cap set at a jaunty angle. It perched high and uneasy on his curly head and the cap undid most of his elegance. He had affixed a large black satin bow to the front of the sidecar and he led the Nimble Motley procession with obvious pride.

Behind came the hearse with Jay, Deirdre and Mac. Jay was resplendent in his Naval dress blues, though his jacket and hat were draped over his father's casket in the back. Mac was dressed again in all of his MacGregor plaid finery. Deirdre had on a dark green frock with her grandmother's white wedding dress hanging in the back. She wore her best family jewels and for good luck she also wore the *Shian bao* Jay had given her for her protection. All of her finery was hidden under her long black cloak, 'we really shouldn't even be seeing each other,' Deirdre thought. 'We don't need any bad luck on this special day, our wedding day.'

Behind the hearse came the car that Declan had gotten for them from the good doctor. Dermot drove with Donal sitting next to him and on the floor between them was Donal's rifle, loaded and ready. This was a holiday for them; the soldiers had all gone away. Still and all, you could never be too careful. The two men were dressed in their best and their best would do alike, for a wedding or a funeral. In honor of Sean O'Neill, they were wearing black arm bands, which they would take off during the wedding, and the motor car itself had black satin ribbons tied on the bumpers, both front and rear.

The Nimble Motleys were on their way to a wedding and a Requiem Mass, and they had expectations of adding two gentlemen from the continent as new members of the Motleys before they arrived at the Mass Rock. The burial itself would be delayed until Sean O'Neill's body arrived in New York. He would rest in America next to his Polish born wife.

They received no more than a passing glance from the local citizenry. Wakes, funerals, processions and the color black had become a part of life here since the Lusitania went down.

Swallowtail Terns and black backed Gulls swooped and fed in the flooding bay while the stately Cormorants stood on the rocks with their wings outstretched and dried their oily feathers. Life went on while it was able.

Declan led them left up a side street, then right and right again and they came to a stop facing the main street next to the pub where Rene and Fritz were last seen. Across the main road, groups of men stood on the quay talking about the early morning doings. So many soldiers, and lorries and coffins, and more coffins aboard the ship, and so much rain, and so many things they had to talk about. But the conversation kept coming back to the one question that was never really decided in a seaport town. If you were bound for Kinsale or Cork City or were going up to Dublin itself, would you prefer to make the journey by sea or by road?

Rory left the men at the quay and came across the road as soon as he saw Declan and the group. "Your timing is right on, Declan. Wee Willy Burke and my boss, Big Billy Conklin just left by car for Timoleague. Rene and Fritz decided, at least Fritz decided and Rene agreed, just as soon as the rain stopped, that they'd stretch their legs and walk back."

"Ah, that's grand Rory, climb into my sidecar, so."

"Let me just go back and tell Jay in the hearse and then I'll tell Dermot in the doctor's car."

"RORY. There's no time, man. Will you just get in and we'll be off and away, so."

Rory did as Declan bid. He really was delighted to climb in. He had never in his life ridden on a motorcycle, much less sat in a sidecar.

Jay pulled the hearse to a stop next to Rene and Fritz who were walking along the road and Rene said to all of them. "*Mon Dieu, Fritz,* You are again so correct. Wee Willy wanted us to ride, but my dear friend Fritz says no. We must stretch the legs. I, Rene said, Fritz, you cannot walk. He said to me, Rene, we will not walk far. They will find us and we will ride. And *voila,* you 'ave found us and now we will take the ride."

The two newest members of the Nimble Motleys climbed into the hearse and sat on the bench seat with Deirdre between them.

She held hands with both Rene and Fritz and Jay's smile grew wider. "Will you marry me, Deirdre Ni DalCas?"

"Yes and you know I will, but you'd better watch your driving, Jay O'Neill."

Just before Timoleague there was a lay-by with a grand view of the water and all the turbulence caused by the river meeting the bay. Dermot signaled a stop and one by one they pulled off the road and into the place for resting and viewing. Declan steered the motorcycle alongside Dermot who was driving the good doctor's car.

"Listen to me now, Declan. We must pass this last hurdle and we've made it alright. Go by the Pastor's house. Make sure Devil Burke is plenty busy with no inkling of our presence. Send Rory inside if you must, and then it's time for the white scarf again. As soon as we see that bit of white, we'll go through town and Rory will lead us on to the Mass Rock. We'll have a wedding at last; we'll attend Sean's Funeral Mass and then we are safely away."

"Aye Dermot. I'm with you all the way. Begod, Dermot. Will you ever look over there. Isn't that the two Coveney girls in their father's motorcar?"

"It surely is Mary Rose driving that motorcar and that's Maura Ni Coveney in the seat next to her." Dermot looked hard at Declan, who sat on his motorcycle and looked very innocent. "Now how in the world did they know to come down here this very morning. 'Tis raining so hard, and there's angry wet soldiers at every corner and bridge along the way".

"Shall I send them on home, then, cousin Dermot?"

"Not in this lifetime, Declan. If they came for a wedding, then it'll be a wedding they'll not soon forget. Have them follow us, so."

"I'll do better than that. Just watch me."

Declan, ever the operator, induced Father Rory out of the sidecar by offering him a chance to drive the Coveney automobile. Father Rory, like many people who had never owned a motorcar, loved to drive and would do so at the drop of a cardinal's red hat. Mary Rose Ni Coveney said she'd never at all mind riding in a sidecar, especially one that was attached to Declan's motorcycle. This game of musical chairs and cars was further enhanced when Declan talked Rene out of the hearse and into the Coveney auto to keep Rory company. The two priests shared a love of history and mystery and were delighted to continue a conversation begun the night before.

He next escorted Maura Ni Coveney out of her family car and into the back of Dermot's automobile. Declan's final and most difficult maneuver involved getting Dermot to allow Donal into the driving position and Dermot himself to open his collar, loosen his tie and sit in the back with Maura. As it happened, before they ever crossed the Argideen River into the town of Timoleague, the two were holding hands and long before the Mass Rock was reached they were hugging and kissing. Donal kept singing a local song, 'Something about goin' to a weddin' and the dire consequences for all single men.

Mary Rose stood up in the sidecar, took the cloth cap off of Declan and pulled it onto her own head with the front facing back so that she looked like a racing jockey. She leaned in to him and gave him a big wet kiss on the lips. Declan, knowing he was so visible at the head of this Motley parade, at first resisted her, then succumbed to Mary Rose and kissed her back with a passion that surprised them both.

Several people passing by actually cheered and clapped for them. Declan bowed and Mary Rose curtsied and then they were off, over the bridge, into town and up to the Pastor's house.

"You'll go in the back door there and ask for cook. Now say it back to me, Mary Rose, just the way I told you"

"Grand day cook. I am Anna Grace McCall. I live over the way near Harbour View and I've heard you have dinner parties and guests over and sometimes hire a girl to help you with the serving and clearing up, so."

"That's it. That's grand, Mary Rose." He regarded her with new respect in his blue eyes. "You're brilliant and good looking too." He kissed her full on the lips. Declan was getting better at this kissing thing. "We need to know if they have any guests over and where are they now? Go on now, please."

Mary Rose was back in less than four minutes with welcome news. "Cook asked where in the world did I ever hear such nonsense, dinner parties, indeed. I said a friend of my sister heard it from the girl who cleans for the Protestant Minister. Well, she says, I've only the one guest and he and Father Conklin are resting in their rooms after supervising the loading and blessing of all them coffins this morning and no, I have no need of any more help. Thank you and goodbye, and she slams the door on me."

"You're a rare one, you are. Here Mary Rose", Declan handed her his white silk scarf. "Tie it around your neck with the tail end over your shoulder, loose like, and hanging out in the breeze as we drive."

She leaned close in and said, "you tie it for me." This time he took the initiative and kissed her while tying his white silk scarf around her lovely pale neck.

Mac had his brass telescope fixed on the far end of the bridge. "Aye, there is the white scarf flying in the wind, but it's around the girl's neck, not his. Anyway, drive on laddie. We're off to a wedding." He turned and winked at Deirdre who, while still holding hands with Fritz was breathing down Jay's neck again. Jay didn't seem to mind it at all.

Just outside of town, Declan and Mary Rose on the cycle slowed a bit and allowed Rory and Rene in the dark green Coveney car, to overtake them. Behind Declan and Mary Rose came the black hearse with Jay and Mac in front and Deirdre and Fritz in back on the bench seat and the shiny new casket and dark coffin held fast to the floor behind them all. Last in the wedding-funeral parade came Donal driving the car that Declan got for them from the good doctor.

The Motley's still referred to this four door black sedan as the good doctor's car. Behind Donal was Dermot, half sprawled on the back seat with Maura Ni Coveney sprawled on top of him. They didn't say much. Mostly they hugged and squeezed and kissed and gazed long into each other's soul after a brief stop at the eyes.

Rory himself was magnificent as the lead driver of this Nimble Motley Procession. He was so very aware that the success of this entire venture depended upon him. His local knowledge of the roads, the approach, and the final location of the Mass Rock were crucial. And even though he would not officiate, without Father Rory Beechinor the DalCas-O'Neill wedding could not happen. Indeed the love and lives and future of this couple were now entrusted to him. Any children of this union, indeed, perhaps the fate of the entire world could be changed by his driving of this dark green car on this day. Rory felt the pressure but stood up under it quite well.

Rory tried to share these thoughts with Rene, but the old priest turned diplomat just nodded and tapped his hands on the dashboard to some private inner melody. Rory looked left and right and left again. He admired the stone walls, the enclosing pastures, and the black and white cows grazing on the lush green grass. He enjoyed the woods and meadows of the passing countryside but he was disappointed that Rene was not interested in talking nor did he want to hear about local history and oddities. Perhaps he should've had Fritz to ride with him instead of Rene, but Fritz was interested mainly in military history.

Fritz, riding in the hearse behind Rene and the Coveney car, was indeed interested in the military history of this area. As they rode along, he measured elevations and distances. Fritz knew just where to place his cannon and what heights were needed and the site line they would have for clear firing. He imagined that he could explain it to Mac and Jay.

"*Ja herr MacGregor*. See that hill. *Vell*, had I been here at that time, even a small battery of cannon right there." He stuck his cane out of the window and used it as a pointer. "No no, Cromwell never could succeed. Never could he sail up the river and destroy your lovely Abbey if I had even two cannon on that hill.

Ja Jay. I could never be a Naval gunner. How do you hit something when your gun platform is moving, up and down and side to side. And even more so difficult, your target also is moving, up, down, side and side." Fritz moved his cane about with his words. "Naval gunnery is more sorcery than science, *ja Jay?*"

Deirdre and Mac and Jay smiled at Fritz. They enjoyed the way he bent history and wove plausible outcomes with his imaginary interventions. History and life itself could often benefit from a do over.

Rory and Rene in the lead car turned off the main Bandon road and the group followed them along a smaller one lane road that led them deeper into the countryside. Very soon they turned off the road onto a rutted two wheel track with grass growing between the wheels as they moved along. Some places were still soft from the mornings downpour and they went slow and easy, with the Coveney car and motorcycle in the lead and the hearse and the good doctor's car following behind.

Soon there were plowed fields on one side of them, woods on the other side and in the distance they could see a house and farm buildings. Rory stopped and the other drivers got out and gathered close to hear him.

"There is a foot path here through the trees and down into the small bowl like place of the Mass Rock. A bit further on there is a wider and less steep pathway that will allow the cars and the hearse down near to the old sacred place."

Dermot, back in charge now, spoke up. "I'd not like to be trapped down in there if someone comes looking for me. Donal, take this footpath and see do we have a way out of it if the need arises." Donal nodded and moved away toward the footpath.

Maura chimed in and her sister confirmed it. "We've been here to this Mass Rock. My Da had us both here, some years back." Mary Rose nodded yes and both sisters were off down the path. "Come Donal, we'll show you this path down to the rock.

"Go on then. I'll keep the good doctor's car parked separate just in case." Dermot backed up and looked for a spot to hide his car in the bushes while the rest of the vehicles went along to the less steep path that led down to the hidden place of the Mass Rock.

Deirdre was wide eyed in anticipation and she was not disappointed. Down the hill the path became less steep and opened out in a level place of larger trees. Mac stepped out and guided Jay as he drove the hearse in among the trees. Without a word they all gathered at the hearse and began walking into the glen and under the large trees.

The priests Rory and Rene went first followed by Deirdre and Jay, then came Mac and Fritz, who struggled a bit and placed his cane carefully down in the grass and twigs with each step. On either side the hills rose up forming a small glen. Ahead, the glen narrowed and the hills met and mingled a short distance in front of them. The hills resembled two giant hands, held sideways, palms open and fingers extended and touching to form a cup of welcome as the Motleys entered this ancient and sacred place of worship.

Just before the hills met there was a small clearing and large oak trees on the flanks of the hills grew high and overhung the cleared space in the center. Parasite sprigs of mistletoe appeared in bunches on the limbs of the oak trees and the sunlight filtered down and bathed everything in the clearing with a soft green glow.

Ahead, cradled in the palms of the two hands, and centered in the clearing was the Mass Rock. The mottled stone was massive, man sized, almost shoulder high and just as wide. It was level on top. The stone was wide and long, and big enough for a large man to lie full out upon it with room to spare. It was speckled with moss and lichen and at the base of the Mass Rock was a wide stone step. It too was overgrown except at the center where it had been worn smooth and shiny as though from constant use.

Jay and the two priests and the Coveney sisters held back as Deirdre walked slow and stepped gently upon the grasses of the green hued little meadow. She approached the Mass Rock in awe tinged with apprehension and fear. As she had hoped, here in this place she and her man would be joined in holy matrimony. The church would bless their union. She would be married here at home in Ireland, in spite of the Bishops and their decree against it.

Deirdre ascended the step and placed her hands on the stone altar. It was warm to her touch. Her eyes followed the oak branches where they reached up and laced together to form a wicker-work roof on this small green cathedral. Unbidden, her two arms rose up following her gaze, her two feet shifted into the well worn treads on the stone step. She was away in time; rooted to the place of a Celtic priestess before her ageless stone altar. Above her, growing on the oak branches Deirdre saw the mistletoe, another symbol of the old Druids. She remembered the stories of how the ancient pagan priestess would use a special golden knife to cut sprigs of the plant to use in religious ceremonies. Deirdre then thought of the modern usage of the mistletoe, the kissing ritual. It brought her back to herself and to this day. She turned to her man Jay and the priests and her friends and Deirdre laughed aloud.

"Jay. Come to me, love. Come now, please and see." Jay came and saw where she was pointing above them and he laughed. They kissed each other there on the step, at the place of the priest before the ancient stone altar. They held nothing back in their kissing and Deirdre and Jay promised themselves to each other, again and forever.

Truly, they were married to each other now. In a short while, Rene as a Jesuit priest would witness their union and bestow upon them the sacrament and the official blessing of the Holy Roman Catholic church.

Declan with Mary Rose at his side drove his motorcycle under a fine old oak tree with low hanging branches in just the right places. Standing up on his saddle, he began hanging an old sheet. Mary Rose held it up to him and Declan fixed it to the branches, then moved over and fixed another and repeated it until they had boxed in a private area, an outdoor dressing room for the bride and her ladies-in-waiting.

"There you go, cousin of my cousin. In these woods and by this sacred old stone we have fixed for you and your ladies a private dressing room." Declan made a deep bow.

Dermot, Donal and Mac returned from scouting the area and they looked glum. Dermot held up his hands and they quieted to hear him. "This is not an ideal location. I don't see how they held secret Masses here and escaped capture by the English soldiers."

Mac laid out the precise problem for them. "We're down here in a sort of depression, a low spot between those two hills. The only way out is back the way we came in. It could well become a trap for us all." He pointed in back of them and up the gradual slope they had come down into this special place of the Mass Rock.

Donal added, "myself and Declan can be posted up there on either side and away from the opening to this lovely glen or bowl as Dermot calls it. We'd give you some warning and some little time, but you'd still come flying out of here, up the slope and into the open, into the waiting arms of your pursuers. It would be quite dicey, I'd say.

"Much too dangerous," Dermot announced. "I'd never feel right if anything happened. So then. Deirdre love, let us have your wedding. Jay, your Da Sean O'Neill, is here in body and spirit to be witness at your nuptials. And with your permission Jay, we will cancel the Requiem Mass. I feel so strong that we should not stay overlong in this spot, lovely as it is."

"Dermot love. I, Maura Ni Coveney have information which will please you and put ease into your mind." The Nimble Motleys all turned to Maura who had just stepped out from behind the white sheeted dressing area.

"Tell me Maura, please. Tell us all." Dermot had no idea, not a clue, what she meant.

"There on the left of the stone is that huge old oak, and at the feet of the oak is a spring of clear water. The water forms a tiny pool and then runs along the base of the hill and seems to disappear back there behind the big Mass Rock. Dermot, the water does not disappear and the hills do not quite meet and close off this tiny glen. There is an opening. An escape way. A hidden exit to a safe passage." Maura's eyes sparkled and she smiled at Dermot

"Donal, Declan, run you, and see what's there. How big? Where does it lead?" The two men ran past the stone to see the escape route and Dermot continued to Maura. "Maura, love. How do you know this? And what else can you tell me about this ancient and holy place?"

Maura walked over and hopped up onto the stone step in front of the huge rock, the place of the priestess where Deirdre had stood a moment ago. "I'll tell it to you as it was told to me."

Declan and Donal rushed back, both saying, "Yes. Yes." Donal described it thus: "The way of this glen is like two open hands with fingers extended and touching. But see, they don't quite touch or meet or close off this glen. The fingers of one hand extend behind the fingers of the other hand, so to speak. The one hill runs behind the other, so. There's a narrow opening, with the wee stream flowing and a path beside it. It would easily take two of us together, side by side like, with the one getting wet feet and him walking in the water."

Declan, ever the clown chimed in, "Maura Ni Coveney you are a seven day wonder. To please her man Maura has conjured up a magical path leading us all to safety. Dermot og O'Rourke. You have it all now, a woman with beauty and brains and even magic."

Maura, blushing, raised her arm for attention and called out, "Dermot, I know you wish to give orders in light of this new situation, but please everyone, hear my story before you move away from this sacred place." Maura told her story and she seemed to take on the aura and become each person, each part of the tale, as she wove her *Shanachie* magic.

Deirdre and Mary Rose slipped out from behind the sheeted area and joined the men standing and listening. Deirdre stood between Jay and Mac and joined arms with both men. Mary Rose went to Declan and put her arm around his waist. The two priests, Rory and Rene were eager to hear this latest bit of local history that promised an element of mystery and pagan rituals.

Dermot, as Jay had been with Deirdre, was delighted to find a totally unexpected side to this woman who had begun to take a prominent place in his thoughts, his desires, indeed, the way he saw his life unfolding. He knew she was a hard working, competent businesswoman. He knew as well that she was a stunning beauty and could be very passionate at the right time; and now he was treated to the sight and sound of her being a spell binder, a story teller and actress as she became all the people in her tale.

Maura Ni Coveney began. "I give you this story as it was given to us by our father and as it was given to him by our grandfather." Here Maura held out her arm and included Mary Rose as part of her tale. "He brought us here and told us this bit of truth and wonder on this very spot." She seemed to grow taller and almost mannish as she assumed the role of her father and grandfather before him. Maura's voice deepened and echoed between the low hills.

"I was here at this altar, praying and humming a spiritual sort of a tune, when he made a noise and I turned and saw him. It was an old man. He sat quiet and restful upon the ground and he leaned against that huge old oak tree. His legs were out before him, crossed at the ankles, and his gnarled hands held each other on his lap. His old fashioned clothing had been cleaned by the rain and pressed by his form, and it fit him the way the bark covers a tree.

I stepped down and moved towards the old man, when he raised his arm and pointed at me, and the force of his manner held me fast and I could not move." Maura stepped down from the stone before the altar and moved towards the old oak tree, then she stopped.

"He spoke to me, but I do not know the sound of his voice. Perhaps the words came only to my mind. He said this to me in a rhyme.

Bal and Lugh were worshipped here And from the sea, Man'nan MacLir

Many Gods in ages past. Stain on stain, Christ but the last.

God is one, diverse his fate This stone and I, man await.

He pointed with a sprig of mistletoe and I moved as in a trance to the spring and the small pool of clear water by it. It was so quiet, I could not hear even the birds singing or rustling in the leaves. Perhaps my ears had stopped working. Close by the pool there was a small cup. I rinsed and filled the cup and it seemed to be of silver or pewter, and the water in it was shiny and dancing."

Here Maura moved trancelike to the spring and mimed filling her cup. I brought the cup of blessed water to him and he drank. He smacked his lips and drank again. He blessed me with his Druid's wand of mistletoe. I took the cup and drank and I made the sign of the cross, protecting us both. He nodded and spoke again in a younger, stronger voice and the wrinkles all left his cheeks and his hands grew smooth and young.

Hunter and game oft here met. Wet red stream, blood of the lamb.

Lamb of God, race of Cain

Again, sacrifice or roam Homeless, hungry, bones and hide.

The old man stood and he appeared young and strong and he stood straight and his bark-like clothing changed into chain mail and his voice rose. It was clear and commanding.

The stranger came, strong, guilt free. Leg'cy of shame, Penal Law

Raw his gift to native son.

Won he Erin, cleaving God

God pity you, oh stranger.

Suddenly, he brandished a sword and menaced me with it.

Wide your legs. Accept my thrust, Just my cause, submit you must.

Thus planted the stranger"

Maura suddenly slumped against the tree and she seemed to shrink before their eyes.

"And then he was as before. The conqueror's armor faded and he was an old man in tattered clothing again. He opened his two arms wide, with his palms facing me in a Christ like welcome and blessing. Then he began to fade and I could see through him and I saw the tree behind him as he spoke these last words and put them into my mind.

This rock, bloody and ancient. Anciently stained and waiting,

Waiting for you, oh stranger. Danger gone; you are blest.

Maura crouched down and held up her arms in defense. "The sky clouded over and this green air before me became dark and cold. A slow wet rain fell on me and I left this place. It wasn't until I was well away from here, that I realized I still had the shiny silver cup in my hand. So said our grandfather to his son. So said our father to his daughters. And so, out of love, we give this truth and this story and this blessing to all of you now."

From a deep pocket, Maura drew forth an old tin cup, dented and discolored. She walked to the pool of clear water, rinsed and filled the cup and brought it to the two priests. Rene drank and blessed her in his native French. Rory drank, extended his hands to her head and gave her his blessing. In this silent ritual, she refilled the cup and brought it to the bridal couple. Deirdre drank and with tears flowing she kissed and thanked Maura. Jay drank and gave Maura a gentle kiss of thanks for this gift of a story on their wedding day.

Maura filled the cup once more and moving very gracefully she approached Dermot with the cup held out before her in both hands. She made a deep curtsy and raised the cup near to Dermot's lips.

"If my love takes and drinks from this, we shall be married before the four seasons pass."

She stood before him, a beautiful, smart, willing and patient woman. He covered her two hands with his own and together they raised the cup to his lips and he drank all of the clear water. Maura's eyes sparkled and her walk to the spring was exultant as she filled the cup again and went to her sister and handed the cup to Mary Rose. "Drink sister." When Mary Rose finished drinking, Maura asked, "Will you help me share and bring our gift to the rest of this group." She gestured wide, "our beloved Motleys, here assembled."

Mary Rose repeated her sister's path and she brought the first cup of water to her Declan. She curtsied and proposed to him with her cup of clear water held high. But he, Declan, brushed her away spilling some of the water and refused to drink.

"Mary Rose, stop it will you. I'm not at all big on this magic, so." He backed further away from her. "When it's our time, we'll know. We don't need field water from an old dented cup."

She threw the rest of the cup of water in his face and in a fury she turned and marched back to the spring where she knelt with her back to the group and gathered herself before filling the cup again. Mary Rose, her eyes overflowing, brought the cup to Donal, who drank and gave her a bashful kiss on the cheek. "Pay him no mind, darling Mary Rose. He has a bit of growing up yet to do."

She went to Mac and he drank and hugged her tight and thanked her for her part in all of their exciting adventures. Almost stumbling now and beginning to cry, she carried the cup to Fritz.

He adjusted his monocle and said loud enough for all to hear, "Ask again your question, lovely Mary Rose and I vill say *ich will,* I will. Yes. Yes. And again yes. I vould be honored to have such a woman as you are." He took the cup and drank all of it. He clicked his heels and bowed deeply, then he gave her his handkerchief.

Mary Rose, still sniffling but managing much better, went to fill the cup one last time and offer a drink of the clear water to her sister. She gave a venomous glare at Declan as she passed him in the small green glen.

Declan, embarrassed and sorry for his response to her, sought redemption in a joke. He bellowed out, "BeGod almighty, girl, next thing you'll be telling me you believe in the Little People."

Mary Rose, kneeling at the spring and crying quietly to herself, shouted out, "I do not believe in the Little People, Declan O'Mahon." She paused. "But they are real, all the same." She carried the filled cup to Maura. "Thank you Maura for making me a part of this. I barely remember being here with you and Da, but I'll remember now. I will remember all of this." And she glared again at Declan.

Dermot, after conferring with Mac and Fritz, had a plan. "We need the hearse turned about. I want it facing out, uphill and ready to go. Also, your Da Sean will have a better view of your wedding. Jay, you and Deirdre and Mac are assigned to the hearse. Next, we'll have the Coveney car, Rory driving. Then the motorcycle with Declan and Donal need to be out of this glen, now before the wedding. Rory, I want you to follow Declan, he'll show you where to hide the automobile where it can be reached by using the secret passage behind the Mass Rock. Lastly, I want the good doctor's car turned and pointing out. When we've finished our tasks, everyone back here. Oh and Deirdre, how long will it take you to get dressed and get married"? Dermot smiled at his cousin to soften that hard question.

"Dermot O'Rourke. If your mother were here…"

"Sorry Deirdre darling. I know. I'm far out of bounds on this, and I am sorry, but I feel uneasy. We've been here overlong and I wish we could hurry things along a wee bit."

The Coveney sisters each took one of Deirdre's arms and the three of them went behind the sheets and into their green dressing room. Three dresses were hung from an oak limb and a small picnic table held Deirdre's oak and leather jewel case, a mirror, makeup bags, and combs and brushes. The ladies went to work on each other, with Deirdre the bride first.

"Before you all move away," Rory held the men together. "Can you make sure when you turn the hearse around that the casket, that is Sean O'Neill in the casket, has his feet facing the altar. Church law requires it. Only the clergy may have their head towards the altar."

Rene took the small grip that Rory had brought and set aside the black vestments for the now canceled Requiem Mass. He put on a white surplice and around his waist he tied his cincure, a long white rope-like cord whose ends fell down along his leg. The surplice was of a fine linen with exquisite lace along the collar, the bottom edge and the ends of both sleeves. He took his white stole, kissed it and hung it around his neck. Father Rene was almost ready.

"Maura *mon cher*, I must 'ave a cup of holy water for this wedding ceremony. May I borrow your small chalice?" Her hand, with the cup in it, appeared from between the hanging sheets. "*Merci, Merci mon cher.*"

Holding the cup from Maura, Rene poured the last of the holy water out of the bottle brought there by Rory. Wanting more, he went and added a bit of the clear spring water to the cup. He ascended the stone step, placed his cup upon the altar and said his prayers. While praying his mind wandered and he pictured himself saying mass before a crowd of his people, when red coated soldiers ran into the glen, shouting, shooting and bayoneting his people. Rene shook his head to clear away that bloody vision. He had no idea how he, Father Rene Jean Batiste de la Salle would react. Would he run? Or would he fight? Could he, as Rory has said he would do, offer a blessing to the soldiers? They too were children of God.

Mary Rose came through the dressing room sheets all done up in her new rose-colored dress. She had a pert little matching hat that sat forward on her shiny hair and gave her a pixie look. She carried her fiddle and asked Rene if she could play while he prayed.

"Ah, mais oui. Prayer and music are like bread and wine, or like a man and a woman. Alone they may exist, but together, ahah!" Rene kissed his fingertips. "They were always meant to be together. I will pray and you will play. This is life, yes?"

To the group Mary Rose said, "Because we are in an ancient and holy place, and because the ancient ways are mostly ignored, I will begin with an offering to those 'Old Ones'." Here she looked directly at Declan, "I will play, 'The Faeries Lamentation and Dance'."

Mary Rose played with wild abandon, moving and swooping her body in time to the tempo and spirit of her music. She moved and played from the altar to the spring; in a circle she moved through the green sun dappled glen, spreading her Faerie music completely around and behind the altar, where Mary Rose disappeared and only her music was visible under the canopy of tree branches. She ended halfway between the altar and the dressing room. Mary Rose sank to one knee and played soft music and waited for her sister and Deirdre to emerge.

Jay, resplendent in his full dress Navy uniform, moved to one side of the altar and next to him as his Best Man was Gregor MacGregor in his bright, colorful MacGregor clan plaid. Mac took a plain gold band out of his pocket and placed it into Jay's palm, then closed his fingers around it. "My wife's wedding band. She took it off before she died and made me promise I would not bury it with her. She had the second sight you know, my Regina, my wonderful black haired Welch woman. 'Put it to good use,' she said. 'You will know when and where.' So, Jay. This is where and now is when.

I want you to put this on the hand of your bride, and she will partake of and add to the love that is in it." Jay wanted to protest, but Mac stopped him. "I am your Da, now." He grinned at Jay, "and you must be a dutiful son. Obey me in this."

Declan was again dressed in his half aviator half messenger outfit while Donal was in an Army Tunic and plain black trousers. Dermot was dressed in a new dark green military uniform with an I.R.B. shoulder patch and lieutenants shoulder bars. Rory was attired as a simple parish priest and Fritz wore a dark blue outfit of military cut but with no emblems, badges or national insignia. He could have come from any continental armed force, but no country was identified. The group wore a motley assortment of clothing and was well and truly named The Nimble Motleys.

Dermot gave his last instructions. Rory and Fritz were to be in the meadow of the glen near the stone altar and at the first sign of trouble they were to rush the ladies behind the altar and away through the secret passage.

Donal and Declan would go up the hill into the woods, one on each side, and keep an eye out for any intruders. "Pick a place where you can see the approaches to our glen, and also see down through the trees to the stone altar. Watch the wedding, indeed, but watch our safety first. Go now and be careful. Donal you have your rifle and Declan you have that long barreled pistol on the lanyard. Be ready. Be careful. Our lives are in your hands."

Dermot walked over and took his place alongside Mary Rose who was still crouched down and holding her fiddle ready to play. The sheets parted and Maura stepped slowly out as her sister began to play the Wedding March. She had on a pale green dress that showed off her fine figure and a matching hat that was a feminine adaptation of a man's slouch hat with a small veil attached.

Maura took Dermot's breath away and he almost forgot to look at Deirdre as she emerged from her sheet-hung woodsy dressing room in her grandmother's Ivory Paper Silk wedding gown. She wore the ancient family heirloom gold and emerald brooch at her throat, the matching earrings, and the ring to the set was on her right hand. Deirdre took Dermot's arm for the short walk across the green glen to the primitive Mass Rock altar stone.

Jay felt his knees tremble at the sight of Deirdre. Mac, his best man, stood next to him and squeezed his elbow to steady him and Jay watched and heard his bride approaching. Her two-piece gown was very crisp and the paper-thin silk made a crinkly sound as she came toward him.

Everyone seemed to hold their breathe and even the music was muted, so the crinkly sound of her silk gown filled the space around them.

Delicate Irish lace and a full veil muted her beauty and her dark flowing hair but it gave her an air of mystery. The lace adorned the low neckline and was worn again at each wrist. The full length skirt was superb with the lovely fly-tie silk trim and delicate silk flowers sewn down each side. It swept to the ground hiding her feet and she appeared to float across the small glen towards him. Rene stood behind the men, waiting to unite the couple.

Jay's heart leapt in his chest and he did not breathe. He thought of his first sight of her on the Trans Siberian Rail Road and how he couldn't take his eyes from her. He remembered how he must have dozed off then, for the next time he looked up, she had changed seats and was now facing him. She was incredibly beautiful. From her long dark hair, her eyes up tilted at the corners, her wide generous mouth now in a half smile and her peaceful posture as she dozed in her seat. Jay was enthralled and even more so when he learned later, after they were lovers, that she had been awake and through slitted eyelids she had watched him watch her.

Thoughts of the two of them making love got him excited, and he was impatient for the ceremony to be over and for the two of them to be on to more basic carnal endeavors. Jay sighed and told himself to slow down. Standing next to his priest friend and being at an altar, even a pagan one, called for a different line of thinking. He inhaled deep down to the bottom of his lungs and let his breathe out slow and smiled at Deirdre. Jay wondered what she was thinking as she moved toward him step by slow step in time with Mary Rose's fiddle playing the Wedding March. Still, he wondered where they would spend heir first night together as a married couple. The Coveney's Inn was close. That would be a good choice.

Dermot lifted Deirdre's veil, gave her a cousinly kiss and handed her over to Jay. Now the four of them, Deirdre on the left and Jay on the right, flanked by Maura and Mac as witnesses, stood before Rene.

"My dear friends: You are about to enter into a union which is most sacred and most serious." Rene looked upon the couple before him with affection and raised his eyes to Dermot who had moved back and stood next to Rory and Fritz. "In the interest of brevity we will dispense with the rather lengthy 'Instruction Before Marriage', part of the ceremony."

"John Joseph O'Neill, wilt thou take Deirdre DalCas here present, for thy lawful wife, according to the rite of our Holy Mother the Church?"

Jay looked at Deirdre, smiled and looked up at Rene. "I will."

"Deirdre DalCas, wilt thou take John Joseph O'Neill, here present, for thy lawful husband, according to the rite of our Holy Mother the Church?"

"I will." Deirdre smiled at Jay, turned to Rene, and said it again in French. *"Oui, je le veux."*

"Join together your right hands." Rene next motioned them to turn in towards each other.

Together and to each other, they repeated after Rene. "I Jay O'Neill, 'I Deirdre DalCas', take thee for my lawful wife, 'husband', to have and to hold from this day forward, for better, for worse, for richer, for poorer, in sickness and in health, until death do us part."

Rene smiled so broadly his face seemed in danger of coming apart. "You may kneel and face me, my loved ones. *Bien.* I join you together in marriage, in the name of the Father," He made a large, high and wide, sign of the cross over them. "and of the Son and of the Holy Ghost, Amen." Rene took Maura's cup, now his chalice, and sprinkled them quite liberally with holy water. "If you have a ring, I will now bless it and you Deirdre, who will wear it." Mac pointed to Jay's pocket, and Jay gave the up ring to Rene.

Deirdre gave Jay a gentle nudge and he remembered to take the old Spanish ring Deirdre had given him off of his right hand and give it to Rene.

"Our help in is the name of the Lord…" Rene continued with the blessing of the rings.

There was a distraction out in the meadow of the glen. Declan came down the hill leading two men and in a hoarse whisper heard by everyone, he explained that they were musicians he had invited to play for the wedding. One carried a flute and a bodhran, a sort of native Irish drum. The other was a piper. He carried the uilean concert pipes. Declan handed around a bag of rice and told them all to take a handful. Dermot kept hissing at him to get back to his post up on the hillside.

Rene carried on with his blessing of the rings. He crossed himself and the rings and the couple kneeling "…Bless oh Lord this ring, which we bless in Thy name, that she who is to wear it, keeping true faith unto her husband, may abide in Thy peace and obedience to Thy will, and ever live in mutual love. Through the same Christ our Lord, Amen." Rene then did the same for Jay and his ring.

All the Motleys repeated the 'Amen's'. Some whispered it low and fervent, while some others sang out 'Amen' with great gusto.

Rene sprinkled her ring with holy water in the form of a cross and handed it to Jay. Jay took Deirdre's left hand and placed the ring on her third finger. "With this ring, I thee wed, and I plight unto thee my troth."

Rene then blessed his ring and handed it to Deirdre. She took Jay's left hand and placed the ring on his third finger. "With this ring, I thee wed, and I plight unto thee my troth."

Rene blessed them again, "In nomine Patris, et Filii, et Spiritus Sancti, Amen. You may kiss your bride, my son."

A great shout of joy rose up from all of the Motleys and Mary Rose broke into a spirited reel. The flute player joined in and the piper sat on the rear fender of the hearse and tuned up his pipes. Rory grabbed the bodran and began beating time with the small bone used to beat the ancient skin drum.

The reel was followed by a jig, then a hornpipe, a mazurka and finally a waltz. The group danced and high stepped; they kissed the bride, and shook the hand of the groom and hugs and kisses flew from one to another and over it all the music colored the green glen and it all seemed so together, so wonderful, so right.

From somewhere, Maura had a bottle of whiskey. Mac asked Rene if the chalice could become a tin cup once again. Rene nodded yes and poured the last of the holy water over the flat top of the massive stone that was the altar of their Mass Rock and he said a prayer of thanks and last, he gave a blessing for holy places.

He handed the cup to Mac, who had Maura fill it, and Mac handed it back to Rene who smiled and took a tiny sip. He smiled wider and nodded as Mac and Maura moved with the bottle and the cup to the dancers. Each of the Motleys had their measure, from Jay who took a fine wedding day swallow, to Deirdre who was already so high with excitement, she had only a tiny sip, to Dermot whose sense of duty allowed him to barely wet his tongue with the good twenty-five year old whiskey.

The waltz music was achingly beautiful. Mac and Fritz watched with approval as Dermot whirled Maura round and round in front of the spring and little pool of water. Jay and Deirdre had eyes only for each other as they dipped and twirled around the glen and moved from deep shadow to sun dappled grass meadow and back again to the front of the altar.

Mary Rose announced a song special for Deirdre and began to play The Green Fields of America. The flute and the piper joined in and the newly weds danced on.

Declan came down the hill and to the edge of the clearing. He motioned to Mary Rose to bring him the cup at her feet so he might have his wedding toast. She shook her head no at him and kept on playing. Declan strode into the small meadow and went over to Mary Rose.

BANG. A pistol shot rang out. CRACK. CRACK. Two rifle shots came in quick succession.

Declan crumbled down the way a rag doll would and it being discarded. He lay in a pool of his own blood. Deirdre sagged back against Jay. Her Ivory Paper Silk wedding dress had a red stain high up on her chest and she never made a sound.

CHAPTER ELEVEN

Declan went down in a heap and Mary Rose screamed and ran the few steps to him. She knelt in a widening pool of his blood and cradled his head in her arms. Then she held her hand hard against his neck to stop the spurting blood, but it was to no avail. He died in her arms very quickly.

Rene came the few steps over to give Declan the Last Rites. He stood over Mary Rose and blessed her too as she knelt crying in the pool of Declan's blood but he knew that no amount of blessings would take away her pain and loss nor lessen her sorrow.

"Is that Declan's blood on Deirdre?" Mac came running to Jay who was kneeling almost alongside Mary Rose who was holding Declan. He held Deirdre on his knees.

"No. My Deirdre's been shot. It's her own blood. But she's alive." He was pressing his shirttail against the wound, but the red stain kept spreading across the ivory gown.

Dermot came down one side of the hill and Donal the other. "I saw only the two men, Dermot. One fired his pistol and the other fired a rifle. I killed the rifleman, but he did get off a shot. The one with the pistol ran away. Are we hurt? Is any one of us hurt?"

"I heard Mary Rose screaming." Dermot shouted. "I think Declan is shot, maybe dead. And Jay is holding Deirdre, but listen to me now, Donal. You're my best man and we must protect the rest of the Motleys. Go you now, out through the secret passage. Take Declan's bike and circle all around us. Look carefully. Make sure there are no more of them, and by Christ do capture that one bastard who ran away from here if you can."

Donal turned, hefted his rifle and trotted toward the altar stone. He knelt and made a quick appraisal of Declan's body. He moved two steps to Deirdre where an ashen Jay assured him Deirdre lived and Donal ran then behind the stone and out through the secret passage to Declan's motorcycle.

Rene turned and knelt alongside Jay and Deirdre. "Sed libera nos a malo. But deliver us from evil, Jay and Deirdre." He prayed for her and called out for Rory.

Mac answered, "what do you need, Rene?"

"Rory's kit, the,...the,...his bag for Extreme Unction. I need oils and ointments for the Last Rites, for Declan and maybe for our dear bride, poor Deirdre. Just in case."

Mac called out, "Fritz, Dermot, there's a stretcher in the hearse. Bring it here, for Deirdre. Rory went up into the woods, Rene, with his bag. He said he would anoint that damned soldier if he was dead, or pray with him, if he is alive. I hope he's anointing him."

Mac helped Jay out of his jacket, ripped off Jay's shirt and made a bandage out of part of it. Next he tore down part of the wedding dress neckline and exposed the wound. With the bandage held in place by Jay, Mac used the shirtsleeves to tie it tight around Deirdre's chest and under her arms. Mac studied Jay; he was whiter even than Deirdre.

"It should hold now and stop the bleeding. There's no wound in her back, just in her chest and it never got her heart. Thank God, me boyo, thank God and thank whatever pagan spirits inhabit this glen and crowd around this ancient stone altar."

Rene nodded in agreement, made the sign of the cross and blessed all of them again and this time he included the pagan spirits.

Dermot stood frozen in place, halfway between Declan and Deirdre. He could not move nor could he speak. His cousin Declan was dead and his beloved cousin Deirdre was down and bloody and badly hurt. She had been more like a little sister to him and he was devastated. How could he tell Fiona? What would he say to her?

He blamed himself. He had failed as leader of this group, his wonderful, trusting Nimble Motleys. He had let them down.

Maura came and led him the few steps to the Mass Rock and sat him down on the stone step. She found the cup in the same spot, just in front of where Mary Rose had been playing her music, before the shots rang out and changed their lives forever.

Slowly she urged Dermot to taste the whiskey, and she soon had a half cup inside of him and he stopped shivering. He set the cup down on the stone beside him, took her hand and kissed her fingers and then he kissed the warm palm of her hand. They looked at each other and he whispered to her, "My God, Maura was it only yesterday at your house?"

"Aye Dermot. And that is where we all shall go right now. We will get a surgeon in for Deirdre and we will prepare Declan for a proper wake and a funeral. He went away from us much too young and he will be sorely missed by all of us and 'twill be a wrenching blow to poor Mary Rose. She had picked Declan to be her man, reluctant though he was."

Dermot stood up and made believe he was himself. "All right Nimble Motleys." He gulped and caught himself almost crying as he called out the name given to them by Declan. "We leave now, my Nimble Motleys, what's left of us," he added. "We are headed back to Coveney's Inn. And we shall go together and as a proper funeral caravan.

The bike goes first with Donal diving. The hearse goes next. Jay, you and Mac, Deirdre on the stretcher and Declan..." Here he stopped and wiped his eyes, and blew his nose. "Some of you please place Declan in the black wooden coffin. It's there in the hearse, next to Sean O'Neill. Pray to God we won't need a third coffin."

"It's done already, Dermot." Mac took charge. "Declan is in his coffin. Maura, will you ride with us and take charge of Deirdre, and Mary Rose can ride...."

"Mary Rose is already in the hearse with Declan," Maura said. "She will not leave his side. She will ride along and be next to Declan, next to his body."

"Rory and Rene will have the Coveney car and they should keep their vestments on and drive ahead of the hearse. You two priests want to be very visible."

"Good Mac. Fine idea and thanks." Dermot was becoming himself again. "I'll drive the good doctor's motorcar and Fritz will be my companion. Take everything people. Leave nothing behind, please. We don't know if this is over yet."

Dermot stopped and watched as four men approached them. They walked slow and easy down the slope into the glen. Two carried rifles and one had a revolver tucked into his waistband and he was pushing and prodding the fourth man ahead of him. "The two with rifles are friends," Dermot whispered to Mac.

"The one being pushed at us, him with his head down, that's Wee Willie Burke," Mac said.

"Devil Burke." Dermot looked him up and down and curled his lip. "His trousers are wet."

At that moment Rory came down the hillside, into the meadow, "There's a dead soldier up there. I gave him the Last Rites, but his body should be taken care of." He saw the newcomers and held out his hand to the man with the pistol, "Well, how good to see you..."

Dermot cut Rory off. "No names here father. We all know who we are."

Rory came close and whispered to Dermot and Mac, "That's Wee Willie Burke and the other with the hand gun is my friend the owner of this land where the Mass Rock sits, where we are standing just now."

Rory's friend, the landowner spoke up. "I found him skulking along with this still in his hand." He pulled the revolver from his waist, reversed it and handed it butt first to Dermot. "It's been fired today. You can still smell it. The one shot only."

"Thank you, that's grand. Perhaps some day I may repay you for your effort and courage. Right now we must be away."

"I understand," the landowner nodded his head sideways and stepped back a few paces.

Donal drove into the glen and appraised the situation. He smiled at the two riflemen and nodded at the landowner.

To the two riflemen Dermot indicated Wee Willie. "We'll take charge of this baggage if you will carry off the soldier on the hill. He's had his Last Rites, he deserves nothing more than to be put into the ground."

The leader of the two riflemen looked at Dermot's uniform and grinned. "We'll take care of your little problem, Leftenant, we sure to God will."

Dermot realized these men from the West Cork Brigade had never seen the new uniform he was wearing and he appreciated the smile. He flicked a bit of imaginary dust off of his sleeve and smiled at the newcomers.

To Donal he said, "Put Devil Burke in your sidecar and secure his hands down below the cowling. I want no one to know he's our prisoner. Take his gun and tell him you'll shoot him with it if he makes a sound." Dermot handed off the gun. "And get him out of our sight now before Jay or I decide to take his head off."

After Burke was gone the silent one of the two riflemen spoke up. "Dermot, do you want the dead one's papers or anything?" Dermot shook his head no. "Well now, a way out in the back of beyond, there's a wee small quarry, out past the crossroads at Beal na Blath. He'll be residing there if you ever need him." As they were leaving he spoke again. "Had he a rifle, Dermot, or a pistol?"

"A rifle. It should be near his body. He killed Declan with it, and wounded Deirdre."

"Sorry Dermot." The man crossed himself. "So sorry, and on this, her wedding day. And poor Declan gone, altogether." He nodded. "Grand meeting all of you. When Ireland is free we'll have a drink together. Ach Dermot, was there not an automobile with them?"

Dermot nodded yes, then said, "You keep it. It will be found not far from the body."

The two rebel soldiers walked uphill into the woods to pick up the dead soldier, his rifle and to find Wee Willie's car, which would be found not far from the body.

They shook hands all around and the landowner, a good Protestant and fierce Irish patriot, smiled, "I must fade away now and become a good subject of the English King once again. It's not yet time for me to be open about my real loyalty to my own country."

William Burke was thoroughly cowed. He sat in the sidecar in his wet trousers with his hands tied and could not even scratch his nose when it itched, as it often did when he went out of doors and into the countryside. He did not like Ireland, not one bit.

Of course he was born here, on his mother's estate. But he had never liked it here, and especially not out in the wilds of Western Cork County. There were a few mildly interesting places in Dublin but the rest of the country was all one big bog as far as he was concerned. And the people were, almost without exception, uneducated bog trotters and rebellious louts.

Dermot came and spoke to him like a Dutch Uncle and told him how it would be if they were ever stopped. "Burke you are an Oxford Don. You have vast estates up near Kilkenny. You are part of the Lusitania investigation and you are part of this funeral cortege because you are going to bury a very dear friend who went down with the ship. His name is Sean O'Neill and he died a hero, trying to save infants aboard the Lusitania."

Wee Willie agreed to everything. "Could I have my hands free, Please?" Willie thought of arguing but the look on Dermot's face scared him. "One hand. Please." He pleaded for mercy but neither Mac, nor Fritz would even talk to him and Rene stayed far away.

The ride out of the glen was slow and painful. Dermot didn't like bringing up the rear but he saw the wisdom of having the two priests out front and visible. Once they made it back to the hard road their speed picked up but Dermot was very troubled and Fritz had a good ear.

"I am the leader, Fritz. I am responsible."

"Ja. Who leads is always responsible."

"I should've had more men out there, watching, standing guard."

"Ja."

"At least four more. Two close in and two more posted a ways out."

"Ja."

"And..."

Fritz patted his shoulder. *"Ja herr Dermot O 'Rourke. Ja.* And they should be alert sentries. And they should be non-drinker sentries. *Ja, Ja."* He patted Dermot again.

They were silent for a long time. They drove into and through the walled city of Bandon without incident, each lost in private thoughts, when finally Fritz said, "In war, for the leader, it is the wounds we cause in others that hurt the most and stay the longest."

With a few quick adjustments the hearse had been converted into an ambulance. Maura, ever practical and always competent, had filled two bottles at the spring, knowing they would need water on this trip. She had removed the wooden slat backrest from the bench seat so she could sit facing backwards. Now she could help Jay tend to Deirdre and hold the stretcher steady and keep it from sliding and slipping as the hearse moved along.

Jay was half sitting on the foot of Declan's black coffin and half kneeling on the floorboards between the coffin and Sean's new casket. Deirdre, on the stretcher, had been carried in head first and laid upon a pile of blankets on top of Sean's casket. The stretcher tended to slide and move around with every curve in the road. It had to be held and steadied to protect Deirdre, and keep her wound from opening.

Jay, facing the back of the hearse, took a bottle of water, wet his finger and passed it slowly over Deirdre's parched lips. He did this again and again and some water seeped into her mouth. Deirdre swallowed and licked her lips. Jay quickly put more water on her tongue and lips. She licked her lips again and opened her eyes. His eyes were so filled with tears he couldn't focus on her face. Deirdre managed to lift her right arm and guide Jay's face down to her mouth. She kissed his mouth, his nose and his eyes, once again tasting his salty tears.

"Are we married now, my Jay?" Deirdre's voice was low and hoarse.

"Yes Deirdre. We're married now." Jay choked but managed to get the words out.

"Oooh good. I'm safe now. You said I'd be safe once we were married. Am I safe, Jay?"

Jay swallowed his sobs so not to alarm his bride. "Yes. Yes my love. We're both safe now."

"Happy wedding day, my love," she whispered to him and licked her dry lips.

He couldn't answer, but he tried to hold her close without holding her so he wouldn't hurt her wounded chest. "Thank God you're alive," he managed after a bit. "I love you, wife of my heart." Jay wet his fingers and dabbed at her lips, spilling water as the hearse moved ahead.

In the back, Mary Rose knelt on the floorboards with her head resting on her one arm, which she had around Declan's black coffin. She kept crooning to him in a sing-song musical litany about forgiveness and love. "Did I scare you, darling Declan. My passion is so strong. I had no patience. Should have waited. You would've caught up. Forgive me my love." With her other arm, Mary Rose helped to steady the stretcher. She kept moving between dreams of what might've been with Declan to strong reality whenever Deirdre's stretcher began to slide.

Mac, alone in front, drove as he had never driven before. He heard Deirdre moan in pain whenever he went over a bad spot, and so he pictured the road ahead paved with eggshells. "Come on you bastards. Fix these roads. Slow now MacGregor, around this curve. I'm going very careful, Jay. Sorry Deirdre. I must make haste for you, but very, very gently."

They were around a bend in the road when Dermot pulled to a stop behind the hearse and Donal on the cycle came back to him. "A quarter mile back, our big expensive touring automobile is parked outside a pub, the motorcar Declan sold for us. If it is indeed the good doctor, Rory wants to go back and get him. Have him come to Coveney's for Deirdre. He's a military surgeon. The man is used to treating gunshot wounds, the way I'm used to making them, so." Donal's voice rose up and his eyebrows followed. His face was sad but hopeful.

Mac stuck his head in the other window. "I like it, Dermot. What say you?"

"I like it as well." Dermot pulled out a wad of bills. "Here's some of his own money back to him. Tell him we have a gun shot victim to be treated. Discretion and haste is the way to go, Mac. He must come now and there's more money coming to him. You go Mac. You and Rory. And bring his nurse as well. Nothing but the best for Deirdre. We'll have The Cracker Jack surgeon for Deirdre and with him we get the best surgical nurse in seven continents."

Under his breath he added, "and you my darling Declan were a pure seven day wonder. We will miss you something fierce." Now that the immediate danger was past, the death of Declan was becoming real to him.

He handed Mac a pistol. "Last resort. Shanghai him if you have to. We'll push on ahead to Coveney's Inn. I'll drive the hearse; you ride with the good doctor and his nurse. Don't let him get lost or get away. Deirdre needs him." Mac agreed and went with Rory to get the doctor. Dermot turned to Fritz, "Can you drive, Fritz?"

"*Ja. Ja.* Bad leg, my cane, my limp and all, I can drive. You go Dermot and be the leader you are." Fritz locked eyes with Dermot. "Every leader suffers losses and you have just been tested. Go. You will lead us to the Inn."

"Thank you Fritz. For everything. You really understood."

"*Ja. Ja.* You go lead. I am now a follower *und* a driver." He shifted into the drivers seat with some difficulty, waved goodbye to Dermot and rubbed his hands together in sheer glee in anticipation of driving this fine modern automobile. "I must let Rene see me driving," he said to himself. "He vill see his friend is not just a limping old warrior."

Soon, on a straight stretch of road, the large touring car zoomed past them. The good doctor sat alone in the open front seat. He leaned forward and seemed to be urging the big car to go even faster. He had a look of total joy on his face. In the enclosed rear compartment the nurse held onto the side strap with both hands. She looked scared to death. Mac, also in the rear, grinned at the Nimble Motleys as he passed them by.

When the caravan arrived at the Inn, the big car was parked at a crazy angle directly in front of the main entrance. The cook had tried to keep him out, but the good doctor bullied his way in and barked out orders. Mac explained to her what the doctor needed, then joined him in pushing tables together, flinging chairs out of the way and looking for lamps.

"Blankets, towels and sheets," the good doctor yelled. "Boiling water, and the best lights you have, I need light. Nurse!" He looked around for his nurse. "What's wrong with you?"

Mac went to the door and helped her in. She was quite shaken from the wild ride here.

"Come on, dear. Get a move on. I need my operating clothes. Bring the kit with all my knives, and bring bandages, and the anesthetic. Well you know what we need, just bring all of it. Now." He saw her face and softened his tone. "Please hurry Nurse. I need you."

In a flash the best surgical nurse in seven continents began living up to her name. She quick marched out to the car, captured Father Rory and loaded him up with bags, cases and grips. "And do not forget that small bag with his knives. He must have his knives."

"Yes my dear, of course. Leave that now," Rory indicated a large bag that nurse was struggling with. "I'll make another trip and bring it in for you. You just go and be nurse to the good doctor. We must give poor Deirdre our best. Today was her wedding day."

Jay and Dermot with Donal and Rene lifted Deirdre on her stretcher out of the hearse and with great care they got her into the dining room of the Inn. "Careful now." With the nurse directing they lifted her off the stretcher and onto the makeshift operating table

Maura, once she stepped back into the Inn, was again in her element. She took charge of everything that was not medical or military. Her first move was to give her grieving sister something to do. "Mary Rose, go change your clothes. I want you in the dining room. You will do everything to assist that nurse. Try to anticipate her needs, and the doctor's needs, same as you do with our guests. Think like them and try and be in front of them. God knows, the way things are going in this world, medical skills will be in great demand."

Next she stopped in the kitchen and gave the cook a brief outline of the situation and told her what needed to be done. "Food, tea, constant boiling hot water for the operating room, set up a long table in the sitting room lounge, service for twelve, and get in two of your nieces to help us. I want the best two."

Next she intruded onto the military side. "Dermot, for God's sake bring all the men out to the enclosed garden, especially Jay. He is in there hovering about and getting in the way. And, I'd suggest the hearse and all should park around the back just like before. Can you step in here for a minute, please Dermot?"

Once they were in the scullery with the door closed, she pressed herself against him and their kiss became a long and passionate embrace and they made promises to each other for more. "Now, what do you need for Devil Burke? How can I help with that amadan".

"Maura you are the grandest woman. You can swing from passion to business in the blink of an eye. I need a room with a good secure lock on the door and one that has no windows."

She moved close again and slid her leg in between his two legs. "I have a room like that, but I was saving it for us." She laughed and wriggled in his embrace. "Do you think I am a hussy Mr. O'Rourke?"

"Indeed I do, Maura Ni Coveney. And I intend to marry you as soon as possible so you're not out ruining any other innocent young man." He held her close and caressed her body.

She kissed him again and whispered in his ear, "we will see tonight just who ruins who." Maura stepped back into her business role. "Suppose I take Jay on a tour of the Inn and let him select a room for Burke."

"That's grand. He knows what we need and it will ease his mind to be doing something. How is Mary Rose?"

"The same as Jay. She is busy now helping the good doctor's nurse and so she has put her grief into the back corner of her mind."

Dermot left her rummaging in the scullery for the Inn's emergency medical kit. He assembled all the men in the walled garden, with the exception of Donal who stood guard over Wee Willie in the sidecar. Willie's hands were now free and he was busy scratching his nose and ears and under his chin. Any flies or biting bugs were long gone but he still itched.

"Jay is with Maura on a search of the Inn. He'll pick out a small room, no windows and easily locked." Dermot had all the men assembled, but he relied for advice on the two old soldiers, Mac and Fritz. He turned first to MacGregor. "Mac?"

Mac slammed the garden table they were sitting at. "When you anticipate an attack and it finally comes, it is a shock, of course, but it's almost a relief as well. A feeling of 'let's get on with it'." The other men nodded agreement except Rory who jumped at the violent slam and the noise it made.

He looked puzzled, and Mac tried to put it in perspective for him. "Rory look, you train for years, you expect to be put to the test but when it comes it's a shock and a relief too. You wonder will you do what's expected of you, and then your training kicks in and you succeed. Do you remember after your ordination, the first time you sat in the confessional and some person told you their closely guarded secrets and you had to forgive their sins. That was a serious matter, wasn't it?"

Rory agreed. "More serious than the shooting death of Declan and the wounding of Deirdre. I deal with the immortal soul and make decisions about others that will last for all eternity."

"Amen, Rory, well spoken." Rene encouraged Rory.

"What really astounded me," Mac went on. "No one bolted behind the altar stone and out the secret passage to safety. Everyone stayed and helped another in our group. I am so proud of you, every one, and I am pleased to be one of the Nimble Motleys." Mac looked at each in turn. "Now let us reconstruct the attack. Did anyone hear four shots? Rory half raised his hand. Did anyone hear two shots?" No one responded.

Jay entered the garden from the Inn followed by one of the new helpers. The girl carried a tray loaded with tea and cups for everyone. When she left Jay declared, "There were three shots. A small one first, probably a pistol, followed very fast by two rifle shots."

Dermot agreed. "Donal killed the rifleman, but only after he got off that one shot. That's the shot that killed poor Declan. That accounts for the two rifle shots. Devil Burke must've shot Deirdre with his pistol."

"*Ja, drei.* Three shots. I think you are most right except for Villy. He is not capable of shooting anyone himself. He hires it done for him. I think he fired in the air. Rifle man shoots at Deirdre, but Declan steps into the line of fire. Bullet takes him through the neck and goes into Deirdre. Yes? Mac? Is it not so?"

"I think you are correct, as usual, Fritz. We'll know for sure when the good doctor has finished patching Deirdre. Jay, make sure you get the bullet from him."

"I will indeed. I intend to have it mounted on my watch chain. When Deirdre and I are old and sitting in our rockers I'll pull out my watch and say to her, remember that time out in West Cork, when we got married and then you were shot?" They smiled and laughed and the tension eased somewhat.

"This Inn is quite the place. We found a small locked room where Maura keeps the wine and spirits. No windows, either. After moving everything drinkable to another room, it's like a monks cell. Just big enough for a cot, a table and two chairs. Wee Willy is in there, pleading for mercy, and he is ready to talk. He's all yours, Dermot."

"*Ja,* You Dermot must question him most carefully, especially how he connects to the war office in London. What is on paper against Deirdre?" Fritz banged his cane on the ground for emphasis. "Who knows her name?" The garden was very quiet.

"Mac"? Dermot wanted advice from his other main advisor as well.

"It sounds ideal, a small room, a small table and two chairs facing each other. You must press him hard, Dermot. At the end, I want his story, on paper, in his hand, signed and witnessed. This is what I want him to say: He pursued this young woman, out of some misguided romantic notion, and used his own money to bribe two or perhaps more, enlisted soldiers. Subsequently he got one of them shot and disabled and another one ran away out of fear of Burke, after taking his money. He hasn't been seen since."

Fritz held up his hand. He was deep in thought. "Is better maybe to press Villy strong, Dermot. Did he shoot? Or order rifleman to shoot. He is then guilty of killing, yes?"

"Murder," Jay pronounced. Rene and Mac winced but Jay went on. "Willie Burke has acted beyond the law, has caused two deaths and innocent people were seriously hurt and he has destroyed government property in the person of two soldiers, during war time."

"In addition, according to Mac, this is not the first time he has done something like this. However, since time has passed and no real evidence of his former misdeeds remain, he will not be charged with any other cases of fraud, bribery and misuse of His Majesties assets." Jay sat back satisfied.

Rene spoke up. "Is any of this true, Gregor? And even if it is, I would not like to see Wee Willie hanged. Would you Gregor? See him hanged? Is this your wish?"

"It's close." Mac smiled. "Close enough that Wee Willie will believe that we can make it very uncomfortable for him if we made this document public. I share Rene's view, I'd not like to see the man swing, though he does deserve it if he gave the order to fire on her."

"He must resign from this Lusitania commission. That should be a separate document." Mac ticked items off on his fingers.

"*Ja, und* from his university position." Fritz added. Rene and Mac agreed.

"*Oui*, and relinquish all titles, rights, money and inheritance from the Burke estates," Rene was emphatic.

Mac seemed satisfied. "We will have stripped him of everything he holds dear. Now, we should give him something to look forward to, a sort of a reward. He will be held as a prisoner, gently enough, after he has signed his confessions and three other papers."

"Sort of a guest of the nation." Dermot was beginning to see daylight in this situation.

"Aye, an honored prisoner guest. However, if Deirdre were to die, he will be executed." Jay spoke with passion tinged with venom.

Rory jumped up. "But Deirdre will live. The good doctor assured me."

"True enough, Rory." Mac smiled. "But Wee Willie doesn't know this."

"How long will he be held, Gregor". Fritz liked to begin with precise dates, numbers and places. He knew from experience that things would go awry anyway, but if you begin with solid plans the chaos might be contained, or at least lessened.

"When Deirdre has recovered enough to travel. When she has sailed away from these contentious islands, Wee Willie will be released the next day into his mother's custody."

"His mother?" Rene exclaimed.

"*Das mutter?*" Fritz was puzzled.

Mac explained. "He will be so damned embarrassed being in a sort of prisoner exchange and given into his mother's care, he will never talk about it. Billy Burke is a good sort and she'll help us keep it quiet, especially after she sees what he has done, what his penalties could've been, and the just punishment he has himself agreed to."

"What about poor Declan?" Dermot asked softly. "Can we get some satisfaction for him? Mac, what do you think is fair?"

"Good point." Mac thought for a minute. "The Burke's are well off and Wee Willie controls most of it. In the document where he relinquishes all monies and titles, add a paragraph saying, an amount shall be given to Declan's family and heirs, which will give them an annual income equal to what he would have earned. Plus, he will pay a generous lump sum to Declan's family for burial and final expenses. You pick a figure, Dermot."

Maura came out and whispered to Jay. He jumped up and ran inside. Maura slumped onto the bench seat next to Dermot and he put his arm around her. "The good doctor is just about finished. The wound is clean; her stitches are in, and they are bandaging her chest now."

"Did he get the bullet?" Mac asked.

"He said they would turn her half over and make a small incision in her back. The bullet almost came clear through. It is just under the skin in her back. Poor dear, she will have to learn to sleep on her right side. Her left side, both front and back will be sore for some time to come." Maura drank from Dermot's teacup; set it down and slipped her hand under his.

"Fore and aft, like." Dermot muttered and Maura looked puzzled. "Fore and aft is how Donal described the wound on that soldier he shot on the way here from Cobh. It was a shoulder wound, clear through. He was bleeding fore and aft, Donal said."

"Heavenly retribution?" Mac looked a bit uneasy. "If that is the case, it should've been me got shot. I've a lot more to answer for than that lovely innocent lass."

Rory, a bit tentative said, "I've become quite good in the confessional, Mac. Whenever you feel the need, I'm ready for you." He looked hopeful.

"Ah Rory, I wish it were that easy for me. I would have to believe and I do not. But thank you for the offer." Mac turned to his old friend, "See, Rene. At least he offers me absolution. All you do is laugh at me and condemn me to some place worse than this."

*Ah, mais oui, mon ami. "*I think that you and I have adjoining seats, down below." Rene laughed and Mac joined him.

"Three seats may be required, mon ami, Rene. Perhaps we must make room for our Fritz, too, yes?" Mac turned to Fritz.

Fritz smiled but did not join in the laughter. It would require much more information for Fritz to believe or disbelieve, and solid facts about the afterlife were hard to come by.

The two new serving girls began bringing out food and Jay came out right after them. "God I'm famished. She's wonderful, Deirdre is." He gulped some tea. "The good doctor finished the operation and when Nurse and Mary Rose had her all bandaged, she opened her eyes and looked at me. I wet my finger and put it to her lips. She kissed my finger. Then they chased me out. She will need to go under once more and they'll turn her and take the bullet out of her back. Can we eat now?" In true male fashion, Jay's anxiety was replaced by hunger.

Fritz had been quiet for some time. He set down his knife and fork and queried Dermot and Mac. "High on your list must be, 'what orders did he give to the marksman.' You must press him, Dermot. Vee Villie is quite, ah like an eel, slippery, yes. He'll try to viggle out from criminal charges. And Mac, perhaps you and I could be near the room and listen, then you and I, we advise Dermot, yes?"

"I'd like to take a whip to that two faced bastard." Jay looked around at the others, but no one encouraged him. It seems there had been enough violence for one wedding day.

"Easy son." Mac laid a hand on his arm. "We have an old saying at home, revenge is a dish best eaten cold. Wee Willie Burke will get his, I guarantee it."

They ate in silence for a while, and then Dermot stood up "We have some business before us. I'm going to ask Maura to bring some whiskey out. I ask that you have one drink, just a nightcap only, and turn in early." Dermot surveyed his Motley group and missed Declan's easy, joking, but to the point banter. "We will set up a revolving watch. Two hours on and two off. I've got the first watch. Donal you and I are outside on the perimeter, and Rene is inside. Second watch is Mac and Fritz with Rory inside. Jay, my lad, since this is your wedding night and your beloved wife is inside, wounded but mending, you have twelve hours off duty. Any questions?"

"As soon as my Deirdre is doctored and tucked into bed, I'll take a watch. I couldn't sleep now anyway."

Dermot continued. "My friends out in West Cork are sending two more men to help Donal and the ones already here. When they get here we can change our duty roster and ease up a bit. I will not repeat my mistakes of earlier today."

Jay spoke up, "no one blames you, Dermot. We all let our guard down, including myself and especially Declan, and he paid the highest price for a momentary lapse." Heads nodded in agreement all around the table.

Dermot went on, "When the good doctor in finished, Maura will have her girls turn the dining room from an operating theatre, into a chapel. We'll have Sean in his casket and Declan in the black coffin brought in, candles will be lit and perhaps Rory and Rene can show Maura what else should be changed. We will have a Requiem Mass tomorrow morning, first thing."

Dermot looked around at his steadfast group. "The Motley's will attend, religious or not, no exceptions. Please. When I finish and get everything we want from Devil Burke, he'll be taken away to a safe house and held prisoner until Deirdre has mended and is safely away."

Jay groaned and held his head in his two hands. They all turned to him and Mac asked, "are you all right, son?"

Jay was completely drained. The last few days had taken a heavy toll on him. "My God. I've got everything I asked for. I wanted answers. Where is my father? Is he alive or dead? Where is my woman? If I find my love, will she marry me? And now I have my answers.

Here is my father, he's with me but he's dead. Here is my beloved. We're married and she is with me, but shot through the chest at our wedding. On the ride up here in the hearse, my new wife, all shot and bloody was sliding around on top of my father's casket. Good Christ Almighty." Jay lifted his head, looked from one to the other and finally settled on the two priests. "I'm afraid to ask for anything ever again." Rory and Rene looked away from Jay.

Maura came with the whiskey and went to Jay first. "Let me strengthen your tea, Jay." She poured a healthy splash of the whiskey into his hot tea. "Deirdre is fine, the good doctor has the bullet and he will come to you shortly. He and Nurse will stay the night and see her again in the morning. We moved her to small room off the dining room. Mary Rose is with her and perhaps in a few minutes you will sit with her yourself." Jay nodded yes and Maura moved around the group pouring the whiskey and comforting her men.

Donal joined the group and held out his teacup to Maura. To Dermot he pointed and held up two fingers. "One is upstairs with Burke. The other, your good friend, is out on the perimeter. And Dermot, he's had word, your Mam will be here by first light."

Dermot smiled and Jay brightened. "That's Fiona? Your Mom. The one Deirdre considers her second mother."

Dermot's smile widened. "Indeed. Now she'll heal even faster."

"If that's whiskey you're holding? I could do with a tot." The good doctor said to Maura and turned to his nurse. "Will you have a splash, love?"

"Yes, I need a double. Treating a beautiful young woman for a gunshot wound makes me jittery. Especially if it's her wedding day." Nurse set down a dish and a specimen jar.

"Can we have that other light over here?" The doctor picked up the dish. This is the bullet out of her back. It's from a rifle." Donal and Jay, Dermot, Mac and Fritz all had experience with firearms and they all agreed with the good doctor. "Lead from a rifle bullet. It's much different than that from a pistol."

Dermot spoke for them all. "So it was the one shot through the neck killed Declan as he moved in front of Deirdre and the same bullet caught her high in the chest. He saved her life." He looked at the good doctor and his nurse, then at his Motley group. "We'll sort this all out in the morning."

"Who was this Declan?" asked the good doctor.

"A young man who worked for me, in a manner of speaking," Dermot said. "Declan is the one who bargained with you in the swap of our motorcars."

The good doctor winced. "Too bad. I liked that young chap. He could've gone far. Had a good head on him." He held out his hand. Nurse handed the specimen jar to the good doctor and he turned to Jay. "You are the American Navy man, her husband?"

"I am."

"Then that bit of lead is yours to keep and so is this." He took the jar

213

and poured the contents into his large, steady hand. "I found this chain in her clothing. It had been around her neck. This dust I pulled from the wound. It looks like ashes."

"Incense," Jay whispered softly.

"And this tightly wrapped red silk."

"Deirdre wore an Incense Fire Pack on a chain. It hung down from her neck."

The good doctor finished Jay's sentence. "Between her breasts and undoubtedly saved her life. You gave her a heart shaped Shian Bao?"

"It was diamond shaped. It was given to me by a...a friend and I gave it to Deirdre for protection. How do you know about a Shian Bao?"

"I served in the Orient for many years. I have two myself, both heart shaped. So a Chinese woman gave you a diamond shaped one. That is very intriguing." He held up a shiny bit of twisted metal. "This was a silver heart. It was inside the diamond shaped Shian Bao."

Jay was very quiet for a minute. A vision of Wan Lee leaped from his heart up into his head and he heard her lovely sing-song voice, 'See Jay man, Wan Lee give you friendship with love hidden inside and you give love and friendship to your woman, keep her safe. Now everyone happy. Wan Lee love you and you love your woman. Long life and happiness. Good bye, Jay man.'

Mac broke the silence. "Are you all right, Jay?"

Jay bobbed his head yes to Mac and looked at the doctor. "So Declan took away the speed of the bullet and the Shian Bao with the silver heart inside, deflected the lead from Deirdre's heart, and both saved her life." He held his cup out to Maura and without saying a word she poured him another tea with whiskey.

The good doctor agreed. "Yes. Passing through soft tissue like a neck would have slowed it some and the Shian Bao and the silver heart deflected it just enough to miss the heart. Your woman is young and healthy. With some rest, she should live a normal life." He poured everything back into the specimen jar, including the bullet. He tightened the cap and handed it to Jay. "I saw two caskets inside. Can you enlighten me?"

He looked around the long wooden table and finally Donal spoke up.

"Ah, Jasus Doc. If we tell you we'd have to put you down, so. You and your lovely companion."

The good doctor laughed. "I'll have a taste of that whiskey laced tea. Listen, I've been cashiered out of the British Army. I'm officially persona-non-grata with the present government, although they do need my skills and call on me occasionally. That's the only reason I still have a license. I see what I see and I hear many things that I probably should not hear. In one way, I am as much an outlaw as any of you. And I am her doctor and cannot reveal anything about my patient. So, tell me who and what is this Motley bunch and what are you all about. The truth please, or if it's to be lies, at least make them interesting."

Jay stood up. "I'll sit with Deirdre and send Mary Rose out, if she'll come." He set down a small diamond in front of the good doctor. It was the smallest of the lot and it was his last. He didn't even know he still had one, until he felt it in the lining of his cap. Again he silently thanked Wan Lee. He stuck his hand out, shook with the good doctor and thanked him and Nurse for Deirdre's life.

"That's a hell of a nice fee, young man."

"That's also to buy your silence. I don't want Donal to be shooting anyone else tonight. The noise will disturb my wife." They both smiled. "The black coffin holds our young hero, Declan. The larger one is my father, Sean O'Neill. He was on the Lusitania." Jay took his jar and walked away, then looked back. "Dermot, tell him as much as you want. I think we're all right. Maura, I'll pay their bill, too. My Deirdre is worth every penny of it."

Jay tiptoed upstairs and saw the guard on Wee Willie's locked room. He gave a one fingered salute and went quietly back down to the dining room, where the two bodies were laid out. He sat for a moment and said a prayer for the two dead heroes, his father and Declan. I'll be back later, he promised them and went to Deirdre's recovery room.

It was a small room with Deirdre in a single bed. She was propped onto her right side, by a big pillow behind her. Mary Rose sat resting in an easy chair facing the bed. Her eyes were puffy and red from prolonged weeping. Jay took off his shoes and went past her. He placed a pillow on the floor and half sat, half knelt in front of his wife and kissed her hair and her cheeks. As he had done in the hearse on the ride here, he dipped his finger in a glass of water and wet her parched lips. Deirdre licked her lips and he repeated this several times. She murmured in her sleep and kissed his finger. He bent and kissed and moistened her lips.

"Me too," came softly from behind him. Mary Rose had her eyes open.

Jay took the water to her. He dipped a cloth into the water and gently bathed her eyes, then her lips and her face. She mouthed a thank you to him.

"Thank you Mary Rose, for everything. You are a good woman and I'm so sorry for your loss. I know we will all be friends." He bathed her eyes again. "There's food and tea and whiskey outside, and friends too. Will you join them. They'd like to have you with them."

"I'll go to my room first and change. I have blood on me and I need a change of clothes, and....and." She caught herself and stood up. "There's a packet of sleeping medicine, on the table there. When she wakes, give half in a small glass of water and she'll sleep again. Sleep is good. It will help the healing after the violence done to the poor dear. Thank you, Jay." She kissed his cheek and left the room.

Jay silently moved the table and placed the chair so he could sit turned towards her and their faces were just inches apart. The one candle gave enough light so he could see her clearly. Once in awhile the candle would sputter and send shadows dancing in the room. Deirdre's breath was slow and even and Jay tried to match it with his own life affirming force, in and out, in and out. It was almost mesmerizing.

He spoke softly to her, not quite sure he was speaking aloud. Maybe it was in his head. But he was sure that she understood him. "My father says hello, and Declan too. They're glad you're here in your room and not laid out next to them. Me too. And Wan Lee sends her love. You see there was a tiny silver heart inside the Shian Bao. It deflected the bullet away from your heart. I wondered about that. I almost opened it once to see if the diamond held a heart inside. I'm so glad I never opened it, never looked in it.

That good doctor is a very good surgeon. He says soon you will not even have a scar. In the front near your lovely enticing breast it may look like a dimple, and on your equally lovely back there won't even be a line, nothing. You are my beautiful wife and I love you so much. And I thank you for loving me.

I can't wait to show you my home, my country. The first thing you'll see is that grand big lady in the harbor. She welcomes everyone. You will love her and all that she stands for. We Americans don't always measure up to her, but she's always there, showing us, reminding us, helping us to be better people, better citizens. She's French you know. She's a real lady.

And that's only the beginning. Did I tell you, Fiona is coming. Dermot said she'll be here at first light. I know you will love having her here and I'm anxious to meet her, your second mother. I hope she likes me."

Deirdre's voice came very faintly and Jay put his ear to her mouth. "Fiona will love you. I love you. Still thirsty."

Jay fixed her water with the sleeping powder and held it for her until she finished it. "Good night, my love. Sleep. Rest. Heal."

He turned so his head was touching hers and smiled as fiddle music drifted in from the garden. Soon a concertina joined in and then the bodhran pulsed out a low beat. Voices were singing, but he couldn't make out the words or identify the singer. 'Sometimes,' he thought, 'a person's singing voice did not sound like that same person's speaking voice'.

The good doctor looked in, and Jay kept his eyes closed as he took Deirdre's pulse and felt her skin for a temperature check. He overheard him say to Nurse, as they left, "Do you know what they call you, my dear?"

"What do they call me?"

"They say you are the best surgical nurse in seven continents."

Nurse laughed. "And do you know what they call you?"

"No, what do they call me?"

"They refer to you as, The Good Doctor, and they call you a Cracker Jack of a surgeon." They both laughed and moved away out of Jay's hearing.

"Jay. Jay me boyo." Mac spoke softly and shook him a bit, then covered Jay's mouth so he wouldn't speak and disturb Deirdre. "I'll take the next watch. It's about two hours to first light. Go on up to my bed and catch a few winks. First door on the right."

The cock crowed and kept at it. Mac could also hear the morning wind pick up and rustle the tree branches outside. They tapped against the windowpanes. Through half slitted eyes he could see the darkness give way to shadows and images. The latch clicked and the door opened a few inches. "Come in, it's all right," he said and kept his voice low.

A woman came in and went past him, right to Deirdre. She stood without a word and watched her niece breathing easy and slow. Mac got up and pushed the chair closer to the bed, the way Jay had it in the night. She gestured thank you and perched on the edge. After a few minutes she held out her hand and in a low musical voice said, "I'm Fiona O'Rourke, Dermot's mam and Deirdre's aunt. You must be Mac."

He took her hand in both of his. "I'm Gregor MacGregor, and yes, they call me Mac."

"I'd like to call you Greg. Do you mind?"

He started a smile that soon took over his entire broad face. "I'd like that, Fiona." In the dim candle glow and half morning light, he saw a handsome woman, an older version of Deirdre and a softer feminine version of Dermot. The family resemblance was striking. "I'll leave you two together now. I need a bit of the morning air."

"There's tea on the fire in the kitchen. Dermot and Maura are starting the day." She chuckled. "The pair of them. They act like they invented lovemaking. They can't stop touching and grinning at each other. I'm so happy for my Dermot. And she looks a proper match for him. I'm thinking they'll be busy for a lifetime, finding everything within and without each other. The battles are hard but the making up is grand. And my Deirdre and her man, Jay? Do they touch a great deal and grin at each other?"

"The same, Fiona. Perhaps a bit more so. They've been busy dodging enemies and trying to find and marry each other, but yes, they can't keep their hands off of each other. And yes, they too grin a good deal. I do enjoy watching them at it."

"And you, Greg." Fiona laughed. "Do you have a sparring partner, yourself?"

"She's gone these five years, now. I'd better find that tea. Perhaps we can talk, later, Fiona." Mac slipped out the door and Fiona watched him go and watched the place he'd just vacated.

"Fiona." Deirdre's voice was hoarse and full of tears.

"Deirdre my child, my love, shah, shah, shah, *tosca sin inis mavorneen, macushla.*" Fiona ran her hands over Deirdre's face and petted her hair and her head, then reached down and took her good hand and kissed it. "Your left arm in that sling, is it broken, then?"

"No Fiona. It keeps my shoulder from moving. The wound is down at the swelling of my breast." Deirdre's mouth was so dry she could barely talk.

Fiona took a cloth and dipped the corner into the water glass, then put it against Deirdre's mouth. "Here now, suck on this and get some moisture into your mouth. If you stay silent for more than two minutes, I will not know who you are, surely."

It was a long-standing family joke that Deirdre as a girl never stopped talking. She talked to her toys and to her dolls, she talked to the cats and the dogs, she carried on with plants and trees and sometimes she just talked to herself. She was never without words.

"Put your hand on my pillow, Fiona." Deirdre, as she had done so many times before, laid her cheek in the palm of Fiona's hand and kissed it.

"Now, tell me about your Jay. No, don't talk, just nod to me, my all grown up little one. He's an O'Neill." Deirdre nodded. "He is left handed?" She nodded again. "Then he's one of the lucky O'Neills. There's one in each generation born left handed, born lucky. His Da is laid out inside, dead on the Lusitania." Deirdre nodded her head. "And his Mam is dead in New York," another nod. "Then you two have a great deal in common." She nodded. "Child you will wear out your neck. Just stop me if I say it wrong." Fiona caressed her face and wet the cloth once more for Deirdre to suck on and wet her mouth from it.

"His name is John Joseph and they call him Jay. He's smart, and handsome and he loves you," Deirdre smiled and felt silly smiling with the wet cloth hanging from her mouth and draped over Fiona's wrist. "And you love him something fierce." Deirdre's eyes gleamed and she nodded. "And you'll go away with him to America." Fiona's voice trembled.

Deirdre eyes filled with tears and the tears overflowed and ran down her face. She spit out the cloth and reached for Fiona. "Oh Fiona, I love you. You're my Mam and I'm your Deirdre. And I love you and I love him."

"Hush now, hush."

"I love him so and yes, I will go away with him to America."

"I know, I know. Hush now, Deirdre my love. We've had so many American Wakes in our family and in our town and in this poor country, one more won't harm us at all."

The two women held each other and cried with each other and finally Deirdre dozed off into a peaceful sleep. She had a dream of contentment with her Jay on one side of her and Fiona on the other. Later, she remembered feeling puzzled in the dream. Was she a young girl or was she a woman? It didn't seem to matter. She was both and she was content.

Fiona held her Deirdre, her twin sister's daughter and whispered to her. "I think you have always resented your mother dying and leaving you. And though you thought of me as your mother you never called me Mam, always Fiona. I think you wanted to be my sister; wanted to take my Fionnoula's place. I thank you for that. And I love you for wanting me to be both mother and sister to you."

Fiona laid her head back on the chair and thought to herself. 'But now I must let her go. She grew up so grand; she had been a free spirit just like Fionnoula and myself. She met her lifetime mate, and now she would complete this cycle we call life. Deirdre and Jay would raise children of their own and though a half-world away they'd be a part of her family.'

Fiona smiled and closed her eyes. 'And she would have children again in her own house, that lovely home on the Fergus River. Her other child, the only child of her body, her own Dermot, will bring his Maura into the house. I will be a mother-in-law.' Fiona's smile widened in anticipation of the coming battles between Maura and herself.

'Oh it will be grand, and our love for Dermot will bring us back to harmony. And oh yes, I'll have my way with his children, I will indeed.' Fiona smoothed the sheets and caressed Deirdre's hair and her brow. "Hush Deirdre, I'm only talking to myself. Sleep now child, sleep and heal yourself my darling Deirdre."

CHAPTER TWELVE

'The sick room will soon need a revolving door,' Jay thought as he entered, 'and a name for it too. If Declan were here, he'd name the room in a flash. The WarRoom,' he thought and liked it, 'we'll call it the WarRoom.' He kissed Deirdre and he fussed over her. He was introduced to Fiona and Jay liked her immediately. 'She was so much a combination of his Deirdre and her cousin Dermot. And it was like a peek into Deirdre's future. In time, she will look like this, a vibrant, charming woman holding untapped depths of love and creation.'

Fiona kissed him as she would a son-in-law and chased him off to the Requiem Mass and breakfast after. "Eat well Jay, you'll need all your strength for my Deirdre. And you can bring us a cup of tea, after."

When the Mass was over, Rene came into the WarRoom and brought communion to Deirdre and Fiona. With a typical Gallic shrug he waived away the fact that neither had fasted since midnight. Rene gave absolution to them, then he held up the wafer and said, *"Ah, mais oui.* Catholics must always make a double leap of faith." He held up the host. "Here in this wafer is the body and blood of Christ. This we believe. We also believe that this thin flat round wafer is made from real bread." He smiled and the two ladies laughed. He gave them communion, and he blessed them in Latin, French and English. "I will go now, before I ask that you two bless me. I think you are both much blessed."

"Adieu mon pere," Deirdre whispered.

"I like that priest," Fiona declared. "And he's the one who married you and Jay."

Nurse came in and undid the bandages. As if on cue, the good doctor came in when the last bit of cloth came off the wound. He looked and probed. He clucked and hmmmed and finally said he was very pleased. "You are healing quite well, young lady. You must have had a Cracker Jack of a surgeon." He laughed out loud and Deirdre chuckled. She held her side and blushed in spite of herself. Fiona was puzzled and Deirdre said it was an in-house Nimble Motley joke. She would explain it later.

The good doctor paused at the door; "I must ask Jay about that Shian Bao he gave you. Those ashes seem to help your wound heal faster than normal. It is quite amazing."

Nurse put on new bandages, restored the sling and was gone out the door. Deirdre encouraged Fiona to go have her breakfast. "If you're going to care for me properly, you will need to be strong." They laughed and hugged and Deirdre whispered words from her childhood. "Thank you for coming, my heart."

Fiona answered her, as always, "You knew I'd come, my light." And she finished the childhood chant, "And who is our strength, my Deirdre?"

"Dermot is our strength," Deirdre softly said. Fiona closed her patient's eyes and left the room. She wished with all her strength that she had been at the wedding, maybe, maybe.

After eating, Jay came back and was pleased to see how she looked. "A night's rest and with Fiona here and some food. You seem so much better."

"And you. Mostly you. You are my healer, my Jay."

"And you ate?"

"An egg. I had a soft egg. Well, most of an egg. And a bite of toast and a sip of tea."

"She's eaten almost nothing at all." Fiona came in the door and put on a stern face. "How in the world will you clean his house and cook his food, and...."

"Enough." Deirdre grimaced and then they laughed together. "Don't make me laugh. It hurts." She held Jay's hand and motioned Fiona to put her hand in between their two. "Jay, do you remember when you met Dermot?"

"Yes. You said we had to like each other because you loved us both."

"Yes. And I love the two of you, Fiona and you, with all that I am."

Jay kissed Fiona' cheek and then Deirdre's lips. He sat on the small folding chair he'd just brought in and urged Fiona to take the soft armchair. "I have news. The good doctor will leave tomorrow, Nurse too. Up to Cork. He's been offered a high paying contract job for the Army, Special Cases Surgery, or some such. Before this World War is over he'll be a wealthy man." Jay looked at Deirdre and Fiona, but they seemed just barely interested.

"And more news, Nurse asked Mary Rose to go with them. She'll assist Nurse who of course assists the good doctor. Nurse was very impressed with the way she helped with your operation, Deirdre. Nurse said in six months or so Mary Rose could get a certificate and come back here to help Maura turn this Inn into a wounded soldiers convalescent home.

Two heads turned to Jay. "More on that later, but it seems the Motleys have gone from being hunted by the authorities to now helping heal the British Army. And with the good doctor's guidance and help from Mac, the Coveneys too will become well off." Jay held up his hand. Both of the women were firing questions at him. "Hold on. Wait, let me finish, please."

Fiona subsided; having raised children, she had great deal of patience and knew that Deirdre, wonderful talker that she was, would fill in all the delicious details later on.

"John Jay O'Neill, you tell me everything, or I'm up and out of this bed."

Fiona held her down and urged Jay to hurry. "Speak Jay lad, tell her everything."

"I have lot's of news. It seems the Motleys are all taking their leave, or most of them anyway. Declan is leaving. Or rather his family will take him home for a proper wake. They were here in time for the Mass, and they will stop in and say hello to you both before they go. He'll be buried out of his own parish chapel.

It seems my Da and Declan will travel together a bit longer. Donal will

223

drive him home in the hearse and then he'll take my father's casket to the port in Cobh to a cold storage place. They'll hold my Da there until we take him home to New York. Then Donal will return here.

And Dermot has the papers, giving Declan's family a generous settlement from Wee Willie Burke's estate. "A sum in cash, more that enough to bury him; and a sum invested to bring in pounds sterling each month to equal what Declan would make in a lifetime."

"Money will not bring him back. He's a bastard that devil Burke," Deirdre almost sat up.

Fiona held and soothed her. "Hush, hush, love. He'll get his. Dermot will see to him."

Jay hurried on, "Dermot says Burke is a broken man and is giving us nearly everything we want from him. But he'll be in here soon to tell you himself. Dermot was here in the night, but the good doctor chased him. Said only your husband and your mother should be in here now."

"Indeed Jay, I'd say he told that good doctor a thing or two," Deirdre looked from one to the other of them.

"No love. He turned white as that sheet when he saw you lying there. He went all quiet and left when he was asked. He was very frightened for you and now he hangs on every word the good doctor says. He's all right now though he's not too happy that his wife will run a home for wounded British soldiers."

The women exploded and Jay was aghast. "Oh Jesus, I've done it now."

"What wife," came from Fiona.

"Maura Ni Coveney?" Deirdre almost sat up and again Fiona held her.

"Shhh. Don't say I told you. Oh Jesus Christ Almighty. He and Maura will be in here to see you and tell you and you have to act surprised. Please," Jay pleaded with them.

Deirdre's eyes were half closed and she looked at Jay as though she could devour him whole. "That's grand news Jay. I think everyone should be married, don't you agree Fiona."

Fiona looked from one to the other and said in a stern voice, "enough, you two." Then she laughed. "Healing first. There's gobs of time for

224

tumbling in the hay, so. First you must have a good healthy body, my darling Deirdre."

She rose and kissed Deirdre then kissed Jay warmly and told him, "welcome son. Welcome to the family. Now I must go and find my other son and let him tell me his news. Then I suppose I'll have to bid welcome to my new daughter. Be on your best behavior you two. I'm leaving the door open." Fiona laughed again and left the room.

Jay and Deirdre kissed for long time and with much passion. "I'm still dry. Wet my mouth again." He obliged, and used his tongue instead of his finger. After a bit she called a halt. "I want you so much, but we better stop. Tell me more news." Deirdre paused and with her good hand, she pulled his head down to her face, "between kisses."

"Wee Willie has agreed to everything except directly saying he gave the order to shoot you. He claims the marksman fired after he, Burke fired his pistol into the air; says they just wanted to scare you, but that's a lie. Declan, of course stepped into the line of fire. He slowed the bullet that nearly killed you."

"He saved my life."

"Yes he did. Most of us, including Dermot, think he was after the cup of whiskey, and was shot by mistake. However, he'll have a hero's funeral. The I.R.B. will give him full honors for having saved the life of another hero; a woman honored for her role in a very secret operation." He looked at her with love and true admiration. "Somewhere, before we go home," Jay paused at her reaction, "to your new home that is, there will be a ceremony honoring you and your heroic efforts. I am so proud of you, Deirdre."

She kissed him and ran her fingers into his hair. "More news. Give me more."

"Dermot had a notary come in, right after the Mass. We all, that is, the two priests Rene, and Rory, Fritz and myself, as well as Mac, Maura and Mary Rose; we all gave depositions that Burke had been stalking you, made another attempt on your life, up near Cobh, and we assume it was he, Burke, who gave this order to shoot. It killed poor Declan, wounded you and the soldier ran away. We all signed and the notary stamped it so our testimony could be used in court, if needed.

But it won't be needed. Wee Willie is a broken man. He resigned from the Lusitania commission. He resigned his place at the University. He renounced all claims to the Burke estate, all moneys, all honors, everything. He's finished.

Mac, who knows the family, says a younger son will now inherit everything and the new Burke heir has no regard for Wee Willie. So your Devil Burke will be dependent upon the charity of his mother, Billie Burke and she will keep him on a tight leash."

"Will Burke be released?" Deirdre asked in a small panic.

"No, no. Not until you are all mended and we have sailed for America. This bit should cheer you. Dermot's pals sent us two men who will take Devil Burke deep into West Cork, out near the Kerry border. He'll be held in a cottage there and the ironic part is they'll drive him out there in his own car. The one Wee Willie's man drove to the ambush at the Mass Rock."

There was a tap on the open door and Dermot and Maura came in. Jay stood and made room for them. Maura knelt on the floor at the bedside and Dermot sat on the chair, his face just a foot from Deirdre's.

"Thank God in heaven above, Deirdre." His voice caught in his throat and he almost cried at the sight of her. "You look grand." Dermot kissed her and smoothed her hair.

"*Ah Diarmuid macushla.*" Deirdre took his hand and kissed it. "My brother, my strength." She took his hand and reached for Maura's and the three held hands and Deirdre blurted out, half crying, half laughing. "I'll miss your wedding, won't I?"

"This is a secret." "Who told you?" Maura and Dermot asked at once.

Deirdre looked at Jay. "My Jay. Sure the Yanks can't keep a secret the way us Irish can." Deirdre blubbered and her eyes leaked again; since her wedding and being shot her emotions were so close to the surface. Dermot wiped away her tears and caressed her face. Deirdre looked at Jay again and smiled through her tears. "But I love you anyway, my Yankee Jay."

On that note, Jay blew her a kiss. "I'll leave all you Irish to swap secrets. I need to talk to Mac." He stepped out of the WarRoom and looked back. Maura and Deirdre were hugging and Dermot sat with one hand on

Deirdre's dark hair and the other on Maura's golden head. He looked like an ancient Celtic Chieftain blessing the women of his Clan.

Jay went into the garden and saw the Motleys sitting on cushions, as all the benches were wet. The morning rain was gone and all the bushes, flowers and herbs were washed clean and looked vibrant in the mild spring air. The men were easy, drinking tea and gabbing, but a feeling of expectancy filled the air.

Rory was packed and ready to head back to his lovely parish by the Argideen River and Courtmacsherry Bay. His pastor, Father Big Billy Conklin was clamoring for his quick return and making promises of no more penalty retreats plus a bit more freedom for the young curate. The actions of Wee Willie Burke had stunned the Pastor and made the transgressions of Rory seem pale in comparison. Big Billie had no wish for the bishops nor anyone else to know that he was so close to Wee Willie and indeed had brought him into the parish as an honored guest. Father Rory Beechinor, it seems, now had the upper hand.

Jay asked him to hang back for ten minutes before going in to say goodbye to Deirdre. "She has Dermot and Maura in with her now."

Rene and Fritz were packed and waiting for the American, Jay's replacement on the Lusitania commission. He was the same young man who had traveled with them on the Frigate and took down the story of Jay's travels. He would take Rene and Fritz in the opposite direction, back to Cobh and thence on to London to write their report. They too waited to bid a fond farewell to Deirdre.

Jay shook hands and then hugged Fritz. He thanked him again for that private message from Deirdre, which kept his hopes alive. To Rene, Jay gave a great hug, kissed him three times on his cheeks and then he asked for his blessing. Jay knelt on one knee and Rene placed his hands on Jay's head and blessed him as he would his own son.

Rene felt very close to this young man and also to his lovely young wife. And he was grateful to them. Rene had not performed a wedding for years and it brought back memories of his early days in the priesthood when many of his friends had asked the young Jesuit to marry them. He would ask MacGregor to keep him informed about their lives in America.

Between the kitchen and just off the entry out to the walled garden was a short passageway. Maura's father had installed a door at each end of this hall when he had the telephone installed and now it was a tiny room about the size of a closet. It held a shelf and a chair, a reservations book, a telephone on the wall, a mirror and a few maps hung about on the sidewalls. Mac sat there with the phone in one hand when Jay walked by.

"Jay, if you have a minute, I'll place that telephone call now. Maura gave me permission."

"You'll want Killybegs in County Donegal, Mac. You'll need whoever is in charge of the graveyard. We need permission to open the family plot there."

"Good Christ, me boyo, I know your Da's hometown and his county. He must've mentioned it to me seven hundred times."

Jay laughed. "All right, go ahead and call. And thanks Mac, for bringing this up. I wanted to mention it to you, but with so much going on, and then I guess I was afraid. When you say it out loud, it sounds sort of gruesome. The fact that my father said the same thing to you so many times made it easier for me.

Not easy, but easier. I felt kind of foolish asking the good doctor to take out my father's heart so we could bury it in Ireland while the rest of him would go home to New York and be buried with my mother. The good doctor just shrugged, and he held up that small diamond."

"Jay, he's a doctor and a military man. An autopsy is not that unusual for him and the good doctor is delighted with that fee. He'll operate in an hour he said?"

"Yes. My father's casket is still in the dining room and Maura is bringing me some of that dark green linen she uses for the aprons. I have to finish my report to the Admiral and after that I'll be back in Deirdre's room, but I'll join you in an hour for the operation." Jay started away but turned and came back. "We're just barely married and now I'm going to leave her for a few days. But at least she's mending well and she has Fiona with her. I hope when we get back I'll be able to sleep in a room with my wife instead of sharing a bed with my father's best friend." Jay grinned at Mac. "If you need me, send one of the new girls."

"That's fine, Jay." Mac nodded, picked up the telephone and rang the operator.

Mac was on with the operator. He spoke very loud. "I'd say give me the postmaster in Killybegs. He'll know who I need to open a grave there." Mac covered the telephone, "go on then, Jay. I'll make the arrangements for tomorrow. We'll need one of the Motley autos, and…Hello. Hello. Aye, I need to open an O'Neill grave. You are the postmaster. And you are the Warden of the Killybegs Graveyard, as well. That is fine, you're the very man I need"

Mac covered the telephone. "Go on, Jay. I can handle this…. And your brother digs the graves. No sir, not at all. My name is Gregor MacGregor. I am a close cousin. Yes, that is correct. Yes indeed, I am one of the 'Children of the Mist'. You know the MacGregors then? Oh, your family was involved in fighting with MacGregors. Did you fight with them or against them? Ah, sure, you are correct again. That was so long ago it doesn't really matter whether your people fought with the MacGregors or against them. 'Tis all the same, now.

Yes, the name of the deceased is Sean O'Neill of Killybegs, son of Joseph, grandson of John. He left Killybegs at the age of fifteen. Yes, years ago. So you knew the family, then. We need only a small grave, the size of a child's coffin. We have only a part of him to bury. He went down with the Lusitania. Aye. Correct again. Yes. This was his first trip back."

Mac shifted the telephone to his other ear. "Tomorrow I'd say, in the late afternoon. We're coming up from Cork. And yes, we would like to have a piper. You have a good one, do you? A cousin, is he? No I do not know how long it takes to make a piper." Mac covered the phone again. "Dermot, how long does it take to make a piper?"

Dermot shrugged as they passed by but Maura spoke up, "it takes twenty one years to make a piper. Seven years learning, seven years practicing and seven years playing before you become a piper."

"Twenty one years," Mac yelled into the Killybegs connection. "How long has your piper been at it? Hmmm. We will take him in any case, and we will see you tomorrow late in the day and thank you."

"His man has nineteen years and eleven months piping. Says he'll take a wee bit off on the fee because his man is not yet a full fledged piper and we do know the difference."

Dermot and Maura smiled; they hugged each other and walked on out into the garden.

Upstairs in the bedroom he shared with Mac, Jay finished his report. He went over it for the third time, signed it and put it in an envelope for his fellow Naval officer to carry up to his Admiral at the Embassy in London.

He had a quick wash, a shave, and a change of clothes and Jay felt he was ready to see his father's body cut open and the heart wrapped in new linen for burial in Killybegs, Donegal, the town his Da left so many years ago.

Just outside of the WarRoom he ran into Rene and Fritz and they said another heartfelt goodbye. Rory came out too and gave a frosty farewell handshake to Jay. He blurted out, "In the name of Jesus Christ, Jay, don't desecrate the body of your own father."

"Got in Himmel, Rory Beechinor. Even your own church has saints who have body parts, which lie buried in many places. They are venerated." As he spoke, Fritz stomped his cane on the floor for emphasis.

Rene spoke in a reasonable tone, "Father Rory. This is Nineteen-fifteen. Autopsies are no longer unusual. Organs are removed. This man Sean must lie with his wife in far off America, but his heart belongs in Ireland. His son is dutiful of his father's wish. Yes?"

Jay was aghast. Deirdre and Fiona had the door open and had heard everything. This was not the way Jay was going to explain it to his Deirdre and her Fiona. Besides, a part of Jay agreed with Rory. He knew this was right. It was what his father wanted; yet he felt uneasy removing his father's heart and leaving it behind. "I am following his wish, Rory." Jay said lamely.

Rory was not easily detoured from his chosen path, "are you quite sure there is holy and consecrated ground in Killybegs, up in Donegal?"

"Yes I am sure there is consecrated ground in Donegal." Jay finally found his footing. "Good God Rory, the O'Neills have been burying O'Neills in Killybegs for hundreds of years."

Mac came in and filled the small hallway as he put an end to the discussion. "Christ almighty Rory, Killybegs is where the King of Spain sent his ambassador to meet with Red Hugh O'Donnell and Hugh

O'Neill. They hoped together to throw the English out of Ireland. Even a MacGregor knows that much history. Yes the graveyard is consecrated. I just spoke with the man in charge and they'll open the O'Neill plot on the morrow."

The two priests and the German soldier-scholar took their leave. The Nimble Motleys were decreasing in numbers, even as they reached their all of their goals.

Mac clapped Jay on the back and sent him forward into the room and into Deirdre's outstretched good right arm. When Mac entered, Fiona took another long look at this big Scotsman and declared she would go and get tea for them all.

"Will you walk with me Greg, and help me carry it back." Deirdre's second mother left the recovery room on the arm of Jay's second father.

Deirdre pulled Jay down till his face was nestled into her neck and he kissed her again and again. "We heard all of it, Fiona and I. You sounded uneasy, Jay. Is this what you really want to do for your father, your Sean?"

"I honestly don't know. It's what he himself wanted"

"Remember the cave up on the Hill of Fires, we sheltered from the storm and I told you your Da was dead." She stroked his hair. "I held you and you cried for your Da. Have you the need? Do you want to cry for him now, Jay?"

"I am crying. Yes I have the need. Hold me." He kissed her neck and moved her gown down and kissed the swell of her breast. "It was in that place, I asked you to marry me. And I hit my head and you kissed the bump, and then you said yes, you would be my wife. I want to kiss your wounded breast as well, my Deirdre. I love you so much." He groaned and she held him tighter. He whispered to her. "Ever since we've found each other again, my emotions are...well, my tears are flooding up there right behind my eyes. All the time."

"Oh, Jay. Me too. My eyes well up and tears spill over at almost nothing." They studied each other's eyes and read the love that was strong in them. "I know you want me, and I want you as well. Can you wait while I heal, my Jay?"

"I can. I will. Yes, of course." He kissed her lips and she dried his eyes and his face with her sleeve. "I will do this for my Da, because it is what he wanted." He smiled at his wife. "I hear the tea things coming."

"I hope you are decent, because we are coming in, regardless." Mac entered pushing a tea trolley. Fiona was right behind and she carried several new, dark green, linen clothes. The trolley held a fine old flowered porcelain teapot, a creamer and sugar bowl and matching cups, saucers and small plates. There was a large platter filled with oatmeal biscuits with currents, folded napkins and a spoon holder. "I am sure Fiona thought of everything," Mac smiled and poured milk first, then tea, into four cups.

"Jay, Maura gave me these new linens for you. Give them to the good doctor or Nurse when you go in there." Fiona indicated the dining room where the operation would take place. "Greg, will you tell to Deirdre that story of the gold fields up in the far North."

Mac held them all spellbound as he spoke of that long frozen winter he and Sean had spent in a tiny ice bound cabin in the gold fields of the Yukon. They had gotten to know each other's deepest desires and innermost thoughts during those long dark days and nights.

"I love my wife and young son," Sean had said. "But by God I am torn. I miss my homeland. My heart will always be there. Surely, this must be the lament of every exile in all the foreign lands in this world. When I die, if you have any say in it Mac, my body is for my family, but my heart should be in Ireland." Mac looked at them one by one. "I made him that promise." He stopped speaking and drank some of his tea. "I had no idea how to do it. Nor when, nor if."

Deirdre, with her eyes overflowing, called to Fiona. "Will you ever bring me our jewelry case, Fiona".

Fiona brought the Old Spanish oak and leather case to the bed and handed it to her. "This is your case, Deirdre. I gave it to you along with all of the jewelry." The two women regarded each other for a long moment. Fiona nodded her assent, and suddenly her eyes glistened and they were as moist as her little sister Deirdre's were.

Deirdre unlocked the oak and leather case and took out the contents. She selected the emerald and gold brooch with the matching earrings and ring and handed them to Fiona.

"Thank you my darling Deirdre, but the emerald ring is yours." Fiona placed the ring on Deirdre's middle finger and lifted up the other jewels. "These will stay in Ireland and on behalf of Dermot and Maura, we thank you for the brooch and the earrings."

Deirdre, with her good hand, lifted the Old Spanish case and gave it to Jay. "This too shall stay in Ireland, Jay. You will take and bury your father's heart in this old case brought here by the Spaniards so long ago. Our families truly will be united, and in so many ways."

"Thank you Deirdre. Thank you Fiona." Jay, overwhelmed, accepted the Spanish case.

"Come Jay. It is time to see the good doctor. Ladies, from the bottom of my own MacGregor heart, I thank you for what you have done for both of these O'Neills."

"What time have you," Dermot asked. "And what are you pouring into that flask, Jay?"

Mac answered him, "it's half five in the morning and that foul smelling stuff is supposed to be coffee. Jay found some in the back of a cupboard. God knows how old it is."

Jay had a dreamy smile going on and off his face, and said, "I'm having an American quick meal. Some bread and some coffee as we drive. You just caught us Dermot, we were almost out the door."

"I wanted to thank our Scottish Motley here and bid him farewell." Dermot and Mac clasped hands and acknowledged their mutual fondness and high regard for each other. "Maura asked will you come back for our wedding? And yes indeed, I want you here as well."

Jay's smile got wider, "I think Fiona too, is curious. Will you be back?"

Mac tried to keep a straight face, but he too smiled and grabbed Dermot's arm on his way to the door. "Send me an invitation, Dermot my lad, and you'll see just how fast a Scotsman can move."

In the Motley car, the one they all called the good doctor's car, Jay drove and sipped bad coffee from his flask. They were already through Cork City and headed North on the road to Mallow before most of the countryside was awake.

"You never came up to our shared bedroom, last night."

Jay's grin got much bigger. "Maura's new girls took out that easy chair and fixed me a single cot in the WarRoom. With a bit of maneuvering, I spent last night with my new wife snug in my arms. Mac, it was so great to just have hours and hours holding each other; talking and sleeping and talking." He shook his head and stayed silent for a long time. He was lost in his memory of the night before, and all the hugging and kissing he never mentioned to Mac.

"My father always loved the time he got to spend with my mother. He said there was never enough of it. His marriage to her was the center of his life; she was his world."

They left Mallow behind and took the road North to Limerick. The drive was peaceful for both men, and the memory of Sean filled the long silences between them. Jay would tell a story from his childhood, like the first time Sean took him fishing in a boat. Sean liked the fishing and Jay enjoyed being in and around boats, and fishing and boating became the only activity that Sophie, Jay's Mom, would not enjoy with them. She railed against the water, never did like it, and she would not go near it. Sean said something happened on her voyage to America that she never got over. She would not talk about it.

Beyond Limerick they turned more Easterly on the road to Nenagh and Roscrea and the land changed as they moved away from salt marshes and seacoast and into the saucer-like interior of Ireland where freshwater lakes and different birds and crops filled the eye and the ear.

Mac drove for a while and he told stories of Sean as a young father on assignment for his government in various and strange places. "He'd say to me, 'Mac, it's almost like we should be grateful to the English for oppressing us. They drove me out. Without them, I never would have left Ireland.' As a child, Sean was taught to be wary of the government. The Officials were often the oppressors and they were always the enemy. Once in America, Sean said he loved working for his government and being a part of his new adopted country.

"And that's the way he put it, Jay. He'd say, 'This is My Country Now and by God, I will help to build it and shape it and make it my own.' He dearly loved being a part of it."

These wondrous foreign locales where the two of them met and worked fired the imagination but increased a longing for family, a wife and a child. "Sean had his Sophie and you. I had my Regina and young Maria. We helped each other weather the loneliness, but I will admit there were times when we wallowed in it. We absolutely reveled in it. I remember one night, 'with a drink taken,' as your Da put it, we actually had a contest to see which one of us was the loneliest. Can you believe that, Jay? We almost fought over it, the loneliness."

They had fallen into a pattern where the driver did most of the talking and the passenger most of the listening. As they headed up to Athlone, Mac looked over at Jay, and discovered that his passenger, his audience, was fast asleep.

"My fine young friend, I think you did more talking than sleeping, last night." Mac laughed.

When they were nearly into Roscommon Mac found a country pub with several autos and tractors and horse drawn farm wagons parked out front. "Come on my boyo, I think we have a good place for our dinner. We'll take a break here."

After a good country meal, a pint of Guinness, and a stop out in back at the outdoor toilet, Jay took the wheel and pointed them to Sligo. Soon, Jay and Mac smiled at each other when they heard the first gulls call out as they neared the salt water again and sea birds wheeled overhead, while others flocked into a field and dug in the soil for a land meal.

"I seem to be most comfortable when I can smell the salt air and see the black and white gulls diving for a meal," Jay declared. Mac agreed, and soon it was his turn to doze off. Once out of Sligo, Jay took the road to Ballyshannon.

"Look Mac. That yawl over there has classic lines to her. There's nothing in the world like a small vessel, with her sails filled on a good tack and a strong following sea. I too, long to be home, Mac. My home in America. Strange isn't it. It's like we are fixed at birth. Whammo. Something or someone slams you on the head and you're marked for life.

Here you are child. This is your home. Enjoy it or not, it doesn't matter; you will idealize this place, and wherever you go you will long for your birthplace for the rest of your life. There, see the sign, Mac. Donegal town is close, then we turn left and go just a short ways into Killybegs."

Once in Killybegs, Mac had Jay pull over at a shop. "Whenever Sean described a burial, he always talked about whiskey for the men and sherry or port for the ladies. I'll get a bottle of each, just to be prepared."

"Do you think anyone else will come? It's over thirty years since my Da left here."

"My boyo, we have no idea if anyone at all will come. And I don't want to have too much with us. Sean said the custom is the bottles must be finished, consumed, emptied there in the graveyard itself, else bad luck will come to the dead and even worse to the mourners."

"I'd say Mac, that you and I and my Da have had our share of bad luck and don't need any more. A bottle of each should do us fine."

"Aye. You and I, the priest and the piper, the gravedigger and probably the postmaster I spoke to on the telephone. He sounded the inquisitive type and I'm guessing he'll be there. No one else, Jay?"

"I can't think of anyone. My father had a younger brother but he died as an infant. His mother died after he left school, about age fourteen. His father remarried a year later and my Da came to America soon after. He claimed the stepmother ran him out of the house. A few years after that, around the time I was born, he had a letter from Killybegs, from her, the stepmother. It said my Da's father died in a boating accident. My God, Mac. My father, and his father before him, both dead at sea. I never made that connection."

"I know, son. I thought of it the minute I heard the Lusitania went down. I was quite sure he was gone at sea, though I didn't want to broach the subject with you. Are you all right?"

"Yes, I'm fine. If you will get the spirits," Jay smiled, "the bottled kind. Then I'd like to just drive the streets a bit and get a feel for my father's town before we go find the graveyard."

After driving the town and close in areas they headed south from the town of Killybegs, up a hill and then along a peninsular that jutted out into the Atlantic.

"A finger of land juts out and points the way to America," Jay said softly. "My father used to say that, every time he talked of Killybegs."

On the westerly side of the peninsular the land fell away in a series of drops down to the rocky strand and the tumbling surf of the Atlantic

Ocean. In the distance the winding coast road led away into the wild beauty of this southwest corner of Donegal County.

The setting sun had an hour or so of good strong daylight remaining, though a band of dark clouds parallel to the horizon covered it, and muted the sunlight.

Jay stood for a moment and admired the western view. The clouds hiding the sun were rimmed all around with a rose pink glow and the colors were mirrored down in the water and up into the sky. It was a beautiful place and a lovely time of the day to bury his father's heart and just where he always wanted to be, at home in his Killybegs, Donegal.

Sean's heart was wrapped in new linen and it filled Deirdre's oak and leather case. The case was locked with the key in Jay's pocket. He would keep that key as a reminder of this day. The Old Spanish case nestled in a cloth carry bag that Jay held tight against his chest. He turned and stepped eastward under the iron archway, which guarded the entrance to the graveyard, and he caught up with Mac.

On this side of the peninsular the graveyard sloped easterly down to the bay and the town. All around were green fields set off by gray stone walls and the blue water of the bay had small dancing white points all over it, as an onshore breeze set the bay in motion. The boats and the people in them moved up and down on the waves. Killybegs was a fine small port and seafaring town. In other times it had been the setting for pirate raids, town and crop burnings and battles, both on the land and out at sea.

They made a brave sight as Jay in his Navy dress uniform and Mac in his MacGregor war plaids joined the small group around an open grave. The priest, at the head of the grave, wore a black stole over his white surplice and he held an open prayer book in one hand and a holy water dispenser in the other.

His server standing behind him was an adult rather than an altar boy and he held the incense pot on a long chain in both hands. Periodically he would step back and swing the pot so the burning coals stayed glowing red hot and ready for the priest to apply the sweet incense.

There must have been old incense in the pot. The smell reminded Jay of the sandalwood in the Shian Bao. It also brought back memories of his childhood as an altar boy at home.

The piper stood off to one side. He blew into his bag and tuned his chanter and then began a low mournful tune. Mac whispered to Jay, "I would've said twenty two years playing, at least." He winked at Jay and the younger man felt himself become less stiff and solemn.

Jay fought off the impulse to laugh out loud. He had noticed this before about himself. At the most solemn moments, he would get an urge, almost an insane impulse to laugh or smile. He had fought this urge as long as he could remember.

They had to step around a large stone Celtic cross to reach the graveside. The cross had the large distinctive ring encircling the arms and the upright and it stood well over seven feet in height. There was an O'Neill name on it and a date from two centuries ago.

The grave itself was much too large for the small package Jay carried. It was cleanly dug and it was all white sand right down to the bottom. Next to the grave was piled the dug up sand and behind the sand stood the digger. On the other, open side of the grave stood two women, one was old and the other young. Twenty or so yards away, behind the priest an old man in tattered clothing leaned, almost lurked, against a stone marker.

Mac lifted his chin, pointed and whispered, "here for a free drink, no doubt."

"Will the deceased be here, soon?" The priest demanded looking at Mac and then at Jay.

Jay removed the wood and leather case from the carrying bag and held it up in his two hands. "Father...This is Sean O'Neill, father."

"Was this an unborn child, my son?"

"This is my father, Sean O'Neill of Killybegs, though he left here many years ago." The priest began to speak but Jay held up the case in his two hands and cut his objection short. "My father went down with the Lusitania. We have just a small part of him to be buried in his birthplace." Jay waited. He hoped the priest would not object further.

"This is consecrated ground, my son. Have his remains been blessed?"

"Aye father." Mac joined the theological discussion. "In Cork, yesterday, we had a requiem mass. A parish priest and a visiting Jesuit concelebrated that mass. We trust we have not kept you waiting." Mac paused and gestured with an outstretched arm behind him towards the westering sun. "We have only so much daylight left to us, father."

As though by magic the sun fell below the obscuring clouds and bright sunshine fell on the grave and illuminated the pure white sand within the grave and the white sand piled alongside. The white sand glistened in the sudden sunlight. Then the large Celtic cross cast its shadow over Sean's grave. A perfect encircled cross fell at the feet of the priest and ran the length of the open grave. The two women on the side, the gravedigger and the server behind the priest all gasped and stepped back. The priest stayed his ground but he immediately began casting holy water into the grave and on the case held forth by Jay.

"Subvenite Sancti Dei, occurrite Angeli Domini." The priest recited in Latin.

"Come to his assistance, ye saints of God." The server repeated it in English.

The priest again sprinkled the case with holy water and exchanged the dispenser for the censer on its chain; he put incense in it, and began blessing Sean and the grave. He went back and forth, then left, then right, and front again. Jay liked the smell and was wafted back into his childhood when he had assisted at mass and the incense was always his favorite part.

Jay surrendered the case to the gravedigger. He affixed a rope with a slipknot and lowered Sean's heart down into the grave. The priest used the incense and holy water again, then he chanted, "Et ne nos inducas intentationem."

Jay translated for Mac, "And lead us not into temptation."

"Sed libera nos a malo."

Mac smiled and translated this time, "but deliver us from evil."

The priest then sprinkled holy water over the white sand pile, which would cover the remains and he closed with a short prayer; after that the priest nodded to the piper who went back to playing. The music this time, though mournful, was a bit livelier. He began with 'The Minstrel Boy' and went on with 'Come To The Bower'. 'A good choice, thought Jay, with words about a "free boundless ocean" and "stupendous waves", and "the fierce tempest gathers" to "Erin the Green, the dear land of our fathers".

Jay liked the next verse, "Will you come to the land of O'Neill and O'Donnell, the patriot soldiers of Tirowen and Tirconnaill." It seemed a good fit with his father's end of life journey.

Jay thanked the priest, shook hands, and pressed an offering into his hand. He repeated this with the server who, as it happened, was also the postmaster, and then he paid the gravedigger.

Jay dropped to his knees and prayed for Sean. He prayed for Sean's father, lost at sea and missing from this O'Neill gravesite. Sean's mother came next in his prayers, and then more O'Neill family members going back to that hardy O'Neill who became ruler of this land by cutting off his right hand and flinging it ashore to win the race and the kingship by being first on the beach. His bloody red hand still adorns the flag of Ulster Province.

Mac was busy offering the two women some sherry and the priest and server some whiskey. Before they had left the Coveney Inn, Maura had pressed the old dented tin cup, her chalice, into Mac's hand. "You will need this at the graveyard," she said.

The priest drank first, a small tot, and then he left. The server and digger deferred to the women who had their sherry out of the cup, then the men had their first drink from the cup and stayed for more. The piper stopped playing long enough for his turn at the cup and to accept a fee. Jay paid him his full fee. He was a fine piper, though shy of twenty-one years.

"You are a grand piper," Jay said. "On behalf of my father, thank you." Jay and Mac took their turns at the cup and Jay waved over the tattered old drinker. "My father would not have any one go dry while he was laid to rest. Join us for a drink, please." After the drinker had a pull at the cup, Jay pressed a half crown into his hand.

The old woman was the child of Sean's stepmother and a different father. She was born long after Sean's father had died. The younger woman was her daughter. Neither had known Sean nor his father, but came out of respect, they said. More like just nosy, Mac said later.

The women, after more sherry, drifted out of sight to a grave of their own relatives. Jay took the remaining half bottle of sherry and gave it to the old drinker, who promised to stay and finish it in the graveyard. The server and the digger stayed while the digger did his job and as light faded, Sean's heart was covered over by the white sands of the Killybegs graveyard.

The piper, standing up near the entrance arch was silhouetted against the dying sun while he played 'The Flowers of the Forest'. Jay and Mac walked up near the piper and straddled a stone bench facing each other. They could look east and watch the darkness creep into the bay and the town and uphill into the graveyard. By looking the other way, they could see the sun setting out in the western ocean.

They sat quiet and fulfilled on the stone bench. After a bit, Jay took the bottle sitting between them and poured a dollop into the tin cup. Mac took the cup, raised it in a salute to Jay; he raised it again towards Sean's grave and drank down the whiskey. They were quiet for another while. Finally Mac took the bottle and poured a dollop into the cup. Jay took the cup and repeated the process, toasting Mac and his father, before drinking.

The piper saluted the O'Neill grave; wheeled about and saluted the setting sun. He turned smartly and began marching back to the town of Killybegs. A drummer, a young lad, joined him and together they played 'O'Sullivan's March'. The two men drank again and soon the pipe and the drum and the music were gone out of sight and out of sound. Only the memory was left to the two men on the bench.

Mac cleared his throat and began talking to Jay. He kept his head turned seaward to the setting sun. "I was the one, Jay. I was the one sent to find the gun runners." He stopped and drained the last few drops directly from the bottle.

"You remember our meeting in that, oh-so-elegant men's club I brought you to. All four of us men at that meeting, from time to time, we assist our governments in various ways."

"What has that got to do with us? With me? With you? With all of us, Mac?"

"The four of us men in that group, both individually and as a group, are dedicated to promoting peace in the world, or at least in our corner of the world."

"I repeat, what the hell has that got to do with us?"

"We each have our areas of expertise. Wee Willie has wealth and education. Fritz has a fierce intellect and he's a warrior. I am a soldier with investigative experience and Rene has great moral attributes. We could help you solve your problem, find your woman." Mac said.

"I accepted a job, an investigative job, from the Home Office. There were rumors of Irish Rebels buying guns from one of the combatants. It could've been France or Germany or Russia, maybe even the Turks. I went to Paris to pick up the trail. Jay, easy Jay."

Jay was rocking back and forth on the bench. "Then I saw you, and you were the exact image of Sean when we first met, up in the Yukon. It hit me like one of those trains. You are young Jay-Jay, son of my best friend, Sean O'Neill and you're all grown and manly now.

You told me your story about a beautiful young woman, a train in Eastern Europe. I wondered had you gone to your mother's people in Poland. But no, you met your young woman way out East of Poland, somewhere in Russia. We ransacked the station, you and I together, looking for her." Mac paused and watched Jay who was very still.

"Then that detail about the train stopping briefly just outside of Paris popped up and I began to wonder could we both be looking for the same person. You for your young woman, and me for someone buying guns from a foreign power."

Jay stood and from a half crouch, whispered very low to Mac. "What the hell are you saying?"

"You looking for your new lost love, me looking for an Irish rebel looking to buy rifles. Could your love be my gunrunner?"

"You spied on me? Me Mac?" Jay was shouting now. "Sean's son. You used me to find her?"

"After our search there was nothing in Paris, so I took you over to London, my next area to investigate." Mac turned and faced into the graveyard. Perhaps his dead friend Sean could help the son Jay understand his dilemma.

Mac took off his bonnet, loosened his tie and collar and slipped the knife out of his stocking. As he had done with Deirdre that day when they first met, he flipped the dirk end for end, held it by the blade and offered the handle to Jay.

"Hear me out, Jay. When I've finished you may stick it in my throat if you like."

"My father's best friend, you said." Jay's voice rose and cracked. Mac nodded. "His almost brother. Loved me as a son, you announced."

Mac nodded again. "All that you say is true Jay me boyo. Now, hear me out."

Mac stood up and put one foot on the stone bench. He faced west and looked to the ocean and the pink sky where the sun had just set. Jay sat and faced east. He looked toward his father's grave and the encroaching darkness that was fast filling the graveyard.

"As a younger man I had two ongoing loves. The Empire and the British Army. Oh aye, I loved my wife and my child, but always I was attracted to the next posting, some new and exciting place or adventure. There was always that difference between us, your Sean and myself. He would speak of Sophie and you. He couldn't wait to get back to you. I, on the other hand, couldn't wait for my new assignment, a whole new challenge. My Regina did as other Army wives did; she waited; she accepted, she was always there when I came back."

Jay eased down till he sat on the ground, his back against the bench. His father's grave was lost in the gloom, but the large O'Neill stone cross stood up tall and glowed in the twilight. "So you did love my father and by extension, my mother and me."

"Aye Jay. That love was real. It still is and stronger now and larger because it includes you and your lovely bride, Deirdre." Mac stepped around the bench and lowered himself to sit facing the ocean, his back leaning against the bench. "After my Regina was gone and I almost lost my daughter as well, I began to value your father's ways."

"Mac, why the hell didn't you tell me on the boat-train to London?"

"Tell you what, laddie? That I was a temporary agent for the government; that I was looking for an arms purchaser; that your lady, the love of your life, was my prime suspect? First, I wasn't sure that guns were ever purchased or if indeed they were purchased and if so, were they destined for Ireland. With this war raging all over Europe, everyone is buying arms.

Last year it was the Orangemen in the North of Ireland. The Carsonite

Volunteers with the connivance of some in high Government places, brought in a great deal of smuggled arms."

Mac paused, picked up and shook the empty whiskey bottle. "We suspected they landed at Larne and they had secret fast motorcars. Each night they drove all over the province, until most of the Orangemen in the North were armed. Then. THEN this excuse for a government passed a law banning all arms into Ireland.

They feared that men like Dermot and Declan might obtain guns. They never even made an attempt to disarm the Carsonite people in the North. That's when I began having my doubts about this present bunch of laddies running our Empire. Ruining our Empire, I should say.

I could not be sure your woman was the purchaser. I kept my counsel, heard your story and brought you to London to tell it to our group. Indeed if anyone could solve your dilemma, it would be us four older men acting together."

"You deceived me, Mac. Christ almighty, how can I ever trust you again?"

"Jay, lad. You said you'd tell us the entire story and you deceived us as well. You left out a good bit of information."

Jay flared in anger, "only things personal to Deirdre and me."

"Which may have given me vital clues as to her real name, her real nature, her mission. In any case, Jay, it became clear that Deirdre most likely had a hand in the purchase of arms, that you were not involved, that she had indeed disappeared and that you were sincere in your desire to find her."

"So you spied on me and you hoped I'd lead you to her and to the guns."

"Believe me when I say, I didn't give a damn about the guns. Long ago, I became fed up with this government and what they were doing to my beloved Empire. I accepted this job mostly out of boredom. I became a neutral in your case. I could help you in your search, protect you along the way and keep you out of trouble at the end.

You are Sean's son and the more I saw of you, the stronger I felt that your Da had been right all along. It's family that matters the most. Governments change, the Army changes, in time the Empire itself will change and crumble of it's own weight. Family is there when all else is gone."

"Mac, why didn't you trust me enough to tell me?"

"Tell you the woman of your dreams is probably a spy, an arms merchant in time of war and subject to the harshest penalties. Would you have believed me?" They both shook their heads, no. "Jay, your Da was coming and soon would be with us. The three of us together could sort this out and try to slip you out of any mess and keep your Naval career, intact. I would tell Sean. He could guide you and you would certainly believe your own father."

"I wish to God, it had gone that way." Jay was quiet for a while and Mac knew he was sorting through events, trying to get his mind around these revelations. "What about Burke? Wee Willie Burke? Was he part of your team?"

"No Jay,.never. Wee Willie is an avaricious bastard. He controls, or at least he did control, a great deal of wealth, but the man was never satisfied. He confided to me on the sly that the War Department was about to offer a large sum as a reward for information or arrest of any arms being smuggled into Ireland.

After hearing your story, he was sure that your mystery woman was guilty and would be an easy capture. All he needed was more information and so he decided to follow you to find her. He had no official standing with any department. He figured he'd get the goods on you and capture her and collect the reward."

"As did you, yourself."

"Nay Jay, never any reward. I was a consultant on a flat fee. I'd get my pay whether I found anyone or not. But I saw my job as threefold. Keep you safe while you searched for your woman. Determine if she could be involved with Irish Rebels. And third keep Wee Willie out of your way. All of this in addition to my investigative job which became less and less important and in the end of no importance what so ever."

They were silent in the fading twilight and both men knew the dark night was coming. Jay broke the silence first. "So, you were looking out for me?"

"Aye Jay. As soon as Wee Willie read the message that the Lusitania went down, I knew Sean had met the same fate as his father. He was dead at sea. I knew I could no longer be neutral. I had to look out for you, protect you and help you. We were family now, you and I.

On the frigate that morning before we landed in Cobh, I made my final decision. I am a true MacGregor, a real 'Child of the Mist'. Family has become more important than King and Empire and much more important than this corrupt government we have.

If I am to help you, to protect you, then I must embrace your woman and help and protect her as well. I think my Regina would be proud of me and some day I'll have a sit down with my daughter Maria and tell her all this. I hope she will approve of me too."

"And what happens now, Mac?"

"Tomorrow, you'll go down to County Clare to Declan's burial. I'll catch a bus, a ferry and a train to London and file my report." Mac turned and leaned across the bench to Jay.

"What will it say, Mac?" Jay too turned and they faced each other in the fading light.

"I have it written already. 'There were no suspicious persons found in Paris. The train in question made an unscheduled stop just east of the capital but it was due to a mechanical failure. Nothing of interest was found in London.

I traveled to Queenstown in Ireland, chased several rumors to no avail. Explored the South coast where smugglers are known to do business, especially the area from Kinsale down to Skibereen and centered on Clonakilty.

I chased another rumor up to the old pirate center at Killybegs. I have nothing to report. There is at this time, no solid evidence of arms smuggling into Ireland. Enclosed are a list of my expenses.' End of my report"

"And my Deirdre? What of her?"

"My God, Jay. I feel the same for her as I do for you and your Da. If you will allow me, I will become part of your family, as all of you are a part of mine. Someday, I expect my daughter Maria Scotland will perform on the New York stage. I hope we can all be at her opening night together, Jay."

"Mac, what of Dermot and Donal and the Brotherhood? How about the things you saw and the other people you met? What of the Nimble Motleys?"

"The things I saw are things I participated in. I'm as guilty or more so, as the rest of the Motleys. Before we landed in Cobh, I made my decision. Once in, I was in right up to my neck." He stopped and pulled at his clothes to bare his neck. "This is where the rope fits, me boyo, and several times I had a terrible itching in this part of my anatomy. It was especially bad when Wee Willie was near us."

First Mac and then Jay left the soft earth of the graveyard and once again they sat on the opposite ends of the stone bench, and faced each other. But this time there was no convivial bottle of whiskey between them. Jay was hurt and suspicious.

"In a week or less, I'll have an American Passport for Deirdre O'Neill and she'll be safe. Now Mac, what of Wee Willie's confessions, where are they?"

"Dermot and I each have a set of the original confessions, signed and notarized. The Nimble Motleys are safe as a group and safe individually."

"So is this goodbye?" Jay paused and Mac held his breath. Jay was afraid he would choke on his words. "Is this goodbye or just a short, 'so long for now' sort of parting?"

Mac let out a long slow breath. "In a week or so, I expect an invitation for Dermot's wedding to Maura."

"Will that change when I tell Deirdre about this evening, Sean's burial, the trip up here, your disclosure. She'll press me for every detail. You know how she is. And what Deirdre knows, Fiona and Dermot will know before the tea kettle boils."

"Jay, I'm just guessing, but I think Dermot already knows or suspects, just about everything. Some of his looks, his questions, said he thought I might be wearing more that one hat. And somewhere along the way, he accepted me as full-fledged Nimble Motley. And truth be told, Jay, I was and I still am grateful to him and all the Motleys for that acceptance."

Jay leaned across the bench toward Mac. "Do you fancy Fiona?"

"I'd like to dance with her at her son's wedding and I think she'd enjoy dancing with me. Do you know, she calls me Greg? My God, Jay, my own mother called me Greg when I was a wee bairn, a hundred years ago or more." Mac laughed and Jay joined him.

"There's another invitation I'm expecting. The one to your going away party be it on land or aboard the ship that carries you and Deirdre to America. Jay, I want to be there."

In the fading light Jay held his eyes on Mac's two eyes and finally he stuck out his hand and Mac crunched it in his own and then they were hugging and clapping each other on the back.

"Maybe I'll let Deirdre talk me into staying for Dermot and Maura's wedding." Jay declared.

CHAPTER THIRTEEN

Jay dropped Mac at the bus station. He offered to drive him to Londonderry or even clear across to Belfast but Mac said no. He too needed some time alone to sort through his thoughts and feelings. Jay didn't press the matter. They shook and hugged and patted each other's backs and promised to be together again soon. Be it at the wedding or at Jay and Deirdre's leave taking, their American Wake as Fiona called it.

Well before noon Jay had everything he needed, copies of certificates of his father's birth, his grandparents' births and dates of marriage and deaths. He would file these certificates at home along with his own and Deirdre's important papers. It will be a comfort to future generations. Jay made a mental note as soon as he reached New York, he would begin a search for his mother's people and her records in Poland. She'd never talked about it to him.

'It was as though, now that his future life together with Deirdre was secure; he felt the need to anchor his past. He needed names and dates and places of origin and the search took on more urgency because he knew he would never have faces to go with his new information. He had a few old photographs and his mother and father's images burned into his mind. It was good that Deirdre had had a chance to see his father.'

Jay made it to Sligo in good time and he enjoyed being alone with his thoughts. He still struggled to separate feelings from thoughts and he remembered words from some professor and even from Wan Lee, saying that we control our thoughts, but feelings just happen. We are not responsible for them. We are responsible only for how we deal with those feelings.

Just beyond Sligo, Jay veered a bit west of south on a road, which would take him to Galway. Suddenly he pulled over in astonishment. He was hearing Wan Lee's teachings in his head, but it was Deirdre's voice he was hearing. He pulled back onto the road and as he went through the gears he laughed at himself. Now he had the best of two worlds, sage advice from his oriental teacher and his lover's sweet voice in his head, his wife's voice.

'Grand' he thought. 'I wish Deirdre was with me now. She'd enjoy this drive and the countryside and she'd share my debate. I guess I'm tired of being alone already.'

Mac's story last night had opened his eyes. Perhaps he had been taking family for granted. The depth of feeling between Dermot and Deirdre and Fiona was heartwarming and astonishing. It was the same with the Coveney girls. As happened at the dinner in the Coveney Inn garden, Jay once again saw what he had missed growing up an only child with no aunts, uncles or cousins. Suddenly, he sorely missed that which he'd never had.

In Tobercurry he stopped for a meal and immediately missed the big Scotsman. Mac was terrific company. He always made an observation or two that were dead on the mark, and they usually contained a bit of absurdity. Eating alone wasn't near as much fun.

Jay pushed on through Castlebar to Galway and Ennis. He followed Dermot's directions beyond Clarecastle to a small road, which led him right to the adjoining properties of Dermot and Deirdre's family holdings. It was a lovely spot including a point of land between the Fergus River and a small tributary that fed into the river. Just a bit downstream from their land, the Fergus flowed into the large Shannon estuary.

There was a house nearby and beyond a field and stand of trees he could see another house. In between, a track led down to the river's edge. There was a long dock, with a sail powered fishing boat and several smaller craft tied up.

Jay went to the first house. He knocked and entered and found a painting of a woman, an older Deirdre or a younger Fiona, he then realized it must be Deirdre's mam, Fionnoula. She had been a twin to Fiona and the resemblance among the three women was so very strong.

Knowing this was the right house Jay pulled an ottoman next to an easy chair, shed his shoes and sat back with his feet up. It was good to relax after two days of driving and the emotional turmoil of burying a part of his father; then came the revelations from Mac and the various feelings those disclosures had aroused in him.

Jay awoke with a start. A strange man stared down at him and a smiling Dermot had him by the foot. "The right place Jay, but the wrong house altogether. Jay this is another cousin, Tomas Cummins. Tom is working this place on shares with Deirdre. He farms the land and fishes the Shannon waters and keeps this house till Deirdre decides what she'll do with it.

Now, of course, that question has been settled. Tom, this is that Yank I told you about. He has an Irish mug on him, but he's thoroughly American the way he stole away Deirdre's heart before any of the local lads had a chance with her.

Jay O'Neill of the Killybegs O'Neills and the United States Navy, meet Tom Cummins, a Clare man and a fierce hurler. You'd not like to meet him on the field when he has a hurley in his hands. Now, just as soon as Deirdre's husband has put on his shoes we'll be off to my own house. Maura is fixing the tea and your welcome to come, Tom."

"I won't but thanks. I'm headed over to Sixmilebridge." He smiled at Jay, "My Sheila is helping Declan's family prepare for tomorrow. I'll see you both at the church. They're having the 'Laying In', tonight."

On the ride over to Fiona's house, Dermot explained while Jay drove. "The body is taken from the house and laid in the church the night before the burial. The family will keep a vigil all night, praying and remembering. You don't do that in America?"

"No, the wake is held in the house and the body taken to the church in the morning in time for the requiem Mass."

Fiona's house where Dermot grew up and where Deirdre came after her mother Fionnoula died was a large two-story stucco house. Maura greeted him with a hug and a kiss and directions to a bedroom, upstairs.

"Come back down, Jay and we'll have our tea out in back and you can tell us all about Killybegs. And Jay, listen to me now, there are some things of Deirdre's she asked for. It's all there in a pile in your room, boxes and cases and a small folding desk. You may want to pack it into the motorcar tonight. It will save time in the morning, love."

They sat outdoors in the mild evening with the long lingering twilight that was so enjoyable here, as the days came closer to the Summer Solstice. Jay recounted the burial, the pure white sand and the unexpected mourners and the reactions of those people.

He described the scene at the graveyard, when Mac pointed and the sun broke out and the shadow of the large Celtic cross fell across the grave. The mourners all fell back in fear except the priest, who used the holy water to ward off any unwanted entities. Dermot smiled and Maura crossed herself as Jay told about the shadow falling onto his father's open grave.

For the last part, Jay went slow and picked his words carefully. He described the graveyard on the hill, the rich red glow in the west and the gathering darkness to the east. He recounted Mac's disclosure and tried to use Mac's own words. "When we met in Paris, he was a contract agent for the government chasing down a rumour of an arms purchase by Irish Rebels. As I told him about my Deirdre gone missing and my being in a panic to find her, Mac began to see that we could be both chasing the same mystery."

Jay went on and gave Dermot and Maura a full accounting of the conversation there in the Killybegs graveyard as darkness settled in around them. Jay told of his own shock, anger and lastly acceptance, and he told about Mac's journey from being an agent of the British Empire, to a neutral observer and protector and finally a full fledged Nimble Motley.

"Yes, I did have him pegged right from the start," Dermot sounded pleased. "What do you think, Maura love?"

"I have two almost conflicting thoughts." Maura poured more tea for the three of them while she assembled her words. "Regardless of your religious beliefs or lack of them, I think Mac gave you that disclosure because of the sun popping out the way it did. The pure white sand in that seaside grave must have glistened in the sunlight and made the sudden shadow of that ringed Celtic Cross seem that much darker and more frightening. These things touch something deep within us, our soul, if you will. People react in different ways. Some jump back; some fling holy water; Mac was moved to tell the truth. He examined his conscience and told you the truth, Jay. He was being honest with himself and with you."

They were silent and drank tea while digesting Maura's conclusion. After a bit she said, "Jay, there is a telephone here. You won't be able to speak to Deirdre in her bed, but you can get news of her and give her some back. It's in that little office by the front door."

Jay nodded and moved toward the kitchen entrance. "Thanks, Maura. After I speak to Deirdre, I'll turn in. It's been a long day and another one tomorrow." He poked his head back out and said, "listen you two, perhaps I should sleep in the middle of your bed. As an old married man, I could keep you both from temptation."

Dermot threw a biscuit at his head and Maura blew him a kiss. "Jay dear, if we were determined to have our way with each other, we would just wait till you were snoring. But just in case, I think I will lock you in your room." They laughed and Dermot waved him away.

"Ah, one last thing Maura. You said you had two thoughts about Mac's story. What was your other thought?" Jay waited for her words with wonder and some apprehension.

"What would Mac have done, had Devil Burke not been in pursuit of you and Deirdre?"

The day began clear and bright with a strong breeze off the Fergus River and a bright red band along the eastern horizon. Jay double checked his load and untied a case and the folding desk from the roof and stuffed them inside the car. The old seaman's adage ran through his head, 'Red in the Morning, Sailor take Warning.'

Dermot came out dressed in his military uniform. "If it's no burden Jay, Maura will ride along with you. I have some special business needs doing. Here she comes now."

Maura kissed Dermot, "And remember to eat something, my love." Dermot drove away in the Coveney auto and she got into the good doctor's motorcar with Jay. "If we hurry, I can help the ladies with breakfast, and after you men eat, we will all be off to the church."

"Maura, I've been wondering about something ever since I'm in Ireland." She turned to him and he went on. "When do you women get to eat? You're always serving the men."

She smiled a secret smile and replied, "standing, walking, running, and mostly in small bites." They both laughed, he at the absurdity of her answer, she at the truthfulness of it.

He really liked this young woman. She was a great catch for Dermot. She was smart, witty, ambitious and hard working. And maybe she was just a tad officious; not quite bossy, but close. Jay smiled to himself and wondered what their relationship would be like five years from now. For that matter, who would he and Deirdre be, in five years'?

Declan's family home was quite small and very crowded. A long plank table outside was filled with men eating, while women in twos and threes rushed more food out to them from the tiny kitchen. Jay went to the table to eat and Maura went inside to help.

Donal came and hugged Maura and shook hands warmly with Jay and then he went to the church. There were only a few people left inside or outside the house when finally Maura came out leading her sister. Mary Rose Ni Coveney's eyes were red and swollen from weeping and she hugged Jay and began to cry again.

"Your wedding was so beautiful, Jay. And now this funeral," Mary Rose spoke softly. Her voice was almost hoarse. She had told and retold the tale of she and Declan and their budding romance and their 'would've been marriage,' had the heroic Declan not been slain by the 'stranger' in his effort to save Deirdre's life.

Jay held her and soothed her. "When do you start your medical training?

Mary Rose brightened, "next week. And then the week after, I'll be back for another wedding, our Maura and Dermot. And the day after is your big Departure Party. You and Deirdre are sailing away to America. I will miss you so." She hugged Jay again.

"We will? Sail away?"

She laughed and wiped her eyes. "Indeed you will. My Maura and your

Deirdre have your lives mapped out for the coming fifty years." Both of the Coveney sisters laughed and Mary Rose darted back inside to change clothes and repair her face. "Dermot is coming here for her and will take Mary Rose to the church."

The wood and stucco church was small and crowded. 'Jay had to keep reminding himself that this was a chapel. In Ireland, a church meant a Protestant house of worship, while a chapel was a Catholic one.' He and Maura knelt in a pew while up in the choir loft they could hear Mary Rose's fiddle. The parish was too poor for an organ, but someone had donated a harp and the two instruments together made heavenly music.

Declan lay in his closed black coffin and the priest blessed him with prayers and incense and holy water. Jay tried hard, but as always, the droning of the Latin, the soaring harp and swooping fiddle led him away from the Mass and into his private world. He remembered Declan, the jaunty, boasting, lovable young man of so much promise. His quick mind, his jokes, the way he could get to the neat little kernel of truth inside a problem and make a joke out of it. All of this and more flooded back into Jay and he missed Declan intensely.

A life so full of promise, snuffed out by a death so meaningless, so unnecessary, so insane. Was there a God? Could there be? Jay shivered and one bit of the Latin penetrated, 'Sed libera nos a malo'. But deliver us from evil. Jay shivered again. Thankfully his mind wandered once more and he came around to the main point.

Dermot and Maura have a date for their wedding. Great! And his Deirdre, his new wife has decided to remain here in Ireland until the wedding. The decision was made without him. However, it is entirely logical to stay for the wedding if their sailing was the next day. But who booked the sailing and what is the date and on which ship of what line? What's the date for the wedding? And why were these important matters settled without him?

Then he heard Deirdre's voice inside his head. "But Jay my darling, you were so long away up in Killybegs and Sixmilebridge. Someone had to do something. And you were going to suggest we stay for the wedding, anyway. You know you want me to have this memory, my Dermot's wedding. We'll be so far away, in America. And he's my brother, well almost my brother. And with Maura's help, I booked us a very nice inside cabin. It's quite inexpensive, my love. You should be proud of us, of me."

Jay gave Deirdre a kiss and ushered her out of his mind. He'd have to check the shipping line and get a better cabin. They were, after all, bringing a Lusitania victim back home. And this was a honeymoon voyage. And he was a full Lieutenant in the U. S. Navy, and a Yank.

Mary Rose rode to the graveyard with Declan's family while Jay and Maura rode in the good doctor's car, together. There was no sign of Dermot, not yet at least.

They were driving along in a slow procession following the coffin while many of the mourners walked behind and before them. On the left was the iron fence of the burial ground and on the right was a low stonewall. Suddenly, out of a gap in the stones of the wall, stepped two donkeys. They were true Irish asses, with a line running down the back from head to tail and another across the shoulders, forming a perfect cross on their back.

"They say an ass carried Mary when she was carrying the baby Jesus, and another ass carried the man Jesus into Jerusalem and that's how they got the cross on their backs." Maura smiled as she told this to Jay.

"And these two asses were particular friends of Declan's, I suppose." Jay smiled in return. "Will they stay for the burial do you think, Maura?"

"They will, but they will not take a drink, after." Maura brandished the dented tin cup. "And thank you for bringing this back to me."

When the incense, the Latin prayers, the holy water and all the crying was finished, Declan was lowered down and the burial was almost finished. The priest stepped back to make room and Dermot and a squad of men, all in the uniform of The Irish Republican Brotherhood, moved to the graveside. Dermot stood at the head and Mary Rose stood at the foot of the grave of Declan O'Mahon. She was dressed in a ladies version of the Brotherhood uniform.

Dermot gave a short eulogy. He praised the deceased as a gallant soldier who gave his life protecting the life of another. "There is no higher calling. He gave his life for an Ireland free of foreign domination and whole unto itself. Sinn Fein. Ourselves alone." Dermot saluted and Mary Rose repeated the eulogy in Irish and then she too saluted.

The squad raised their rifles and fired three volleys in quick succession over the grave. A bugle played and when the echoes of the guns and bugle fell silent, the squad filed out, led by Dermot and Mary Rose. A lone piper played "The Minstrel Boy", as the Irish Republican Brotherhood marched out and away from a fallen hero.

Jay was moved to the depths of his being. No one he knew, Irish or American, so perfectly fit "The Minstrel Boy" as the dead Declan O'Mahon. In deference to Declan and his family Jay stayed and had one drink. As soon as decency allowed he bade goodbye to Donal and Maura and was back in the good doctor's car and headed home to his poor, wounded, lonesome wife.

He screeched to a halt by the front door, ran in and through the dining room; down the hallway and burst open the door to the WarRoom. There was his Deirdre in a bright new nightgown, her hair was brushed and in place, her eyes were alight, and she had a smile on her lovely wide mouth. Her good arm reached out for him. Jay went to his knees beside the bed, kissed and hugged his bride and looked into her eyes. "I love you," he whispered.

"I love you back," and she grinned. "Did you bring my things from home?"

Jay was dumbfounded, but Deirdre called out over his head. "Girls. Now, right away, please." The two new girls brought in a sturdy chair with wheels on the two back legs. They half lifted Deirdre out of the bed and settled her into the chair. By tilting it back just a bit, they could wheel her into the dining room where Deirdre sat comfortable and impatient at a table as the girls unpacked the good doctor's car and brought her possessions in to her and laid them out on the table.

Jay unpacked the boxes and laid package after package on the table in front of her. Deirdre unwrapped her treasures and delighted in each one. Jay was enchanted. He watched her expressive face and it went from suspense to surprise to tears and back to pleasure and laughter. For Deirdre it was Christmas, her birthday and her wedding all at once. Some packages Jay had to help her with. They were too much for an excited one-armed girl.

Some few things Fiona had wrapped last week, others had been in storage for years. There was one large case marked Fionnoula, and Deirdre set this aside. She saved it for last. Deirdre knew she would cry and she knew she had to make peace with her mother, dead these many years, before she sailed away from Ireland with her new husband.

Jay sat and watched and marveled as expressions chased across his wife's face. He could never, in his mind, capture all of the different looks she had stored inside of her. He was captivated and in love and wondering how long his good fortune would last. If he had a rabbit's foot, he would be rubbing it. Quietly and out of sight he knocked three times on the wooden table leg.

He made room at the table as the girls brought the tea trolley with snacks and biscuits and jam and a bottle of lager for him. Deirdre was too excited to have more than a nibble and a sip of the tea. Jay too was excited and he kept looking at that chair on wheels and wondering if there was some other way to use it. They were an old married couple now, but had not yet consummated their marriage. He was getting desperate.

"Jay." She beckoned him closer. "I've been doing a bit of thinking."

'Sweet Christ, what now?' He thought. "Tell me Deirdre. I want to know all your thoughts."

Deirdre held the back of Jay's head and pulled him close to her so she could whisper into his ear. "My back is fantastic. It's almost healed. I can lie on it, but my left chest still has pain and will take no weight. But. Listen now, I've done some thinking. If you lay me crossways on the bed till I'm almost hanging off, and you support my two legs, you can, I mean you cannot put any weight on me, but. Oh my God, Jay. I want you inside of me. Tonight my love when they've all gone to sleep."

Jay stood and just as quickly he sat down again as one of the girls came in for the tea things. Deirdre grinned at him. She had seen the bulge in the front of his trousers.

Before the girl left with the tea trolley, Deirdre spoke, "dear, can you set that gramophone in my room, in the WarRoom. I'm going to take a rest and a bit of soft music will help. Since there're no guests, I'll leave my things here, for now."

"Yes Deirdre. Sir, shall I set up that single cot the way it was?"

Jay made a quick calculation in his head. He figured the size of the room, the cot versus the easy chair and he pictured Deirdre crossways on the bed. "No, I'll nap in the easy chair, and I can manage Deirdre in this chair and into her bed, and our thanks to you both." He wanted Deirdre with all that he was. Every ounce of his being cried out but he could not hurt her.

And Deirdre wanted him regardless. She had some idea about fulfilling her wifely duty but she also wanted him physically and she needed him emotionally. It was very important to her that they consummate their marriage. She would suffer any pain, even a chance to open her chest wound, to have Jay love her and make love to her, now.

Jay got her onto the bed and had her laying crossways. Gently he maneuvered her to the edge and supported her legs. Her planning was brilliant, and they were both ecstatic. Their lovemaking could best be described as urgent slow motion After all the emotional storms and stresses they had both been through, the heightened strain and physical exertion of their love making was magnificent. After the lovers made wondrous love, he sighed a great big, full sigh, and eased down onto the bed next to her. They held hands and laughed together.

"Now I remember why we got married." He lifted her legs and draped them over his own so she wouldn't slide off the bed and he kissed and caressed her as if it were the first time.

"Well Jay O'Neill, that wasn't bad, but can you do it again? I dare you." She teased him.

"Be careful who you dare, you willful wanton DalCas woman. We O'Neill's always rise to the occasion." He laughed out loud at his pun and Deirdre grinned at him.

Deirdre as though in a dream, said. "Put more music into the room Jay, before you rise too far. Just turn the recording over and we'll hear the other side, so."

"Was the music playing? I never heard the first side."

One of the new girls was polishing silver in the scullery when Maura passed by, "Maura, shall I take the tea trolley to the O'Neills in the WarRoom?"

"Is the gramophone playing?"

The girl went into the hallway and listened. "Yes, I can hear music and John McCormack is singing. He has such a clear sweet voice."

"Do not bring any tea to them now, but keep the kettle humming. They will call whenever they are ready." Maura smiled as she passed her Dermot.

He sat in his favorite spot in the kitchen, feet up, reading stories from the *Tain Bo Cuilgne.* "We've an awful lot of music in this house, lately." He pulled Maura onto his lap. "That gramophone will be worn out before they ever sail to America."

Deirdre was getting stronger each day and Fiona, feeling herself in the way, and not wanting to put any roadblock in her son's blossoming love affair with Maura, invented some urgent business at home. She left for County Clare and her home on the Fergus River.

"I'll be here again in time to help you with the wedding," she promised as she kissed Deirdre and Maura and Dermot and Jay goodbye.

The healing of Deirdre's wound was almost miraculous. Another miracle was the chair with wheels embedded in the back legs. Jay had her up and into the dining room for at least one meal each day.

On every good day they would spend time together out in the walled garden. Jay would show off his expertise in pulling weeds and harvesting ripe fruit and vegetables. Deirdre would name the flowers as she had him cut them for a dining room bouquet; and she would name the birds as each flew into the garden for a bit of the bread she threw to attract them.

Some days Jay would leave Deirdre and drive to Cork on business. Some days Dermot would go along. Jay would go into the solicitor's office where they gave him desk space and use of the telephone and telegraph. He was in constant communication with his Admiral at the Embassy in London, the shipping line in Cobh, his father's attorney in New York and Mac MacGregor in London.

Dermot was just next-door in an office reached by a dim hallway, which appeared to end in a porters closet but was really a hidden entrance to a suite of rooms maintained by the I.R.B. Dermot never discussed any of his activities there and Jay never asked. Dermot was waiting for a new assignment, but first he and Maura would marry and the newlyweds would spend a fortnight holiday on the Southern coast of Spain. They would be close to Jerez de la Frontera and the Quadalquivir River, the sherry capital of the world in a place well known to both Irish and British smugglers alike. Flor Sweeney made all the arrangements for them.

Jay was technically on detached duty for the U.S. Navy. Once on board ship and homeward bound he would begin a month's leave. It would give him time to bury his father, settle Sean's estate and house in New York, take his bride by train to Niagara Falls for a honeymoon and report to Washington D.C. for a new assignment. He and Dermot had so much in common. They were both awaiting new assignments; were both newly wedded and of course the strongest link by far was their love for Deirdre.

Guided by Dermot, Jay went to a jeweler's shop on The Grande Parade in Cork City and brought in with him the remains of the Shian Bao including a bit of the red silk, a dusting of the incense ashes, the little silver heart, all mangled, and the lead slug from the bullet that killed Declan and had to be dug out of Deirdre's back.

Jay was entranced by the piece this clever jeweler wrought. On a fine chain hung a small silver heart backed by two red silk wings of many layers. Behind these was mounted a silver cylinder which held the lead slug and sealed inside the lead was a pocket of the ashes. Jay would present this to Deirdre on the day of Dermot and Maura's wedding. He hoped she would wear it.

Deirdre treasured these days with Jay and the dinners with all four of them; although sometimes it was just herself and Maura and these hours were good too. It gave the young women a fine chance to gossip, swap stories and clothes, and make plans for the unknown. They knew their futures would be different though the paths they trod would be very similar. They each hoped for a stronger bond with their chosen man. Each of them expected to bear and raise children. They both wanted an active life beyond husband and home and that was very important to them. Deirdre was fierce about equality and the rights of women and Maura had a liking for commercial ventures and wanted to seize every opportunity.

She was very business minded. "I can see this as a sort of soldier repair center. We are close to the City; close enough to Cobh and incoming ships and yet we can offer the peace and quiet of a country setting. This war is on nearly a year now and if it goes much into Nineteen Sixteen or beyond, why we will need to add a wing onto the building." She paused and poured tea for them both. "Mary Rose will handle the medical side and I will do the feeding, the housing and the business end of it."

Deirdre was more interested in politics and the role of women in the new world order, which surely must happen, after such widespread devastation. "The coming changes Maura, will be so exciting and all pervasive. I do believe the role of women in politics holds enough work for me for at least two lifetimes." She waved her arm and indicated the Inn. "But what will you do when the war is over and the troops are all mended and gone home to their wives?"

Maura had a dreamy look on her usually down to earth face. "And after the fighting ends? There are four large empires involved in this war and they will be changed, entirely."

"Deirdre we have men fighting in Egypt and the Holy Land, in Syria and Turkey, the Balkans and in Russia, France and Belgium. My God, people will want to travel and show these battle places to their families. When we get to Spain, I will do a bit of exploring. Think of a well run Inn or Hotel with grand Irish hospitality in some of these exotic far off places."

"A few Coveney Inns strung out along the Mediterranean Sea? Is Dermot with you on this?"

"Not yet." Maura laughed. "We agree on the plight of Ireland. We must be free to chart our own destiny. We agree that Ireland, after the war, should be included in any peace treaty, settling national borders and so on." She sighed. "He has not the same drive for business as he has for politics."

Maura smiled at Deirdre, "It must run in the family. We will, of course, compromise and I may never reach the lofty heights that I can foresee." She regarded Deirdre seriously; looked into her teacup and swirled the tea leaves. "I foretell an interesting life for each of us." The two women laughed and got onto plans for the coming wedding.

One afternoon when Jay and Dermot were in Cork and Maura and the serving girls were inside planning the wedding feast, Deirdre sat in the garden alone as the sky darkened and a fast moving storm began dumping a torrent of rain on the garden and on Deirdre. She could not move her chair. She was cold and shivering and completely wet. She couldn't stand and her cries for help became lost in the howling wind and thunder of the storm.

Deirdre became afraid, and she almost began to cry. Then she got angry and cried even harder. Her tears of fear and rage mixed with the rain and she beat on the arms of her chair. She cursed the man who had shot her. She railed at herself for not healing faster and she vowed to never again be caught helpless and dependent upon others.

At last the girls and Maura saw the storm, realized her plight and ran out to her. They brought her into the kitchen and undressed her. They hung her wet clothes near the hot stove and rubbed her dry with big fluffy towels from the hot press. A glass of brandy warmed her from within and still shivering under a wool blanket she announced, "tomorrow I will begin standing. Maura, I will walk and dance at your wedding on Saturday next. Now, girls, will you wheel me to the WarRoom and bring to me that case marked Fionnoula. Oh and yes, bring another brandy, please."

Alone in her room Deirdre sipped her brandy. She set it down and with tears still leaking down her cheeks, she opened her mother's case. On top was an envelope and the writing on it was Fiona's.

"My darling Deirdre.

This letter is from your mother, who was my dearest and best friend as well as my twin sister. She said to me, 'Give this to my daughter. I leave it to you to know when she is ready. I love you both, Fionnoula.' It is time now for you to have this letter and these things. Deirdre, please know that you have been well and truly loved. I am, your aunt, your sister, and most of all, your friend. I love you so much. Your Fiona."

Deirdre held the letter between her palms as though she could divine what was inside. She put it down on her pillow for later. The first things in the case were from her two years at school in France. A white beret, her brown and white school uniform, a midi blouse, a sailors scarf, brown skirt, stockings and shoes. Someday, when she had a daughter she'd get these out…A ships menu, but no date on it. Was it going to France or coming home? A train ticket stub and timetable, a student pass to the

Eiffel Tower, The Louvre and the opera and a program of La Boheme, were spread across the case. Four school progress reports from France and her Leaving Certificate were tucked inside her favorite sweater.

She had been sent away to school soon after her mother died, and she was numb about her life with Fionnoula. The twins looked so much alike and she had spent so much time with Fiona and Dermot that memories of her real birth mother were fuzzy at best. Deirdre knew this would be painful, but she plunged ahead, regardless. Next in the case and hiding everything else, was a long woolen cloak. It was custom made for her when she was half grown, maybe ten or so. Her mother had made it. Fionnoula was the twin with needle and thread talent. Fiona had other skills but it was Fionnoula who made all of her clothes.

Deirdre held the cloak up and examined it; she smelled it with deep breathes; she rubbed it on her face and arms and clutched it to her breast as the times came flooding back to her. She remembered the little stool she stood on, as Fionnoula on her knees, pinned and shaped and tugged at the garment. That last fitting she had to keep her eyes closed until she finally stood before the mirror and saw herself in the cloak. She was so pleased. She wore it and showed it to everybody. She had hugged and kissed Fionnoula and begged to wear the cloak everywhere, even to bed.

Within a year, and it seemed to Deirdre almost at once, Fionnoula became ill, took to her bed and died within a month. Deirdre bereft, and in a rage, blamed her mother for leaving her. In anger she cut up all the fine clothes her mother had made, all except the cloak. Some one must have hidden it from Deirdre in her rage. It was most likely Fiona who hid it away.

Now she had the cloak and with it came all the memories, both good and bad. With a great effort of willpower she was able to picture the twins side by side, her mother and her aunt together at the table, together in the boat fishing, together laughing and singing as someone cut a cake, together at Christmas and on St. Stevens Day, Easter and Deirdre in a new dress and bonnet. Each summer Fionnoula made new light frocks in bright colors for her.

One mother sick in bed, another mother healthy and worried. The trouble was the images were interchangeable. She could not distinguish her Fionnoula from her Fiona. And so, in order to make peace with herself, she would have to love them both and forgive them both.

Jay came in just as she struggled to her feet for the first time since the shooting. The blanket fell away and she stood, nearly naked, swaying and crying and laughing. He grabbed and held her, then managed to get them both seated on the bed. She told him about her entire nightmarish day; the storm, her fear, being wet and alone and unable to help herself. Jay soothed her and calmed her with caresses and hugs and told her he understood.

"Ah Jay. I can love them both now. My Fionnoula and my Fiona. They were mothers to me, both of them. And as I grew I became a sister to them. Now my Jay, I can leave Ireland. I can and I will go with you to America."

Jay was puzzled and quite amazed. There was never any question about Deirdre not going with him, but he didn't say that. He was learning every day. He learned from Dermot and Maura. He watched how Fiona handled situations. He remembered his father and his mother and how they gave small signals to each other and stayed clear of damaging storms. The way a big ship would signal a smaller vessel and establish who had the right of way, thus avoiding a collision. And so he recognized Deirdre's signal in time to respond correctly.

"I'm so glad, Deirdre. You know I've loved you since that day I first saw you on the train. I want you with me always and everywhere, especially in America."

She smiled and nuzzled into him on the bed. "I want to go home to Clare. I'll visit my mother's grave and see my old home once more, before we sail away. Will you take me?"

"Yes my love."

"I need two days to practice standing and taking a few steps. You'll help me?"

"You're getting better aren't you? Yes, of course I'll help you. It's what Naval officers do."

The Coveney Inn was in an Irish uproar, a real Donnybrook, with wedding plans, and departure plans and there were so many decisions to be made and by so few people.

The guest lists were drawn and redrawn, revised, cut back and added to until Maura and Fiona were each satisfied. Maura arranged for the food and drink and leaned on all of her suppliers, reminding them of how important Coveney's Inn was to their business. They were all allowed to hear the rumor that Coveney's might become an Army Convalescent Center and thus be busier than ever. The suppliers were quite generous, and they were especially interested to learn that Maura's husband-to-be held a commission in a not to be mentioned army and he might have a future in Irish politics. That is if he stayed alive and out of jail.

Maura promptly hired the owner of a neighboring Inn to serve in her place as hostess and operations manager for the weekend. The neighbor was pleased to be asked and readily agreed to help. Though they were rivals, Maura often sent this woman her overflow business and they were respectful of each other's talents.

The wedding was Saturday. Many of the people would stay over or return for another go on Sunday. That was the departure party for Deirdre and Jay. They called it an American Wake, a Farewell Party or a Feis, and in the time honored Irish way, the more sad an occasion was the longer the event would be treasured and remembered.

The entire weekend would be nonstop feasting, dancing, and drinking with laughter and tears enough for everyone. There would be solemn promises of eternal friendship made between strangers who would never see each other nor hear of each other ever again.

Marriage vows would be exchanged and love and a marriage bond would be created strong enough to withstand rebellion and a civil war, bleak and hard economic years, good times, and the ravages of time itself.

Mary Rose put herself in charge of the music for all the festivities. She was to be the maid of honor for her sister, but she would also play at the wedding and for the dancing to follow. She rounded up a half dozen fellow musicians and one of them owned a portable wooden dance floor. It would arrive and be erected in the garden early Saturday morning.

Jay had two duties for the festive weekend. He ran all of the errands and brought in any supplies, which could not be delivered. His second job was as a physical therapist for his Deirdre. He'd massage her, help her stand, and provide resistance for her as she pushed her arm and shoulder against him. Deirdre's young body healed well and improved each day.

The only problem was the young lovers vibrant lust for each other. Each time Jay massaged and worked on Deirdre's arm, shoulder or breast they had to 'put music into the room.' The others in the house smiled whenever they heard the gramophone playing.

Deirdre did most of the sit-down work. She would write lists, keep a progress chart, cross off jobs finished, and write thank you notes for the steady stream of gifts that arrived every day. Between these chores, she would go with Jay on his trips, and sometimes they would be gone for hours on the simplest errand.

They cherished their time alone together. Jay called it Sinn Fein time, ourselves alone time. He was getting good at attaching names to people and things. Nicknames he called them and did it in memory of poor dead Declan. The two new girls at the Inn were Bernadette and Stephanie and of course Jay named them almost at once.

On the Thursday, they had the new girls, Bernie and Steve, pack a lunch for them and Jay and Deirdre headed up to County Clare and Fiona's house on the Fergus River. They would visit Fionnoula's grave and bring Fiona back with them. The two new girls were old hands at the Inn now and they were busy instructing a temporary staff of a half dozen who would work right through Monday and the big clean up after all the festivities were over.

Fiona was packed and waiting when they arrived. After hugs and kisses, she showed Jay the way to the graveyard, and he parked as close as possible to the site. Then with Fiona on one side and Jay on the other they helped Deirdre to the place where her mother lay buried. Fiona stepped aside to visit with her long dead husband and infant child. She knew Deirdre needed to be alone with Fionnoula and she was overjoyed that the two would make up and find peace and love before Deirdre sailed away to America with her chosen man.

"Help me down, Jay. I want to kneel and pray." Jay did and stepped away so his wife could pray and tell her mother she loved her and they were at peace with each other. "And thank you for giving me my life," she whispered. "I am so sorry I was not older and more help, more understanding, when you went away from us. Goodbye Fionnoula my dearest mother."

The ride back to Cork, Bishopstown and the Inn began rather quiet and sad and so the three of them began telling stories of family and life and loved ones, and soon laughter overtook the sadness. Finally, shyly, Fiona asked about all their 'doings' before she came down to help her wounded Deirdre. She wanted to know everything.

"Tell me all there is to know about those motorcars."

Deirdre had been in the dining room of the Inn for most of the bargaining between Declan and the good doctor, so she told that entire story with Jay nodding and grinning as Deirdre hit all the high points. "…And our Declan clearly had the best of that mental jousting."

"And what of that other car. The grand big expensive one, surely you should've kept that one. 'Twas worth a fortune wasn't it, so."

"The car was too hot," Jay explained. "We had to get rid of it to keep Deirdre safe from Devil Burke. Wee Willie's man had seen us and the car, just after the road block."

"Ah, the road block. Tell us about that and the grand singing and all." Fiona was trying to sound casual.

Jay watched in the rear view mirror and could see a smile flitting across Fiona's lips. Deirdre turned to face Fiona in the back seat, "You've heard about the road block? And the singing? And the terrible danger we were in?"

"Dermot mentioned something about it, but do tell us the full story, Deirdre love."

Deirdre and Jay, taking turns recounted the full story for Fiona. The roadblock, the machine guns, the rifles and pistols, Donal scrunched up like an invalid under the blanket with his finger on the trigger of his hidden rifle, and Mac out on the running board in full Scottish attire saying, 'we'll use guile, not guns.' Then together Deirdre and Jay sang out a rousing rendition of, "It's a Long Way to Tipperary."

Fiona joined the singing and before the last notes of that grand marching song had faded away she asked, "and has he a good strong voice?"

"Who?" Jay and Deirdre asked together, playing innocent.

"Greg MacGregor," Fiona answered, "and what are you two laughing at?"

"He'll be at the Inn when we get there," Jay told Fiona.

"Well then, Jay darling, drive on and don't go slow on my account. I enjoy a speedy ride, so." Fiona smiled and leaned back against the cushions.

Deirdre turned in her seat and faced Jay. It helped ease her stiffness a bit with her right shoulder against the seat back and in that position she could see Fiona too. "I have some juicy gossip I was saving for you both." She paused until Fiona was bursting with curiosity. "Father Rory will marry Dermot and Maura after all."

Jay swore and Fiona gasped. "How is this possible?" She asked, "when he made such a fuss about the edict from the bishops and refused to marry the two of you."

"Listen now. He went to his pastor, the one they call Big Billy Conklin, and told him the whole story, or perhaps only select parts of the whole story. When Big Billy heard that his dear chum and old school mate, Wee Willie Burke was in hot pursuit of a woman, and that woman is me, and he had that poor woman shot and a man was killed and a British soldier disappeared, and all at his, Burke's instigation. Ah, can you picture it. Big Billy as white as that tablecloth in his dining room where I served him dinner and where that lecherous bastard Burke fondled my breast." She paused for breath and changed her position again.

"Fondled you?" Fiona was aghast. "How, what did he do? Deirdre?" Her voice rose up.

Deirdre waved it away. "In any case, Rory insisted that he be allowed to make amends by performing the marriage of Maura, a good Cork woman, and her man, even though a rumor has it that the man is a member of The I.R.B. Big Billy relented and will allow this one lapse from the order of the Bishops, but…but it cannot happen in a church. Rory can marry them in a catholic ceremony outside the church, treating the marriage as though one of them was a Protestant." Deirdre laughed and Jay joined her.

Fiona was not amused, and they rode in silence for a while. "Well in God's Holy Name, Deirdre what does poor Maura think of all that?"

"Ah Fiona. Maura is delirious. The same way your Dermot himself is. She doesn't care a tinker's damn about any of it. She says, 'we've had a

Requiem mass for Declan and Sean right here in this same dining room we will be married in. The room and the house are blessed, surely. Except perhaps for the bedrooms and especially Deirdre and Jay's room. That WarRoom they sleep in is more carnal than catholic, she says.'" She gave Jay a dig in his ribs.

Fiona didn't laugh; she had a worried mind. "Deirdre you will help me surely, with Maura and the wedding dress?" Deirdre turned again and Fiona went on. "The skirt you wore at your wedding is fine, there was no damage at all. And the sleeves survived the mayhem that the deranged man visited upon you. But the top half is ruined. Between the gaping bullet hole and all the bloodstains and the ripping and tearing they did to get to your wound, the top had to be remade entirely. And nothing matched, you see. None of the materials today will match the color that is in it, from years ago."

"What's to be done, Fiona?"

"'Tis done already. I had the cleverest dressmaker, and she is the best since my Fionnoula is gone, she took apart the two large puffy sleeves and used that material and made a new blouse for the top. Then she added some nice lace for the sleeves and it is brilliant, Deirdre. It is absolutely better now than when you wore it. That dress will go now for another three generations of weddings, I dare say."

"That's grand, Fiona. But what then is the problem?"

"The problem is Maura. Will she like the dress? I am to be her mother-in-law. Will she accept her wedding dress from Dermot's Mam? Women tend to be touchy about weddings."

"Fiona, you gave that dress to me and so 'tis mine to give to Dermot's bride. Let me give her the dress and see it fit to her form. Surely, she will not resent my wedding gift to her."

On Friday afternoon before Maura fully relinquished her authority at the Inn, she had the girls gather all the religious statues and holy pictures in the house. The collection included several crucifixes, the Blessed Virgin, and St. Joseph. Saints Patrick and Brigid were there along with St. Jude, St. Christopher and the Sacred Heart. She had them all put outside on the windowsills. "We do not want the rain on us tonight or tomorrow.

These should help keep us dry. With all these exposed outside, it will never rain a'tall."

The supper that night was a small family gathering, including Mac and Donal and Rory who offered a blessing for the coming union and the future well being of the Nimble Motleys wherever they might go. Father Rory, wanting to make amends, gave a special prayer. "Lord we ask a special blessing for Jay and Deirdre, just recently married and we give thanks for her speedy recovery from her wounds. Thank you O Lord Jesus Christ, Amen."

Mary Rose sat next to Donal and with her encouragement he spent most of the dinner telling tales of Declan and his heroic and antic escapades. She never tired of hearing about the fine young man she had chosen for her mate and whose young life was cut short when he saved the life of another by jumping into the path of a bullet.

Mac was seated next to Fiona who was in rare form. She had with her all the people she cared about. She had her son Dermot and his new love, Maura. She had her Deirdre who filled the roles of niece and daughter and sister. She had her for two more days, anyway, but Fiona was pleased and knew her sister Fionnoula would be pleased too with the direction Deirdre was headed.

And last, Fiona had a new admirer, this big Scotsman with the ready smile, keen observations and easy manner. Greg MacGregor knew who he was and that gave Fiona a feeling of well-being and a grand jolt of confidence.

While the wine was being served, Jay handed Deirdre a small box. She didn't know what to make of it. "What's this, a gift for me? I am well and truly married already, kind sir." The way a child would, she quickly ripped off the paper and opened the box. At first she had no idea what it was, then Deirdre recognized the layers of red silk wings around the little heart as a part of her Shian Bao. "Ooh Jay. My Shian Bao, my lucky charm."

"The little silver heart there was hidden inside the red silk diamond. It saved your life. It deflected the bullet away from your heart." Jay kissed her fingers. "May this Shian Bao and myself, protect you forever, my Deirdre, my wife."

Everyone clapped and cheered them and she passed the box around the table. When it came back, she took it out of the box. "Will you clasp it around my neck Jay, please. I want to wear it always."

The rest of the evening was devoted to Maura and Dermot and their plans, which were still being formed. "We'll probably live here at the Inn and I'll drive in to Cork each morning." Dermot was quite relaxed about it all.

Maura jumped into it with, "unless the Inn is filled with wounded soldiers. Then we likely will live in Cork and I will drive out here each morning."

Mac chimed in, "in any case, one of you will be on the move each and every day."

Donal added, "or you could live in the middle in Bishopstown and both of you could be on the move every day in two directions." It sounded like Declan and he meant it that way.

The evening ended early and on a quiet note. They all knew the next day would be long and very busy.

In the WarRoom Jay helped Deirdre undress and hung up her clothes with care. "Yes, I will, yes. I'll be very careful and not crush your gown for tomorrow. Now, Deirdre, shall I put a bit of music into the room?" He smiled at her.

"Jay O'Neill, don't you dare crank up that gramophone. You'll wake the entire house." She smiled back at him. "Everyone here knows you're a big strong Yankee sailor who can make love every damn night of the week and stop grinning so I can kiss you goodnight." They kissed and hugged and he caressed her to sleep.

"Thank you for my new Shian Bao. I love it."

CHAPTER FOURTEEN

The wedding was beautiful. Every bit of it followed the script as envisioned by Maura and it all turned out even better than planned. Although Maura had relinquished her 'Head of the House' status she still maintained tight control over everything that happened and everyone who made things happen.

The dining room and indeed the entire Inn was resplendent with cut flowers and blooming plants, bunting, flags and weddings bells and other decorative items of silk and fine paper wrought into exotic shapes. There were two potted palms flanking the makeshift altar and Father Rory wore his most festive vestments.

The guests wore their best and the ladies were especially colorful in frocks of every shade and nuance of spring.

The harp and fiddle music began and the mother of the groom entered. Fiona wore a stylish frock of Wedgwood blue, which matched her eyes and she used accents of light blue and a bit of lavender. She kept a slow steady pace on the arm of Mac MacGregor. He wore his formal tuxedo as though he was born to it and the two kept smiling at each other and made eye contact all the way down the short aisle.

Deirdre stepped out of the doorway and took Jay's arm. The seated guests gave oohs and aahs and applauded Deirdre as she came down the aisle on Jay's arm. The applause was for her overcoming the violence done to her by a madman, but the surprise exclamations were for her dress and for her looks. Deirdre was almost an exact but younger version of Fiona. They could easily have been sisters. Her frock was light blue with accents of lavender and Wedgwood and was cut from the same pattern as Fiona's.

Jay was handsome and manly in his formal attire and he looked from his Deirdre to Fiona and back again. He too was amazed all over again at the family resemblance and the great beauty of these two women. Deirdre was young and vibrant and like a budding rose she was full of promise. Fiona had the beauty of a rose in full bloom. She was the promise fulfilled.

As they came up the aisle and were half way to their places, the good doctor caught Deirdre's hand and Nurse reached out with her hand, so the three held hands briefly and exchanged smiles as Deirdre and Jay passed slowly by.

The fiddle music stopped and Mary Rose came down the aisle on the arm of Donal. He looked wonderful and wore his formal suit with pride. Mary Rose as Maid of Honor wore a long lavender gown with rose pieces at her throat and waist and gloves. She was so beautiful in an ethereal way, that the guests, knowing her story, her loss, whispered words of praise and encouragement as she slowly passed by. Donal hugged her arm.

A young flower girl came next, spreading petals on the bridal path and carrying Mary Rose's fiddle and bow under her arm. The friends and family all cheered as the little one handed the fiddle to Mary Rose, who gave it a quick tune up and joined with the harp in The Wedding March. She played as though her heart would break, and tears glistened in her eyes as she watched her sister come slowly up the aisle to marry her chosen man.

Father Rory winced as he remembered the Wedding March music and that scene outside in the garden when Mary Rose played the tune and he, Father Rory Beechinor, announced to all the Motleys that he could not marry Deirdre and Jay because of the Bishops decree.

Maura was the bride and she was the most beautiful woman in the room. The wedding dress, remade since Deirdre's wedding showed no sign of any mishap. It fit Maura like a custom gown, made from scratch for just her. The women, those in the know, all agreed the lace sleeves and other changes only added to her beauty. Maura wore the gold and emerald brooch and earrings, the old Spanish family heirloom that Deirdre had given back to Fiona for Dermot and Maura to have and so it would remain in the family and stay in Ireland.

She was on the arm of her uncle, Ned Coveney, the youngest brother of her deceased father. His wife and two daughters sat up front and the three women all wondered the same thing, 'will that dress be available for our side of the family when we have a wedding.'

Rory married them and blessed them and blessed the two rings. And then for good measure, he blessed the entire audience of family and friends and even all of the staff who stood in the back of that so very versatile dining room, operating theatre, and Chapel for a wake, a requiem mass and now a wedding.

The wedding party lingered for photos in the dining room and then moved outside to the enclosed garden where the guests were busy at the table of finger food, or *hors d'oeuvres,* as Maura called them. A table with wine, punch and whiskey stood to one side of the food and a smaller table of non-alcoholic drinks was on the other.

A bower had been erected at one end of the garden, near the fountain and the fishpond. It was covered with flowers and vines, and the wedding party had more pictures taken there.

Deirdre and Jay had extra photographs taken. Maura was very generous with Deirdre. She remembered how Deirdre's wedding was interrupted, and she was so happy to marry her Dermot that she was glad to share the limelight, share her special day with Deirdre and Jay.

And Deirdre was grateful for this generosity. The two young women had grown quite close in the fortnight since Dermot brought his small group, his Nimble Motleys to Coveney's Inn.

The good doctor and Nurse went with Jay and Deirdre into the WarRoom where he examined the wounds one last time. The damage to Deirdre's back was almost gone and the wound on her chest was healing well. There was very little pain and just a bit of discomfort when she stretched and exercised to regain her full range of motion. The good doctor was pleased. He wished her and Jay God Speed on their travels and he left. It was now Nurses turn to instruct Jay on how to bandage Deirdre and care for her against any infection.

"You must keep the wound clean and bandaged and here's some cream to rub on her chest so her skin does not dry."

"I promise to rub her chest each night." Jay grinned and Deirdre would've kicked him except Nurse was in the way.

Nurse gave a small smile. She'd heard these jokes before. "At the slightest sign of infection, stop the cream and use this ointment. Then give this powder in a glass of water morning and night. Infection is the enemy. Time is your friend."

She surprised them and kissed Deirdre and then Jay and wished them well in America. "I wish we were going with you. I swear to God, all of Europe has become a nightmare." On the way back out to the garden, Jay saw the good doctor at a table in the dining room conferring with Dermot and Maura and Mac. Mac waved them over and made space for Deirdre's chair and for Jay. Mac told them just where they stood with the proposed Army Convalescent Center.

"Maura and the good doctor drew up a plan of operations and it has been well received here in Cork and up in Dublin. It's been moved on over to London for final approval."

"That is where MacGregor comes in." The good doctor said. "He has connections near the top of the pile in London and will present our plan in person, next week."

Maura spoke up, "They love our plan here and up in Dublin. The Army is simply overwhelmed. Those poor men are still too sick to go back home; they cannot be put out onto the street, and more wounded come in by ship each day. They need every bed they can find."

"So," Dermot grinned, "While you two are off to America and we," he grabbed Maura in a hug, "are baking our bones on Spanish sand, Mac and the good doctor will have the paper work cleared for us. Maura will begin work as soon as we return."

"That's grand, Dermot." Deirdre was overjoyed for them. "Jay and I have something to share with you."

"Two things, Dermot," Jay began. "And this is off the record, but we, the U.S. that is, will be in it with the British and French and Russians. It may take awhile, but after what I've seen across the length of Europe, and after the Lusitania's destruction, I have no doubt of it. However, even before we commit to this war, there are young Americans soldiers and flyers fighting now, and of course being killed and wounded."

Jay paused while a new young server brought a tray of champagne and passed drinks around. "Just as soon as you are open for business here, wire me at the American Embassy in London and they'll forward it to me wherever I am. I'll arrange clearance for you to care for any American wounded."

"Yes," the good doctor added, "They will be shipped back to America as soon as they are well and they would go from Queenstown, anyway" he paused, "Cobh, I mean."

"The second thing, Dermot," Jay went on, "Flor Sweeney will try to buy back the hearse or ambulance or whichever that vehicle is. The Navy doesn't expect any money back so it's yours to deal with. However, Deirdre and I talked about it. We think you or rather Maura should keep it and use it to convey your wounded here. Another service for you to offer to the government."

"And charge for. Ah Jay. Deirdre. What a grand idea." Maura was delighted. "We will charge the British to house and care for the wounded, and we will add a charge for carting the poor wounded boys here. I like it and I thank you both."

"One final thought, now." Jay added as he and Deirdre and the newly weds clinked glasses. "Flor Sweeney will see you making a great deal of money and his nose will be bent, so you might have him build you a dozen or so of his fine coffins and some of those rolling chairs that Deirdre used so well."

"Aye Jay," Mac was intrigued. "I was impressed with his operation. He has some fine mechanics and wood workers at his command."

"Finish carpenters and shipwrights, they are indeed some of the best." Dermot agreed. "And, of course, we can get him the most of the burial and mortuary work. He'll be well pleased, he will. Anytime Flor Sweeney is pocketing coins, he's a happy man, indeed."

"Dermot, we should join our guests." Maura linked her arm through Deirdre's. "Mac, Jay, come out you, to the garden with us. Deirdre, I am so pleased that the weather recognized our festivities, aren't you? Have the staff bring in all our religious statues after your party."

The young staff people of Coveney's Inn were fairly flying about. They carried drinks and replenished food outside in the garden, even as they converted the wedding chapel back into a large buffet and dining room. There were stations for both hot food and cold food. There were several meats and fowl, two kinds of fish, a multitude of vegetables, platters of salads and fruits and several kinds of tarts, jellies and sweet biscuits for the young ones.

Another table held stacks of plates, flatware, napkins, cups and saucers and glasses. It also held several giant urns of hot tea and smaller carafes of coffee.

When all was ready, the dance music stopped and the lead musician announced a buffet dinner was being served in the dining room. As most of the guests moved inside, the staff went outside and collected used wine and drink glasses, old plates, and anything soiled or out of place.

Some of the guests remained inside to eat and others came back out to the garden. Many of them sat with relatives or friends, others made their way to any open seat and sat down with strangers, where in the free and easy atmosphere of a wedding feast; they quickly became acquaintances.

The wedding guests were a varied, congenial and mystified group. This union between Maura Ni Coveney and Dermot O'Rourke was a total surprise to almost everyone. The traditional reading out in church of the marriage banns for three weeks before the ceremony, had been waived. The wedding plans were made. Family and friends were notified; and now on such short notice, here they were married and ready to go away on a trip.

Upon their return they would go into a whole new business venture and a new way of life. Some shook their heads in amazement, a few were angry at these sudden and upsetting events but most were delighted and wished the two of them well.

Mary Rose played her fiddle and circulated among the guests. She smiled to herself at all the varied comments she overheard.

"And who is this Coveney girl he married. I never in my life heard of the family."

"Ah now, ye edjit, this is the Coveney Inn were sitting in. The girl he married owns it, or half anyway. He's done quite well for himself, marrying a woman of property."

"I've heard he's a member of some secret society."

"He's a real hard case, they say. Liable to end up in a prison cell or worse."

"Why would he pick a fight with the King and Government when our own lads are over there fighting the Kaiser?"

"The English are getting their arses kicked over in France."

"Indeed. 'Tis our best chance to be done with them. As de Valera says 'England's troubles are Ireland's opportunity.'"

"Sure, that Dermot, he'll be heading our own Irish Government one of these fine days."

Flor and Florrie Sweeney watched Dermot and Maura swirl and dip through a waltz. "They make a handsome couple, don't they," Florrie said and smiled as Jay wheeled Deirdre over to join them.

"Florrie, I'm so happy to see you again. You were like a mother hen to me that night. Jay this is Florrie Sweeney. Florrie meet my husband Jay, and you two men know each other."

Jay shook hands with Flor and watched as Florrie hugged Deirdre and fussed over her and shook her head at how well and healthy she looked after her close brush with death.

Flor spoke in a low voice. "You'll be happy to know Deirdre, all those lorries made it up to Cobh in fine shape and the goods were delivered as planned." Flor Sweeney was extremely pleased at the way things were developing. "And you'll be missing some big doings hereabouts in the next year or so. We've everything all laid on. But then you will have your own grand doings over in America, I suppose."

Mac and Fiona danced by and chided Jay and Deirdre. "Come on now Jay, get your wife Deirdre up and out of that chair. She promised Dermot she'd dance at his wedding."

Deirdre held up her good arm and through a twinge of pain she raised her left arm too and Jay lifted her up onto the dance floor and into a slow round of swirls and steps. She regarded her husband with her head tilted to one side, as though she was surprised. "This is our first dance." And she kissed his cheek. "Am I a good dancer?"

"Superb. You are sublime. You're a sweet dream in my arms.

"Oh stop it you fool," she chuckled low in her throat and leaned back in his arms to look at him. "I'm stiff and clumsy and you yourself are a dream dancer. It's you should go and dance with some healthy girl."

"Ah but I love you and you're not too bad for a beginner. But this is not our first dance. Don't you remember? We were dancing like this when you were shot."

"I must have blocked out that memory, Jay O'Neill along with the shooting. Now you wait until I'm fully healed. I'll show you dancing."

"I can't wait and I won't." And he wheeled her faster and held her tighter and she laughed and danced and finally admitted she had better sit down.

Maura and Dermot appeared in their traveling clothes and made the rounds of 'thank yous and good byes'. Mary Rose came and announced a special send off for her sister and new brother. She came with her fiddle to the edge of the dance floor and began to play a spirited Flamenco. One of the young girls on the staff came running out to the middle of the floor and danced to the raw Spanish music. She was a student of dance and had won many medals in local competitions and she had the feet, the hips, the elbows and hands to make the Flamenco work. She was very good. The crowd was pleased; they gave both of them a big hand and the musician and the dancer gave the wedding crowd an encore.

Mary Rose pointed with her bow, first to Deirdre, then to Jay and announced, "For the other newly wedded couple." She played a lively Russian Folk tune and the young dancer broke into a dance where, her arms folded across her chest, she almost squatted on the floor and kicked her feet out in front of her, one after the other. Again everyone cheered, and again there were questioning comments.

"She's Irish, from County Clare. He's an American, from New York. For God's sakes, why a Russian folk dance?"

"What in the world was that all about?"

"Pssst. I heard his mother was a Russian, probably a gypsy."

Then the wedding was over and it was time for goodbyes. Fiona and Mac kissed and hugged the newly weds, then Deirdre and Jay embraced the newly wed couple and said goodbye. "Dermot, I can never repay you for helping me find and care for my father's body. And you brought me to my Deirdre. A thank you is not near enough."

"Take care of my Deirdre Jay, and we will always be brothers. Good luck."

Deirdre was misty eyed but kept herself from crying. Kissing and hugging Dermot and saying goodbye was one of the most emotional, most difficult experiences of her life. She had no idea when, or if ever, they would meet again. Her going off to America was bad enough but Dermot was in a risky profession. Young patriots in Ireland did not normally live to a ripe old age. Perhaps marriage to Maura would change his outlook or mellow him a bit.

After Dermot, she turned to Maura, hugged her and whispered, "I give you my brother, my Dermot. I know he is in your good hands and I will always love you both. Goodbye and God Bless." Deirdre turned away and the tears came, but she bit her lip and did not cry out.

Finally Mary Rose, in a flood of tears kissed Dermot and cried and kissed her sister and cried again. Dermot and Maura ran to the motorcar and away they went. Dermot would retrace his steps from a few weeks ago and drive back to Cobh. They would stay overnight in a hotel and be on a ship to Spain in the morning.

The wedding guests began to leave, as the evening became nighttime. Candles and lamps were lighted on the tables outside and the harpist and Mary Rose with her fiddle took turns entertaining the dwindling number of merry makers.

Fiona and Mac came back after taking a walk to a favorite spot. A while back Maura had shown them her secret hideaway. Just down the road from the Inn was a hidden place where you could step around behind some bushes and be sheltered under a large Rowan tree. There on the bank of a small stream, you had a grand view of the flowing water and the sun setting out to the West. Maura's father even had one of his workers install there a bench for two. Maura's Mam and her Da would often end their day at this quiet place.

Fiona came and sat down by Jay. Mac sat on the bench next to Deirdre's rolling chair. She asked where had they been.

Mac answered. "We went for a stroll and a sunset. You should've come, the pair of you. Jay, you could roll her chair most of the way and the two of us could've lifted her to the stream bank." Fiona smiled in a relaxed way and reached out to hold Deirdre's hand.

Jay grinned and said, "and then what Mac? Would I sit on your lap?"

Deirdre squeezed Fiona's hand and smiled at Mac. "Fiona dear, Maura gave you her secret place so you and Mac would have somewhere to go and be together. Alone together."

"My own Deirdre, Maura gave me her secret spot to get me out of her way for a wee bit each day." They all laughed and the two women agreed that this was one of those fine two-edged gifts, and it was so typically Irish. They laughed again.

Fiona stood and asked, "will I bring everyone a drink? Tea? Whiskey? Anyone in need of something to eat?"

Jay answered first. "No more food, thanks. A brandy will end the evening for me. Can I help, Fiona?" These four, Deirdre, Fiona, Jay and Mac had an easy way with each other.

"A sip of Jay's brandy will do me fine," Deirdre said. "And have me right into my bed. What are you all smiling at? You think we'll be playing the gramophone?"

Mac stood. "I'll come and help you, Fiona. I might sip on a small whiskey to round out such a glorious day." Fiona took his arm and they walked back into the house.

Jay took Deirdre's hand and watched the older couple go arm and arm out of the garden. "Do you think they'll get serious?" He asked his wife.

Deirdre laughed deep in her throat and pulled Jay close so she could kiss him. "I think they have that in mind. Yes, they are already serious."

Mary Rose began a new song and the music soared as she played from her heart. Deirdre sang a bit of it for Jay. "Our love was on the wing, we had dreams and songs to sing. It's so lonely 'round the fields of Athenry." And then she told him the story in the song. "A young man caught up in a rebellion. He's now aboard a prison ship bound for Botany Bay in Australia; while his young wife, on shore, sings to him of love and the hope that their child can grow and live in freedom. 'The Fields of Athenry,' she said."

Fiona and Mac came back with a tray of drinks and assorted fruit and sweets. The four raised their glasses and drank to the future. Jay called out then to the music makers and they raised their glasses in a salute to Mary Rose and Delia, the harpist. Mary Rose thanked them all for their encouragement and announced her final song for the night.

"I will play this for a dear friend who went away from us." She closed her eyes for a moment and began a slow and haunting performance of Thomas Moore's "The Minstrel Boy". She played and moved to the music; she swooped and turned and centered her playing on an older man who stood and sang while she played. "This is an uncle of my Declan," she announced. He had a strong, clear voice, much like Declan's had been but with greater range and his voice was much more mature.

"The Minstrel Boy to the war is gone, in the ranks of death you'll find him; His father's sword he has girded on, And his wild harp slung behind him; Land of Song, said the warrior bard, Tho' all the world betray thee, One sword at least, thy rights shall guard, One faithful harp shall praise thee."

As the playing and singing ended, it became very quiet and those few remaining guests gave a silent thanks or a nod of approval to Mary Rose and Declan's uncle. But no one spoke and it was very quiet in the walled garden of Coveney's Inn.

"He has a fine voice," Fiona whispered low to her three companions, "as had Declan himself. The two would often sing together and you could be moved to tears by the singing they had in them." Fiona stood and put a hand on Mac's broad shoulder. "Mary Rose has become very close to Declan's family, since. They say, sure the two of them would themselves soon marry had Declan not been slain in ambush by those strangers." Fiona blew kisses to Deirdre and Jay. "Greg, will you come inside and say goodnight with me?"

Mac stood, took Fiona's arm and smiled at Jay and Deirdre. "Good night, you two."

They sat alone for a short while, and Deirdre spoke from her heart. "Oh my God, Jay. One part of me asks how can I leave my home, my people, my country? Can I really go?"

"Deirdre I love you."

"Yes. I know and I love you. And that's it right there, *mo leir*, my grief.

The other part of me says, Jay, get me out of here. Get me out now, my love. I'm tired of running and hiding and being shot. I want us to make our home. I want to be your wife and be together with you for all time, my Jay. You are *mo cushla mo croí*; you are the joy of my heart. Come now. Wheel me in. We'll put some music into the WarRoom, but we must play the gramophone low, I don't want to compete with Mary Rose."

"She's finished for the night."

"No. I often hear her playing into the wee hours of the night. Sometimes I could cry with the sounds she brings out of that fiddle. I have to reach out and touch you to make sure we are together. She must lose herself entirely inside the music." Deirdre reached up to caress Jay as he pushed her chair into the WarRoom.

CHAPTER FIFTEEN

"What are you doing up so early?" Jay looked over at Deirdre. She was in her chair with a writing tablet on her lap.

"I'm making a list of things that I must do. I did learn so much from Maura. She's a wonder at things of this sort, lists and charts and tables and such like"

"Come back to me in bed. You don't need lists, I have it all in my head."

"That isn't what you said last night. Last night, you said you had it all down there," and Deirdre pointed to her lap. He groaned and she giggled and carried on. "Jay, I heard someone working in the kitchen. If you put your robe on you could bring us some nice hot tea into the dining room." She smiled sweetly at him. "And you can push me there on your way into the kitchen."

They sat alone in the dining room. On the table were tea and toast and an eggcup sat in front of each. Jay took a spoon, cracked his egg, lifted off the top and began to eat his soft-boiled egg.

Deirdre worked on her lists. "Your father is there in Cobh, ready to be hoisted aboard. Will they hoist him or carry him on, do you think?" Without waiting for Jay to answer, she went on. "My desk is crated, our large steamer trunk is crammed full. It's mostly my own belongings, Jay. Yours all fit into your sea bag. Why did you buy us that grand steamer trunk, anyway? Will we travel? In any case all of that is up in Cobh with the shipping agent. So all we need worry about is your bag, my two cases and my new jewelry box. Thank you again for that. I love it."

Jay had bought her a fine leather case for her jewels to replace the Spanish one she gave him to bury with his father's heart. "Deirdre my love, if that were Maura now, she'd be finished with her list and she'd be over here on Dermot's lap thanking him properly." He patted his lap and smiled hopefully at Deirdre.

"Oooh no, me boyo. You're not getting me back into bed on this fine morning. We, that is, we as in the two of us, have much to do. Today we are leaving. There will be our Going Away Party, our American Wake as they call it, and I will have everything ship shape, as you sailors say, before our guests arrive." She leaned over and consoled him with a kiss. "Tonight *astore*. Do you know *astore*? Treasure. Tonight, my treasure."

It was Sunday and the staff had an easy day of it. The guests would begin arriving just after noon. The meal would be served at two and judging from yesterday, only a few would stay into the late afternoon. Jay and Deirdre would join them all in a parting glass as the evening came on and then be on their way to Cobh and their ship before full darkness set in.

Declan's brother and sister came back and the uncle with the grand voice also came to wish them God speed. Two of Deirdre's childhood girlfriends arrived. One had a beau and the other had a husband and Deirdre remembered both of the young men. It was a tender, sentimental meeting. Fiona joined the young women and they had a fun time telling tales and repeating gossip about their long ago schools and chums, teachers and priests and their favorite *Ceili* bands and singers and Friday night dates and old flames almost forgotten.

The young men formed another group with Jay and Declan's family and talked mostly about jobs and the weather and of course the big war. They were too shy to ask directly, but they were dying with curiosity about the Naval officer, Deirdre's husband, her secret wedding, her wound and now her leaving for America.

Deirdre knew they were all bursting with curiosity. "I'll tell you how it all happened," Deirdre announced in a loud voice and the men and the ladies became one large group clustered around her. Mary Rose came, hand in hand with Declan's sister. Mary Rose was anxious to hear Deirdre's new version of the events that took Declan's life. She might even use it herself. In her mind, she and Declan were all but betrothed and now she would forever be Mary Rose Ni Coveney, Mary Rose, the unmarried daughter of the Coveney's

"It was all so strange," Deirdre tried to keep her story very general with almost no specifics. "We were planning to marry, Jay and I; taking our time we were, and enjoying our courtship. Then Jay lost his father on the Lusitania and he had to come here to Cork, to identify him and claim him and take his body home to America.

It was so tragic. Of course, we had to rush everything. I suppose we could've just waited and had the ship's captain marry us at sea, but I wanted it done in a good old Irish way. I wanted a proper wedding, one with a priest to marry us. My Jay has a dear old family friend, who is a Jesuit, a French Jesuit by the way, who obliged us and that was it." She looked around with innocent wide eyes but her audience clearly wanted, needed to hear more.

She reached up to hold Jay's hand and gave them more of her story. "We set a date and he married us. The wedding was rushed indeed, but we are properly married. And, oh this," she indicated her wound. "That was purely an accident, a coincidence. We were out in West Cork to claim Jay's father.

Did you know the Lifeboat Service out of Courtmacsherry rescued him. They were too late, of course, but those oarsmen, rowing a small boat out onto the wild Atlantic; they are so brave, so gallant, and they were the first rescuers to reach that tragic scene.

Ach, my wound. A madman mistook me for his runaway bride and shot at one of us." She looked around with an air of wonder. "We are never sure, who was it, that the madman was shooting at. But brave Declan shielded me and took the bullet himself. He died in her arms." Deirdre reached out toward Mary Rose, who stood taller and accepted the admiring glances. "I had a glancing wound only, but it's mostly healed, and now it's all right for me to travel, so we're off to America." She smiled so sweet at her listeners, and they smiled nervously back. They knew that her story had left more out of it than she had put into it.

Jay leaned down and kissed her. He whispered, "you and cousin Declan would've made a fine pair of grifters."

The group drifted and clustered around Mary Rose who appeared both larger and more tragic at the same time. "…And I have the dress at home. Indeed, I kept it, for the blood on it is all I have left of my darling Declan O'Mahon."

Fiona broke the silence that followed Deirdre's story and Mary Rose's revelation. "Ah grand, the food is being served. We have whiskey, wine and porter or there is tea and lemon squash. Hard or soft, what is your pleasure? Come now and fill your glasses, so."

The harpist was back and began playing light airs as they ate and drank and talked. Mac took his food and guided Fiona, Jay, Deirdre and Donal to a small table set off by itself.

Fiona was concerned, "Should we not be mingling with our guests?"

"They'll never miss us. Deirdre's story and Mary Rose's bloody dress will keep everyone happy and busy gabbing." Mac looked at the remaining Nimble Motleys gathered around him. "And I have some gabbing of my own to do. Has Dermot said anything about after their wedding trip? His plans?"

"Well the wounded soldiers hotel, or convalescent center will be all laid on and that will keep the pair of them busy," Deirdre ventured.

"I meant up in Cork City, in that office that doesn't exist, the one on the Grande Parade."

"Greg darling, that's secret. Dermot never talks about the I.R.B. He doesn't admit there is such an organization, not even to his sainted old mother." Fiona smiled at them.

"Sainted indeed. You've finally admitted it, Fiona." Deirdre smiled with her.

"Be serious, please." Mac covered Deirdre's good hand with his and reached for Fiona's hand with his other. "Has he said anything to either of you?"

Donal spoke up. "Sure it's no tale out of school, I'm telling you. But he did say I might have a new assignment, so. And be marching alongside someone else, after his trip to Spain. With Declan gone, like; I'm his right hand, d'you see. And if I'm to be working with someone other than Dermot, than what will become of Dermot himself?"

"Strange." Jay spoke slow and careful to Deirdre. "I didn't give it much thought then, but after Declan's funeral he clapped me on the shoulder and said he hereby anoints me, Jay O'Neill, as the new Chieftain of the Nimble Motley Clan. I said, Dermot, I'm off to America soon. He said back, light hearted, 'then your tenure will be a short one, my brother.'

We both laughed and then he grabbed my arms, looked me in the eyes and said, 'maybe you'll start a new Nimble Motley Clan in America'." Jay looked from Deirdre to the others. "I assumed he was so very upset at burying Declan, a friend, a cousin, a fellow rebel and companion. Maybe there was something else worrying him."

"Let me share my thoughts with you." Mac looked around the table. "We're not all I.R.B. members, but we are all family." He squeezed Fiona's hand. Jay and Deirdre saw the squeeze and exchanged knowing looks. "Almost all family anyway. Now. Here's the way I read it." Mac cleared his throat and sipped his tea. "The action with the rifles, if indeed there ever were any rifles, has passed quietly and unnoticed. That is to the good."

"Wee Willie and his pursuit of Deirdre and the elusive rifles, not so good. An active duty soldier, shot and wounded. A civilian young man was shot dead. A young and extremely beautiful young woman has been shot and wounded." Mac tried to lighten the tension a little. "This beautiful young woman, by the way, looks remarkably like another woman sitting right here next to me." Fiona covered Mac's hand, which was holding hers.

They all smiled and Mac became serious again. "Another active duty soldier has gone missing in West Cork and a well known London figure, a university don is missing, last seen in Cork County. His mother, Billie Burke knows all but says nothing. Others know nothing but their tongues are wagging. Questions are being asked." Mac sat back and sipped his tea. He wanted the others to absorb the information and see the problems as he saw them.

Jay spoke. "We sail tonight. We'll pick up her American passport on the ship and Deirdre will be out of the country and safe. Completely safe.

The British authorities can't touch her. Wee Willie can be let free, and we have the documents."

Jay's voice trailed off. He knew better than most that no one is ever safe. Those in power will act and justify their actions later, and even apologize if need be. He had a recurring nightmare of British Marines storming their trans-Atlantic luxury liner and taking a handcuffed Deirdre away in a small patrol craft, with himself held helpless at rifle point.

Donal spoke then, and slowly, thinking his way through the problem. "Yes we have documents, signed and witnessed and enough to put old Devil Burke into prison for a good long time. But, and here's the rub, so. As soon as we use those statements, the whole shebang becomes public. Then what about the Brotherhood, Dermot and myself and even Declan lying dead in his heroes grave."

Deirdre's face became white. "Those documents are of no use? I'll be away in America, but what of the rest of you, here or in Scotland or England?" Deirdre was shaken. "Will devil Burke get away with it, then? Will he try and reclaim all that he has lost?"

"Will my children never be safe?" Fiona voiced the fear of mothers everywhere when there was trouble in the land.

"Hold, hold, now." Mac held up his two hands to stop any further slide in thoughts or words. "Wee Willie Burke is finished. As we speak, the new heir to the Burke family estates and wealth is settling in and adjusting to his sudden good fortune. Wee Willie when freed will retire to a small cottage his mother owns. He's out of his university position, his wealth, and his exclusive men's clubs. He is finished. Yes, we have the documents. Yes they are good and usable. And yes, we will use them if the need ever arises."

"Here's our problem. The whole shebang, as Donal calls it, is already public or at least well known, to those in power. When people get dead or go missing the police get involved. Yet, there have been no police investigations up to this point, neither official nor unofficial. And that is mystifying to me and a wee bit scary."

"The powers that be know about it and have put a lid on it." Jay offered.

"Aye. The kingdom is at war. They worry about subversive actions in their back yard, Ireland, in this case. Soldiers shot and others missing, but no official action has been ordered. That means unofficial action. Who ordered it, who supplied it, whose bloody hands are all over this and which budget did it come out of? I've lived, marched with and been a part of this Empire for most of my life. I know how they operate.

Yes, the Irish Republican Brotherhood is a secret organization, but you can bet your laced up boots that the Crown is aware of it. They will be almost certain that the Irish will make a move for freedom while this World War is raging. It is common sense from a military point of view. And I'm just as certain that the Crown knows or strongly suspects that our Dermot O'Rourke had a hand in all this shebang." Mac looked at Donal.

"Now Donal, we must get Dermot through these next few years. Get him beyond the war and the following peace negotiations. We must help him get on the other side of all of this unpleasantness. Someday there will be normal times and normal lives to be living."

"Dear God in heaven, Greg," Fiona cried out. "How do we accomplish all this getting beyond and getting on the other side?" Fiona looked stricken. She was equating 'beyond', and 'the other side' with death.

Mac calmed Fiona and turned back to Donal. "Look now. I know how they think Donal, and you must talk to Dermot and have him convince his bosses to leave him be. He must remain in plain sight. His face will become the face of that secret, rebel, Brotherhood.

The Crown will watch him and believe they have a line on a major subversive group. The Crown will allow him to operate freely, hoping to thwart the Rebels and stop their activities. If the I.R.B. brass hats move him or hide him, they will paint a target on his back. That will only verify what the Crown suspects and they will hunt him down. If Dermot can convince his bosses to leave him in place, he should be safe."

Mac swung back to Fiona and held her hands in his two large capable hands. "Dearest Fiona, we will help your Dermot through this. And it will not be easy on him, or yourself." Mac searched her eyes for clarity past an instinctive mother's fear for a child. Satisfied with what he found in her, Mac included the rest of the Motleys.

"There will be sacrifice and great risk for Dermot." Mac paused and waited for questions.

Jay looked at Deirdre. She was squeezing and pulling his hand. She wanted to hear from her love Jay, concerning Dermot, the only other man she had ever loved. "What sacrifice Jay? What risk?"

Jay responded to Deirdre but spoke to all the Motleys. "If the I.R.B. keep Dermot in place and allow him to be the public face and voice for a secret rebel Army, he will be excluded from any important meetings, any decision making. In effect, my Deirdre, he will become a front. I don't know if Dermot can stand that sort of change in the way he sees himself."

"That's it exactly, Jay. There's the nub of it. Will Dermot be able to make this sacrifice." Mac looked with affection from Fiona to Deirdre. "You must keep a silent face on you, both of you. For if you say to him go up; he'll be inclined to go down. He has to come to a conclusion that he can live with, he himself and now Maura, his wife, as well."

"That's the sacrifice," Deirdre stated in a flat tone.

"What is the risk?" Both Fiona and Deirdre asked at the same time.

Donal answered. "The Crown. They could decide to pick him up at any time. They'd have him up to Dublin Castle and down into the deepest dungeon. I know two chaps who worked there and they say 'tis not for any sane man, or woman, so. The screams and groans and crying out, remain with you long after. That's what they say."

"You've said it, Donal. It's not the British Army." Mac was clearly upset. "It's the others, the torturers with black masks and the bully boy tactics. They use methods would make any man say anything against any person, even his own mother." Fiona shuddered and Mac put his arm around her.

"The information they get is almost all lies. What they produce is mostly broken men, battered in body and soul. And unfortunately they are doing the same thing to our once magnificent Empire. It is becoming battered and broken. It no longer has a soul."

Fiona held herself as though coming up out of icy cold water and stood up. "We must now rejoin our guests," she held out a hand to Deirdre and Jay. "Come please. And Greg, will you ever go and get me my shawl. It's in the kitchen on the back of my chair." Mac nodded and rose to go inside.

"I feel a chill and I'm afraid the sun must go down behind the stream and the trees without us tonight."

Mary Rose stood in a circle of admirers seated all around her. She was playing for them and telling stories as she played.

Donal brought her a cup of tea and asked her, "Mary Rose, will you become a nurse and bring us good health, or are you becoming a *Shanachie*, bringing us stories and music from our glorious past?"

"Donal, dear Donal, I will be both." She smiled at him and looked to the group of Nimble Motleys approaching her. "Is it time to go?"

Jay nodded and Mary Rose moved over in front of two empty chairs. "Here, sit here please. You two are our guests of honor and I will play for you, before we all go to the ship."

Deirdre asked, "are you all coming with us to the ship, then?"

"Indeed we are. We haven't finished saying goodbye to you". Mary Rose curtsied and began to play. "Now here's just for the two of you, who are a part of my family in America." She closed her eyes and played, "The Wind That Shakes the Barley." Mary Rose swayed in time to her music and she sang soft and low to Jay and Deirdre.

"I sat within a valley green, I sat me with my true love. My sad heart strove to choose between. The old love and the new love."

"This song was written about the rebellion of 1798. A man named Robert D. Joyce. He later fled to America to avoid arrest by the Crown. This next verse was written for myself and for you, Jay. And if I can hold steady my bow and my voice, I'll sing and I'll play it for ourselves." Mary Rose planted her two feet and she swayed as she sang and she played.

"While sad I kissed away her tears, my fond arms round her flinging. The foeman's shot burst on our ears, from out the wildwood ringing. A bullet pierced my true love's side, in life's young spring so early. And on my breast in blood she died while soft winds shook the barley."

As the music and Mary Rose's singing faded, Jay had to reach down and untwist Deirdre's fingers from his own. She was holding on so tight, her ring had dug in and left a perfect mark of the emerald stone deep in his palm. He pulled her to him and she whispered, "I'm fine, my love. I was thinking of us, but mostly I thought about poor Declan."

When they looked up, Mary Rose had her back to them, the fiddle held out to one side and her bow out to the other. She held this Christ like pose for a moment and when she turned back to her audience, her face was clear. She had a half smile on her soft mouth and her green eyes glistened. "And now my Deirdre, this is for you. Someday, when your house is a shambles and your four children are screaming and fighting, and your husband, with a drink taken, is pounding the table for his dinner. Think back and remember this fine evening and your farewell at our Coveney's Inn. I will miss you, fair Deirdre." Mary Rose played and sang to Deirdre, 'The Green Fields of America'.

"I've heard that song before," Jay whispered.

"Yes love. Mary Rose was playing 'The Green Fields of America' at our wedding when Declan and I were shot. I remember it all now. We were dancing; there was a loud crack and I was shocked to see his blood on me. And then you held me and I felt a tremendous pain and I knew it was my own blood I was seeing. Declan was down and I was shot.

You held me and rocked me and I thought, we are truly married. Shouldn't I be I safe now? You said I'd be safe, Jay. Is this the full length of my marriage, a few moments, only? Will I ever go to America with you?" She paused. "It is a lovely song, indeed, but I never want to hear it again."

They drove to Cobh harbour with Fiona and Mac in the back of the good doctor's motorcar. Jay was almost numb with emotion. He was married to his true love and he was taking his father home. But the cost was so high to everyone involved. He couldn't begin to know what Deirdre was feeling. Their talk inside the car was mostly of small things, and though they were exhausted and on edge, they were all easy with each other.

Mary Rose and Donal followed on the motorcycle. Donal, of course sat in the sidecar, but instead of a rifle, he held her fiddle and her bow. Mary Rose drove the motorcycle with wild exuberance and her new white silk scarf streamed out behind her. She knew she could never catch Declan, but she seemed determined to try. Donal counted himself lucky that he would pick up the Coveney car that Dermot had driven and left at the hotel yesterday. Donal would drive it back by himself to the Coveney Inn.

The third vehicle in the Motley caravan held Deirdre's two girlfriends from her growing up years and their men. They, of course, were busy discussing the day's events, the wild stories they had heard and the very real tension in the air, which centered upon Dermot, who wasn't even there.

"Dermot is involved in something dangerous. I overheard them talking about it."

"No, no, he and Maura are going to open up an Old Soldiers Home. How dangerous can that be?"

"Deirdre is your best friend, Nell, but I did not believe a word of her tale. Two weeks in bed from a flesh wound? What did happen to her?"

"I haven't a clue, but if that's what she wants us to know, then I for one will believe her."

"And what's this talk about Deirdre getting a medal? Who would give her one and for what, I ask you."

"You'd never believe me in any case, so why should I tell you."

"Tell it all, Nell. We may not believe it but we'd all like to have the story anyway."

"'Twas the night before Dermot and Maura's wedding." Nell began. "They'd a fine rehearsal dinner and were out in the walled garden. Sudden like a man appears and wants to know who's in the house? Dermot says, just us, just family and the Motleys."

"Who in the name of God are the Motleys?" Is it another family? Are they related?"

"Hush, let Nell tell us."

"Now listen to me. Into the garden comes six more men in uniform. They form up and salute and present Deirdre a medal and some papers. Sealed and embossed, papers. There's not a question from anyone. The one is charge says, 'for your own safety, do not wear this medal in public.' They salute again, wheel about and they march on out. And that's it. She would not tell me any more than that."

"It had to be something military. But she wasn't in the war. Dermot is not the only one doing something dangerous, I'd say."

"And poor Mary Rose. Playing her fiddle at Deirdre's wedding and her fiancé Declan is shot and killed. She's the one with rare courage. Do any of you remember Declan Meehan?"

"Not Meehan, O'Mahon, Declan O'Mahon. I saw the death notice in the paper. But no, I did not know him at all. Sure he was much younger than Nell and Deirdre and me."

"And the older man, that Greg, is surely sweet on Fiona. Isn't he somehow related to Deirdre's Jay? But he's a Scot, not a Yank."

"His name is Mac, not Greg. I heard several of them call him Mac, including Deirdre. And yes, he's an uncle to that Jay O'Neill fella. I think they're related on his mother's side."

"I haven't a clue what the real truth of any of these matters is. But, if they do sail away on that ship, then we know for sure that they're off to America."

"Not a bit of it. Listen to me now, the one and only thing we'll know for sure is that Deirdre and her Jay are on a ship bound away from Ireland. Where they go is another question."

They were between Cork City and Cobh when Mac pointed away and up hill to the left. "I think that's the hill we were coasting down when Donal fired and shot that soldier who was following Jay and myself."

"And Deirdre," Jay added. "I'm sure he saw we had a woman in the car with us. She was the main target."

"It was so quiet, Fiona." Deirdre turned and almost whispered. "We rolled down hill. The engine was off. No one spoke. We could hear the blackbirds in the trees and even the cows in the fields. There was not a sound in or around us. BANG. The shot rang out and we all jumped. Including you, big Mr. Mac Greg MacGregor."

"Yes. I admit it. I jumped too." And he joined the rest of the Motleys laughing.

Jay slowed the car, "This is where the road block was. The machine guns were right there." He pointed to the intersection. "Come on Mac, sing out and we'll join in."

"It's a Long Way To Tipperary. It's a long way to go." The Motleys joined voices with Mac as the lead singer and sang the rousing marching song and the good doctor's car seemed to rise up off of the pavement and speed along on the very air itself.

They drove directly to the quay and Deirdre kept looking, "Jay where is our ship?"

Jay pointed way out into the harbour at a large ocean liner. "She's much to big to tie up in here. We'll take the tender out to her." He parked at the harbour's edge and the two following vehicles swung in next to him. Jay unloaded his bag and Deirdre's cases. He paid an attendant to park both cars and the motorcycle; and then he called out, "Come on, one and all. We have an hour before sailing, let's make the most of it."

As soon as they boarded the small ferry-like craft, the skipper cast off, and they stood or leaned against the rail and watched the ocean liner come closer. At the same time the shoreline and the lighted city scene grew smaller behind them.

Deirdre watched the shore, then turned and watched the ship. Her trips to and from France had been on much smaller coastal steamers, and she was impressed. She leaned back against her Jay and declared. "My God Jay, the size of it. It surely is a huge, grand big ship. It's a ship, right? Not a boat?"

In true sailor fashion he had told her, "A boat is small, something you mess around in close to the shore. A ship is large, big enough to carry men, machines or cargo around the world." He answered her, "Yes, she is a ship alright, a magnificent ocean going liner."

But Deirdre had turned and was watching the lights of the Town of Cobh and St. Colman's Cathedral and the entire waterfront panorama. "Oh look you Jay, it's just grand to see Cobh from out here in the bay." He started to tell her about his arrival here, but she had turned again and was in thrall at the size of the Trans-Atlantic liner, as they cruised closer to it.

He held her close and Deirdre called against the wind to Fiona who was nearby, standing and leaning against MacGregor. "Look you, Fiona." She pointed up at the ship looming above them. "'Tis as big as a city and yet it floats on top of the water." The ship now rose up into the darkening night sky above them. They could hear the rumbling of the ship's engines and feel the vibrations. It seemed as though the entire ship was alive and alight. 'Deirdre wondered would the ship welcome them or devour them?' She shivered in Jay's arms.

Their stateroom was on the port side, amidships, and three levels below the mezzanine deck. They had a porthole and a private toilet and shower. There was a double bed, two easy chairs with reading lamps, and ample closet and storage space. It was almost luxurious and Deirdre was delighted. "Oh Jay. It's grand, we'll cross the wild and wide Atlantic in style." She turned around and around taking in the room and touching Jay as she turned.

Donal looked everywhere in amazement. He examined the fine walnut paneled walls, the brass lamps, the artistic plumbing in the bathroom and finally the porthole. "BeGod, Fiona, Cleopatra didn't travel any finer than this. Shall I open the window, Deirdre?" He grinned at the women as he unlocked and opened the small round 'window'.

Jay left to find a steward for a few more chairs and extra glasses. When he returned the room was full. There were two on the chairs, four sitting on the bed and four more people standing. The cabin was full and noisy with excited talking; yet it was comfortable.

The steward came with three extra chairs and a tray of glasses. Jay thanked him and slipped him a coin. At once Mac opened his travel bag and brought out a bottle of Redbreast whiskey.

Fiona clapped her hands. "Oh thank you Greg. You brought the Priest's Bottle." He looked puzzled at her and Fiona explained. "You brought the good twenty five year old whiskey. At home it never comes out of the cupboard except when Himself comes to bless the house or visit the sick and the dying."

Mac looked at the bottle and grinned, "the priest's bottle is it? All right then, hold out your glasses. We'll drink a holy toast to The Nimble Motleys. By God, where is Rory when you need him."

They toasted and talked and drank. The steward came back with two bottles of champagne. "Complements of these two fine gentlemen and their ladies." He indicated the four old friends from Deirdre's childhood. They talked and laughed and drank and Mac watched his two women in fascination as the older beauty never took her eyes off of the younger one.

Fiona drank but little of the whiskey or the wine, but she drank in every look, each facial expression, and every movement made by Deirdre. Fiona's entire body seemed to be absorbing Deirdre's laugh, her voice, her gestures, indeed her entire being. Fiona was storing it all for future remembering. Her little Deirdre was leaving her, going to a far off foreign land. Would she ever in this world, see her again?

Mac leaned down to Fiona, "I know you will miss her, this younger version of yourself, your little sister. We will see them again. On my life, I promise you Fiona, we will be together again, the four of us."

She reached up and took his hand, in much the same way as Deirdre did with Jay. "Thank you Greg. I could not have survived this day, this leaving, were it not for you." She kissed his hand and kept holding it as she continued to absorb everything about her Deirdre.

The ships whistle gave three long blasts and a young steward came down the passageway. He clanged a bell and cried out, "Ashore. All ashore. All ashore that's going ashore. Now please, now. Ashore." His voice and the bell faded as he went on giving his warning.

There was a general rush to finish drinks, and shake hands, or hug, kiss, or cry and wipe away tears. Nell, the friend closest to Deirdre all through her girlhood and early woman years came out of the bathroom wearing her boyfriend's raincoat and holding her dress in her hands.

"Deirdre, you are my best friend. You've been admiring my new frock all day and evening and so my dear, I want you to have it. Take it to America with you and when you wear it, think of me." She handed the dress to a surprised Deirdre.

They hugged and kissed and Deirdre said, "Thank you Nell, but what will you be wearing home tonight. Will I give you something of mine?"

Nell boldly opened the raincoat and showed off a bit of leg in stockings, and a white slip. "They'll be another wedding, quite soon, I'm thinking." The girls laughed and Deirdre stood and held her new dress up to her body.

Nell admired her new frock against Deirdre's curves. "It lights up your eyes, so. Wear it in good health my Deirdre."

Donal stuck his head back into the cabin. "We're away now. Come along so, and let this grand ship be off on its way to America."

The Nimble Motleys went down to the open hatchway and walked out the gangplank to the small tender, which would take them ashore. Jay and Deirdre went up to the open deck and stood at the railing. There they looked down at the small craft bobbing in the water below them.

"Is that them, Jay. I think I see them in the back of the boat."

"The stern."

She mimicked him with a low voice and a big frown, "The stern, Deirdre. The back is the stern." She laughed and kissed him. "I am so excited. We're really going to America."

She turned herself in his arms and got into one of her favorite positions. With her back to Jay and his arms around her she could lean against him, rest her head on his shoulder and kiss him by turning her head. "Listen Jay."

Faintly at first and then more distinct as the wind abated they heard singing and fiddle music. Still in his arms, they moved back to the rail and looked over the side. There below, looking up at them were the four Nimble Motleys and the four temporaries. Mary Rose had her fiddle and she was playing and swaying as the small ferry rocked upon the waves and the eight people all sang out. The wind dropped and Deirdre and Jay could hear the tune and the words.

"Come back to Erin, Mavourneen, Mavourneen. Come back again to the land of thy birth. Come with the Shamrocks, and Springtime Mavourneen. And it's Killarney shall ring with our mirth."

The wind picked up again. The ship gave a blast of its whistle and the small tender moved away headed back to shore. Jay and Deirdre waved and waved and they could see hats and hands waving back at them from the stern of the small craft. Mary Rose waved her fiddle in one hand and her white scarf in the other, then it was too far and too dark to see any more.

"It's anchors aweigh and we are away, Mrs. O'Neill." From behind he hugged her tight and held her breasts in his two hands. "Can you feel the ship through your feet? The engines are making top revolutions per minute and the screws are turning." He stopped and looked at her. "Those are the propellers, my seagoing wife; the screws are turning fast and churning the water to take us out of Cobh. Shall we go below to our cabin? Shall we put music into it?" Jay was feeling very nautical now that he was on a ship and headed out to sea. He was also feeling very romantic. This was, after all, their honeymoon.

"A few minutes only, my Jay. I want to see Cobh and Ireland, and plant it into my mind so I'll never forget it. Be patient with me." She wriggled her bottom and moved against him. "I will make it worth your while."

"Will you put music into our stateroom?"

"An entire orchestra, for you my love."

"That's wifely blackmail."

"Yes my Jay. Does it work?"

"Yes it works." He held her closer.

The both saw it at the same time and exclaimed together. "Oh Jay." "Oh Deirdre, look."

A spear point of bright red flames shot skyward from the hill up behind the Cathedral. The fire seemed to come from the very spires of St. Colman's itself.

"Jay, we made love on that hill. That's the Hill of Fires, where Dermot took us when you found me, came back to me." She moved against him. "Oh God Jay. I want you now, but we must stay and see this." She giggled. "And you need me just as much." She felt his excitement and she could feel the throbbing of the ship rising through her legs into her body.

"There's no holiday or Celtic celebration today is there?"

"No Jay. That fire is for us, and it must be the work of the Motleys. Declan is dead, but, Oh Jay. This is the work of Dermot and his lads. They have the people and they know how to make it happen. And they did it for us, as a send off. He must have laid this on before he and Maura sailed for Spain."

"And that's not the only thing he arranged." Jay turned her to face him. "Kiss me and I'll tell you what else your Dermot managed as a send off."

"Now that is husbandly blackmail. And yes it works." She groaned and kissed him and pushed herself against him. "Tell me or I'll take back my kiss."

"How do you take back a kiss? Never mind. You know Mac and Fiona are staying over tonight in a hotel." She nodded. "Well your brother Dermot paid the desk clerk to give them one room only, to say the hotel was full and nothing else available, and make sure the room they got had only the one bed, a small bed."

Deirdre began to laugh and held on to Jay and kissed him and laughed again. "Ah Fiona. Good for you, and hooray for the big Scotsman." She raised her arms and shouted into the darkness. "I am Deirdre, a woman from Clare, and every woman should have her man. And good for you my Dermot."

When she looked shoreward again they could still see the lights of Cobh but the hill fire was just a tiny point above where the Cathedral should be. "Take me to your bed, my prince and we'll make an heir to our throne."

"Will you settle for a Congressman or a Governor? In America we don't have princes or thrones. But we do have heirs."

"Speaking of heirs, Declan told me a strange story. It was out in the woods at the Mass Rock. We girls were behind the screen getting changed before the wedding. Declan was headed to his lookout post up on the hill, but he stopped to tell me this story. I suppose the rock and the woods and Maura's story got him thinking about the Shee, the Faerie folk, like the Bann Shee, or Banshee.

It seems The Hill of Fire is also called *Mulacant Sidhe*, or Mullacha Shee, the hill of Faeries. Declan said to me, 'Ach Deirdre, I know you and your Jay got together on the Faerie Hill. After your long separation, 'twas only natural, like. But know this and be warned. Any child conceived at those stones, that Faerie place, is certain to be a changeling.' That was Declan's parting gift to me. Before he saved my life, that is."

"Changeling or not, any child of ours is sure to change something." Jay took her arm and they went down the next staircase and along the passageway to their cabin. The extra chairs and glasses and debris from their little Bon Voyage party were all gone. The cabin had been cleaned; the bed covers turned down and a sweet lay atop each pillow.

"Oh Jay, I could get used to this kind of living," Deirdre called from the bathroom. She came out wearing a revealing nightgown and headed for the bed.

"Hey. Slow down. Why wear the gown if you're not going to let me see you in it." She smiled and twirled and modeled the gown and herself in it, for him. "And I could get used to you looking like this." He led her to a chair and they sat, Jay first, then Deirdre. "Listen, don't take all this luxury too seriously. I'm a government employee and we could end up living in a grass shack on a tiny South Sea Island somewhere."

"Just as long as we're together, Jay. I don't care." This was not going the way she planned it. There would be long afternoons at sea for these serious talks.

"We may not always be together. You might have to live in a small flat while I'm out at sea patrolling the cold North Atlantic."

"Take me into bed Jay and patrol my warm body. Now. Please." She wanted a relaxed love making session with plenty of romance. Later, when her desires had been fulfilled and her Jay had fallen asleep, she would get out the letter from Fionnoula and read what her mother had to say, those many years ago. If she decided to toss it, the porthole was there and it was already open. All of the past would be left behind tonight. She had her new husband and they were headed to a new land. It was time to look ahead, not backwards.

Their lovemaking was slow and almost awkward at first. Then the rhythm of the ship altered and together they hit their stride.

It was wonderful and Deirdre laughed and held him tighter. "What happened to us?"

"The ship has passed out into the open ocean and the waves are deeper and longer. The rhythm has changed and..."

"Shhh. No more talking. Just love me. You can tell me why tomorrow."

Later, when Jay had fallen asleep, she went to her leather jewel case and got out the letter from her mother. She took it into the bathroom and sat down to read it.

> My darling daughter,
>
> I will go away from you soon and my heart is breaking. My Fiona will give this to you and I suppose you will be all grown up when you read it. Please forgive my anger but I will miss so much and it isn't fair. I will not see you blossom into a woman. I want to see your face when you tell me you have

met your man. I want to watch you while you are in love, hear your voice change and see your eyes alight when he is near. I will miss your wedding, and I will miss seeing you big with child as I was. Deirdre, I love you so. You are my child, mine and your beloved father's. You are not part of someone else, not anyone else.

From the moment I knew you were growing inside me, I treasured you. I almost resented birthing you, knowing I would have to share. I was resentful even of my own twin, my Fiona, my best friend. She had recently lost her second child and I knew she would claim a part of you. Even a small part was too much for me. I would have to share and I didn't want to. God help me. Can we love too much?

They tell me I will be very sick and in a great deal of pain. I will be cranky and may push you away. Forgive me, Deirdre. Please think of me as I was. When I was whole and able to hold you and help you and play with you. I wish I could make you another cloak, a real grown up cloak. One to keep you warm through the years, until you give it to your own daughter.

I love you my child, my own sweet Deirdre.
Your mother.
Fionnoula Gilmartin DalCas.

Deirdre sat still and it was so quiet she could hear her own breaths coming in and out. Finally she rose, went into the bedroom and over to the open porthole. She stood a moment then slammed the small round window shut, turned to the bed and then went back to the porthole. She locked it securely and returned her mother's letter to her jewel case. She whispered, "I will take a bit of my past out of Ireland and carry it with me. There is my man. This is my future." Deirdre got into bed and lay down next to her husband.

It felt so good to lie down in a nice large bed with her man, her Jay. She listened to the rumble of the ships engines and felt reassured. It was grand to be taken somewhere we wanted to go, with no effort, no struggle, only comfort and joy. Deirdre thought she could hear the sounds of the ships propellers turning. She smiled and put her hand on Jay. 'The screws he would call them; are turning, pushing the water, taking us home to America.'

She could hear his breathing and Deirdre tried to match her breaths to his. Soon she was struggling and gasping. His breaths were deeper and longer than hers. 'No matter, she reasoned, he's bigger the I am, and we're different in a lot of ways.' She giggled and moved closer to him. 'But I am the *Bean na Tighe*. I am The Woman of the House.'

Deirdre turned on her side and moved back against Jay. He turned and draped an arm around her. She took his hand and placed it around her breast. Her mind roved and she thought about the waves. 'She knew when she stood on the strand in Ireland the waves broke upon the sand. She knew too that when she would stand on the shore in New York, the waves would roll into the land there, as well.

Was there a place in the ocean, she wondered, where the waves were parted. One set of waves going East to Ireland and another set going West to America? If there were a divide in the middle of the ocean, they would have to cross it. She would talk to Jay about it tomorrow. And the lady, the one in New York harbour with the torch, she wanted to know more about her. Was she really French?'

Deirdre lay quiet and held her hand against the *Shian Bao*. She pressed it to her breast. Perhaps the remains of the very bullet that pierced her breast and almost ended her life would now erase the scar and bring her good luck on into the future.

Deirdre drew her breaths with the ship. She found a rhythm in the vibrations and engine sounds that was pleasant and matched her mood. It lulled her into a state where everything lay open to her, even their future. She could nearly see herself and Jay, as they would be in the years ahead. It was so close. She could almost see their future life together.

THE END

IRISH WORDS & PHRASES

Ard na Grienne	Ard nah green yuh	The height of the sun
Astore	As thor	My treasure
Bean na Tighe	Bann na tee	The woman of the house
Ceili	Kay lee	Dance, party, festival
Diarmuid	Deer ma duh	Dermot
Gombeen Man	Gom bean	Landlords rent collector
Go raibh maith agat	Gorruh ma huh gut	Thank you.
Grainne Ni Mhaille	Gron yuh O'Malley	Grace O'Malley, pirate queen
Mavourneen	Ma vore neen	Darling
Mo cushla	mah cush lah	Beloved
Mulacant Sidhe	Mulla ka Shee	Hill of Faeries
Amadan	ohm ma don	Fool
Praties	Pray tees	Potatoes
Ruari, mo lier	Ror ee mo lear	Rory, my grief
Samhain	Sow in,	Halloween
Shanachie	Shawn a key	Story teller
Shian bao (Chinese)	Shee on Bowe	Incense Fire Pack, luck
'S rioghal mo dhream.		My race is royal.
Tain Bo Cuilgne	Tane Bo Coolie	Ancient heroic tales
Tosca sin innis a warra,"	Tosha shin inish a wah rah.	A comforting; not to worry.

also available from publishamerica

IGNITED VERSES

by Felicia Rogers

Life is poetry. Poetry is life. *Ignited Verses* is a collection of poems that contains a piece of the author's heart and soul. It is intended to ignite your passion to life and love.

"Poeta nascitur, non fit…A poet is born, not made."

Felicia has been a poet most of her life but has taken her God-given talent more seriously the past several years.

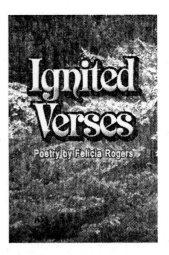

Her poem "Sydne" appeared in poetry anthologies, *TIMELESS VOICES* and *INTERNATIONAL WHO'S WHO IN POETRY*, published in Maryland, USA, last 2006. She received an Editor's Choice Award for this poem. It is also one of the poems included in a *CD-SONGS OF POETRY* released this year by http://www.poetry.com

Paperback, 63 pages
6" x 9"
ISBN 1-4241-7974-2

About the author:

The daughter of a doctor and an insurance underwriter, she works as a nurse in a local community hospital and a nursing home.

Felicia wants to be remembered as a child of God who has learned, loved and left a legacy through her poems.

available to all bookstores nationwide.
www.publishamerica.com

SECRET SACRIFICES

by Cynthia Hall

Maggie Brown's ten-year-old secret is in danger of being revealed when her daughter Tracey is abducted. Desperate to find her, Maggie contacts Tracey's biological father, Matt Sanford. The unsuspecting father uses his law enforcement skills as he would with any routine kidnaping case to help locate Tracey. Maggie and Matt rush against time and a powerful tropical storm to get to Tracey before she is taken away forever. While Maggie and Matt's undercover journey leads them into dangerous twists and turns involving a devious Caribbean kidnaping ring and a bad cop, Tracey is fighting her own battle when she is brought into a questionable environment of abuse and uncertainty. Maggie's frantic search forces her to make decisions that could shake the stability of her private world. Tracey is faced with finding strength beyond her comprehension, and Matt must decide if he is able to forgive.

Paperback, 195pages
6" x 9"
ISBN 1-4241-7257-8

About the author:

When Cynthia L. Hall began work on her debut novel, *Secret Sacrifices*, she worked for a local sheriff's department, which gave her great insight into law enforcement and helped with the details. Cynthia's writing includes human interest stories and freelance photojournalism. She and her husband live in Ohio. They have one daughter.